THE KILLING GROUND

In the same series

THE ULTRAMARINES OMNIBUS
by Graham McNeill
(Contains the novels NIGHTBRINGER, WARRIORS OF
ULTRAMAR and DEAD SKY, BLACK SUN)

By the same author

STORM OF IRON

· **HORUS HERESY** ·
FALSE GODS
FULGRIM

A WARHAMMER 40,000 NOVEL

THE KILLING GROUND

Graham McNeill

To Jimmy, Dave and Pete of the 1st Battalion of the Royal Anglians, and Commissar Chris from the RMP. Thanks for chat and the info. Come back safe, guys.

A BLACK LIBRARY PUBLICATION
First published in Great Britain in 2008 by
BL Publishing,
Games Workshop Ltd.,
Willow Road,
Nottingham,
NG7 2WS, UK

10 9 8 7 6 5 4 3 2 1

Cover by Karl Kopinski.

A CIP record for this book
is available from the British Library.

ISBN 13: 978 1 84416 562 9
ISBN 10: 1 84416 562 0

Distributed in the US by Simon & Schuster
1230 Avenue of the Americas, New York, NY 10020, US.

Printed and bound in the US.

This is a work of fiction. All the characters and events portrayed in this book are fictional, and any resemblance to real people or incidents is purely coincidental.

See the Black Library on the Internet at
www.blacklibrary.com

Find out more about Games Workshop
and the world of Warhammer 40,000 at
www.games-workshop.com

IT IS THE 41st millennium. For more than a hundred centuries the Emperor has sat immobile on the Golden Throne of Earth. He is the master of mankind by the will of the gods, and master of a million worlds by the might of his inexhaustible armies. He is a rotting carcass writhing invisibly with power from the Dark Age of Technology. He is the Carrion Lord of the Imperium for whom a thousand souls are sacrificed every day, so that he may never truly die.

YET EVEN IN his deathless state, the Emperor continues his eternal vigilance. Mighty battlefleets cross the daemon-infested miasma of the warp, the only route between distant stars, their way lit by the Astronomican, the psychic manifestation of the Emperor's will. Vast armies give battle in his name on uncounted worlds. Greatest amongst his soldiers are the Adeptus Astartes, the Space Marines, bio-engineered super-warriors. Their comrades in arms are legion: the Imperial Guard and countless planetary defence forces, the ever-vigilant Inquisition and the tech-priests of the Adeptus Mechanicus to name only a few.
But for all their multitudes, they are barely enough to hold off the ever-present threat from aliens, heretics, mutants – and worse.

TO BE A man in such times is to be one amongst untold billions. It is to live in the cruellest and most bloody regime imaginable. These are the tales of those times. Forget the power of technology and science, for so much has been forgotten, never to be re-learned. Forget the promise of progress and understanding, for in the grim dark future there is only war. There is no peace amongst the stars, only an eternity of carnage and slaughter, and the laughter of thirsting gods.

'Regiments that have served for more than ten years are usually transferred from protracted war zones into armies of conquest. Not only are these the best troops, but they are also the oldest, having fought gallantly for the Emperor for a decade or more. Their reward is to take part in the conquest of a new world. If they are successful the entire regiment earns the highest honour the Imperium can bestow, the gratitude of the Emperor and the right to settle a new planet. All over the Imperium there are worlds that were originally populated in this way. Their people are the hardy descendants of victorious Imperial Guard regiments.'

Tactica Imperium – Commanders' notes
on protracted service.

Sometimes the ghosts of the past won't let you go...

THE BAR WAS crowded and the simmering air of resentment that filled its smoky depths was like a current running through Hanno Merbal's body. He could sense the hatred of what he represented in every muttered syllable, every furtive glance and every hostile stare. He lifted the glass before him and knocked the harsh spirit back in one gulp.

The crude liquor burned his throat and he coughed, wondering for a moment if the sour-faced bastard behind the bar had simply served him a glass of promethium as some kind of sick joke. He slammed the glass down onto the beaten metal bar and looked into the man's yellow eyes, seeking confirmation of his suspicions.

Yes, the man wore a mask of ungrateful resentment etched into his face, just like all the other locals. Hanno wouldn't have put it past him to try and poison a decorated Imperial soldier of the Achaman Falcatas, but as the heat of the liquor spread through his gut, he smiled as the strength of the drink eased the frantic screaming inside his skull.

Hanno lowered his head until it rested on the cool metal of the bar.

'Another one,' he said, and another measure was duly poured and set before him. Hanno took a deep breath, inhaling the stink of his own sweat and guilt, and closed his eyes against the sight of his rounded belly and sagging chest.

He lifted his head, studying the bar and the drink that sat upon it.

From the pattern of the rivets and the faded markings along its length, Hanno could tell that the bar had once been the side of a Chimera. Slots that had once been fitted with integral lasguns were now repositories for spent and crushed lho sticks. The drink was a cloudy, gritty concoction distilled in a corroded drum that had once been a Hellhound's fuel tank. It was lethal stuff, but it was the only thing that helped Hanno Merbal blot out the memories of the Killing Ground.

He lifted the drink and again drained it in a single swallow, coughing at its potency.

'Damn, but that's good stuff,' spluttered Hanno, tossing a crumpled handful of the new Imperial currency onto the bar. 'Give me the bottle, you robbing bastard.'

Hanno heard the rustle of conversation drop a notch and he looked around, a soldier's instincts for danger not yet completely obliterated by the alcohol he'd consumed. Through the haze of hookah smoke and stinging eyes, Hanno saw that virtually every face in the bar was turned towards him.

'What are you looking at?' he yelled, his resentment overcoming the deeper desire that gnawed at his sanity. 'I got every right to be here. We beat you. You lost. Deal with it.'

'Here's your drink,' said the barman, slamming an unlabelled blue bottle down beside him, 'and keep your damn cash, I don't want your blood money. Now get out.'

Hanno snatched up the bottle, but made no attempt to retrieve the notes from the bar. He pulled the cork from the neck of the bottle with his teeth and poured himself another drink.

'Why do you keep coming here?' asked a voice beside Hanno. He spun unsteadily on his stool to see a tall, rangy man with a shaved head and a long, forked beard tied in braids looming over him. A knot of pale scar tissue creased the left side of his head. Hanno knew enough veterans to recognise a las-burn when he saw one.

The man wore the same faded brown work tunic as everyone else, but where most others on this dismal world favoured ash-grey storm cloaks, this stranger wore the green and gold double wrapped cloak of the Sons of Salinas.

'I could have you arrested for wearing that,' said Hanno.

'I'd like to see you try,' said the man. Hanno's eyes focused as he took a closer look at the man. He was unarmed, but wore the threat of violence like a weapon and his eyes shone with controlled anger.

'What's your name?' asked Hanno.

'You know my name, I think.'

'I think I do,' said Hanno, seeing a number of men behind the stranger slide their hands beneath their storm cloaks. 'There's a reward for your capture, or death. I forget which.'

'Are you planning on collecting it?'

Hanno shook his head. 'Not tonight. It's my day off.'

'Very wise,' said the man, 'but you never answered my question. Why do you keep coming to this place? I hear you come in every night and get blind drunk on raquir before insulting everyone and staggering back to your barracks alone.'

'Perhaps I like the company,' snapped Hanno, waving his hands at the walls, 'or perhaps I like the aesthetic of rusted battle tank interior.'

'Are you looking to get killed?' asked the man, leaning close and whispering.

'And if I was, would you be the man to do it?' Hanno whispered back. 'Would you?'

'I think you should go. A lot of people here want to kill you,' said the man, 'and I'm not sure I should stop them.'

'Then don't, please.'

The man leaned back with a curious expression on his face. 'Is that it?' he asked. 'Did Barbaden send you here to get killed so he can unleash Kain and her Screaming Eagles?'

'Barbaden?' spat Hanno. 'He's got nothing to do with me, not anymore.'

'No?' asked the man, reaching out and lifting a flap of Hanno's long trench coat to reveal the faded scarlet uniform jacket of a lieutenant in the Achaman Falcatas, the silver buttons straining to hold in his generously proportioned belly. 'Last I heard, the Falcatas were still Barbaden's old regiment.'

Hanno snatched his trench coat closed and returned his attention to the bar, rubbing a hand over his stubbled jaw and bleary eyes. He

looked back at the man with the forked beard and said, 'I'm sorry. I...
We never meant–'

'Are you apologising to me?' interrupted the man, his anger even
more plain.

'I'm trying to,' said Hanno, but before he could say more a series of
knocks sounded at the entrance to the bar and the man turned and
ran for the back way out. Within moments it was as if the incident had
never happened, the shadowy denizens of the bar returning their
attention to their drinks and studiously avoiding Hanno's gaze.

He turned on his stool as the tall, stoop-shouldered form of Daron
Nisato ducked under the iron girder welded to two wrecked tank chassis that served as a lintel and stepped into the bar with an expression
of disappointment. He flicked a piece of floating detritus from the
lapels of his enforcer's tunic and looked around the bar until his eyes
fixed on Hanno.

'I thought I'd find you here, lieutenant,' said Nisato.

'What can I say?' replied Hanno. 'I'm a creature of habit.'

'Only bad ones,' said Nisato, and Hanno was forced to agree.

'You'll never guess who was just here,' said Hanno, by way of conversation.

'Who?'

'It doesn't matter,' giggled Hanno, looking over to the rear of the bar
as Nisato took a seat next to him. 'No one important.'

Daron Nisato was a handsome man in his fifties with sharp features, quick eyes and dark skin. His hair was tightly curled and had
turned to grey at the temples at an early age, giving him a distin-
guished look that had served him well when he'd been a commissar
in the Achaman Falcatas.

'You want a drink?' asked Hanno.

'Of raquir? No, I think not. I don't think you should have any more
either.'

'You're probably right, Daron, but what else is there?'

'There's duty,' said Nisato. 'You have yours and I have mine.'

'Duty?' barked Hanno, waving his hands around the bar. 'Look
what duty's done for us. Made us the enemy on our own world, a
world we fought and bled to win. Some prize, eh?'

'Keep your voice down, Hanno,' cautioned Nisato.

'Or what? You'll arrest me?'

'If I have to, yes. A night in the drunk tank might do you some good.'

'No,' said Hanno, 'there's only one thing that'll do me any good.'

'What's that?'

'This,' said Hanno, drawing an immaculately polished pistol from beneath his trench coat.

Nisato was instantly alert. 'What are you doing, Hanno? Put that away.'

Hanno reached into his trench coat again and pulled out something that gleamed gold beneath the flickering globes strung on looped wires from the corrugated metal roof of the bar. He tossed the object onto the bar, where it spun like a coin, rattling on the metal as the image of a fiery eagle wobbled on its golden surface.

'You still keep your medal?' asked Hanno.

'I never received one,' replied Nisato. 'I wasn't there.'

The medal ceased its rotation and lay flat on the greasy surface of the bar.

'Lucky you,' said Hanno, his eyes filling with tears. 'You don't see them then?'

'See who?'

'The burned ones… The ones… The dead?'

Hanno saw the confusion in Nisato's face and tried to speak, but the awful, unforgettable smell of seared human meat rose in his nostrils and the words died in his throat. He gagged, tasting ashen bone and smelling the acrid reek of promethium as though a soot-stained flame trooper stood right next to him.

You were there.

'Oh no… No, please…' he sobbed. 'Not again.'

'Hanno, what's the matter?' demanded Nisato, but Hanno could not reply. He looked around as searing flames leapt to life all around the bar, hot, yellow and unforgiving. As though fanned by some unseen wind, the flames displayed an appetite beyond measure and greedily devoured everything in their path with a whooshing roar. Within moments the entire bar was aflame and Hanno wept as he knew what would come next.

The patrons of the bar rose to their feet, clothes ablaze and faces transformed from surly and hostile to molten and agonised. Like some monstrous host of fiery elementals, they marched towards him, and Hanno turned to Daron Nisato, hoping against hope that the former commissar was seeing what he saw.

Daron Nisato was oblivious to the flaming carnage filling the bar, looking at him with an expression of worried concern and pity.

Hanno cried out as black smoke boiled from the ground, choking and reeking with chemical stink. Shadows moved through the haze like fiery marionettes jerking to the dance of some lunatic puppeteer.

He heard Daron Nisato's voice, but the words were lost to him as he saw a horrifyingly familiar form emerge from the smoke and fire, a girl child, no more than seven years old.

Her dress was ablaze and her arms were, as always, held out to him, as if seeking his affection or rescue. Her skin bubbled and popped, meat and fat running from her bones like molten rubber as her limbs creaked and contracted in the terrible heat.

'You were there,' said the little girl, her face a searing mass of bright flame that ate through her skull and into her brain-pan. A dreadful, spectral light filled her eyes, all that the fire had not yet dared to consume.

'I'm sorry,' said Hanno, as a suffocating wave of guilty remorse clamped his heart.

He drew in a deep breath and in the blink of an eye the inferno of the bar, the melting child and the burning men vanished. All was as it had been moments before. Hanno snatched at the bar to steady himself as the world spun crazily around him, his senses trying to reorient to normality in the wake of such horror.

'What the hell was that?' demanded Nisato beside him, completely unaware of the nightmarish things that Hanno had just experienced for the thousandth time. The enforcer took hold of his arm and said, 'Let's get out of here. You're coming with me.'

'No,' wept Hanno, shrugging off Nisato's grip, 'I'm not. I can't go on like this.'

'You can't,' agreed Nisato. 'That's why you need to come with me now.'

'No,' repeated Hanno, snatching up his pistol and the medal from the bar. 'There's only one place I'm going: Hell.'

Hanno Merbal thrust the pistol into his mouth and blew the back of his head off.

'I should never have believed that death had undone so many.'

PART ONE
REBIRTH

ONE

Do PEOPLE SHAPE the planets they live on or do the planets shape them? The people of Mordian are melancholy and dour, the folk of Catachan pragmatic and hardy. Is this the result of the harsh climes and brutal necessities required for survival, or were the people who settled the planets in ages past already predisposed to those qualities? Can the character of a world affect an entire population or is the human soul stronger than mere geography?

Might an observer more naturally attribute a less malign disposition, a less frightful character, to those who walk unconcerned for their safety beneath the gilded archways of a shrine world than to those who huddle in the darkness of a world torn apart by war and rebellion?

Whatever the case, the solitary heaths, lonely mountains and strife-torn cities of Salinas would have provided an excellent study for any such observer.

RAIN FELL IN soaking sheets from the grey, dusky skies: a fine smirr that hung like mist and made the quartz-rich mountainside glisten and sparkle. Flocks of shaggy herbivores fed on the long grasses of the low pastures, and dark thunderheads in the east gathered over the looming peaks.

Tumbling waterfalls gushed uproariously down black cliffs and the few withered trees that remained on the lower slopes surrounding a dead city bent and swayed like dancers before the driving wind that sheared down from the cloud-wreathed highlands. A brooding silence, like an awkward pause in a conversation, hung over the dead city, as though the landscape feared to intrude on its private sorrow. Rubble-choked streets wound their way between blackened buildings of twisted steel and tumbled stone, and ferns with rust and blood-coloured leaves grew thick in its empty boulevards.

Wind-weathered rock and spars of corroded metal lay where they had fallen, and the wind moaned as it gusted through empty windows and shattered doors, as though the city were giving vent to a long, drawn out death rattle.

People had once lived here. They had loved and fought and indulged in the thousands of dramas, both grand and intimate, common to all cities. Great celebrations, scandalous intrigues and bloody crimes had all played out here, but all such theatre had passed into history, though not from memory.

Hundreds of streets, avenues, thoroughfares and roads criss-crossed the empty city, wending their way through its desolation as though in search of someone to tread them once more. Open doors banged on frames, forlorn entreaties to a nameless visitor to enter and render the building purposeful once more. Rain ran in gurgling streams beside the cracked pavements, flowing from grates and gathering in pools where the land had subsided.

A tall church, its façade of stone scorched black and greasy, stood proud amid the ruins, as though whatever calamity had befallen the city had seen fit to spare the mighty edifice the worst of its attention. Tall spires cast long shadows over the city and the great eagle-winged pediment that had once sat proudly above the arched entrance now sagged in defeat, its wings dipped and streaked with green corrosion.

High windows that glorified the Emperor and His many saints were shattered and empty, fragments of coloured glass jutting like teeth in rotted frames. The heavy iron doors that had once protected the main vestibule of the church lay twisted and broken on the cracked flagstones of the esplanade. Shattered statues lay beside the doors, fallen from the roof and left to crumble where they lay.

The wind collected here, as though drawn by some unseen imperative to gambol in the open square before the church. Wisps of mist were dragged along with the wind and fluttering scraps of cloth, paper and leaves spun in miniature whirlwinds as the strength of the wind gathered force.

The gaping blackness of the church's entrance seemed to swallow what little light was left of the day, and though the wind pulled the leaves and debris of the city back and forth with ever-greater vigour, none dared violate the darkness within the abandoned building.

A hollow moaning issued from the church, though nothing lived within it – or indeed in the entire city – and a gust of air, colder than the depths of space, blew into the square.

Beginning as spots of brightness against the black, rippling streamers of light oozed from the arched entrance and flowed like ghostly lines of mercury along the ground in two parallel tracks. Before, the church had seemed relentlessly solid and immovable, now its fabric seemed to ripple and warp as though in the grip of a monstrous heat haze.

The moaning built, rising from a far distant sound to something much closer, a shrieking howl of a thing in agony that fought to hold itself together as though its very sinews were being unravelled with every passing second.

The darkness of the church's interior swelled, billowing outwards like an explosive ink stain. Then it retreated, spilling back over something that had violated time and space to enter this world, a churning, seething remnant of a thing first given form in another age.

It resembled a great juggernaut machine of pistons and iron, its brazen flanks heaving with unnatural energies as it thundered from the church. Steam leaked from every demented, skull-faced rivet as wheels of rusted, dissolving iron ground the mercurial tracks beneath it.

Deep within its fragmenting structure, it might have once resembled an ancient steam-driven locomotive, but unknown forces and warped energies had transformed it into something else entirely.

Whatever power had once fashioned the monstrous, terrifying amalgamation of machine and dark energy now appeared to be working to unmake it. Flaring whoops of light streamed from it, peeling back like the layers of an onion. The very air seemed toxic to its existence, hissing clouds of stinking vaporous light billowing from its every surface.

The terrible machine screamed like a wounded beast, but deep within the aching agonies of its dissolution, there was a keening note of welcome release, as though an eternity of torment had come to an end. Its passage slowed until it came to a halt, like a hunted beast that had reached the end of its endurance and could run no more.

Within the tortured end of the machine, there was the suggestion of voices, a hint of things within it that were not part of its decay. The sounds of the voices grew stronger with each passing second, as though their owners called out from some freshly unlocked, yet still impossibly distant chamber.

As a portion of the juggernaut dissolved, it revealed a dreadful glimpse of the machine's red-lit interior, a stinking meat locker that reeked of unnumbered slaughters and debaucheries, roaring fires and an eon's worth of bloodshed.

Shapes moved within the light, a handful of figures that stumbled like newborns or drunks as they spilled like entrails from the dying machine. Tall, broad and humanoid, they scrambled and crawled from the light as though in pain.

The figures emerged from the armoured leviathan that had brought them to this world, wreathed in coiling wisps of smoke. Their steps were feverish and unsteady, but even unsteady steps were welcome, so long as they carried them away from the dissolving machine.

As the figures put more distance between themselves and the heaving engine, their shapes resolved into clarity, though, had an observer been watching this incredible arrival, he might have wished that they had not.

They were monsters: the Unfleshed.

They were twisted freaks of nature, the bastard by-blows of hideous surgery, failed experiments and dreadful power of unnatural origin. No two were alike, their skinless bodies massive and grotesque, their heads swollen, encephalic nightmares of distended eyes, ripped faces and gnashing fangs.

To see such things would have driven many a man mad with fear, but had anyone had the courage to look beyond the physical deformities and hideous malformations of bone and flesh, they would have seen something else, something that would no doubt have horrified them even more: the glimmer of human understanding and awareness.

Two other figures followed the monstrous creatures, as stumbling and as dazed as the monsters, but without the horrifying aberrations of the flesh that afflicted them. Both had the bulky, gene-built physique of Astartes. One was broader and more powerfully built than the other, although his right arm ended abruptly at the elbow.

One was clad in blue armour; the other in fragments of armour the same colour. The first wore his dirty blond hair tight to his skull, his features wide and open, while the other, dark haired, grey-eyed and wolf-lean, had a face that was stern and patrician.

Both warriors, for it was clear from the wounds and weapons they bore that these were men to whom the crucible of combat was no strange and unknown place, staggered away from the disintegrating machine, collapsing to the ground and heaving great draughts of cold air into their lungs.

With the disembarkation of its passengers, the mighty engine that had carried them squealed with the sound of metal grinding on metal as the burning wheels of iron dragged the strange and terrible machine away from the place.

Confined so long to realms beyond the material universe, its substance was unused to the assault of the elements that made up this existence, and the abrasive banality of reality was undoing its unknowable, warp-spawned structure as surely as a flame devours ice.

Its former passengers watched it gather momentum, moving slowly at first and then with greater speed as its form became ever brighter, as if some infernal power source within was drawing close to critical mass. Its brightness soon became too much to bear, even for those whose eyes were genhanced to withstand such things. With a tortured scream, though whether one of death or release none could tell, the living engine vanished in an explosion of light.

No violence or blast spread from this explosion, but a glittering rain of light fell and saturated the air with the sense of an infinite power having been released into the world.

With the final dissolution or escape of the great, immaterial engine, the gloom and dread of the dead city smothered the world once more, the rain bathing the bedraggled travellers in cold, clammy wetness.

The two Astartes warriors found each other in the rain, embracing like brothers at the simple joy of having returned to a world where the air was not a toxic soup of pollutants, ashen bone matter and the hot, sad smell of burned iron and war.

The bigger warrior ran a hand through his hair, frowning as he took in the dismal nature of their surroundings.

'Thank the Emperor,' he said. 'We're not on Medrengard!'

His companion smiled and tilted his head back, letting the cold rain run down his face, as though such a sensation was a rare and precious gift. 'No, Pasanius,' he said, 'we're not.'

'Then where are we?'

'I think we are almost home, my friend,' said Uriel Ventris.

Though it was dusk, Uriel's eyes could easily pierce the gloom enveloping the city once the afterimages of the Omphalos Daemonium's departure or destruction had faded. No trace remained of its passing, and Uriel was grateful to be rid of the vile daemonic creation.

Once it had been the infernal conveyance of a mighty creature of the warp, an engine by which it could traverse the dreadful regions of warp, time and space to wreak havoc on mortals throughout the galaxy. That daemon was gone, destroyed by another of its diabolical kind, allowing Uriel and Pasanius to escape the daemon world of Medrengard in its blood-soaked interior.

'Where do you think it's gone?' asked Pasanius, his hand resting on the butt of a purloined boltgun. Though his right arm was gone below the elbow, Uriel knew that Pasanius was equally adept at killing with his left. Uriel too was armed, a golden-hilted sword that had once belonged to Captain Idaeus, his mentor and former captain of the 4th Company of the Ultramarines, gripped in one fist.

'I don't know and I don't care,' said Uriel, breathing the crisp air and relishing the fresh, wild scents carried from the forests that circled the mountains towering over them. He saw flocks of grazing beasts on the rugged flanks of the peaks, and the sight of something so unthreatening was absurdly welcome. 'I am just glad we're free of it.'

'Aye, there's that,' agreed Pasanius. 'Now we just have to figure out where it's dumped us. I certainly wasn't steering, were you?'

'No, but I don't think the Omphalos Daemonium was ever meant to be steered by the likes of us.'

'So we could be anywhere,' said Pasanius.

'Indeed,' said Uriel, as curious as his friend to know where they had been deposited. Though he had no idea why the daemon engine had chosen to end their journey upon this world, whichever world it was, he had spent the unknown period of time within its depths visualising Macragge and his home world of Calth, hoping against hope that thoughts of familiar places would somehow guide the mighty engine's course towards them.

It hadn't worked. This world neither looked nor felt like either of those worlds. The sky above was leaden grey, with brooding and dissatisfied clouds scudding around the peaks of the high, craggy mountains that looked down on the strange, abandoned city they found themselves within.

Uriel turned from the mountains to survey their more immediate surroundings, a wide, marble-flagged square choked with rubble and weeds. The buildings around the edge of the square had been cast to ruin by time and, unmistakably, the brutal effects of war. Bullet holes, laser scarring and promethium burns marked almost every inch of stonework and the cold sense of the lingering dead hung heavy in the air.

'So I wonder where this is?' said Pasanius, turning in a circle. 'It's Imperial at least.'

'How do you know that?'

'Look,' said Pasanius, nodding towards the building behind Uriel.

Uriel followed Pasanius's nod to see a double-headed, bronze eagle hanging at a forlorn angle from a tall building of blackened stone. The arched niches and statuary, though broken and in a state of gross disrepair, were unmistakably those of an Imperial temple. The Unfleshed gathered beneath the eagle, their heads craned back to stare in rapt adoration at the symbol of the Emperor.

'Or at least it *was* an Imperial world,' pointed out Pasanius. 'This place is dead.'

'Aye,' agreed Uriel. '*This* place is dead, but there will be others.'

'You sure?' asked Pasanius. 'I hope you're right.'

'I am,' said Uriel. 'I don't know how, but I just am.'

'Another one of your feelings?' said Pasanius. 'Emperor preserve us. That always means trouble.'

'Well, wherever we are, it has to be better than Medrengard.'

'That wouldn't be hard,' pointed out Pasanius. 'I don't know many places that wouldn't be a step up from a world in the Eye of Terror.'

Uriel conceded the point, trying to blot out memories of Medrengard's continent-sized manufactories, its impossible fortresses, the billowing clouds of hot ash that seared the throat with every breath and the vile, dead things that soared upon the thermals of hellish industry.

They had endured all manner of horrors on Medrengard in the service of their Death Oath, but despite everything the home world of the Iron Warriors could throw at them, they had triumphed and escaped.

But where were they?

Uriel's thoughts were interrupted as those of the Unfleshed that could, dropped to their knees before the church of the Emperor. Those with anatomies too twisted to kneel simply bowed their heads, and a low, keening moan issued from their distorted throats. Uriel could only imagine what these poor, pitiful creatures might be feeling.

As if sensing his scrutiny, the largest of the creatures turned to face Uriel and shuffled over towards him, its steps heavy and its sheened body rippling with monstrously powerful muscles. A pungent, animal odour came with the creature, the Lord of the Unfleshed, his body raw and crimson, the soft rain dripping from him in red droplets.

As always, the sight of this creature brought a mix of feelings to the surface: horror, pity, anger and a protective urge to see that they were not treated as their appearance would suggest, for the Lord of the Unfleshed was, by any definition of the word, a monster.

Taller than Uriel, the Lord of the Unfleshed's body was grossly swollen and built beyond the power of a Space Marine. Once, not so long ago, he had been a child, a captive taken by the dreaded Iron Warriors to Medrengard, where daemonic magic and the cruel attentions of the Savage Morticians had wrought him into a freakish beast.

In an attempt to hothouse fresh warriors, the diabolical surgeon-creatures of the Warsmith Honsou had implanted stolen children in grotesque daemonic wombs and fed their developing anatomies a gruel of genetic material concocted from fallen Iron Warriors and captured Astartes gene-seed.

A capricious and unpredictable alchemy at best, this process resulted in far more failures than successes and those pathetic, mutant offspring deemed too withered or degenerate to be further transformed were flushed from the hellish laboratories like so much excrement.

Most such abortions died in Medrengard's nightmarishly polluted wastelands, but some did not, living as skinless monsters driven into the darkest abyss of madness and despair by the horror of their own existence.

Uriel and Pasanius had first seen the Unfleshed, as other inhabitants of Medrengard had dubbed them, as they slaughtered the degenerate prisoners of an Iron Warriors' flesh camp. He had been horrified by their savagery, but later came to realise that they were as much victims of the Iron Warriors as any of those lost souls whose bodies had been tortured beyond all endurance in the camps.

When Uriel had come to realise the truth of the Unfleshed's existence, he had been horrified and filled with pity for these towering monsters, for they were creations of flesh and blood that carried the essence of Space Marine heroes in their veins.

They all boasted physiques reminiscent of carnival grotesques in their unnatural anatomies, with flaps of dead skin pulled over their deformities as if such paltry disguises could hide their warped flesh. One creature's jaw was kept forever open by distended fangs like splintered bone, another was cursed with the withered, still living body of its conjoined twin fused to its chest, another's skeletal structure was so warped that it no longer resembled anything human and moved with a locomotion never before seen in man nor beast.

'This Emperor's world?' asked the Lord of the Unfleshed, his leathery tongue having difficulty in forming the words over thick, razor-edged fangs.

Uriel nodded, seeing the pain behind the creature's eyes. 'Yes, it is. One of them anyway.'

'More worlds like this?'

'Millions,' agreed Uriel.

Seeing the confusion in the Lord of the Unfleshed's face, Uriel understood he probably had no concept of so vast a number. 'There are many worlds like this,' he said, pointing up to where hundreds of stars shimmered in the darkening sky. 'Each of those lights is a world like this.'

Uriel knew that wasn't exactly true, but as the Lord of the Unfleshed looked up, a slow smile spread across his face.

'Sky black.'

'Yes,' smiled Uriel, only now realising how much he had missed the natural diurnal cycle of a habitable world. 'The sky is black, and in the morning it will become light again.'

'Like world of Iron Men?'

Uriel shivered as he pictured the dead, unchanging skies of Medrengard and the unblinking, black sun that held sway over it all. 'No, not like Iron Men's world at all. The sun is golden and warm. You'll like it.'

'Good. Iron Men's world bad,' said the Lord of the Unfleshed. 'This world smell bad too. Not bad like Iron Men's world, but still bad.'

Uriel's interest was piqued. 'This world smells bad? What do you mean?'

'Bad things happen here,' said the Lord of the Unfleshed, looking around the square with an apprehensive gaze. 'Blood spilled here, much blood. Not all gone yet. Making Unfleshed hungry.'

Uriel shared a look with Pasanius, both warriors all too aware of how dangerous the hunger of the Unfleshed could be.

The Unfleshed had fought alongside them on Medrengard through brutal necessity and desperate circumstance, but how long such an alliance would hold against their terrible appetites was something Uriel was not keen to find out.

He looked up into the mountains, where the faint outlines of herds of animals could still be seen. Uriel pointed upwards and said, 'You see those beasts on the mountain?'

The Lord of the Unfleshed nodded and Uriel was reminded that their physiques were, at least partially, made up from Space Marine gene-seed, which included superior eyesight to that of mortals.

'You can hunt them,' said Uriel. 'That is good meat, but only that meat. You understand?'

'Yes.'

'Human meat is bad meat,' said Uriel. 'You cannot eat it. The Emperor does not want you to eat human meat anymore.'

'We understand,' said the Lord of the Unfleshed. 'No eat humans.'

'If you see any humans you don't recognise, hide from them. Don't let them see you,' added Pasanius.

The Lord of the Unfleshed bobbed his massive head, thick ropes of drool leaking from around his fangs, and Uriel knew he was already thinking of the taste of fresh meat and hot blood. Without another word, the mighty creature turned and barked a string of guttural commands to his fellow creatures, who rose from their obeisance below the temple's eagle and followed their leader as he set off in the direction of the mountains.

'Will they be all right left to their own devices?' asked Pasanius.

'I don't know,' admitted Uriel. 'Emperor help me, but I hope so.'

Uriel and Pasanius watched them as they vanished from sight, swallowed up in the darkness of the dead city.

'Now what?' asked Pasanius.

Uriel turned to his sergeant and said, 'Now we talk.'

TWO

NIGHT CLOSED IN on the dead city as Uriel and Pasanius sought shelter from the drizzling rain and biting wind. Pasanius was still clad in his stained blue power armour, albeit severed at the elbow, while Uriel's skin was largely bare to the elements. Portions of Uriel's armour had been stripped from his upper body by the brutal ministrations of the Savage Morticians, and though fragments remained of his breastplate, the armour was essentially useless.

Without power feeding the fibre bundle muscles that augmented the wearer's strength, it was heavy and cumbersome, impeding where it was designed to enhance. Without conscious thought, both Space Marines gravitated towards the Imperial temple. Of all the buildings around the square it was the most intact and therefore the most defendable.

The city felt dead and abandoned, but it did not pay to take such things at face value. A fuller exploration of the city could come when the sun rose, but for now, shelter and somewhere to lie low was Uriel's priority.

The doors lay twisted and melted on the ground, and Uriel recognised the telltale impact striations that spoke of a melta blast.

'Someone barricaded themselves in here,' said Pasanius, following Uriel's gaze.

'Looks like it,' agreed Uriel.

'Now why would someone do that?'

'If you were a citizen of this city and you were under attack, where would you seek refuge?'

'I wouldn't be seeking refuge,' said Pasanius. 'I'd be fighting, not hiding while others fought for me.'

Uriel said nothing in response to the simple, yet wholly under-standable sentiment, recognising the same lack of empathy for the fears of mortals in Pasanius's tone as he had heard in so many others of his kind. To be so elevated above ordinary men brought the risk of arrogance and though he had heard that egotism given voice by many other Astartes warriors, he had never thought to hear it from Pasanius.

The temple's vestibule was cold, a chill that reached out to Uriel beyond the sensations pricking his skin. He had stood in many tem-ples from the most magnificent to the most humble, but even the least of them had a sense of the divine in their architecture and sense of scale, but this building had none of that.

It felt empty.

Uriel pushed open the splintered remains of the doors that led to the nave, the echoes of his footsteps thrown back at him like those of a shadowing twin. Dust motes spun in the air, but his vision easily pierced the gloom of the temple's interior as he made his way inside. A vaulted ceiling arched overhead and thick pillars of fluted stonework marched the length of the nave towards a toppled altar.

Fallen banners that reeked of mould lay curled on the flagstones and broken wooden pews filled the floor between the vestibule and the raised altar. The walls were faced with dressed ashlar and the last of the day's light illuminated thousands of scraps of paper fastened to every square inch.

Intrigued, Uriel made his way towards this unusual sight, breaths of wind through the empty window frames making it seem as though the wall rippled in anticipation. The papers were old and faded and many had rotted away to fall on the floor, piled up like snowdrifts. Of those that remained, Uriel saw they were a mix of scrawled prayers for the dead, scraps of poems or simple lithographs of smiling men, women and children.

'What are these?' whispered Pasanius, his voice loud in the still-ness of the temple as he made his way along the wall and peered at the sad pictures and words.

'Memorials,' said Uriel. 'They're prayers for dead loved ones.'

'But there're so many... Thousands. Did they all die at once?'

'I don't know,' replied Uriel. 'It looks like it.'

'Emperor's blood,' hissed Pasanius. 'What happened here?'

A cold breath whispered across Uriel's neck.

You were there.

Uriel spun on his heel, his hand reaching for his sword.

'What?' said Pasanius as Uriel's blade hissed into the air.

'Nothing,' said Uriel, relaxing when he saw there was no threat.

He and Pasanius were the only trespassers in the temple, but for the briefest second, Uriel could have sworn that there had been someone behind him. The temple's crepuscular depths were empty of intruders, and yet...

Uriel's warrior instincts had been honed on a thousand battle-fields and he had not stayed alive this long without developing a fine sense for danger. Though he could see nothing and hear nothing within the temple, he had the definite impression that they were not alone.

'Did you see something?' asked Pasanius, bracing the bolter between his knees and racking the slide. The noise was ugly and harsh, and both warriors felt a ripple of distaste at the sound. The weapon was from the battlefields of Medrengard and had once belonged to an Iron Warrior. Though he held it before him, Uriel saw that Pasanius was reluctant to employ a weapon of the enemy.

'No,' said Uriel. 'I felt something.'

'Like what?'

'I'm not sure, It was as if someone was standing right behind me.'

Pasanius scanned the temple's interior, but finding no targets for his weapon he lowered the bolter. Uriel could see the relief on his face and the sense that they were not alone in the temple receded.

'There's no one here but us,' said Pasanius, moving along the length of the wall towards the altar, though he kept a firm grip on the bolter. 'Maybe you're still a little jumpy after Medrengard.'

'Maybe,' said Uriel as he followed Pasanius, walking past a proces-sion of smiling faces, votive offerings and fluttering prayer papers.

So many had died and been remembered on these walls. Pasanius was right, there were thousands of them and Uriel thought the scene unbearably sad. The opposite wall was similarly covered in sad memorials, and stacks of fallen papers clustered around the base of every column.

They reached the altar and Uriel sheathed his sword.

'We should study these papers,' said Uriel, pushing the fallen altar upright and beginning to unclip the few broken pieces of the armour encasing his upper body, not that there was much left of it. 'They might give us a clue as to where we are.'

'I suppose,' said Pasanius, placing the bolter on the ground and pushing it away with his foot.

'Are you all right, my friend?' asked Uriel, placing a shorn sliver that was all that remained of his breastplate on the altar. 'We are on our way home.'

'I know, but...'

'But?'

'What's going to happen when we get there?'

'What do you mean?'

'Think about it, Uriel,' said Pasanius. 'We've been to the Eye of Terror. No one comes back from there unchanged. How do we know we'll even be welcome back on Macragge? They'll probably kill us as soon as they see us.'

'No,' said Uriel, 'they won't. We fulfilled our Death Oath. Tigurius and Calgar sent us there and they will be proud of what we did.'

'You think?' said Pasanius, shaking his head. 'We fought alongside renegade Space Marines. We made a pact with cannibal mutants and freed a daemon creature. Don't you think Tigurius might take a dim view of things like that?'

Uriel sighed. He *had* considered these things, but in his heart he knew they had made every decision with the best intentions and for the right reasons.

The Masters of the Chapter had to see that.

Didn't they?

It had been Uriel's wilful deviation from Roboute Guilliman's Codex Astartes that had seen them banished from Ultramar in the first place. Penned by the Ultramarines primarch ten thousand years ago, the Codex Astartes laid out the precise organisational tenets by which the Space Marine Chapters would arise from the mighty Legions of the Great Crusade.

Everything from uniform markings, parade drill and the exact means by which warriors should deploy for battle was described within its hallowed pages, and no Chapter exemplified its teachings better than the Ultramarines.

To conform to the principles of their primarch was seen as the highest ideal of the Ultramarines and so to have one of its captains go against that was unacceptable. Uriel had willingly accepted his punishment, but having Pasanius condemned with him had been a shard of guilt in his heart for as long as they had marched across the surface of Medrengard.

In his time on that hell world, Uriel had often doubted his worth as a hero, but with the casting down of Honsou's fortress and the destruction of the daemon creatures that had birthed the Unfleshed, he had come to see that they had been instruments of the Emperor's will after all. Now, with their Death Oath fulfilled, they were going home.

How could such a thing be wrong?

'We have done all that was required of us,' said Uriel, 'and more besides. Tigurius will sense that there is no taint of the Ruinous Powers within us.'

'What about this?' asked Pasanius, holding up the severed end of his arm. 'What if there's some lingering remainder of the Bringer of Darkness left in me?'

'There won't be,' said Uriel. 'Honsou took that from you.'

'How can you be sure it's all gone?'

'I can't,' said Uriel, 'but once we get back to the Fortress of Hera, the Apothecaries will know for sure.'

'Then I will be punished.'

'Perhaps,' allowed Uriel. 'You kept a xenos infection from your superior officers, but whatever the senior masters of the Chapter decide, you will be back with the Fourth Company before long.'

'I wonder how the company is doing,' said Pasanius.

'Learchus promised to look after the men of the Company in our absence,' said Uriel. 'He will have done us proud, I'm sure.'

'Aye,' agreed Pasanius. 'As straight up and down a sergeant as you could wish for, that one. Bit of a cold fish, but he'll have kept the men together.'

'What few were left after Tarsis Ultra,' said Uriel, thinking of the terrible carnage that had seen much of the Fourth Company dead as they defended the Imperial world against a Tyranid invasion.

'That was a tough one, right enough,' said Pasanius as Uriel placed the last of the broken pieces of his armour on the altar. His upper body was left clothed in a simple body sleeve of faded and dirty khaki, the toughened fabric pierced with holes where his armour's interface plugs had meshed with the internal workings of his body.

'I'm sure Learchus will have been thorough in raising promising candidates up from the Scout Auxillia,' said Pasanius. 'The Fourth will be back to full strength by now, surely.'

'I hope so,' agreed Uriel. 'The idea of the Ultramarines without the Fourth does not sit well with me.'

'Nor I, but if you're right and we get back soon, do you think it will be yours again?'

Uriel shrugged. 'That won't be up to me. Chapter Master Calgar will decide that.'

'If he knows what's good for the Chapter, he'll appoint you captain the day we get back.'

'He knows what's good for the Chapter,' promised Uriel.

'I know he does, but I can't help but feel apprehensive. I mean, who knows how long we've been gone? For all we know, hundreds or thousands of years could have passed since we left. And this place...'

'What about it?'

'The Lord of the Unfleshed... He's right, something bad happened to this city. I can feel it.'

Uriel said nothing, for he too could feel the subtle undercurrent in the air, a feeling that the imprint of terrible calamity had befallen this city, that it hadn't simply been abandoned.

'And another thing,' said Pasanius, 'just what in the name of the Primarch are you hoping to achieve with those monsters?'

'They're not monsters,' said Uriel. 'They have the blood of Astartes within them.'

'Maybe so, but they look like monsters and I can't see anyone with a gun not shooting as soon as they lay eyes on them. We should have left them on Medrengard. You know that don't you?'

'I couldn't,' said Uriel, sitting next to Pasanius. 'You saw how they lived. They may look like monsters, but they love the Emperor and all they want is his love in return. I couldn't leave them there. I have to try to… I don't know, show them that there is more to existence than pain.'

'Good luck with that,' said Pasanius sourly.

THE MOON HAD risen and pools of brilliant white light reflected a ghostly radiance around the temple's interior by the time the Unfleshed returned. Uriel was loath to use the memorials as fuel and thus they had built a fire from the kindling of the shattered pews in an iron brazier they discovered at the rear of the temple.

The Unfleshed dragged the carcasses of three of the mountain graz- ers into the church, each beast's body torn and bloodied with fang and claw marks. The dead beasts were covered in a coarse fur, with bovine heads and long, burrowing snouts of leathery hide. Their legs were slender and powerful looking and Uriel imagined they would be swift on the hoof.

'They've already fed then,' said Pasanius, seeing the bloody jaws of the Unfleshed.

'So it appears,' replied Uriel as the Lord of the Unfleshed dragged one of the larger kills over to the altar. The carcass was dropped before him.

'We eat meat on mountain,' said the Lord of the Unfleshed. 'This meat for you.'

Without waiting for an answer, the hulking creature turned away, his eyes dull and lifeless. Curious as to what was the matter, Uriel reached up and placed a hand on the Lord of the Unfleshed's arm.

No sooner had Uriel touched the arm than it was snatched away and the Lord of the Unfleshed turned to face him with a hiss of pain. Uriel flinched at the suddenness of the reaction and the violence he saw in the Lord of the Unfleshed's eyes.

'Not touch me,' hissed the Lord of the Unfleshed. 'Pain. This world hurts us.'

'Hurts you? What do you mean?'

The Lord of the Unfleshed paused, as though struggling to find the words to articulate his meaning. 'Air here different. We feel different, weak. Body not work like before.'

Uriel nodded, though he had no real idea as to why the Unfleshed should feel different on this particular world.

'Try to get some rest,' advised Uriel. 'When the sun comes up we'll get a better look at the lie of the land and decide what to do next. You understand?'

'I understand,' nodded the Lord of the Unfleshed. 'Emperor happy with us?'

'Yes, he is,' said Uriel. 'You are in a place dedicated to Him.'

'Dedicated?'

'It belongs to him,' explained Uriel. 'Like where you lived before.'

'This house of Emperor?'

'It is, yes.'

'Then we stay here. Emperor take care of us,' said the Lord of the Unfleshed, and Uriel found the simple sentiment curiously touching. These creatures may be genetic aberrations, but they believed in the Emperor's divinity with a simple, childlike faith.

The Lord of the Unfleshed lumbered away to rejoin his fellows and Uriel turned back to the altar, where Pasanius was butchering the carcass they had been provided with in preparation for roasting it over the fire. Space Marines could, of course, eat the meat raw to gain more nutritional benefits, but after the deprivations of Medrengard, both warriors were in the mood for some hot food inside them.

Uriel watched the Unfleshed as they hunkered down before the walls, staring in fascination at the parchment scraps on the wall. Pasanius handed him a skewered hunk of meat and placed his own over the fire.

'It's easy to forget,' said Uriel.

'What is?'

'They are just children really.'

'The Unfleshed?'

'Yes. Think about it. They were taken as youngsters and twisted into these horrific forms by the Savage Morticians, but they are still children inside. I was placed inside one of those daemon wombs. I know what it tried to do to me, but to do that to a child… Imagine waking up and finding that you had been turned into a monster.'

'Do you think any of them remember their former lives?'

'I don't know,' said Uriel. 'In some ways, I hope they don't; it would be too awful to remember what they'd lost, but then I think that it's only the fragments of what they once were that's keeping them from truly becoming monsters.'

'Then let's hope more of their memories return now that they're away from Medrengard.'

'I suppose,' said Uriel, turning his skewer on the fire. 'I know they look like monsters, but what happened to them isn't their fault. They deserve more than just to be hunted down and killed because they aren't like us. We may not be able to save their bodies, but we can save their souls.'

'How?'

'By treating them like human beings.'

'Then I just hope you get to talk to people before they see them.'

'I plan to, eventually, but let's take things one step at a time.'

'Speaking of which,' said Pasanius, lifting his skewer of meat from the fire and taking an experimental bite. 'Oh, that's good. What's our next move in the morning?'

Uriel removed his skewer from the fire and bit into the meat, the smell intoxicating and the taste sublime after so long on ration packs and recycled nutrient pastes. The meat was tough, but gloriously rich. Warm juices spilled down his chin and he resisted the impulse to wolf down his meal without pause.

Between mouthfuls, Uriel said, 'Tomorrow we explore the city, get a feel for its geography and then work out where we might find a settlement.'

'Then what?'

'Then we present ourselves to whatever Imperial authorities we find and make contact with the Chapter.'

'You think it'll be that easy?'

'It will or it won't be,' said Uriel. 'I suppose we'll find out tomorrow, but we need some rest first. Every bone in my body aches and I just want one night of proper sleep before we get into things.'

'Sounds good to me,' agreed Pasanius. 'Every time I closed my eyes on that damn, daemon engine, all I saw were rivers of blood and skinned bodies.'

Uriel nodded, only too well aware of the nightmarish things that lurked behind his own eyes when he had tried to rest on the Omphalos Daemonium. Not since he had stood before the Nightbringer had he seen such horrors or believed that such terrible things could be dreamed into existence.

For the unknown span of time they had spent within its insane depths, both they and the Unfleshed had been plagued by these blood dreams and Uriel knew that his mind had been close to breaking, for who could be visited nightly by such phantasms and remain sane?

OF ALL THE nightmarish visions of death and bloodshed that plagued Mesira Bardhyl, it was the Mourner she feared the most. She never saw his face, she just heard his sobs, but the depths of agony and suffering encapsulated in those sounds was beyond measure.

It seemed impossible that anyone could know such pain and sorrow and live. Yet the mourner's dark outline, stark against the white, ceramic tiles of the empty room, was clearly that of a living person.

Tears coursed down her cheeks at the sight of the Mourner, a measure of his pain passing to her as her treacherous feet carried her towards the iron-framed bed he sat on, the only piece of furniture in this otherwise featureless room.

She knew she was dreaming, but that knowledge did nothing to lessen her terror.

Despite the *khat* leaves Mesira had mixed with the half bottle of raquir she'd downed before reluctantly climbing into bed, the nightmare of the Mourner had still found her.

Step by step, she moved closer to the Mourner, wracking sobs of anguish causing his shoulders to shake violently. As Mesira drew closer, she felt his grief change to anger, and though she tried to will her hand not to reach out, it lifted of its own accord.

As she touched the Mourner's shoulder, the stink of burned meat filled her senses and images danced behind her eyes: burning buildings, screaming people and a firestorm so intense it billowed and seethed like a living thing.

'No,' she whispered. 'Not again.'

The Mourner ceased his weeping, as though only now aware of her.

Without warning, flames suddenly bloomed into life across his body, engulfing his head and limbs with incandescent brightness.

'You were there,' said the Mourner, apparently oblivious to the fire that consumed him.

'No, I...' cried Mesira, falling back from the killing heat.

'You were there,' repeated the Mourner, his voice accusing as the flames slithered over him. In moments, his body was scorched black and the smell of his seared flesh made her gag.

'The dead are watching and you will all be punished.'

'Please,' begged Mesira. 'Why me?'

'You were there,' said the Mourner, as if that explained everything. 'You were there.'

'I didn't do anything. It wasn't me,' wept Mesira.

'You were there.'

'I–'

'You were there,' said the Mourner, turning towards her, 'and you will pay. You will all pay.'

MESIRA BARDHYL HURLED herself from her bed, screaming in terror and clawing at the sheets as she fought to free herself from them. She thrashed on the floor of the room, kicking and shrieking like a mad-woman. Weeping, she curled into the foetal position, her palms pressed against the side of her head and her bitten-down fingernails clawing at her scalp.

She bit the flesh of her palm to stifle her screams, rocking back and forth on the floor.

Her eyes were closed tightly and it took an effort of will to open them.

The room was dimly lit, a weak glow from the haphazardly arranged lumen globes on the street outside filtering through the thin curtains twitching at the window. A stainless steel sink and toilet unit gurgled behind a privacy screen and stacks of papers fluttered on the table in the centre of the room.

Mesira remained on the floor until her breathing returned to normal and her heart rate slowed, before picking herself up using the edge of the bed to steady her shaking legs. Her whole body was trembling and she bent to lift the fallen sheet and wrap it around her skinny, wasted frame.

The vision was still fresh in her mind and she wiped away tears as she made her way to the table and poured a tall glass of raquir. Loose papers lay strewn across the table, a half finished report for Verena Kain detail-ing empathic readings she'd made at a meeting between Governor Barbaden and community leaders. It was a breach of security to have them lying out like this, but she had left the Imperial palace early that day, unwilling to spend any more time in Barbaden's presence than she had to.

The sounds of the city drifted in through her window: the clatter of ramshackle ground cars, the raucous sound of drunks pouring from the bars and the occasional violent oath. She could sense the feelings and emotions drifting in the air behind the sounds, but shut them out, blunting her powers with another shot of raquir.

She poured another, knowing she would get no more sleep tonight and unwilling to close her eyes again after the horrors the Mourner had shown her.

In her dream he had turned his face towards her, his flesh dripping from his blackened skull as the heat of the flames roared hotter and brighter. She had wanted to look away. She had known with utter certainty that to see his face would drive her to madness, but her head was fixed in place and when she saw his eyes, cold and white like the heart of a dead star, she had seen horrors that went beyond even those of the Killing Ground.

Sloshing, corpse-filled tenders shuddered and bumped behind a heaving daemon engine that spurted blood and travelled on tracks of bone. Forests of dead children were impaled on jangling meat hooks. Entire planets were laid waste before a tide of screaming daemons, and galaxies were extinguished by the power that poured into this world from the insane geometry of the monstrous engine.

Dead souls writhed in the depths of its awful, daemonic structure and she could feel the immense warp energy surrounding it, a flood of power saturating the air and earth and water of Salinas with its presence. Whatever this horrifying machine was, it had seen unnumbered slaughters and brought with it the dread memories of every drop of blood spilled in its vile existence.

She had seen them all, every soul torn from flesh, every violation visited upon an innocent and every vile, unimaginable horror wreaked upon the living.

As clearly as if she had stood watching it, she saw the mighty daemon engine appear before the temple in the main square of Khaturian, its bronze, eagle-winged pediment sagging where the bombs had loosened it from the stonework: the building the Screaming Eagles had attacked with melta guns and then stormed with guns blazing and blades chopping.

Mesira closed her eyes, trying to block the memories of screams, the echoing bark of gunfire and the horrifying, unending whoosh of flamers. She moved from the table to stand at the window, looking over the cobbled streets of Barbadus and watching the few people that dared pass beneath her window. They walked by without looking up, for it was well known that Barbaden's pet psyker lived here, and no one wanted to attract her evil eye.

Anger touched her and she allowed her ability to reach out, feeling the ghost touch of the minds that filled the squalid tenements and ad hoc dwellings formed in the remains of a regiment's worth of vehicles that the Achaman Falcatas had abandoned to the elements.

Barbadus was a city built upon the bones of an Imperial Guard regiment's cast-offs.

With the conclusion of the campaign to quell the rebellious system, the planet Salinas had been awarded to the Falcatas, and the regiment had been permitted to keep the bulk of its armoured vehicles, for there had not been the means to transport most of them off world. However, without sufficient enginseers or tech-priests, most had swiftly fallen into disrepair and only a handful of companies were able to maintain their tanks and transports in working order.

Those that could not simply abandoned them, and it did not take long for the enterprising citizens of Barbadus to claim them. Families lived in and around these vehicles, making homes in what had once been instruments of war.

A Leman Russ battle tank could house a family of five once any unnecessary kit had been hollowed out, a Chimera even more. Many other vehicles had been cannibalised for parts and sheets of metal, and entire districts of Barbadus were constructed from the remains of those vehicles that had rusted solid, broken down or otherwise failed.

Her senses were filled with the simmering resentment that bubbled just below the surface of virtually every inhabitant of the city, and it was a resentment Mesira could well understand, for the invasion of the Achaman Falcatas had been brutal and bloody.

The new governor had even renamed their capital city after himself.

No wonder they hate us, she thought. I hate us too.

Though her empathic ability was normally confined to reading humans, Mesira could feel something very different tonight, as though she could sense the planet's deep anger. The air had a charged quality, a ripened sense of importance and impending confluence that she had not felt before and which frightened her a great deal.

Something profound had changed on Salinas, but the sense of it eluded her.

Were the images she had seen in the eyes of the Mourner real or allegories?

She was not skilled in interpreting visions and wondered if Governor Barbaden's astropathic diviners might know what to make of what she had seen.

No sooner had the thought of the Falcata's former colonel entered her mind than she felt a cold breath sigh across the back of her neck.

She shivered and spun around, her hand reaching up to her scalp.

A small figure of light stood in the far corner of the room, a young girl with her hands outstretched.

You were there.

THOUGH HE CRAVED rest, Uriel was unable to sleep, the persistent sense that they were not alone still lingering at the back of his mind. After eating their fill of meat, both he and Pasanius had explored the empty chambers of the church, a crumbling vestry, some abandoned supply rooms and a number of private chapels in the transepts.

They had found nothing untoward and had then made a patrol circuit of the exterior of the church, climbing tumbled masonry and crossing angled slabs of broken roadway as they scouted the area around the temple. With only the two of them, it was impossible to completely secure such a large area, but they had found nothing to make either of them think there was anything living in the city besides themselves.

Pasanius slept sitting upright with his back against the wall, his soft snores making Uriel smile as the cares his friend had carried since Pavonis seemed to melt from his face. Though he appeared to be deeply asleep, Uriel knew that Pasanius could switch from rest to full wakefulness in a second.

The Unfleshed huddled in a circle of bodies, curled together like pack animals with the Lord of the Unfleshed at their centre. Their breathing was a cacophony of rasping, hacking gurgles and whistles through the gristly slits that were their mouths and noses.

Knowing that sleep would not come, Uriel got to his feet and wandered down the aisle of the church, pausing every now and then to examine one of the fluttering prayer papers or pictures stuck to the wall. Smiling faces stared back at him, men and women, the old and the young.

What had happened to these people and who had placed the memorials?

A number of the papers were scrawled with a date, and though the format of it was unknown to Uriel, it was clear that each one was the same. Whatever calamity had befallen these people had come upon them in one fell swoop.

Uriel moved down the aisle, unable to shake the feeling that he was, if not in the presence of another, at least being observed by someone or something. He kept a tight grip on the hilt of his sword, taking reassurance from the feel of the golden hilt and the legacy of heroism it represented. Captain Idaeus had forged the sword before the Corinthian campaign and had borne it to glory for many years before passing it to Uriel on Thracia as he went to his death. Uriel had vowed to do the sword and memory of his former captain honour, and the weight of that promise had kept Uriel true to his course through the long months of suffering and hardship.

Uriel emerged from the temple, his eyes quickly adjusting to the ambient light and enhancing it to the point where he could see as clearly as he would in daylight.

Where before the city had possessed a melancholy, abandoned feel, it now seemed altogether threatening, as though some buried resentment was allowed to roam freely in the darkness. Uriel's every sense told him that he was alone, but some indefinable instinct told him that there was more to this city than met the eye.

Dust scampered around the square as though disturbed by invisible footsteps and the wind moaned through shattered window frames and open doorways. Moonlight glinted on shards of glass and metal. Somewhere, a skittering of pebbles sounded like laughter.

Tapping his fingers on the golden pommel of his sword, Uriel set off at random into the city.

Crumbling buildings hemmed in broken streets littered with the detritus of a vanished populace: cases, bags, pots, keepsakes and the like. The more Uriel saw of such things, the more the analytical part of his enhanced brain that was trained to seek patterns in disorder realised that there was an underlying scheme to the placement of them.

These were not simply random scatterings of possessions forsaken by their owners. They were yet more silent memorials, arranged to look haphazard, but set with deliberate care: coins placed in identical patterns, ribbons tied on fire-blackened re-bars and pots stacked together as though waiting for their owners to return.

It looked as though the people who had placed these things had not wanted someone else to know that the dead were mourned and remembered.

It was yet another piece of the puzzle, but without more information, Uriel could make little sense of it. The buildings to either side of him were scarred by small-arms fire and, here and there, Uriel saw the unmistakable impact of artillery and heavy calibre shells. An army had come through this city, firing at will and killing anything that lived.

Rust brown splashes on the walls could only be blood and Uriel stopped as he saw moonlight illuminate the white gleam of bone. He knelt beside a tumbled cairn of rounded stones that covered a small skull, no larger than a child's.

A faded picture had been set amongst the stones, encased in a clear plastic bag to protect it from the elements. Uriel wiped moisture and dirt from its surface, seeing a young girl with long blonde hair in a simple white, knee-length dress. She stood beside a tall man, presumably her father, who beamed with paternal pride. They posed before a building of plain stone with a pair of shuttered windows behind them.

Uriel turned the picture over. Scrawled in simple letters was the name Amelia Towsey.

'How did you die?' asked Uriel, his whisper echoing from the walls as though he had shouted the question. Startled by the volume, Uriel looked up and caught a glimpse of something at the end of the street: a small girl in a white dress.

♈ THREE

URIEL BLINKED IN surprise, and the girl was gone, vanished as though she had never existed.

He surged to his feet and ran towards where she had been standing.

Uriel reached the end of the street and looked left and right. There was no sign of the girl and he began to wonder if he had seen her at all. The image had been so fleeting that he couldn't be sure he hadn't just imagined her there after seeing her in the picture, but she had been so *real*.

Even as he began to discount his sighting of the girl he heard a soft sigh, no more than a breath, from ahead and a flash of white. Cautious, his every sense alert for danger, Uriel drew his sword and advanced along the street in the direction of the sound. The buildings around him were dark and seemed to lean inwards.

He passed more of the cairns, but didn't stop to examine them as the sighing sound changed in pitch. Instead of a breath, it was a sob: a child's uncomprehending grief.

Uriel stopped as the sound faded away and he found himself before a building of plain stone with two shuttered windows. The shutters hung from rusted hinges and a portion of the building had been punched through with bullets and shell impacts, but it was unmistakably the dwelling from the picture.

Had he been led here?

The thought should have disturbed him, but he felt no fear of this place.

All sounds had ceased and even the wind had fallen silent as Uriel picked his way over the ruined wall and entered the building with his sword held at the ready. Part of him thought to go back for Pasanius, but he felt no threat from within, just an aching loneliness.

Once again, Uriel's eyes adjusted to the changing light conditions and he saw a shattered room with smashed furniture scattered across the floor. Broken chairs and a table lay in splinters, charred and blackened by fire. The room reeked of old smoke and Uriel ran his finger down the nearest wall, feeling the filmy residue of spent promethium jelly.

Uriel looked around the blackened room, seeing the sad remnants of lives obliterated in an instant. Two silhouettes were burned onto the far wall, their arms raised in terror or perhaps in a final, useless, gesture of protection from the flames that had killed them.

He could picture the room on fire and the terror and pain of those within as they burned, and he hoped their deaths had been swift. Glass and ceramic crunched underfoot and Uriel bent down to retrieve something metallic from the ashes and rubble: bullet casings, autogun rounds from the calibre, stamped with an Imperial eagle and a Departmento Munitorum serial code.

'Fired in attack or defence?' wondered Uriel, seeing the melted and blackened shape of the autogun lying in the corner of the room. The barrel of the weapon was straight and silver, though pitted with rust. How had it escaped the molten heat of the fire that had destroyed the rest of the dwelling?

Thinking back to the patterns of votive offerings he had seen scattered through the streets, Uriel saw meaning in the gun's placement, following the direction of the barrel and heading into a back room.

Like the main room, this chamber was blackened by fire damage, the walls peeling and bubbled where the heat had not quite reached to scorch. The room was empty and dark, a bedroom by the look of the rusted iron bed frame collapsed in one corner.

Uriel made a circuit of the room, looking for something that the autogun in the outer room might have been pointing at. Feeling slightly foolish, he was about to leave when he saw the words written on the wall.

Partially obscured by dust, the words were nevertheless clearly visible to his genhanced eyesight, hidden, but visible to someone who was looking for something.

The Sons of Salinas will rise Again!

Uriel frowned as he read the words, wondering what they meant.

Who were the Sons of Salinas?

A cult? A resistance movement? A pro-Imperial faction?

Whoever they were, they had been careful to hide their imprecation to rebellion and that alone made Uriel suspicious of their allegiance.

Was Salinas a person or the name of this world?

Uriel turned as a shadow was thrown out on the wall before him. Crunching, heavy footsteps and a wet animal smell told him who had followed him and he lowered his sword.

He edged into the main room of the house, and as he cleared the doorway, he saw the Lord of the Unfleshed crouching beside the wall where the two silhouettes were emblazoned. The creature's enormous head lowered to sniff at the wall and his eyes widened as he took in the scent.

'These people...?' said the Lord of the Unfleshed.

'What about them?'

'This place... Many families?'

'Yes,' agreed Uriel. 'This was a city.'

'And these people?' asked the Lord of the Unfleshed.

'They lived here,' said Uriel.

'They died here.'

Uriel nodded, sheathing his sword. 'They did, but I don't know why.'

'This world feels wrong, sick. I not think that we be happy here,' whispered the enormous beast. 'Men that killed these people... They are bad men, like Iron Men.'

'How do you know that?' asked Uriel.

The enormous creature shrugged, as though the answer should have been obvious, and turned away from the wall, to where a collection of children's toys lay scattered in the corner of the room. The Lord of the Unfleshed crouched beside the toys, a melted doll with a scorched dress and a pile of blocks with the letters burned from them.

The beginnings of what might have been a smile creased the creature's face and Uriel felt his heart go out to the Lord of the

Unfleshed, wondering what the future might have held for the child he had once been had the Iron Warriors not cruelly abducted him.

'Bad men will want to kill us,' said the Lord of the Unfleshed without looking up.

'Why do you say that?' asked Uriel, though he suspected the sentiment was accurate.

'I know we are monsters,' said the creature. 'A bad man that kills families will fear us.'

'No,' said Uriel, 'I won't let that happen.'

'Why?'

'Because you deserve a chance to live.'

'You think the Unfleshed can live here?'

'I don't know,' admitted Uriel, 'but what chance did you have on Medrengard? I don't know anything about this world, where it is or even what it's called, but I promise you I will do everything I can to make sure you have a better life here. What happened to you... It was monstrous, but you don't deserve to be condemned for it. You just have to be patient for a little longer and stay hidden until I can find the right time to tell people of you. Can you do that?'

'Unfleshed good at staying hidden. Not be found unless we want to be. Learned that on world of Iron Men.'

'Then stay here, stay hidden and when the time is right, Pasanius and I will come and get you. Then you will feel the sun on your face and not have to worry about Iron Men.'

'A better life,' said the Lord of the Unfleshed. 'You promise?'

'A better life,' agreed Uriel.

'And the Emperor will love us?'

'He will,' said Uriel. 'He loves all his subjects.'

The Lord of the Unfleshed nodded and turned his massive head towards Uriel. Such a terrible, twisted face was incapable of guile and Uriel felt the responsibility of the creature's simple faith in him. He had promised them a better future and he had to make good on that promise.

The Lord of the Unfleshed's head snapped up and the folds of flesh above his jaws pulsed.

'Men are coming,' said the creature, 'men on machines.'

* * *

Colonel Verena Kain stifled a yawn and rubbed a gloved hand across her eyes, her body naturally rolling with the motion of the Chimera armoured fighting vehicle she travelled in. Sitting high in the commander's hatch, she had a clear field of view across the rugged predawn landscape that followed the course of the river towards the ruined city of Khaturian.

She could see the jagged outline of the city ahead, stark against the bleak ruggedness of the mountains and a grim sight for this Emperor-forsaken hour of the morning. Moving with a unique, striding gait, six scout Sentinels darted ahead through the gloom, the bipedal machines ensuring that this fool's errand Mesira Bardhyl's warning had sent them on wasn't a Sons of Salinas ambush.

The scrawny psyker woman had arrived at the palace in the dead of night and demanded to see Governor Barbaden, which only served to prove her idiocy. Bardhyl had claimed she had something of great import to tell him, and once ushered into the governor's presence, she had sobbed out some nonsense about monsters and oceans of blood spilling out from the Killing Ground.

A slap to the face from Kain had halted her ramblings and she smiled as she remembered the look of shock on the woman's pinched face. Mesira Bardhyl had once been the sanctioned psyker attached to the Screaming Eagles, but was one of the cowards who had chosen to muster out of the regiment following the partial demobilisation of the Falcatas after Restoration Day. Kain had little time for such cravens and the chance to put Bardhyl in her place could not be passed up.

As a psyker, Bardhyl should have been handed over to the Commissariat following demobilisation, but, for reasons known only to himself, Barbaden had allowed her to quit the regiment without a fuss. Why he allowed Bardhyl to do so was beyond Kain, but she took great pains not to press him too hard on the subject, for Leto Barbaden's cold, diamond-sharp mind was an icy thing that could end her career as surely as his patronage had advanced it to the position he had once held.

When Bardhyl had calmed enough to speak without gratuitous hyperbole, she spoke of a great surge in warp energy that had appeared in the ruined city of Khaturian. Consultation with the Janiceps had confirmed that, and Barbaden had ordered her to take a detachment of troops out to the Killing Ground and investigate.

Behind Kain's vehicle, a further eleven Chimeras spread out in a staggered arrowhead formation, filled with over a hundred of her Screaming Eagles. Veterans of a score of campaigns and the most feared and disciplined soldiers of the Achaman Falcatas, the Eagles were her favoured warriors when order had to be restored with maximum efficiency and speed.

As the outline of the dead city drew closer, Kain felt a shiver of apprehension, but shook it off. The last time she had seen this place it had been completely ablaze and the sights and sounds of that night returned with the force of a recently unlocked memory.

She realised she had not thought of that night in many years, but the recollection did not trouble her as it did some members of her regiment. They had done what needed to be done and the planet had been brought to heel. She had no regrets and unconsciously reached up to touch the eagle medal that hung from the left breast of her uniform jacket.

Her Chimera bounced over the uneven ground and she raised battered magnoculars to her face, scanning the outline of the city as the Sentinels drew near the razor wire fence that surrounded the ruins.

Tumbled buildings filled her view, rendered green and milky by the mechanics of the viewfinder, but there was precious little else to see. Their route was becoming rockier and cut through some wooded hills, so Kain pulled her arms in tight and slid back down inside the Chimera.

It paid to be cautious. The Sons of Salinas had stepped up their campaign of guerrilla attacks and, while it was unlikely they would attack such a well-armed force, it was possible that a number of snipers could be lying in wait within such terrain. This whole endeavour could simply be a ruse to lure out and kill an Imperial officer.

Inside the Chimera, it was noisy and dim. Engine noise roared from the back and the stink of oil and sacred unguents was thick in the air. Cramped and filled with solid iron and dangerous moving parts, it paid to be slightly built as she manoeuvred her body into the commander's seat.

'Anything, ma'am?' asked Bascome, her aide-de-camp, from his position by the vox-gear.

'There's nothing there,' she said, shouting to be heard over the rattling noise of the engine.

'Any idea what we should expect?' asked Bascome.

Kain didn't know what to expect after the frustrating vagueness of Bardhyl's warning, but it did not become a colonel to admit ignorance in front of her junior officers.

'Possibly some Sons of Salinas activity,' she said. 'Or else more fools coming to place their trinkets on a pile of stones.'

Bascome shook his head. 'You'd think they'd learn not to come here, especially after the last lot we shot.'

Kain did not reply, remembering the sight of the three men put before the firing squad against the palace wall for breaking the cordon around Khaturian. Entry to the city was strictly forbidden and punishable by death, something that appeared not to deter the many numbskulls that regularly risked their lives to place memorials.

If Barbaden had listened to her, the ruins would have been obliterated by massed Basilisk fire the hour after Restoration Day, but the newly installed Governor had decided that such a move would only re-ignite flames of rebellion so recently extinguished.

Well, the last ten years had shown how well *that* had worked out: a decade of bombings, riots and discontent from a populace too stupid to realise that it was beaten. Imperial rule held sway over this world and the Sons of Salinas were a spent force, no matter how charismatic and cunning Pascal Blaise was said to be.

All sorts of wild rumours had grown up around the leader of the Sons of Salinas: that he had once served in the Guard, that he had once been Barbadus's chief enforcer before Daron Nisato had taken over or even that he was a rogue inquisitor. Whatever the truth of his former life, Kain had killed enough of his soldiers to know that he clearly wasn't *that* good a leader.

'I hope it is the Sons of Salinas,' said Bascome. 'It's been too long since we had a proper stand up fight.'

Kain echoed her aide's sentiment. Since Restoration Day, there had been precious little proper soldiering for the Falcatas. No intense firefights against xenos or the warriors of the Ruinous Powers, but plenty of civilian rioters and thankless patrols through districts of their own derelict war machines where improvised explosives waited to blow off limbs and snipers lurked to take pot shots at the patrolling Imperial soldiers.

The entire situation made no sense to Kain. Hadn't they liberated this system from the Ruinous Powers? True, there had been no overt outbreak of rebellion on Salinas, but with three other worlds in the system already fallen prey to heresy, it had surely been only a matter of time before Salinas came under the sway of the Great Enemy. Didn't these people realise how lucky they had in fact been?

The Falcatas had arrived in a flurry of pomp and ceremony, an occasion demanded by the Master of the Crusade, General Shermi Vigo (a man who loathed Leto Barbaden and who was, in return, despised), but it had only served to inflame the people, leading to three years of grubby, inglorious warfare.

The result of the pacification had never really been in doubt, for the Achaman Falcatas had fought through the treacherous hells of two of the system's worlds already and were in no mood to offer mercy. As brutal and necessary as the fighting had been, there had been little glory in shooting civilians who thought that holding guns made them soldiers.

'Don't get your hopes up, Bascome,' warned Kain. 'This isn't likely to be anything out of the ordinary.'

'WHAT DO YOU think?' asked Pasanius.

'It sounds like Chimera engines, and Sentinels.'

'That's what I thought,' agreed Pasanius. 'Guard?'

'I think so.'

'Let's hope they're friendly.'

Uriel nodded and ran a hand across his scalp as the noise of the engines drew nearer. Uriel's superior hearing filtered out the distortions caused by the ruggedness of the landscape, allowing him to pick out the different engine noises and pinpoint their location.

The vehicles were perhaps two kilometres away and would be here in moments.

Uriel had raced back through the streets of the city, feeling its character change once more, the wind whipping through the streets as though bearing word of the approaching men with every gust. The Lord of the Unfleshed had long outpaced him, his lumbering gait and long, elastic limbs propelling him through the rubble-strewn streets with uncanny speed and grace.

Pasanius was waiting for him and the two gathered their meagre possessions before heading towards the southern edge of the city.

Whoever these men on machines were, Uriel and Pasanius would meet them with their heads held high.

As they prepared to leave, Uriel turned to the Lord of the Unfleshed. He reached up to place his hand on the creature's arm, but remembered how such a gesture had hurt it before and pulled his hand back.

'You understand what you have to do?' asked Uriel.

The mighty creature nodded, his brood of twisted followers echoing the gesture. 'Hide.'

'Yes,' said Uriel, 'you need to hide, but it won't be for long, I swear to you. Let us deal with these men and find out more about this world.'

'Then you come and get us? Tell men not fear us?'

Uriel hesitated before answering, unsure of what to say and loath to promise something he could not deliver. 'I'll come and get you as soon as it is safe, but until then you have to stay hidden. Move higher into the mountains. It looks like there's food and water there and you should be safe as long as you stay away from any settlements.'

The Lord of the Unfleshed took a moment to process all that Uriel had said, his massive form suddenly seeming to be much smaller than before. Uriel realised that the creature was feeling fear and as ridiculous as that thought was, it was completely understandable. Since their last days on Medrengard, the Lord of the Unfleshed had looked to Uriel as a child looks towards its father for guidance.

Now, that guidance was going away and Uriel saw the fear of abandonment in the creature's milky, bloodshot eyes.

'You will be safe,' said Uriel. 'I give you my word. I *will not* let anything happen to you. Now you have to go, quickly.'

The Lord of the Unfleshed turned and led his followers into the depths of the ruined city and as Uriel watched them go, he hoped they might have a chance of life on this world.

Now, as he stood before a long line of razor wire that appeared to encircle the city, he wasn't so sure. Their explorations of the previous night had not carried them this far south and to find that this dead city was cordoned off was a cause for some concern.

'They sound like friendlies,' said Uriel. 'Looted Guard vehicles don't sound as smooth. The engines are well cared for, I can hear that much.'

'Well, you always did have better hearing than me,' said Pasanius, affecting an air of casualness, but Uriel could sense his friend's unease. 'So, what do you make of this razor wire?'

Uriel looked left and right, following the line of tall wooden posts rammed into the ground and strung with looping coils of vicious, toothed wire.

'They didn't skimp on it, that's for sure,' said Uriel. 'Anyone caught in that fence would be torn to bloody shreds trying to cross it.'

'Aye,' agreed Pasanius, holding the bolter loosely at his side. 'From the scraps of cloth and bloodstains on it, it looks like there's no short-age of people attempting to get through.'

They had reached the edges of the city and followed the road until reaching a wide gate, strung with coloured ribbons and garlands of faded flowers. More of the prayer strips hung from the wire and it had the effect of making the gate look almost festive.

'How are we going to play this?' asked Pasanius.

'Carefully,' said Uriel. 'It's the only way we can. I want to be honest with these people, but I don't want to be gunned down by some overeager Guardsman with an itchy trigger-finger.'

'Good point. Best we don't mention where we've been.'

'Probably not,' agreed Uriel. 'Not yet, at least.'

Pasanius nodded to the horizon. 'Here they come.'

Uriel watched as a trio of boxy, bipedal machines stalked through the landscape towards the city, moving with a wheezing, mechanical gait. Painted a deep rust red, each was, much to Uriel's relief, embla-zoned with a golden eagle on their frontal glacis. Two bore side-mounted autocannons, while the third sported a lascannon that hummed with a powerful electric charge.

'There's more than these three,' said Pasanius, his head cocked to one side.

'I know,' said Uriel. 'There's one on our right and another two in the woods to the left.'

'Autocannons and a lascannon… They'll make a mess of us if they open fire.'

'Then let's not give them reason to, eh?'

'Sounds good to me.'

Uriel watched as the three visible Sentinels slowed and approached the gate with greater caution now that they had spotted the two of them. Guns were trained, hissing hydraulics powered up and arming chambers unmasked the war spirits within the weapons.

'Easy now,' whispered Uriel.

All three Sentinels had their weapons firmly aimed at them.

'If they open fire...' said Pasanius, his grip twitching on the grip of the bolter.

Uriel spotted the gesture and said, 'Slowly. Very slowly, put down that gun.'

Pasanius looked down at the weapon, as though he had forgotten he was carrying it, and nodded. With his truncated arm raised, he knelt and placed the bolter on the ground. The Sentinel armed with the lascannon followed his movements.

None of the other vehicles moved, content simply to cover them with their weapons.

'Why aren't they doing anything?'

'Communicating with their commanding officer I expect.'

'Damn, but I don't like this,' said Pasanius.

'Nor I,' said Uriel, 'but what choice do we have? We have to make contact with Imperial authorities sometime.'

'True. I just wish we weren't doing it with a company's worth of heavy weaponry pointed at us.'

The Sentinels before them didn't move, but Uriel could hear the sounds of the ones out of sight moving around to confirm that they were alone. He hoped the Lord of the Unfleshed had managed to get his followers clear of the city, for if the commanding officer of these soldiers was even halfway competent, he would order a search of the city to confirm that they were alone.

At last, Uriel heard the rumbling of tracked vehicles and a staggered column of a dozen Chimeras came into view. No sooner had the armoured vehicles appeared than the Sentinels opened up with dazzling searchlights. Uriel blinked away spots of brightness from his eyes as they adjusted to the blinding light.

Even though dawn was lighting the eastern skyline, the beams from the spotlights were intense and Uriel had to squint to make out any detail behind them. Mortal eyes would have been blinded, but those of a Space Marine could filter out all but the most searing light.

As Uriel's eyes focused, he saw the Chimeras spread out, a squadron's worth of heavy weaponry aimed squarely at him and his sergeant. Doors cranked open and scores of soldiers disembarked from the backs of the vehicles.

'They're good, I'll give them that,' hissed Pasanius, and Uriel was forced to agree.

The soldiers were clad in armour composed of gleaming red plate fringed with fur-edged mail and short, crimson cloaks tied over their left shoulders. Their rifles were aimed unwaveringly at the pair of them, each soldier advancing with a fluid motion that kept his weapon steady.

Their helmets were conical affairs of bronze metal with angled cheek plates and flexible aventails. Each warrior also carried a heavy sword with a curved blade, and nothing in their appearance gave Uriel the impression that they were simply for ornamentation.

'They've gone to a lot of trouble for just the two of us,' whispered Pasanius.

'I know, and how did they know we were here?'

'I suppose we'll find out soon enough,' said Pasanius. 'Looks like they're coming in.'

A sergeant with ocular implants integral to his helmet waved two squads forward. A heavy, square device was planted in the centre of the gate and a cable run back to the lead Chimera by a robed engin-seer with a heavy backpack of hissing cogs and bronze instruments.

A flickering glow built around the box attached to the gate and a crackle of electrical discharge flared along the length of the fence. Barely had the glow faded than the soldiers were coming through, the magnetically sealed gates swinging open with a booted kick.

The red-clad soldiers spread out, moving in pairs to expertly envelop them in overlapping fields of fire.

'Clear!' shouted one soldier, and the cry was repeated by his opposite number.

Up close, Uriel saw that they were professional soldiers indeed. They kept a precise distance from their targets, while still remaining close enough for it to be impossible to miss if this encounter turned violent. None even seemed fazed by the fact that their guns were aimed at warriors who clearly had the bulk of Astartes.

The sergeant with the ocular implants came forward with his curved sword drawn, and Uriel could see that the weapon was a form of falcata, a single-edged blade that pitched forward towards the point.

Such weapons were heavy and capable of delivering a blow with the power of an axe, yet with the precision and cutting edge of a sword. The hilt was hook-shaped with quillons in the shape of flaring eagle wings.

Using the tip of his blade, the sergeant hooked Pasanius's bolter away from him and gestured a soldier behind him to carry it away. The soldier struggled under the weight of the gun and Uriel watched as it was handed off to the eager looking enginseer.

The sergeant looked Uriel up and down, his face invisible behind a combination vox/rebreather attachment and his bionics. With their only gun taken away, the soldiers relaxed a fraction and Uriel felt his respect for them drop a notch, for Uriel still carried his sword. In any case, the soldiers should know that a Space Marine was as proficient a killer with his bare hands as he was with a weapon.

No one moved until the top hatch on one of the Chimeras opened and a slender figure in the uniform of an officer emerged. Uriel saw that it was a woman, a tall, long-limbed woman who dropped to the ground with the assured movements of someone used to being in the field.

She pulled off her helmet and ran a hand across her scalp. Her hair was dark and cut short, her features angular and chiselled. She marched from her Chimera, trailed by a shorter man bearing a portable vox-caster on his back.

Like every one of her soldiers, she too bore a sheathed falcata. A golden eagle medal shone brightly on her uniform jacket.

The woman halted beside her sergeant, clearly surprised to see two such warriors standing before her. To her credit, her surprise lasted for only the briefest of seconds.

'Who are you?' she asked.

'I am Uriel Ventris and this is Pasanius Lysane,' answered Uriel.

'You are Adeptus Astartes?'

It was asked as a rhetorical question, but Uriel nodded and said, 'We are Ultramarines.'

Again, Uriel saw surprise, but just as quickly it was masked. 'Ultramarines? You are a long way from home. How did you come to be here?'

'With respect,' said Uriel, 'we do not even know where here is. What planet is this?'

Ignoring Uriel's question, the female officer said, 'You are trespassing on prohibited ground, Uriel Ventris. To enter Khaturian carries a penalty of death.'

Uriel shared a shocked look with Pasanius. The sheer physical presence and legendary prowess of a Space Marine was enough to render most mortals speechless with awe and reverence, but this woman seemed unconcerned that she faced two of the Emperor's finest.

Anger touched Uriel and he took a step forward.

Immediately, a host of lasguns snapped up, and the soldiers' posture of vigilance was instantly restored.

'We are Space Marines of the Emperor,' snarled Uriel, the frustrations of the time they had spent exiled from the Chapter boiling to the surface. He gripped the hilt of his sword and said, 'We are warriors of the 4th Company of the Ultramarines Chapter and you will show us some damned respect!'

The woman did not flinch from Uriel's outburst, but her hand flashed to her falcata.

'If you were to try to draw that weapon, I could cut you down before it was halfway drawn,' promised Uriel.

'And you would be dead a moment later,' she promised.

'Maybe so, but at least I would have silenced your insolent tongue,' snapped Uriel.

He felt a restraining hand on his arm and turned to see Pasanius, a look of resigned amusement in his eyes.

'Remember when I asked you how we were going to play this?' asked Pasanius 'You said, "Carefully". Does this fit any definition of careful?'

Uriel's anger vanished and he smiled at the absurdity of his behaviour in the face of so much firepower. He released his sword hilt and returned his gaze to the female officer, who glared furiously at him with her hand still held firmly on the grip of her weapon.

Pasanius stepped between her and Uriel. 'Look, before this gets out of hand and someone gets killed, let's everyone take a breath and we'll start again. We are strangers on this world and didn't know that to come here was forbidden. We're just trying to get back to our Chapter and could really use your help. Can you at least tell us what planet we're on and who's in charge?'

The woman relaxed a fraction and released her weapon. She took a deep breath, smoothed the front of her uniform jacket and laced her hands behind her back.

'Very well,' she said. 'I am Colonel Verena Kain, commanding officer of the Achaman Falcatas, and this world is called Salinas.'

'Who's in charge?'

'Governor Leto Barbaden is the Imperial Commander of this world,' said Colonel Kain.

'Can you take us to him?' asked Uriel.

'You'll have to travel under armed escort until your identities can be verified.'

'Verified?' asked Uriel. 'You don't believe we are Adeptus Astartes? Are you blind?'

'Trust me,' snapped Kain. 'I have spent decades fighting the Emperor's enemies, and some of them looked just like you, so you'll forgive me if I don't entirely trust that you are all you seem.'

Uriel was about to retort when Pasanius said, 'Colonel Kain has a point, Uriel. Come on, what does it matter anyway? We're going where we need to go.'

'I suppose so,' said Uriel.

'You'll travel in the back of a Chimera,' said Kain, gauging their bulk. 'It will be cramped, but you can squeeze in I'm sure.'

'Indeed,' said Pasanius, leading Uriel forward under the watchful gaze and lasguns of the Guardsmen.

As they marched towards the waiting Chimeras, Pasanius turned to address Colonel Kain one last time. 'One other thing,' he said. 'What year is it?'

ひ
FOUR

THE LIGHT COMING through his threadbare curtains and the sound of the city coming to life woke Pascal Blaise long before he heard the metal door to his home banging open. He rolled over and reached under his pillow for the pistol that was never more than an arm's length away from him. He checked the load and flicked off the safety catch as he heard excited voices from downstairs.

From the tone of the voices and the lack of further commotion, he knew it wasn't Daron Nisato's enforcers kicking down the door, but didn't put away his pistol just yet. These were uncertain times and the deadly games he and the Sons of Salinas were playing demanded caution.

He ran a hand over his shaved scalp and tugged at the twin forks of his braided beard, as he always did when thinking. He recognised the voices below; one belonged to Cawlen Hurq, his shadow and bodyguard, the other to Rykard Ustel, one of his intelligence gatherers.

Pascal rolled his head, loosening muscles that had cramped during the night. He was alone and the room smelled faintly of engine oil, but that was inevitable given that it was sheeted with plates cannibalised from the rusted hulk of a Leman Russ battle tank.

Satisfied that there was no immediate danger, Pascal slipped from the bed and pulled on his clothes, a faded grey work tunic and a wide leather belt. He pulled on his boots and was lacing them up when he heard a soft double knock at his door.

'Come in, Cawlen,' he said, his voice strong and authoritative. It was a voice used to giving commands, but had once been more used to calling out tithe numbers, accounts and scribe roll calls.

Cawlen Hurq pushed open the door and nodded respectfully towards him, his every motion controlled and unencumbered by unnecessary effort. He was a big man, broad of shoulder and threateningly built. Nature had made him unsuited for any role in life other than the infliction of violence. Like Pascal, Cawlen wore a simple tunic, but he also carried a short-barrelled lascarbine and bore a scabbarded blade at his hip.

'Rykard Ustel's here,' he said.

'I heard,' said Pascal. 'What does he want?'

'He's got word of troop movements.'

'And he has to bring it to me this early?' asked Pascal irritably.

'It's the Screaming Eagles,' said Cawlen, 'in company strength.'

Pascal's irritation vanished along with any lingering tiredness. The Screaming Eagles were the most hated of all the Imperial forces on Salinas. Their reputation for brutality and indiscriminate violence was well deserved and everyone on Salinas had cause to hate them for what they had done to Khaturian.

'It gets better,' said Cawlen.

'How?'

'Kain's leading them.'

Pascal finished tying his boots and rose from his bed.

Verena Kain.

'Oh, but it would be sweet to take that black-hearted bitch down.'

'That's what I thought,' agreed Cawlen with a wicked grin.

'Where are they?'

'Rykard said they set off towards the north,' said Cawlen. 'Said it looked like they were heading towards the Killing Ground.'

'Do we have anyone there?'

'No; at least we shouldn't.'

'Then why is she leading a company there?'

'Who knows, but Rykard said they didn't have any supply vehicles with them, so they'll be back soon. We should get shooters in place.'

Pascal nodded. 'Send runners to the ambush cells. Six teams of missiles. We'll assemble at the Iron Angel and deploy from there. Go.'

Cawlen nodded and left the room, leaving Pascal alone once more.

Pascal felt his heart race at the thought of striking back at the Screaming Eagles. He fought to control his excitement, knowing that a cool head was needed here. Emotional men made mistakes and he was not a man given to displays of emotion, considering them a waste of energy.

He paced the room, thinking through the situation, unlocking talents for analysis that had once served him well in the ranks of the Imperial Administratum, a duty that seemed a lifetime ago.

Pascal Blaise had been a scribe overseer in the office of Governor Shaara, a cog in the ever-turning machine that was the Imperial bureaucracy of Salinas in the days before the Achaman Falcatas had come. Though other planets in the system had seethed with turmoil and unrest, Governor Shaara had kept Salinas free of malcontents and rabble-rousers in the belief that they could ride out this time of troubles.

How wrong he had turned out to be.

Tarred with the same brush as the system's other worlds, the hammer of the Imperial Guard had fallen on Salinas with no less ferocity and force as it had on the others. Governor Shaara had been executed the day the Falcatas had landed and his officers rounded up in detention camps while the Departmento Munitorum officials decided what was to be done with them.

Pascal Blaise had been part of the delegation chosen from among the surviving administrative personnel to approach Colonel Leto Barbaden, the commander of the Imperial forces moving across the surface of Salinas, to protest at the unnecessary nature of these measures.

The memories of that day were burned forever on Pascal Blaise's mind. No sooner had they spoken against the harshness of the Falcatas and the loyalty of their former governor than a detachment of soldiers, men and women that Pascal later learned were Barbaden's 8th Company known as the Screaming Eagles, had surrounded them.

Colonel Barbaden had spoken of the treachery that infected the system and of how he had heard the same protests of innocence from the lips of every leader on the rebellious worlds.

Then the shooting had begun.

Pascal reached towards the puckered scar tissue at his chest where the first las-bolt had struck him. A second had grazed the side of his head and he had fallen into a black pit of pain and unconsciousness. When he had awoken, he was in a long trench, freshly dug outside the palace walls, which was filled with corpses. He had recognised the faces of his fellow delegates and the horror and injustice of their murder allowed him to plumb reserves of strength and endurance that he had not known he possessed.

Bleeding and on the verge of collapse, he had climbed from the mass grave and lurched through the shot-and-scream-filled darkness until he found his way to the nearest house of healing, where his strength had finally given out.

He remembered nothing of the next few days except pain and the sedative highs of medication. A week after his shooting, he had risen from his bed to hear the sounds of Imperial Guard tanks rumbling through the streets of his city and the tramp of marching feet as red-clad soldiers of the Achaman Falcatas rounded up suspected traitors.

Hatred filled him and, in that moment, the administrative overseer he had once been died and the warrior he became was born. Within a month of the Falcatas arrival, the newly formed Sons of Salinas made its first gesture of defiance, planting a bomb that had killed several senior officers of the Falcatas.

Under the charismatic and fiery Sylvanus Thayer, the Sons of Salinas had enjoyed initial successes and had seriously hampered the work of the Falcatas in securing Salinas.

It couldn't last.

Against the relentless force of the Imperial Guard and the ruthlessness of Leto Barbaden, the Sons of Salinas could not hope to prevail. After the horror of the Killing Ground, Sylvanus Thayer had led the vengeful Sons of Salinas into a pitched battle, a battle they could not hope to win, and the flower of their world's manhood had been wiped out.

Pascal had pleaded with Sylvanus not to meet the Falcatas in open battle, telling him over and over that the destruction of Khaturian had been designed to draw him into such a reckless act, but his leader's fury at the massacre could not be restrained.

And, they had died, pounded by artillery, ground over by tanks and finished off by infantry.

Men called Sylvanus Thayer a hero, but Pascal knew the man was a fool. Blinded by rage and the need for vengeance, he had not seen the trap that Barbaden had laid for him. Or if he had seen it, he had not cared.

Pascal Blaise had rallied the survivors and taught them the value of caution and secrecy. He had taught them that they were not the almighty avenging force that Thayer had told them they were, but the trickle of water that, over time, would split the rock.

Thus the war of the Sons of Salinas had continued.

There were no grand gestures of defiance, but small attacks that gradually wore down the soldiers who occupied their cities and whose former colonel sat in the Governor's palace.

A knock at the door drew Pascal from his bitter reveries and he looked up to see Cawlen Hurq standing at the door once again.

'You coming?' he asked.

'Yes,' said Pascal, lifting his ash-grey storm cloak.

He smiled and dropped the cloak, opening the gunmetal foot-locker beside his bed and reaching for the cunningly disguised switch that opened the secret compartment at its base. Pascal lifted the false bottom and drew out a carefully folded bundle of green and gold cloth.

He swept up the double wrapped cloak of the Sons of Salinas and fastened it to the buckles at his shoulder and chest.

Cawlen nodded appreciatively.

Pascal holstered his pistol and grinned to his bodyguard. 'If we're going to kill Verena Kain, it's only fitting she should know who her executioners are.'

HIGH IN THE mountains above the dead city, the Lord of the Unfleshed sat with the rest of his brethren in the midst of a forest of tall trees. Mist clung to the ground and the wet sensation of it around the exposed musculature was strange and unusual. The softness of the ground beneath him was a joy and the cold air in his lungs the sweetest elixir.

He had never known such things, his every breath before now coated with toxic filth from the belching refineries that covered the desolate plains of the Iron Men's world.

They had brought down another two of the beasts that lived in the pastures below a towering escarpment of rock and dragged them into the concealment of the forest. The carcasses lay torn apart and bleeding in a ring of the Unfleshed. The Lord of the Unfleshed tore meat from the bone with his teeth, the hind leg of one of the animals clutched in one meaty fist.

The meat was like nothing he had tasted before, fresh, bloody and full of goodness. All he could remember eating was the spoiled meat of the dead or the chemically disfigured, the fatty bodies of the ones they had found in the flesh camps of the Iron Men.

The thought that there could be another way to live had never entered the Lord of the Unfleshed's mind, for what other life was there? Fragmentary visions of his life before, like images on the shards of a broken mirror pricked his mind from time to time, but he had always turned from them.

Sometimes, when the pain and exhaustion of his existence grew too great to bear, he would travel deep into the ashen mountains and bask in the smoggy peaks wreathed in caustic pollutants that would send him into the deepest slumbers, where he could cling to the last of his remembrances.

There his body would rest, and he could reach the dreams of another life, another way of living.

Were they memories? He didn't know, but he liked to think so.

He would see a woman's face, kind and full of unconditional love. He hoped she was his mother, but had no memory of her beyond this sight. She would speak to him, but he never heard the words. All he saw was how beautiful she was and how much she cared for him.

As the fumes carried him deeper into the tormented depths of his altered mind, he saw towering buildings of white stone, glorious windows of many colours and a host of statues depicting a golden warrior, his head haloed in stars and surrounded by angels of light.

Of all the fevered visions the Lord of the Unfleshed saw, this one had the most power and, more than that, it had an identity.

This was the Emperor and the Emperor loved him.

This love would never last and these golden memories would shatter, replaced by loathsome visions of horror and blood so terrifying that he would crush rocks with his fists in his dreaming frenzy.

He saw fire. He saw explosions and stuttering flickers of bullets.

In the bursts of light, he saw warriors in iron-grey armour fringed with chevrons of yellow and black.

Heavy, textured gauntlets reached for him, tearing him from the bloody corpse of the beautiful woman, his screams, falling on deaf ears as his world resolved into snapshots of horror: darkness and terror, the taste of blood never far from his mouth; slavering saw-carrying monsters and the giant, drooling faces of monstrous mothers.

Then only pain and emptiness as he felt himself enfolded by moist folds of flesh and dragged down into darkness.

Then, gloriously, light.

But the light was a lie and served only to reveal his hideousness.

A monster he was and a monster he became, flushed away with the rest of the rotten meat into the unforgiving wilderness beyond the Iron Men's citadel.

His revulsion at his own horrible existence would always break the grip of the toxic fumes and he would rise from the mountainside to make his way back down to his wretched band, the unwanted, the rejected and the unloved.

Many of the wailing masses of twisted meat and bone shat from above were howling things without form or mind.

These the tribe would eat, but those with enough semblance of form and strength would become part of the Lord of the Unfleshed's growing tribe.

This was the Lord of the Unfleshed's life and he had known of no other way to live, until the warrior had come.

The Lord of the Unfleshed had watched the latest outpourings from the Iron Men's citadel fall into the pool, imagining the taste of their meat as they struggled to the edge of the black water. Anticipation turned to puzzlement, for they were none of them monsters. His only thought had been to feast on them, but he had smelled the mother meat on the warrior who led the new arrivals.

The Lord of the Unfleshed had taken the new arrivals to the great cavern beneath the earth that was home and presented them to the mighty statue of the Emperor that they had built from the detritus flushed from above. The Emperor had judged the warrior, who called himself Uriel, worthy and so they had become part of the tribe and struck back at the Iron Men who lived in the fortress on top of the impossible mountain.

Much blood had been shed, many Iron Men killed and their fortress brought crashing down. Many of the Unfleshed had died also, but it was a good memory, one the Lord of the Unfleshed held fast to as they escaped the world of their monstrous birth in the bowels of the iron daemon's machine.

The Lord of the Unfleshed did not like to think of the time spent within the daemonic machine's reeking, blood-soaked depths, for it had taken all his power and strength to prevent the tribe from turning on one another in a frenzy of gnashing jaws and taloned fists.

The journey had ended though and they had set foot on this world. The air was clean and the ground soft, but there was something wrong with it. He did not know what it was or how to articulate that wrongness, but a presence of great anger saturated the air of this place.

He could feel it as surely as he felt the blood running down his fleshless face.

The meat from the carcasses was almost gone. One of the tribe, a creature with glistening organs oozing at the edges of its bones and a hideously elongated mouth filled with serrated fangs, snapped bones and sucked the marrow from them. Another scraped the inside of the gutted beast's stomach for the last morsels.

'No,' growled the Lord of the Unfleshed, 'we not need to live like this.'

The tribe looked up at him, confusion twisting their mangled features.

'This a better world for us,' he said. 'Uriel promise us this. We not be feared and Emperor loves us.'

He could see the hope in their eyes, the first rays of sunshine diffusing through the treetops with a soft golden glow. The Lord of the Unfleshed felt it on his skin as a pleasant tingle and looked down as the warmth spread across the raw redness of his arm.

He rose to his feet and made his way from the shadows of the forest, ducking under branches as the sun rose higher over the mountains and spilled its golden light over the landscape. The tribe followed him, captivated by the glow building in the sky.

Walking like recently awakened sleepwalkers, the Unfleshed made their way from beneath the trees to stand in the open. Their faces were alive with wonderment, the sight of this bright orb in the sky incredible and new, yet strangely familiar.

Memories of happier times fought to reach the surface of the Lord of the Unfleshed's mind and he felt the beginnings of hope stir in his breast. Perhaps this *could* be a better place, a new beginning on a world where they were not hated and hunted.

The sensation of the sunlight on his body grew stronger, the tingling turning to something else, something painful. The tribe began to moan, rubbing their arms and bodies as though scratching at a persistent itch.

The Lord of the Unfleshed felt the musculature of his body begin to burn, the sensation like the angry heat that covered his body whenever he had ventured into the filthy waters of the Iron Men's world.

He growled as the burning sensation grew stronger, the meat of his body unused to the strange sun's rays. Black patches began to form on his skin, spreading like droplets of oil on water. Pain grew as the black, blistering marks grew and the Lord of the Unfleshed roared as he scratched one and a viscous pus oozed from the wound.

On the Iron Men's world, the sun radiated despair and hopelessness, but this one... this one radiated pain.

The Unfleshed began to howl, clawing at the meat of their limbs and bodies as they struggled to understand what was happening to them. Their cries were piteous as the sunlight burned their bodies and the Lord of the Unfleshed roared in anger and hurt betrayal.

This world was no good. He had known it, but had allowed himself to forget that everything hated them.

Even the sun wanted to destroy them.

'Tribe!' he roared. 'Back! Back into shadow!'

He turned from the burning sun and ran back to the shelter of the trees, but even there the sunlight found them, slicing through the trees in deadly beams that seared the unprotected flesh of their bodies. The Unfleshed looked to him for guidance, but he had none to give.

There was no better life, not for the likes of them.

The Unfleshed bellowed and beat their chests in agony and the Lord of the Unfleshed cried his frustration to the heavens. Through the foliage he saw the rocky escarpment rearing above them, a vertical slab of glistening black rock with numerous waterfalls cascading from high above.

Against the blackness of the rock, the Lord of the Unfleshed saw a patch of deeper darkness, a cleft in the sheer surface: A cave.

'Tribe must run!' he cried. 'Find shelter in rocks! Follow!'

Without looking to see if any came with him, the Lord of the Unfleshed broke from the scant cover of the forest and ran uphill towards the cliffs. His powerful muscles easily carried him across the landscape, leaping over huge boulders and shutting out the burning pain that threatened to overwhelm him.

Behind him, he heard howls of pain, but also the sounds of the tribe following him, wet, meaty footfalls and the crack of malformed bones grinding together.

The black lesions spread across his body as he ran, but the Lord of the Unfleshed shut out the pain, his entire being focused on reaching the cooling darkness of the cave. He vaulted a fallen slab of rock and slowed his pace as he slid into the shadow. The immediate burning sensation subsided, but the crawling pain in his limbs and body remained.

He turned as the faster members of the tribe completed their mad dash to the cave, howling and gnashing their teeth against the pain. The Lord of the Unfleshed turned to see others making their painful way over the open ground, the golden light searing and blackening the meat on their bones with every passing second.

One of the Unfleshed, a creature with stunted legs and an oversized upper body tripped on a loose boulder. It fell to the ground with a shriek of pain, viscous ooze seeping from burns that tore open as it landed. Its glistening, red body split apart where it was burned and it fought to right itself. Its body was out of balance and it could not get up. Powerful arms sought to haul it to its feet, but the pain and horror of what was happening to it were too much.

The creature collapsed with one final howl, and the Lord of the Unfleshed watched the blackness creeping across its body as the unforgiving sun burned away the last of its life.

'Dead now,' said the Lord of the Unfleshed and the others shuffled over to look at the blackening corpse. They could smell the meat on it and he could sense their confusion and hunger, but none dared venture out into the light.

The Lord of the Unfleshed turned away from the light of the cave mouth. Black, water-streaked, walls stretched off into the distance and the darkness was comforting after the pain of the light. The Lord of the Unfleshed lurched deeper into the cliff, his thoughts in turmoil at this new pain.

Once more they were monsters, lurking in the darkness of the cave, where all monsters should be.

Anger swelled within the Lord of the Unfleshed.

THE TROOP COMPARTMENT of a Chimera armoured fighting vehicle claimed to be able to convey twelve soldiers and their kit into battle. As was typical for spaces designed by the military, it assumed that the soldiers would not need to move so much as a muscle once they were packed in. With two Space Marines inside, that space became seriously confined and five soldiers had been displaced and forced to ride back on the roof of the vehicle.

'And I thought Rhinos were cramped,' said Pasanius. 'Remind me never to complain to Harkus again.'

Uriel did not reply, keeping his eyes fixed on the landscape coming into view through the scuffed vision blocks that punctuated the sides of the vehicle and allowed a little natural light to enter the compartment. Recessed glow strips ran the length of the roof, but their light was a sickly red.

Four soldiers of the Achaman Falcatas sat with them in the back of the Chimera, three helmeted warriors with their lasguns held across their laps and the sergeant who had removed Pasanius's weapon. He alone had removed his helmet and Uriel saw that the ocular implants were integral to it and not part of him.

The sergeant was middle-aged, but had a weathered, deeply lined face topped by a shock of sandy hair. The man's eyes were hard, but not unkind, and he looked at Uriel and Pasanius with an expression that was part awe and part nervous excitement.

'So you're Ultramarines?' he said.

'We are,' nodded Uriel.

'I'm Sergeant Jonah Tremain,' said the man, extending his hand to Uriel. The hand beneath the gauntlet felt hard and inflexible to Uriel and he suspected that the sergeant's hand was augmetic.

His suspicions were confirmed when Tremain held up his hand and said, 'Lost it in a skirmish against eldar pirates. Caught a ricochet and a splinter of something got under the skin. Got infected and the medics had to take it right there and then.'

'I have fought the eldar before,' said Uriel. 'They are swift and deadly killers.'

'That they are,' agreed Tremain. 'That they are. But then the colonel was no slouch either. Outmanoeuvred them and none of their fancy tricks could save them when his Screaming Eagles had them locked in place.'

'His? I don't understand.'

'Ah, of course. Colonel Kain's only been in charge of what's left of the regiment since Restoration Day,' explained Tremain. 'Before that, Colonel Barbaden led the Falcatas.'

'The same Barbaden who is now governor?'

'The very same,' agreed Tremain. 'We won this world fair and square. Did our ten years of service, and after we'd fought through the hell of Losgat and Steinhold we were given the right to settle here once we'd won it back for the Emperor.'

Uriel glanced over at the silent soldiers who sat by the heavy iron assault door at the rear of the vehicle. They were hard, tough men and the notion that the sergeant would be so garrulous seemed out of character.

'So how did you pair come to be all the way out here?' asked Tremain.

'In that city or on this world?'

'Both,' said Tremain, smiling, but Uriel could see that the expression was forced. 'I'm sure it's an exciting story. We don't get many visitors here, let alone Space Marines. So come on, tell me how you came to be out here.'

Uriel could sense Pasanius's unspoken warning of saying too much and wondered if Colonel Kain was listening in. Had she placed Tremain in here to get them to talk unguardedly in front of a friendly sergeant?

'That is a long and… involved tale, Sergeant Tremain,' said Uriel.

'You must have a ship. I mean, how else would you have got to the surface?'

'No, we don't have a ship,' said Uriel.

'So did you just teleport down?' pressed Tremain. 'From a vessel in orbit? Or maybe a drop-pod? You Space Marines use drop-pods, don't you?'

'We do,' agreed Uriel, 'but we did not arrive in one.'

'Then how did you get here?'

'As I said, that's a long story, and one I think I'd prefer to tell Governor Barbaden. I will tell you this, though, we are loyal servants of the Emperor, just as you are. We have been on a mission for our Chapter and all we want is to go home to rejoin our battle brothers.'

'It's just that of all the places you had to turn up, it was there,' said Tremain.

'In Khaturian? That's what that place was called wasn't it?'

'Yes, that's what it was called,' said Tremain, and Uriel sensed the man's reticence to talk further of the dead city.

'What happened to it?' asked Uriel. 'Why does it carry a death penalty to go there?'

'It just does,' snapped Tremain. 'Now we'll have no more talk about the Killing Ground.'

'The Killing Ground?'

'I said we'd have no more talk about it,' warned Tremain, clearly not intimidated by the fact that he sat opposite a warrior who could kill him in the time it took to think it. Whatever the truth of Khaturian, or the Killing Ground as Tremain had called it, it was not a subject he was comfortable talking about.

Seeing he was going to get nothing useful from Uriel, Tremain's volubility evaporated and the next few hours of the journey were undertaken in silence, the sergeant offering no more insights to the world of Salinas or its inhabitants. Uriel made no attempt to engage him in conversation, and, instead, turned his attention to the slivers of landscape that he could see through the vision blocks fitted above the vehicle's integral lasguns.

What little he could see suggested a lush landscape of tall mountains, wide forests and clear skies. To see such things after the nightmarish landscapes of a daemon world in the Eye of Terror was a very real pleasure and Uriel looked forward to seeing more of this world before departing for Macragge.

The thought of seeing the home of his Chapter once more was like a balm on his soul and he could already feel the shadow that had fallen over his normal demeanour lifting.

They had completed their Death Oath and had returned to a world of the Imperium. True, they were little better than willing captives, but that would not be the case for long and Uriel was willing to suffer a little indignity before reaching home. He could not fault the Falcatas for their suspicions, for had they not appeared unannounced and unexpectedly in the middle of nowhere? Had someone done the same on Macragge, they would have been hurled into the deepest dungeons of the Fortress of Hera before being mercilessly interrogated.

Ah… the Fortress of Hera: the great libraries of knowledge, the Temple of Correction where the body of Roboute Guilliman lay in stasis, the Hall of Heroes, the Valley of Laponis… So many wondrous places.

If given the chance upon their return to Macragge, Uriel decided he would visit them all.

A crackling voice from a battered loudspeaker cut through his reverie.

'All units, mount up,' said Verena Kain's voice. 'Everyone get on a gun, we're approaching the outskirts of Barbadus.'

Uriel returned his attention to Tremain. 'Barbadus?' he said. 'Is that a city?'

Tremain nodded, chivvying the four remaining soldiers onto the integral lasguns.

'Yeah, it's the capital,' said Tremain, pulling a periscope-like device with a scratched pict slate down from the metal roof of the compartment. The slate flickered to life, displaying a static-washed image of the approaching conurbation.

Its outline was blurred and the buildings at the edge of the city looked somehow strange to Uriel, but the resolution of the image was too indistinct for him to see exactly why.

Raised high above the outskirts of the city's edge was a tall structure or sculpture that, through the distortion of the pict slate, looked like a winged angel.

As the column of vehicles drew closer, Uriel asked. 'What is that?'
Tremain said, 'That? It's the Iron Angel.'

PASCAL BLAISE CROUCHED behind the low roof parapet of an adobe ruin
as he watched the approaching Chimeras. He had given up trying to
identify in which vehicle Colonel Kain would be travelling, for none
had the distinctive whip aerials of a long range vox or bore any distinctive iconography that might indicate that a senior officer was
aboard.

No, the Falcatas has learned not to make such elementary mistakes.

Three Sentinels roamed ahead of the column and another three
brought up the rear and he had a moment's unease as he pictured the
amount of firepower this force could pump out.

Beside him, Cawlen Hurq cradled a battered missile tube, the pro-
jectile already loaded and primed. Across the street, on buildings to
either side of him and within burned out chassis of tanks, were
another five missile teams and thirty gunmen armed with a variety of
ancient lasguns and simple bolt action rifles.

The men had been hastily assembled and though acting with such
haste and lack of planning went against everything he taught his soldiers, the chance to take out Kain was too tempting to pass up.

The Chimeras were rumbling at speed through the ragged outskirts
of the city, where the buildings became more decrepit and bled out
into the landscape. Even now, Sons of Salinas sympathisers would be
clearing the dwellings below him of innocents. Pascal Blaise was careful not to place the people of his world in any unnecessary danger, but
the Falcatas would not be so careful when they retaliated.

Hopefully, by the time such retaliation was unleashed, he and his
men would have vanished into the maze of ruins and abandoned
vehicles that filled the city.

'Ready?' he whispered, the rumbling of the tracked vehicles growing
louder with every passing second.

'Damn right,' said Cawlen.

'Let the walkers go past and then take out the lead vehicle,' said
Pascal. 'The others are waiting for you to fire.'

'I know,' hissed Cawlen. 'Believe it or not, I have done this before.'

'Yes, of course. Sorry,' replied Pascal, fighting his instinct to micro-
manage.

Confident that Cawlen Hurq would unleash the ambush at the right moment, Pascal looked up at the Iron Angel, the guardian and lucky charm of the Sons of Salinas.

The great sculpture of scavenged parts towered above him. Her wings were those of a crashed Thunderbolt, her body shaped from the crumpled remains of its fuselage and her features formed from engine parts.

She was crude and unfinished, and she was beautiful.

'Watch over us today, fair lady,' he whispered.

Pascal slid his body up to look over the parapet.

The Chimeras had entered the killing box.

Cawlen Hurq rose to his knees and swung the missile tube over the parapet to point at the Chimeras on the street below.

'For the Sons of Salinas!' he yelled and mashed the firing trigger.

℧

FIVE

URIEL HEARD THE explosion through the armoured skin of the Chimera as a dull *whump*, the concussion of the detonation rocking the vehicle back on its tracks. Bright light flashed through the vision blocks and a series of rattling pings sounded as blazing shrapnel smacked the hull.

Another explosion sounded, this time from behind and the internal speakers suddenly exploded with chatter and screams.

'Ambush!' he shouted, before the echoes of the first blast had begun to fade.

A tremendous impact hammered the side of the Chimera, tipping it up onto one track. The soldiers cried out and Uriel snatched for the grab rail as the vehicle slammed back down to earth. A portion of the Chimera's side bulged inwards. Smoke and sparks spewed into the compartment and Uriel smelled blood.

One of the soldiers was down, his neck clearly broken. Another was screaming, his face a mask of red where it had smashed against the interior of the hull. The others lay bruised, but unhurt and Uriel surged from his seat against the hull to hammer the release mechanism of the assault door. Immobilised, the Chimera was a death trap.

Hot fumes blew inside and Uriel caught the reek of burning pro-
pellant and scorched flesh. Outside, morning sunlight illuminated a
blazing vehicle, flames spewing from its ruptured sides and thick,
tarry black smoke billowing into the sky.

'Come on!' he shouted. 'Out!'

Pasanius grabbed the wounded soldier as Tremain helped the others escape the stricken Chimera. Bodies and shredded pieces of meat
littered the ground, the exploded remnants of the soldiers forced to
travel on the roof.

Another whooshing roar made Uriel look up in time to see a missile streak from its launcher and slam into the roof of another of
Colonel Kain's Chimeras. This time the missile punched through the
thinner armour of the vehicle's topside and it shuddered as the warhead exploded inside. Smoke ripped upwards and a rattle of gunfire
barked from the rooftops as previously hidden gunmen revealed
themselves.

Uriel dragged another wounded soldier away from the fire that was
taking hold of their stricken vehicle. The engine was ablaze and it was
only a matter of time before the ammo and power pack on board
cooked off explosively.

Solid rounds and las-bolts smacked the earth and Uriel ducked as
he and the wounded soldier made their way into cover. A hail of shots
tore into the wall next to him. Fragments of rock billowed and he
blinked dust from his eyes.

Pasanius joined him, propping the wounded soldier against the
rough stone of a sagging ruin, and Uriel laid the man he carried next
to him. Shots rattled from both sides of the street, a street that Uriel
could see was composed of rough, adobe brick buildings and what
looked like the shells of abandoned tanks.

Canvas awnings and corrugated iron porches had been built into
the rusting hulks and these ad hoc dwellings outnumbered those constructed of more traditional materials.

'We should get into this fight,' said Uriel.

'With what?' pointed out Pasanius. 'Kain's lot seem like they know
what they're doing.'

That at least was true. Colonel Kain's Chimeras were roaring forward to protect the damaged vehicles while spraying bright bolts of
las-fire into the buildings on either side of the street.

The soldiers were fighting from their vehicles, letting the armour take the weight of small-arms fire while the turrets opened up with the snapping fizz of heavy las-bolts. A Chimera pulled ahead of Uriel in a skid of dirt and fumes as it sought to protect a damaged one.

Hard bangs of gunfire echoed from the turret-mounted heavy bolter, the rounds chewing up the stone parapets of the opposite buildings. Uriel saw puffs of red and heard screams over the incessant gunfire. The shooters had sprung their ambush well, but they were hunkered down behind a parapet that might as well have been fashioned from paper for all the protection it provided against bolter rounds.

Uriel watched as a loping Sentinel unleashed a torrent of autocannon rounds towards a group of men moving between the ruins. The heavy calibre shells exploded among them and they all fell, chewed up and unrecognisable, their blood spraying on the pale stone walls in looping arcs.

A shot rang out, distinctive and high pitched, and the Sentinel pilot's head snapped back, a ragged hole punched in the back of his head. Sniper.

Uriel glanced in the direction of the shot and saw the blurred outline of the shooter through the smoke of the battle. More of the Chimeras were pulling up to the damaged ones and soldiers were helping their comrades from the blazing wrecks to pull them inside those that had, thus far, escaped attack.

Uriel risked a glance around the bullet-chipped corner that he sheltered behind. To stand by and watch a battle being fought around him was anathema to him, and he knew he could not sit idly by while others were dying around him.

He turned to Pasanius, but before he could open his mouth, his sergeant said, 'You're going in, I know. Go. I'll cover you.'

Uriel nodded and slid from the alleyway, running towards a damaged Chimera that listed horribly to one side. Smears of blood and oil streaked its surfaces and smoke spat from its stinking interior. Its main gun was buckled, but Uriel had seen that its pintle-mounted weapon was still intact.

Bullets filled the air, the distinctive whine and buzz of them telling Uriel how close they were. Ricochets spanged from armour and he felt a burning line across his calf of something hot and sharp.

He dived into the cover of the listing Chimera and rolled to his feet in its shadow. He gripped the upper edge of the Chimera's hull and swung himself up onto its roof, scrambling across the upper armour towards the pintle-mounted gun. He snapped off the safety and swung the weapon around, his posture unsuited to firing it, but his strength more than able to bear the brunt of its recoil.

The sniper reared up to take aim at another Sentinel and Uriel pressed down on the palm triggers. The noise of the weapon was deafening, uncompromising, and designed to intimidate as much as wound. Heavy slugs spat from the barrel in a flaring burst. Uriel's target flew apart into flesh chunks and a fountain of blood.

He swivelled the weapon on its mount, raking the pounding thump of heavy bullets across the parapet line of the buildings opposite. Clay bricks dissolved under the impacts, blasted to powder by the high velocity slugs. The recoil was prodigious, but easily controllable by the strength of a Space Marine.

A las-bolt creased Uriel's shoulder and he flinched at the sudden pain, but kept his weapon trained on the roof-lines opposite. Arcs of bronze shells spewed from the smoking breech.

'Uriel!' shouted Pasanius from below. 'Your left!'

He turned towards where Pasanius was gesturing with the stump of his arm, seeing a flicker of movement between two blackened hulks of tanks that were now homes. A group of three men were preparing to launch a missile, and Uriel pulled the trigger as he brought his weapon to bear.

The bullets described a curving line as the weapon discharged, the impacts ringing like the sound of a hundred bells as they ricocheted from metal hulls. One man was hurled from his feet, a hole the size of his torso blasted in his body.

To their credit, neither of the other two men balked at the horrific death of their comrade, but kept the missile tube aimed squarely at the Chimera that Uriel sat upon. He kept the weapon trained on them, but the gun coughed dry, the hammer snapping on an empty chamber.

Uriel could see triumph on the gunner's face as he closed one eye.

Then his head exploded.

Uriel heard the distinctive report of a bolt weapon and saw Pasanius running towards him from the alleyway, the welcome sight of a bolt pistol bucking in his left hand. His sergeant fired again and the second man was pitched from his feet. A tremendous explosion mushroomed skyward as Pasanius's next bolt connected with the spare warheads in the canvas sack he wore.

The gunner's missile corkscrewed up from his fallen corpse, spinning wildly before exploding and smearing the sky with black tendrils of smoke.

More grinding sounds of tracks and the heavier, percussive thump of concentrated volleys of fire filled the air and Uriel released the grips of the heavy stubber. Colonel Kain's soldiers had the situation under control and Uriel could add little to the battle.

He saw a flash of green and gold and looked up to see a cloaked man with a shaved head and forked beard through a pulverised section of parapet. The man was shouting, but his words were inaudible over the roar of gunfire and the mad revving of engines.

Even Uriel's enhanced hearing could make out little of what the man was saying, but the sense of his words was clear as gun barrels vanished from rooftops. The weight of fire fell away as the ambushers disengaged and melted into the tumbled ruins.

The man risked one last glance from the rooftops and his eyes locked with Uriel's.

Uriel knew hate when he saw it. He had seen enough on Medrengard to last a lifetime.

This man hated him and wanted him dead, and not just him, but everyone in this bloody, smoke-filled street: the Falcatas, Uriel, Pasanius and every soldier who fought and shouted to their wounded comrades.

The man vanished from view and Uriel rolled from the roof of the Chimera.

He landed in the dirt beside Pasanius.

'Thanks for the warning,' said Uriel. 'That missile could have really spoiled my day.'

'No problem,' replied Pasanius. 'He'd have probably missed anyway. These idiots didn't know they were beaten until it was too late for them.'

Uriel had to agree with his friend's assessment of their opponents. The Falcatas had taken a serious hit when the ambush had been sprung, but had reacted with commendable speed and calm. The soldiers had followed their training and got into the fight without the confusion and panic that might have handed their attackers a victory.

Instead of retreating after their initial success, the ambushers had fought for longer than was sensible and had suffered the worst of the encounter, unable to match the discipline and firepower of a well-led force of Imperial Guard.

'Did you see the man with the green and gold cloak?' asked Uriel.

'I did,' said Pasanius, awkwardly trying to reload the bolt pistol. 'He looked like the leader. Stupid of him to wear something so noticeable though.'

'That's what I thought,' agreed Uriel, taking the bolt pistol from Pasanius and sliding a fresh magazine home. 'Where did you get this?'

'From him,' said Pasanius, indicating a dead sergeant of the Falcatas at the edge of the battlefield with a chunk of shrapnel the size of a shoulder guard buried in his face. 'Didn't think he'd be needing it again and thought it would be appropriate to use his own weapon to avenge him.'

'Very appropriate,' nodded Uriel.

'It means I don't have to use that other damned weapon…'

'Where is it now?'

'In there,' said Pasanius, pointing at the wreck they had clambered from what must only have been minutes ago. 'I'll let it burn.'

Uriel understood Pasanius's sentiment, for there was no honour and only risk in using a weapon that had been touched by the Ruinous Powers. Better to let it perish in the fire than risk it turning upon you.

Another Chimera pulled up beside them, the hatch in the turret open and Verena Kain leaning on the handles of a pintle storm bolter. The barrels smoked and Kain's face was black with dirt, pink lines streaking her features where sweat had run from her scalp.

'Get in,' she barked. 'They could be back.'

'Unlikely,' said Uriel, but he picked himself up and helped Pasanius to his feet. The armoured door at the back of the Chimera opened and Sergeant Tremain and two other troopers stepped out, their lasguns trained on the roof-lines.

Tremain beckoned them over and Uriel and Pasanius jogged over to the rumbling vehicle.

The street was filled with smoke and five blazing wrecks were abandoned where they had been destroyed. There were no bodies to be seen, the dead and wounded gathered up by the crews of the surviving vehicles. The Sentinel whose pilot Uriel had seen shot had collapsed, its leg broken by a careening Chimera. The pilot was nowhere to be seen.

Uriel shielded his eyes and asked Kain, 'Where to now?'

'To the barracks,' said Kain. 'It's closer and we have wounded.'

He had more questions, but the needs of the wounded took precedence and seconds could make the difference between life and death for some of these soldiers. Tremain clambered inside the Chimera, but as Uriel gripped the sides of the door, he saw that the compartment was full to bursting with wounded men who groaned as they lay on the sloshing floor. Uriel knew that the other vehicles would also be like this, thick with the stench of fear and pain and blood.

Soldiers sat shoulder to shoulder, packed in more tightly than even the most ambitious vehicle designer could have hoped, and Uriel saw a respect and admiration in their eyes that hadn't been there before.

Soldiers shuffled as they made room for them, word of Uriel and Pasanius's involvement in the fight having spread to those who hadn't seen it. Corpsmen cared for the wounded as best they were able in the red-lit compartment and a sullen anger simmered below the surface of every man on board.

'We'll ride on top,' said Uriel. 'You need all the room you can get in here.'

THE CHIMERAS SPED onwards through the city of Barbadus, and Uriel was afforded his first proper look at this Imperial capital. It appeared to have grown up around the ruins of an ancient battlefield, such was the litter and detritus of warfare that lay strewn around. Entire graveyards of armoured vehicles had been abandoned and left for the elements to devour and the people of the planet to colonise.

Buildings of agglomerated stone, brick and metal leaned precariously, supported by iron buttresses that had once been the main guns of armoured vehicles. The further into the city the racing column of vehicles went, the more solid and conventional the structures became, high-walled towers of pink stone and bleached timber.

Buildings of dark iron and tempered glass that were of Imperial origin nestled uncomfortably amongst the pale stone and clay bricks of the city and Uriel saw evidence of the war that had been fought to win this world on every one of the older buildings: las-burns and bullet marks, the latter worn smooth by the elements.

Uriel caught glimpses of green and gold streamers wafting from high spires and sagging clotheslines, the same green and gold that the man with the forked beard had been wearing. Many of the memorials in the dead city had streamers of the same colours attached to them and Uriel wondered what they symbolised.

'Emperor's blood!' hissed Pasanius, looking towards a gently sloping hill that rose to the west of the city.

'What?' said Uriel, fearing another ambush.

'Would you look at that?' said Pasanius. 'I've never seen the like.'

Uriel followed Pasanius's gaze and saw a strangely shaped building on the plateau of the hill. There was a familiarity to its silhouette, but it took him some moments to realise why.

The inhabitants of the city had been thorough in their cannibalisation of the discarded armoured vehicles, rendering many of them into dwellings, but this act of refurbishment was surely the apex of the scavenger's art.

Three towering Capitol Imperialis, mighty leviathans of vehicles used for command and control of entire battlefronts, sat side by side and had been transformed into something else entirely. Hundreds of crewmen and officers could operate from within each of these incredible war machines, directing entire regiments of artillery, hundreds of thousands of men and entire companies of armoured vehicles. To see one such colossus on a battlefield was rare, but to see three, abandoned no less, was unheard of.

They were surely abandoned, for the rust and corrosion on their sides was clear proof that these machines were no longer in use. The Imperial eagles on the sides of the outer two were gone, though it was impossible to tell whether they had been erased by the elements or by design. Swaying walkways joined them and iron-sheathed tunnels connected them at lower levels.

'What do you suppose it is?' asked Pasanius.

Uriel had been wondering the same thing. As he looked closer, he saw what might have been a winged staff encircled by a pair of entwined serpents above the control bridge of the middle vehicle.

A caduceus?

'A medicae facility perhaps?' suggested Uriel.

'Seems a bit excessive to use Capitol Imperialis for that.'

'True, but perhaps that was all they were fit for.'

'What do you mean?'

'Look at everything else we've seen,' said Uriel. 'There is a whole army's worth of abandoned armour here. Half the city's built among the ruined chassis of Imperial Guard tanks. When the Falcatas took this place, I think whatever Crusade force left them here didn't leave them with much to maintain their equipment.'

'Meaning it all went to wrack and ruin.'

'Eventually, yes.'

'Damn shame that,' said Pasanius. 'Not a good idea to show that lack of respect to something that would have saved your life in battle.'

'No, not a good idea at all,' agreed Uriel, remembering the harsh treatment meted out to his armour on Medrengard.

Uriel longed to be enclosed in the battle plate of the Astartes, to feel that he was whole once again and a righteous servant of the Emperor, clad in the strongest armour and armed with the deadliest weapons. Uriel's battle gear was more than simply artefacts of war, they were instruments of the Emperor's will.

At the foot of the hill upon which stood the medicae facility was a multi tiered, colonnaded dome that could only belong to the roof of an Ecclesiarchy temple. The soaring grandeur of the building was no doubt designed to dominate the more lowly structures around it with its Imperial majesty. Its glories had not spared it the harsh ministrations of war, however, for two of the four spires that rose from the cardinal points of the dome were broken stumps of stone and steel.

Eclipsing even this temple in its display of Imperial power was a tall, grim-spired palace that towered over the ramshackle city spread around it like debris tumbled from a mountain. Stark against the sky, it was an austere structure, cold and bereft of the glorious ornamentation that Uriel had seen on many other such buildings.

'The Imperial palace?' he said.

Pasanius nodded. 'Certainly grim enough for this place.'

Uriel nodded at Pasanius's assessment. The forbidding aspect of the palace, with its brutal architecture of drum towers topped with hooded turrets, lightning-wreathed antennae and shuttered hangars was certainly in keeping with the sombre atmosphere of this world, but more than that, the building's architecture gave the impression of power without compassion.

Clearly, Governor Barbaden was not a man given to ostentation. That was a nugget of information to store for later and Uriel wondered what manner of man the Imperial Commander was.

He was certainly not liked, if the people on the streets of his city were anything to go by.

They were a handsome, tall people dressed, almost uniformly, in ash-grey coveralls and long cloaks.

The people hugged the buildings as the Chimeras rushed past, and Uriel saw the same sullen hostility in their eyes that he had seen on the faces of the Guardsmen in the Chimera.

The Falcatas victory in claiming this world as their own had obviously left scars: scars that had not yet healed.

Everywhere Uriel looked, he saw evidence of the peoples' cannibalisation of what the Imperial Guard had discarded: market stalls formed from the beaten sheet metal of tank hulls, carts and wagons dragged on wheels scavenged from supply trucks and barrows with handles fashioned from exhaust pipes.

Colonel Kain's column was travelling rapidly through the streets, taking sharp, veering turns at random.

'She's not taking any chances on a second ambush,' noted Pasanius, giving voice to Uriel's thought and gripping the edge of the Chimera as it skidded around another corner.

Uriel looked at the naked hostility that burned from every face.

'I don't blame her,' he said.

THE SCREAMING EAGLES' journey through the strange streets of Barbadus continued for another ten minutes, ten long minutes during which Uriel expected a shot or streaking missile with every breath. No such violence was unleashed, and each turn took them deeper into the warren of streets and further from the Imperial palace.

Eventually, the Chimeras increased speed as they surged towards a walled compound set apart from the buildings around it. Uriel had noticed the buildings becoming more widely spaced and less complete for a few moments, but only as they passed out into the open did he see why.

Rolled coils of barbed wire surrounded the compound and squat, unlovely bunkers of sandbags and timber flanked the heavy iron gate. A bronze eagle was stamped across both sides of the gate and the column of vehicles began to slow as they negotiated a path between great slabs of concrete laid to prevent any direct approach.

'They're cautious, I'll give them that,' said Pasanius, noting the way the guns at the corners of the compound walls followed the column in.

'They're scared,' said Uriel, thinking back to the hostility he had seen on every face they had passed on their journey towards this place. 'They've pulled back within their walls. I didn't see any patrols on the streets, did you?'

'No, but I wouldn't necessarily expect to see a military presence on the streets,' said Pasanius, 'Local enforcers maybe, but not Guard.'

'I didn't even see any of them,' said Uriel.

'No. Odd isn't it?'

'Very,' said Uriel.

Further conversation was halted as the gate rumbled open, sliding within the fabric of the wall, and the vehicles passed into the dusty courtyard of the compound. There were several barrack buildings inside, of basic Imperial design, portal framed sheds with corrugated iron walls and felt roofs. Similarly drab buildings were spaced at regular intervals around the compound: a mess hall, engineering sheds, fuel dumps, quartermaster stores and an infirmary.

A flag bearing a golden eagle with out-thrust talons flew high over the compound and anxious looking soldiers ran from every building as the battered Chimeras parked up. Shouts were exchanged between men spilling from the vehicles and medics bellowed at their comrades to give the wounded room.

Uriel vaulted from the roof of the Chimera, aware of the strange looks he and Pasanius were drawing. He saw Colonel Kain, her clipped tones easily cutting through the confusion and collective outrage at the attack. With calm efficiency, she directed the work of the medics, ignoring their expressions of irritation at her meddling.

Uriel nodded to Pasanius and they walked over to the colonel of the Falcatas.

'Anything we can do to help?' asked Uriel.

Kain looked up from issuing her orders, her face clean and pristine again.

'No,' she said, 'and I'll thank you to remain with Sergeant Tremain. You are still in our custody.'

'Even after what just happened?' said Uriel, as Sergeant Tremain and a trio of Guardsmen, resplendent in fresh uniform jackets and raised lasguns moved up behind them.

'Especially after what just happened,' said Kain. 'Your arrival and the Sons of Salinas attack coming so soon after... I would be remiss not to wonder what the connection is, would I not?'

'The Sons of Salinas?' said Uriel. 'Who are they? I saw that name scrawled on a building in Khaturian.'

'Another thing I am less than comfortable with,' said Kain.

'But who are they?' pressed Uriel.

'They are nothing,' snapped Kain, her eyes blazing with fury. 'They are traitors who cling to the notion that the forces of the Imperium are invaders and should be resisted at every turn. They are terrorists, murderers and heretics, deserving of nothing less than extermination.'

Uriel was not surprised at her vehemence, for she had just seen scores of her men killed or wounded. Even so, there was a hatred in her steely tones that ran deeper than simple anger at the violence done to her company.

Verena Kain hated the Sons of Salinas with the passion of a zealot.

'Have you any idea how they were able to attack you like that?' asked Pasanius.

Kain flashed him a bilious glance that spoke volumes of her frustration. 'This whole damn city feeds them information,' she said. 'Every move we make, there's someone with a portable vox passing word of it.'

IT TOOK ANOTHER thirty minutes to treat the wounded, secure the battered vehicles and re-equip the soldiers, all of whom had expended a good deal of their ammo load in the battle. A nervous looking commissar took statements from soldiers, selected at random, as far as Uriel could tell, and Kain continued to bark orders with the vigour of someone who dared not stop for even a second in case she had time to dwell on what had just occurred.

Her every command was obeyed with an alacrity that suggested that to do otherwise would result in the severest consequences, and Uriel recognised an officer who knew her trade, and who would never allow others to forget it.

In that time, Uriel and Pasanius sat against the hull of one of the Chimeras, the metal ticking and groaning as it cooled. The sun was halfway through its ascent towards its zenith and Uriel closed his eyes and let its warmth bathe his exposed flesh.

With nothing to do but wait until Colonel Kain decided it was time to leave, Uriel revelled in this unaccustomed time to himself. A Space Marine on active duty had precious little time that wasn't spent in preparation for battle. Weapons practice, strength building, biochemical monitoring and all manner of training drills were the virtual be all and end all of his life.

It was a life of service, a life of sacrifice and a life of battle.

What servant of the Emperor could ask for more?

The question presented its own answer in the shape of Ardaric Vaanes.

Uriel's time on Medrengard had caused him to question his role as a Space Marine, but he had passed his own time of testing and come through it stronger. Others on that damned world had not shown such strength of character, and Uriel bitterly remembered the sight of Ardaric Vaanes as he had turned his back on his duty to the Emperor.

Vaanes had once been a warrior of the Raven Guard, but had, for reasons Uriel never discovered, forsaken his Chapter and taken the path of the renegade. Uriel had offered Vaanes the chance to rediscover his honour and seek redemption, but the warrior had chosen dishonour and disgrace.

Uriel wondered what had become of Ardaric Vaanes. In all likelihood, he was dead by now, a bleached corpse lying in the ashen wasteland of that dreadful world.

Feeling himself becoming maudlin, he put Vaanes from his mind and turned his head towards Pasanius.

Neither man felt the need to speak to one another, the companionable silence of two old friends who had seen life and death and everything in-between allowing them the luxury of silence.

That silence was broken by the approach of Colonel Kain.

Uriel looked up as she approached.

'Governor Barbaden is ready to see you,' she said.

'Good,' replied Uriel. 'I think I'm about ready to see him too.'

PART TWO
FLESHED

'From little spark should burst a mighty flame.'

♅
SIX

VISITING THE IMPERIAL palace of Salinas was an experience Daron Nisato avoided whenever he could. The building was too cold and too blatant a symbol of Imperial power to be relished any more. It served as a focal point for the people's anger, and to see its stark, uncompromising lines against the blue of the sky was to understand your insignificance in the face of the Imperium, and more especially, your insignificance in the face of Governor Leto Barbaden.

Nisato allowed the duty officer of the checkpoint to relieve him of his weapons, though it irked him that the city's chief enforcer could not be trusted with firearms in the presence of the governor.

This was the third security checkpoint he had passed through this morning, a drab, prefabricated building that smelled of damp and neglect. The first checkpoint at the main gate had halted his Rhino APC and the second, barely twenty paces later, had confirmed his identity via a series of painful, blood-sampling gene-matchers. He smiled grimly as he wondered if the gene-matchers explained the pasty, ashen complexions of the staffers that worked within the palace.

'Something funny?' asked the duty officer as he locked away Nisato's pistol.

'No,' replied Nisato, aware that these men lacked anything approaching a sense of humour, 'just happy to see you're doing such a thorough job.'

The man looked askance at Nisato, searching for signs of mockery, but Nisato was a past master at keeping his thoughts to himself. Satisfied that his solemn duty was not being made fun of, the man nodded gracelessly and waved Nisato through the door that led into the palace's courtyard precincts.

Nisato was about to pass through when the door behind him opened and the unmistakable aroma of incense, sweat and guilt wafted in. He knew who had entered the room without turning.

'Cardinal Togandis,' said Nisato.

He heard the intake of breath and turned to see the rotund figure of the Pontifex Maximus of Barbadus in all his finery.

'Enforcer Nisato,' said Togandis, his skin sheened in sweat. 'How fortuitous we should find ourselves together at this juncture.'

Shavo Togandis had never been an impressive man, even when he had served with the Falcatas as its company confessor, his manner too brusque, his appetites too unsavoury and his language too florid. Nisato had never felt the need to avail himself of the man's services, preferring to keep his confessions between the Emperor and himself in prayer.

The decade since Restoration Day had not been kind to Shavo Togandis's physique, his already doughy frame blooming to one generously proportioned in all directions.

'You are summoned also?' asked Nisato.

'Yes, yes,' said Togandis, mopping his brow with a handkerchief. 'We are all servants of our lord and master. Barbaden commands and we obey with alacrity. One does not like to keep the good governor waiting, does one?'

'No,' agreed Nisato, stepping aside to let the cardinal approach the unsmiling duty officer.

As Togandis went through the necessary formalities involved in passing through the palace's security, Nisato took a moment to study the senior cleric of Salinas.

He was not impressed.

Aside from his generously upholstered frame, Shavo Togandis had a nervous manner that, in any other man, would have seen him hauled into the interrogation cells below the enforcers' precinct and broken down for a confession.

The confessor confessing. The thought made him smile.

In addition to his shimmering chasuble of crimson and silver, Togandis wore a tall and elaborately worked mitre with long trailing cords of gold. He carried a long staff, which he was attempting to prevent the duty officer from impounding.

'Now see here, my good man,' began Togandis, 'this postprandial summons to the palace has inconvenienced me greatly and this staff is a sacred instrument of my most valued and not inconsequential status on this planet. You would be advised not to remove it from my personage.'

'No weapons or items that could be construed as weapons are allowed within the palace,' said the duty officer, as though reciting the words by rote, 'except by a member of the Falcatas.'

'Now you listen here, you pathetic little myrmidon, you must understand that there are exceptions to every rule and I refuse to truckle to your purblind devotion. Do you understand?'

'Frankly, no,' said the duty officer, holding out his hand, 'but it alters nothing. You'll need to hand over your staff.'

'I wouldn't bother arguing, Shavo,' said Nisato, adopting a tone as stuffy and self-important as the cardinal's. 'Even I, an upholder of Imperial Law, am forced to relinquish my symbols of office in the face of this panjandrum.'

Togandis looked down at Nisato's empty holster and smiled at the gesture of solidarity, oblivious to the sarcasm in Nisato's voice.

'Well, indeed, one must band together in the face of adversity, what?' he said, turning and reluctantly handing over his staff to the duty officer. 'And if there is so much as a single imperfection visible upon that staff when I return, I shall deliver the fiercest commination upon your head!'

The duty officer took the staff and wearily waved the pair of them through.

Smiling, Nisato followed the cardinal into the courtyard, emerging into bright sunlight on the cusp of the transition from morning to afternoon.

The palace towered above them, dark and threatening. Its guns and defences, though angled to the sky, remained an impressive symbol of the power of the man who commanded them. Constructed from immense blocks of dark stone, the palace reminded Nisato of the great, cliff-top castles of his home world, brooding crags carved from the rock of the coastline.

Scarlet-clad soldiers patrolled the lower skirts of the palace, their falcatas unsheathed at their sides. Their red plate gleamed in the sun and the bronze of their helmets shone like gold, but even these men were not permitted to bear firearms as a matter of course.

Unlike many soldiers who looked ceremonial, the Achaman Falcatas were men he had once been proud to fight alongside. There was no give in these soldiers and they fought with a fire in their bellies that other regiments could only envy. That fire had died since Restoration Day, but its embers still smouldered.

A trio of Chimera transports emblazoned with the insignia of the Screaming Eagles were parked up before the palace, an unusual enough occurrence that it made Nisato wonder who had travelled in them to be afforded such a rare honour.

Once again, Togandis dabbed his forehead with his handkerchief.

'So, did your summons furnish you with any clue as to the nature of this audience?' he asked.

Nisato shook his head, slowing his normally long stride to allow the waddling cardinal to keep up. 'No, it didn't, but then Leto always was a man of few words, wasn't he?'

'Indeed he was,' agreed Togandis. 'Indeed he was. No inspiring speeches before a battle, just orders, precise, never to be meddled with, orders.'

That was certainly true, remembered Nisato. As a cadet commissar when Leto Barbaden had taken command of the Achaman Falcatas, Nisato had summarily executed a number of junior officers who had seen fit to exercise their own initiative in their interpretation of Barbaden's orders.

Leto Barbaden did not like to be second-guessed and nor did he expect his orders to be carried out with anything less than total obedience. As far as Nisato knew, the years since Barbaden's relinquishing of command had not mellowed him and thus he had put aside his current investigations into Sons of Salinas activity and headed straight for the palace upon receiving his summons.

Until he had met Togandis, Nisato had assumed that it had something to do with this morning's attack on Colonel Kain's convoy as it had made its way back into the city. Seeing the Chimeras supported that, but the cardinal's presence suggested that some other business was afoot.

'Such a terrible business with Governor Barbaden's former adjutant, eh?'

'I'm sorry?' said Nisato, surprised at this sudden, unexpected, question.

'Hanno Merbal?' said Togandis. 'He shot himself right in front of you, I hear?'

'Yes,' replied Nisato, his interest piqued, 'he did.'

'He was a friend of yours, was he not?' asked Togandis and Nisato wanted to laugh at the cardinal's attempt at nonchalance.

'He was,' confirmed Nisato. Keep the answers short, he thought. Let Togandis do the talking.

'Hmmm, yes,' said Togandis. 'Have you any idea why he would do such a thing?'

'You tell me, Shavo,' said Nisato. 'You were his confessor, weren't you?'

'I was indeed, Daron,' replied Togandis, scorn dripping from the use of his first name, 'but the fact of which I am sure you are cognisant remains that the seal of the confessional is a sacred trust that cannot be broken.'

'Even in death?'

'Especially in death,' said Togandis. 'The sins of the confessed are in the hands of the Emperor. I can tell you he was having some issues with, shall we say, guilt, though.'

'Over this?' asked Nisato, pulling out the golden eagle medal that Hanno Merbal had shown him right before blowing his brains out all over the bar.

Togandis looked away from the medal and Nisato was enough of an enforcer to know guilt when he saw it. Once again Togandis dabbed at his moist forehead.

'I... I haven't thought of Khaturian in a long time,' said Togandis, and Nisato smelled a lie.

'You were there?' asked Nisato and Togandis flinched.

Nisato already knew the answer; Togandis wore an identical medal on the front of his chasuble.

'I was, yes,' agreed Togandis hurriedly, 'but I took no part in the fighting.'

'From what I gather there wasn't much fighting.'

Togandis did not reply at first and Nisato thought the cardinal was going to ignore the question, but the man whispered. 'No, there wasn't, but...'

'But?' pressed Nisato, eager to learn what he could of this most unspoken of battles.

Before Togandis had a chance to answer, a formal voice said, 'Enforcer Nisato, Cardinal Togandis, Governor Barbaden is ready to see you now. If you will follow me please.'

Nisato cursed inwardly and mustered a smile as he looked away from Togandis to the blandly smiling face of Mersk Eversham.

Eversham's face was thin and angular, but his body, beneath the elegantly cut frock coat, was solid and unbreakable. Nisato had seen Eversham in combat enough times to know that the man was a ferocious killer and he wondered how Barbaden had persuaded him to muster out of the regiment. He was an anomaly within the Falcatas, a man of culture and breeding who could have easily become an officer, but had chosen to enlist in the rank and file.

Now he served as Leto Barbaden's aide, attendant, personal secretary and bodyguard, having long ago replaced the now-deceased Hanno Merbal. Nisato had no doubt that Eversham was armed with a number of concealed firearms and blades.

'Mersk,' said Nisato, nodding. 'You're keeping well?'

'Well enough,' said Eversham. 'Now if you please.'

'Of course, of course,' fussed Togandis. 'Come on, Daron. We mustn't keep the good governor waiting, must we?'

'No,' said Nisato, 'we wouldn't want that.'

He saw the faint suggestion of a smug grin on Eversham's face and resisted the urge to wipe it off. Instead, he followed Barbaden's killer and the cardinal as a detachment of red-jacketed soldiers formed up around them, falcatas bright in the sunlight.

The symbolism was obvious and heavy handed, but Nisato paid it no mind as they were led into the palace, down twisting corridors, up cramped screw stairs and through echoing, cold chambers bereft of warming fires or laughter.

Eversham offered no more in the way of conversation and Togandis's normal extravagant garrulousness vanished in the face of the palace's austerity. They marched in silence until the soldiers halted at the end of a long, portrait-lined hallway. At the end of the corridor, Nisato saw the slight, stooped form of Mesira Bardhyl and felt a familiar protective urge towards the woman.

She had always been a nervous creature and had been treated foully when she had served as Barbaden's pet psyker.

The years since Restoration Day had been no kinder to her as far as Nisato could tell.

'This way,' said Eversham, though the route was familiar to both Nisato and Togandis.

They followed Eversham along the hallway, Togandis making a show of admiring the portraits of previous colonels of the Falcatas, and Nisato wondering what the cardinal had been about to say before Eversham had interrupted.

Mesira greeted them with a shy smile and a nod, and Nisato saw dark hollows beneath her eyes and noted how the skin seemed to sag on her sparse frame. Togandis studiously ignored Mesira as Eversham knocked tersely on the wide wooden doors at the end of the hallway. Barbaden's equerry paused just long enough to hear an imperious command to enter before sweeping into the room.

Nisato, Togandis and Mesira followed Eversham into the room, a spacious and extensive library furnished with long tables and floor to ceiling bookcases.

Governor Leto Barbaden sat, perched on the room's central table.

Tall, lean and dark-haired, Leto Barbaden's ascetic frame was dressed in an immaculately cut suit that echoed the pomp of a military uniform in its brass buttons, lined trousers and gleaming boots, but which was undeniably civilian. A line of medal ribbons decorated his left breast, but they were understated and dignified.

Barbaden's face was handsome, his dark hair and neatly trimmed beard sprinkled liberally with silver, but his eyes were those of a predator.

As commanding a presence as Barbaden was, it was the two figures standing before him that completely captured Daron Nisato's attention. It was left to Shavo Togandis's surprise to give them name.

'Astartes,' breathed the cardinal.

Both were clad in pale robes with the hoods pulled back, the clothes looking absurdly small on their enhanced physiques. Both stood head and shoulders above Verena Kain and the armed soldiers who lined the walls of the library. One of the Space Marines was lean, if such a description could be applied to a two and a half metre-tall giant, while the other was a brute of a man whose arm was missing below the elbow.

To say Daron Nisato was astonished by this strange tableau was an understatement of colossal proportions.

'Ah, Daron, Shavo,' said Barbaden, his voice mellifluous, 'so glad you could join us.'

As if there was a choice, thought Nisato.

'We have guests,' continued Barbaden, 'and they claim to have a most fantastical tale.'

WITH EVERY PASSING moment, the sun had crept further and further into the cave, pressing the Unfleshed back into its darkened depths. Bellowing roars and threatening demonstrations of their physical power had not halted its progress and neither had begging, pleading or wails of fear.

The Lord of the Unfleshed felt the anger that had been growing in him turn to rage as the hateful light encroached on their last refuge. There was nowhere to go, no last hiding place that would protect the tribe from the killing light.

Their betrayal was complete.

They huddled behind him, pathetic and afraid, their monstrous forms and mighty strength no defence against the sunlight that would kill their skinless bodies. Even with their limited exposure to it, their bodies were changing, the lesions across their limbs spreading and turning paler as they went.

As the light grew brighter, the Lord of the Unfleshed narrowed his eyes, feeling a tightness to his body, as though his limbs were wrapped in some invisible film.

His body itched all over and he raised his arm to his face, seeing a strange milky sheen where the sunlight had touched it. His arm had changed from the mottled red and grey of exposed musculature to a shimmering, oily white.

Though the terms were unknown to him, his metabolism had reacted to the sudden and shocking presence of ultraviolet radiation by activating the gene-memory of the biological hardware pressed into the service of his construction. In Space Marines the organ was known as the melanochrome, a biological device designed to darken the warrior's skin and protect him from harmful radiation.

Accelerated and altered beyond reason by the horrific nature of his gestation within the daemon wombs of Medrengard, the disparate fragments of the melanochrome were in overdrive, crafting the only defence its mindless biological imperatives knew: skin.

The Lord of the Unfleshed watched as the milky sheen spread still further, flowing like a rippling liquid as it oozed down the length of his arm, covering his fingers and tightening across the meat and bone of his body.

Amazed, the Lord of the Unfleshed took a step forward, easing his newly sheathed arm into the light that crept like an invader into the cave. His arm tingled, the skin darkening from a soft white to a fleshy pink. He withdrew his arm as he saw the same substance crawling over the bodies of his tribe.

Were they to be whole again?

The nature of this miracle was unknown to the Lord of the Unfleshed, but he dropped to his knees to give thanks to the Emperor for it, for what else could the source of this wonder be?

Emboldened by their leader's change, the rest of the tribe edged forward, their glistening bodies following the example of the Lord of the Unfleshed.

They whooped and howled as the light touched them, for their bodies were more degenerate than their leader's and the light still burned them. They looked to him for guidance, but he had none to give them.

His body was changing, adapting, mutating. He did not know how or why, but the Emperor was giving him a chance to better himself, to become more than simply a monster. His anger, a fiery, volatile thing retreated within him, not gone, but kept in check.

The Lord of the Unfleshed turned his gaze upon his tribe. 'Wait. Changes coming. What happens to me will happen to you, not now, but soon.'

As if to prove his point, the Lord of the Unfleshed stepped into the sunlight to howls of fear and anguish. Step after step, he marched through the light until he stood at the cave mouth on the slopes of the mountain.

He felt the sunlight burning his skin, but it was a sensation to be rejoiced in, not feared. The forgotten memory of skin returned to him in all its glory: to be clad in flesh, to stand beneath the heat of a sun and know the feeling of it on his face!

Far below, he could see the ruins of the dead place, shadows criss-crossing its empty streets.

Except, now that he looked, they weren't empty were they?

URIEL STOOD BEFORE the governor of Salinas and knew he was in the presence of one of the most dangerous individuals he had ever met: Leto Barbaden, a man of whom he had heard only fragmentary pieces of information, a man who, until now, had been a cipher.

As a commander of a regiment and now a world, he had clearly not been a man to underestimate, but Uriel saw the truth of the matter as he looked into Barbaden's cold, pitiless eyes.

In his time as a warrior, Uriel had met all kinds of commanders, some good, some bad, but mostly just men and women trying to do their duty and keep their soldiers alive. Barbaden might be concerned with the former, but it was clear that he had no real interest in the latter.

With the wounded dealt with at the Screaming Eagles barracks, Uriel and Pasanius had once again embarked on a Chimera and been driven at speed through the city. A number of decoy Chimeras had also been despatched, but such precautions had, this time, proven unnecessary.

They had seen little of the city on the journey, simply flashes of brick and metal through the vision blocks. Uriel had tried to follow the sense of the route, but had quickly given up after yet another confusing turn. Then there had been a series of stops and starts, no doubt checkpoints of some description, before they had disembarked within a large courtyard at the foot of the Imperial palace.

Seen up close, the building was even more impressive than it had first appeared, its defences and armaments the equal of many of the outlying fortresses in Ultramar. Colonel Kain had led them into a barracks unit at the base of the palace, accompanied as always by a detachment of her red-jacketed soldiers.

A man in a long black coat had met them, a man in whom Uriel saw the fluid movements and casual grace of a natural killer. This man was introduced as Eversham, personal equerry to Governor Barbaden. Uriel had shared a glance with Pasanius and was relieved to see that his friend had also seen through the man's façade of bland functionary.

Clean clothes were provided and Uriel had gratefully stripped out of the remainder of his broken armour. Pasanius had been less keen, and made no secret of his reluctance to be parted from it. Uriel had displayed a similar reticence when a soldier had come forward to relieve him of his golden-hilted sword.

'This was an honour gift from a captain of the Ultramarines,' warned Uriel.

'Have no fear for your battle gear,' promised Eversham. 'It will be taken to the Gallery of Antiquities. Curator Urbican is no stranger to armour and weapons such as yours.'

It was clear that the matter was not up for debate and their equipment had been taken from them and carried away by a squad of sweating soldiers. Still under armed guard, the two of them had used the ablutions block to wash the accumulated filth of their travels on Medrengard from their bodies, though Uriel doubted that a simple cascade of heated water could ever achieve such a thing.

Their bodies cleaned, fresh robes were presented to them, simple things, hastily altered to fit their overlarge frames. Now considered presentable to the good governor, Eversham and Colonel Kain (also in a fresh uniform) had escorted them through the palace, a gloomy, spartanly furnished abode of wood panelled corridors with little in the way of personal decoration or anything approaching a stamp of the incumbent owner's personality.

That in itself was revealing, for it was a trait common to most people, Uriel had come to realise, that they wished to leave their mark on the world to show that they had existed and to prove that they mattered.

Uriel saw none of that in the cheerless chambers of the palace and he wondered what that said about the mindset of the man who called this building home.

At last they had been led through a portrait-lined gallery and into a large, well-stocked library with a score of soldiers standing to attention around the perimeter of the room. Seated before a roaring, crackling fire was a tall man with dark hair lined with silver. His bearing was stiff and unpretentious and he drank a tawny liquid from a curved snifter.

Eversham had departed, to fetch other arrivals, he claimed, and Uriel and Pasanius had been left in the company of Leto Barbaden and Verena Kain.

Kain had wordlessly taken up position with the soldiers at the walls and Barbaden regarded them coolly for several moments before rising from his chair and depositing his glass on the table next to it.

'I am Leto Barbaden, Imperial Commander of Salinas,' he said. 'Now who are you?'

'I am Captain Uriel Ventris and this is Sergeant Pasanius Lysane,' said Uriel.

'The man does not speak for himself?' asked Barbaden. 'Has he lost the power of speech?'

'I can speak well enough,' said Pasanius.

'Then do so,' suggested Barbaden. 'Never let others speak for you, sergeant.'

Uriel was surprised, and not a little angered, at the governor's tone, for, like Kain, the governor displayed none of the awe or reverence that usually accompanied the presence of warriors of the Adeptus Astartes. In fact, his bearing and body language suggested downright hostility.

'You said you are a captain, Uriel Ventris,' continued Barbaden, perching on the edge of the table, 'a captain of which Chapter?'

'We are proud warriors of the Ultramarines,' said Uriel, 'the Fourth Company: the Defenders of Ultramar.'

'Please furnish me with a concise answer when I ask a question, captain. I do so detest loquaciousness,' said Barbaden.

Anger touched Uriel, but he felt Pasanius willing him to remain calm, and he fought down his rising temper. 'As you wish, governor.'

'Excellent,' smiled Barbaden. 'Salinas is a simple world and I should like to keep it like that. I keep things simple because, as systems become complex, they have more chance of going wrong. You understand?'

Believing Barbaden's question was rhetorical, Uriel said nothing.

'Also, when I ask a question, captain, I expect an answer. I do not waste my breath asking questions to which I already know the answer.'

'Yes,' hissed Uriel, 'I understand.'

'Good,' continued Barbaden, apparently oblivious to Uriel's growing anger. 'Salinas is a world not without its problems, true, but none are of sufficient magnitude to trouble me unduly. However, when two warriors of the Astartes suddenly appear on my planet without so much as a breath of notice, it strikes me as a complexity that could dangerously destabilise the workings of my world.'

'I assure you, Governor Barbaden, that is the last thing we wish to do,' said Uriel. 'All we want to do is return to Macragge.'

Barbaden nodded. 'I see, and this would be your home world?'

'Yes.'

'As I mentioned earlier, Captain Ventris, I dislike complexities. They add random variables to life that I detest. In all things, predictable outcomes are those upon which we rely to facilitate our passage through life. Known facts and predictable elements are the bedrock upon which all things are built and if we upset that, well, chaos ensues.'

'Of course, governor–' began Uriel.

'I have not finished speaking,' snapped Barbaden. 'It strikes me that your presence here is just such a random variable and that it would be better if I were simply to be rid of you.'

Barbaden snapped his fingers and the soldiers around the edges of the room suddenly lifted their rifles to their shoulders and aimed them at Uriel and Pasanius.

Uriel couldn't believe what he was hearing and seeing. Was this man simply going to gun them down? He quickly calculated the number and type of weapons pointed at him and the odds of their survival. Even the legendary physique of a Space Marine would not survive a well-aimed volley from these soldiers.

'You arrive on my world, unannounced and without permission,' hissed Barbaden. 'You trespass upon forbidden ground and you expect me to treat you as honoured guests? What manner of fool do you take me for?'

'Governor Barbaden,' said Uriel, 'I swear on the honour of my Chapter that we are servants of the Emperor. If you will allow me, I will explain how we came to be on your world.'

'Explanations are excuses,' said Barbaden. 'I'll have the truth from you. Now.'

Uriel saw anger in Barbaden's eyes, but saw that it travelled no further through his body.

The governor's anger was perfectly controlled, icy and supported by his internal logic, which made it all the more dangerous, as it was not fettered by other emotions.

With a gesture, Barbaden could destroy them without regret and Uriel found himself wondering at the irony of having survived everything the Eye of Terror could throw at them, only to be killed by a fellow servant of the Emperor.

'Of course,' said Uriel, his voice hardening at this boorish treatment. 'I will tell you the truth of our arrival, and perhaps then we can come to some arrangement whereby we can leave.'

'That remains to be seen,' said Barbaden, 'but I will consider it upon hearing your story.'

Uriel nodded, unwilling to offer anything approaching thanks to Barbaden. 'I warn you that this is a fantastical tale, governor. Some of it you may find hard to believe, but I swear on my honour that it is all true.'

Before Uriel could say more, there was a knock on the door and Barbaden said, 'Enter!'

The door opened and Eversham re-entered the room, leading three others behind him.

Two of the new arrivals were men, the other a woman. One man was tall and ruggedly handsome, his skin as dark as the heavy, black body armour he wore. Uriel decided he must be some sort of local law enforcement.

The second man was grossly fat, to the point of obesity: a corpulent mass of flesh clad head to foot in lavishly ornamented robes of scarlet and silver. Uriel took him for a senior member of the Ecclesiarchy, a cardinal perhaps. The man mopped his glistening brow with a sodden handkerchief and Uriel could smell the rankness of his gushing pores.

The third member of the new arrivals was a spare, tired-looking woman with pensive features and a nervous disposition. Uriel could smell her fear, even over the cardinal's odour.

None of the three could hide their surprise at the sight of them.

'Astartes,' breathed the obese man.

'Ah, Daron, Shavo,' said Barbaden, 'so glad you could join us. We have guests, and they claim to have a most fantastical tale.'

ʊ
SEVEN

INTRODUCTIONS WERE MADE perfunctorily: Daron Nisato, chief enforcer of the city of Barbadus; Shavo Togandis, Cardinal of Barbadus and Pontifex Maximus of Salinas; and lastly, Mesira Bardhyl, former sanctioned psyker of the Achaman Falcatas and private citizen. Uriel could not miss the contempt for all three written across Verena Kain's face.

Leto Barbaden retrieved his snifter and sat back down. He occupied the room's only chair and everyone else was forced to stand as he reclined and crossed his legs.

Barbaden waved the snifter towards Uriel and said, 'You may begin your tale, captain.'

Uriel swallowed his anger and simply nodded.

He began with the Fourth Company's mission to Tarsis Ultra and the battles against the tyranids, a race of extra-galactic predators who sought to devour all life on the world. Uriel's voice soared with pride as he told of the many battles fought before the walls of Erebus City and the courage of the Imperial Guard regiments tasked with its defence.

As he described the desperate fighting to save Tarsis Ultra, Uriel could feel the vicarious pride that the soldiers of the Falcatas felt in the achievements of their brother Guardsmen.

The Great Devourer's hordes were defeated on Tarsis Ultra, but the cost had been high.

Many of Uriel's warriors had died, and the Masters of the Ultramarines had not looked favourably on his cavalier methods of command. No sooner had the survivors of the Fourth Company returned to Macragge than Uriel and Pasanius had been charged with breaking faith with the Codex Astartes, the mighty tome that guided the Ultramarines in all things and which had been penned by their Primarch in ages past.

'What was the nature of your punishment?' asked Barbaden.

'We were exiled from the Chapter,' replied Uriel.

'To what purpose?'

'Lord Tigurius, the chief librarian of the Ultramarines saw a vision of great evil and sent us on a mission to destroy it: a Death Oath.'

'A Death Oath?' asked Barbaden. 'So, you were not expected to return?'

'Few have ever returned from such quests,' agreed Uriel.

'But you have completed your Death Oath?'

'We have. We travelled to a world taken by the Ruinous Powers and fought our way into the fortress of an enemy warlord and saw his citadel torn down.'

'And you did this all on your own?' asked Verena Kain.

'No,' said Uriel, choosing his words carefully, 'not quite. We made allies of some of the planet's inhabitants. Together we were able to complete our mission and now seek only to return to our Chapter.'

Barbaden appeared to consider Uriel's words and said, 'An intriguing tale, Captain Ventris, but it does not answer the question that has been vexing me ever since I was informed of your arrival. How did you get here?'

'I am not sure of the exact mechanics of it, Governor Barbaden,' began Uriel, understanding that he would need to tell at least part of the truth. 'Much of what has happened to us in recent times is beyond my understanding, but we were transported within a craft that somehow travels between this world and the Empyrean. It brought us here and left us in Khaturian. Where it is now or why it chose your world, I do not know.'

Barbaden glanced over to Mesira Bardhyl, who gave a curt, nervous nod, and Uriel understood that the governor was using her as some form of psychic truth-seeker. He was grateful he had chosen not to lie to Barbaden, as he suspected that the governor would order his soldiers to open fire at the first hint of falsehood.

'So here you are,' said Barbaden, 'two heroic Space Marines beginning their odyssey home. I admit, it has the whiff of the epic to it, Captain Ventris. What is it you require of me?'

Uriel let out a soft sigh of relief. While it wasn't acceptance or an apology, it was at least a step in the right direction.

'We ask for the chance to send an astropathic message to Macragge,' said Uriel, 'a message approved by you, obviously. We have completed our Death Oath and it is time for us to return home.'

Barbaden drained the last of the tawny liquid in his glass and set it down next to him.

'And if I agree to this request?'

'Then we are at your disposal until such time as our battle-brothers can bring us home.'

Though the offer was distasteful to Uriel, the idea of having two Space Marines at Barbaden's beck and call clearly appealed to the governor and he smiled. 'It is not often we can call upon the warriors of the Adeptus Astartes.'

The governor snapped his fingers and the soldiers around the edge of the room gratefully lowered their weapons.

'Yes, perhaps your presence here is just the thing we have been looking for in our recent troubles,' said Barbaden, 'troubles that Colonel Kain tells me you have experienced first hand.'

'Indeed,' said Uriel, although he knew fine well that Barbaden would already know every detail of this morning's encounter with the Sons of Salinas.

'I am sure your assistance was most welcome,' said Barbaden.

'We needed no help,' said Verena Kain and Barbaden smiled at her interruption. 'Pascal Blaise is no great commander and his insurgents are amateurs.'

'And yet he ambushed you and cost you several armoured fighting vehicles, Verena,' said Barbaden, 'vehicles we can scarce afford to lose.'

Colonel Kain wisely kept her mouth shut as Barbaden continued. 'Yes, I think it might prove advantageous to be seen as having the support of the Adeptus Astartes. The people of this planet need to see that they are part of the Imperium and that to resist the appointed commander will not stand.'

Barbaden stood and clasped his hands behind his back. 'I will set up a communion between you and my astropath and we shall see about getting you home. In the meantime, I insist you remain as my guests within the palace precincts. You will receive the very best hospitality, but for your own safety I shall have to ask that you do not venture beyond the palace walls without escort. As you have seen, the streets of Barbadus are not as safe as we might wish.'

Although he was surprised by Barbaden's reversal, Uriel wasn't about to reject his offer to help simply because he didn't like the man. He nodded graciously and said, 'That is acceptable to us, governor.'

'Of course,' said Barbaden, waving his arm around the room to encompass the others who had arrived before Uriel's tale had begun. 'Now that the matter is resolved, I have many other things to attend to, Captain Ventris, and I must speak with my senior advisors. Eversham here will find you suitable accommodation within the palace and I will send word when it is possible to transmit your message home.'

'Thank you, Governor Barbaden,' said Uriel, although he could see that the man had already effectively dismissed them.

Eversham appeared at Uriel's side and said, 'If you would follow me, please.'

Uriel nodded, casting his eye around the room one last time.

All through his tale telling, neither Togandis nor Nisato had said a single word and Uriel wondered why they had been summoned to hear it. Why had Barbaden gathered them here?

It was something to think of later, for Eversham was waiting expectantly at his side.

Uriel and Pasanius bowed to the Imperial Commander of Salinas and followed their escort from the room.

'WELL?' ASKED BARBADEN, the mask of civility falling from his face once the two Space Marines had been led away. 'What did you make of that?'

No one wanted to be the first to speak and Barbaden sighed. His reputation was such that no one dared to voice an opinion until they knew which way he was leaning. In no mood for games, he said, 'I believe there is more to Uriel Ventris and Pasanius Lysane than meets the eye, don't you?'

Surprisingly, it was Shavo Togandis who spoke first.

'They are Adeptus Astartes, my lord,' he said. 'What is it you suspect?'

'I was asking *you* that, Shavo,' said Barbaden. 'I do not like it when my questions are rephrased and asked back to me.'

'My apologies, governor,' said Togandis, clearly regretting his impetuous utterance. Barbaden paced among his subordinates, enunciating each word with deliberate clarity so that there could be no misunderstanding. His time in the administrative corps of the Achaman Falcatas, prior to his taking command, had taught him the value of clarity.

'Captain Ventris claimed to have come from a world fallen to the Ruinous Powers. Well, cardinal, might it perhaps be perspicacious to have the quarters assigned to him secured with holy scriptures, wards and the like? I would imagine that there must be some litany you could read that would discern any taint.'

'Ah, well, yes, I'm sure there would be some passage that would fit the bill,' said Togandis, 'perhaps in *Sermons of Sebastian Thor* or *Benedictions and Blessings–*'

'I don't need the specifics,' snapped Barbaden. 'Just find a suitable passage and see it done. If they have brought some taint with them, I do not want it loose on my world.'

Having dealt with Togandis, Barbaden turned his gaze on Daron Nisato, solid dependable Nisato. Barbaden could feel the man's dislike of him, but tolerated it, for he was good at what he did and had an honest soul.

That was why he had been transferred out of the Screaming Eagles.

Putting the thought from his mind, Barbaden asked, 'What of you, Daron? What did you make of Captain Ventris?'

Nisato stood a little straighter. 'I don't believe he was lying.'

'No?' said Barbaden. 'Then your instincts are letting you down.'

Nisato shook his head. 'I do not believe so, my lord. While I don't think Ventris was lying, there was definitely more that he wasn't telling you. He was vague about how they arrived on Salinas and what planet they'd just come from, and when a person is being vague, it's usually because they know that the specifics will hang them out to dry.'

'So you think we should press them for details?'

'That depends on whether you want to create a fuss,' said Nisato.

'No,' agreed Barbaden, 'a fuss is something I should like to avoid, Daron. Very well, look into the ambush this morning, make some arrests, shake the tree and see what falls out. I want some heads on spikes by this evening. I don't care whose, you understand?'

Nisato nodded and turned from him. As the enforcer left he whispered something to Shavo Togandis, but Barbaden could not hear what passed between them. The governor smiled. Poor old Nisato, always trying to tie up those loose ends, but never astute enough to realise that some loose ends didn't want or need to be tied up.

With Nisato gone, Barbaden turned towards Mesira Bardhyl, noting the shabbiness of her appearance and the haggard look in her eyes. He tutted. The least the woman could have done was make herself a little more presentable before coming to the palace.

Barbaden had seen the same look on the faces of many astropaths and wondered if such hangdog expressions of misery were common to psykers throughout the Imperium. He pushed the thought from his mind as irrelevant.

'And you Mistress Bardhyl?' he asked. 'Can you shed any more light on what was said here today?'

Mesira Bardhyl shook her head, keeping her eyes studiously fixed on a point of the floor between her feet. Barbaden reached out and lifted her chin until their eyes were locked together.

'When I ask a question, I expect an answer, Mesira,' said Barbaden. 'It would be such a shame if I was to suspect that your psychic ability had allowed a sliver of the warp to enter your pretty little head and I had to have Daron put a bolt round through it, wouldn't it?'

Tears gathered in the corners of her eyes and Barbaden's lip curled in distaste. Tears angered him, women's tears especially, and he leaned closer as she mumbled something inaudible.

He slapped her hard across the face.

'Speak up, Mesira,' said Barbaden. 'I thought you would have sense enough to know that your hysterics this morning had irritated me to the point where you would curb such theatrics in my presence.'

'Yes, governor,' said Mesira. 'Sorry, governor.'

'There you go,' said Barbaden, wiping tears from her hollow cheeks. 'Now that you are composed, can you tell me anything of value? And, please, spare me the hyperbole you were spouting earlier.'

Mesira Bardhyl composed herself with visible effort, reaching up to rub her eyes and take a deep breath.

'It's... It's hard to describe,' she said.

'Please try,' he said, leaving her in no doubt that this was not a request.

'Enforcer Nisato was right,' said Mesira. 'Captain Ventris wasn't lying, but nor was he telling you everything. He believes his truth, that much I can tell, and I sensed no taint to his words, but whatever he and his friend travelled on...'

'What about it?' asked Barbaden.

'I don't know what it was, but it was powerful, so very powerful,' said Mesira. 'It ripped its way through to this world and then tore a hole back through the gates of the Empyrean, and a lot of energy came through as it did so.'

'What does that mean? In real terms?'

'I don't know,' said Mesira, her entire body pulling in tight at this admission. 'I think that's why they appeared in the killing... in Khaturian.'

'Explain.'

Mesira looked up at the people around her, looking for support in their faces. Finding none, she pressed on, and Barbaden could see the resignation in her eyes as she spoke. 'We all know what happened at Khaturian, what we did... The scale of it... Things like that don't just get forgotten, in this world or any other.

'When a person dies, his... soul, for want of a better word, is released into the warp, and it usually dissipates into the maelstrom of energy there. Sometimes, though, when a person dies, their soul has enough rage, fear, anger or some other strong emotion to remain coherent in the warp, and that exerts its own attraction.'

'Attraction to what?'

'To wherever they died,' said Mesira. 'Whatever it was that brought Captain Ventris here was something terrible, something that feeds on death and bloodshed. Khaturian was like a magnet to it.'

'You say it's gone, this thing that brought Ventris here?'

Mesira nodded. 'Yes, it was barely even here, but its power was so great that the walls that separate us from the warp were worn much thinner, and they were already thin enough.'

'Superstitious nonsense,' blurted Shavo Togandis. 'This is a pious world, Mesira. Yes, we have our troubles, but we are conscientious in our suppression of psychics.'

Barbaden chuckled at Togandis's unspoken accusation.

'Our faith keeps the warp at bay,' said Togandis, 'as it always has and always will.'

'You think so, Shavo?' cried Mesira. 'Then you are a fool. Why do you think this system is so fractious? What do you think brought us here in the first place? The warp bleeds into the nightmares of this system's people, stirs their sleep and twists their dreams with thoughts of death and war! And now it's in ours.'

Mesira was wringing her hands, as though desperate to scrape the skin from her bones or clean them of some imagined taint. Barbaden saw the light of madness in Mesira Bardhyl as fresh tears coursed down her cheeks.

'You must have felt it,' she wailed. 'We were there! Oh, Emperor save us, we were there!'

Barbaden stood before Mesira and took her shoulders in a tight grip.

Her words trailed off and she looked up into his eyes. 'I'm sorry... I'm sorry, please,' she whispered. 'I don't want to live like this, please... I can't.'

'Shhh,' he said. 'Be quiet now.'

She nodded jerkily, hugging herself tightly, and Barbaden shook his head at such a pitiful display of weakness. He returned to his seat and slid into the comfortable leather, a sure sign that the audience was at an end.

Verena Kain handed him a snifter of vintage raquir, the one thing on Salinas he had actually developed a taste for, her desire to please him as transparent as her desire to succeed him. He smiled and sipped the liquor, enjoying the biting crispness at the back of his throat.

'You are dismissed,' he said.

CHIEF MEDICAE SERJ Casuaban had spent so many years in the House of Providence that he no longer noticed the smell of blood. The very walls, though scrubbed regularly by rusting and wheezing servitors were so ingrained with the vital fluid that no amount of labour could completely erase it.

How many lives had ended in this wretched place, he wondered.

The answer leapt immediately to his mind: too many.

His boots rapped harshly on the grilled walkway as he made his way through the wards that ran the length and height of the central tier of the facility. It was a daily irony to Casuaban that three Capitol Imperialis, an example of the mightiest war machines ever created by the Imperium, should be shackled together to create a medicae facility.

He snorted at such a description. True, many people did leave the House of Providence alive, but they were shadows of their former selves, most with limbs missing, their bodies covered in hideous scars or otherwise disfigured by the infernal ingenuity of mankind in wreaking harm on one another.

Ten years of conflict between the administration of Leto Barbaden and the Sons of Salinas had cost the people of Salinas dear.

Casuaban was a tall man and was forced to stoop several times as he made his way through the facility, the sounds of people dying all around him. His hair was the colour of the iron walls and his face was craggy and lined, like worn leather left out in the baking sun. He had the bulk of a former soldier, but age and ten years without weekly fitness standards to meet had added flesh to his bones.

Orderlies and nurses worked the wards, tending to the hundreds of people who filled the place. They nodded to him as he passed. In some faces he saw grudging respect, in others wordless tolerance. He knew that he could expect no less.

He made his way into a side compartment, a room that had once housed the fire control systems of the war machine's defensive weapons. Iron sprung beds were packed in tightly, each one home to a pathetic, broken shape that only superficially resembled a human being.

He nodded to the orderly fitting a drip over the nearest patient. A box bleeped erratically and trailing wires ran from the cracked display to the heartbreaking shape that lay in the bed.

'How is she?' Casuaban asked.

'How do you think?' was the answer. 'She's dying.'

Casuaban nodded and stood at the end of the bed, trying to remain dispassionate as he lifted the girl's notes and read how her condition had changed during the night.

Her name was Aniq and what was left of her stirred on the bed. He had been forced to amputate both her legs above the knee and her left arm was missing from the shoulder down. Aniq's entire body was a mass of gauze and synth-flesh, a desperate attempt to keep her from death, an attempt Casuaban knew was doomed to failure.

Aniq and her family had been caught in the middle of a firefight between the Sons of Salinas and a patrol of Achaman Falcatas that had spilled into the dwellings on the southern edge of Barbadus. Solid rounds and las-bolts had torn through the Chimera chassis that Aniq's family called home, the ricochets killing her parents and ripping into both her legs and her left arm. A volatile mixture of home-distilled fuel had exploded in the fight and had bathed her body in chemical fire.

The girl would die tonight. She should have died days ago, but she was strong and Casuaban knew it was his duty, his penance, to fight as hard to save her as she was fighting to live.

'Increase her pain medication,' Casuaban told the orderly.

'It won't matter,' said the orderly. 'The girl won't live.'

Suddenly angry, Casuaban snapped, 'She has a name. It is Aniq.'

'No, she's just another salve to your conscience, medicae,' snorted the orderly and walked away. Casuaban ignored the man and went to the drip regulator, adjusting the flow of Morphia himself. He might not be able to save her, but he could ease her suffering at least.

Casuaban had seen enough of war in his service with the Falcatas to last any man a dozen lifetimes. He had hoped that when his time with the regiment was at an end he would be able to retire somewhere warm where he could spend the last of his days trying to forget man's capacity for violence. He had never dared dream that the Falcatas would earn the right to claim a world of their own. After all, what regiment ever really got to muster out?

You heard stories about worlds settled by heroic regiments of Imperial Guard, but no one ever actually got to do it, did they?

But the Falcatas had it.

Designated an army of conquest by General Shermi Vigo, they had claimed Salinas as theirs, but instead of an end to war and the establishment of a Falcatan dynasty, the conquest of Salinas had become a poisoned chalice.

And Casuaban's vision of a peaceful retirement had vanished like mist.

He remembered the day his dreams had died.

It had been upon the Killing Ground, amid the ashen wasteland of Khaturian.

In the aftermath of the slaughter, he had walked the hellish warscape in a numbed daze, the streets and few remaining buildings filled with bodies that had cracked and twisted into foetal positions such was the infernal heat that had engulfed the city.

That had been the day his world had turned upside down, when his every belief had been shattered and his quest to atone had begun. He looked down at the small girl once more, trying to stem the tide of regret that he felt every time he saw her.

What had she done to earn the wrath of Leto Barbaden and the Achaman Falcatas?

Nothing. She'd done nothing. She had simply been in the wrong place at the wrong time, like most of the people in the House of Providence.

'You didn't deserve this,' he whispered.

The girl's eyes flickered open at the sound of his voice and her mouth moved soundlessly, her eyes pleading for Casuaban's understanding.

He crouched beside the bed and leaned in close to her, her voice little more than breath on his cheek.

'You were there,' she whispered, and he flinched as though struck.

Casuaban rose stiffly to his feet, his heart hammering in his chest. He backed away from the bed, the girl's wasted form now unutterably dreadful to him. He turned and all but fled the chamber, moving as though in a fugue state.

Serj Casuaban made his way through the wards, adjusting drug levels, making notes on charts and burying himself in a hundred other tasks to keep his mind from dwelling on what he had heard.

Darkness was beginning to fall and exhaustion had all but claimed him by the time Casuaban finished his rounds, the little light that pierced the windows fading to twilight grey before he had noticed. Naked glow strips hung from cables screwed into the corridor roofs and the sickly glow made him feel faintly nauseous.

He made his way back through the central section of the House of Providence and climbed the stairs to the control bridge, where lord generals and warmasters had once plotted destruction on a massive scale. The almost bare room was home to a compact desk, a couple of chairs, the low cot bed where he had spent many an uncomfortable night and a wall of locked drug cabinets.

Casuaban dropped the notes he had made on his rounds onto his desk and slumped into the hard, iron chair behind it. The words he had heard from Aniq's mouth and in his darkest nightmares echoed in his skull and he knew that there was one sure method to dull the ache and pain of them. He opened the drawer and lifted out a tapered bottle without a label and a pair of shot glasses, both of which he set on the desk and filled.

'There's no point in hiding,' he said. 'So, join me for a drink.'

A shadow detached itself from the wall and Pascal Blaise took the seat opposite Casuaban.

'Hello Serj,' said Pascal. 'How did you know I was here?'

'Unlike everything else in here, you don't smell of death,' answered Casuaban.

'Ironic, don't you think?'

'Perhaps,' said Casuaban, 'if I gave it any thought. What do you want?'

'You know what I want,' said Pascal, lifting the glass of raquir and taking a sip.

'I can't spare you any more medical supplies, we're running short as it is.'

'So ask Barbaden for more.'

'He'll say no.'

'Not to you he won't.'

'You love this, don't you?'

'What?'

'The fact that the medical supplies your men use come from Leto Barbaden.'

'There's a certain poetic justice to it,' admitted Pascal, 'but that's by the by. We took some casualties today.'

'I heard,' said Casuaban. 'You hit Verena Kain's Screaming Eagles.'

Pascal grinned. 'Aye, we did. She got away, but we hurt the bastards.'

'How many wounded do you have?' asked Casuaban.

'Too many: ten dead and another sixteen wounded. My men are hurting and we need fresh bandages, morphia and counterseptic.'

'I can't spare that much,' protested Casuaban. 'Bring your wounded here.'

'Don't be foolish,' warned Pascal. 'You think that Barbaden won't have Nisato and his goons watching this place for that?'

Casuaban laughed. 'You're here aren't you? You tell me who's being foolish.'

'I know how to make my way around without being seen,' said Pascal, 'and there's only one of me. I think they might notice sixteen wounded men being brought in.'

'I can't ask Barbaden for more,' said Casuaban, though he could hear the defeat in his voice. He knew he would give Pascal what he wanted, had known it the moment he had sensed the man's presence in his office.

'I know this sits badly with you, Serj,' said Pascal, offering some conciliatory words as he saw the defeat in Casuaban's face, 'but you know you're doing the right thing, don't you?'

'The right thing?' said Casuaban. 'I don't even know what that is anymore. I thought I did when I served with the Falcatas. I'd seen too many young men and women blown apart by your bombs, listened to them scream and cry for their mothers, to do anything but hate you. I hated the Sons of Salinas and everything you stood for. I had the certainty of hate.'

'Then came the Killing Ground,' said Pascal.

'Then came the Killing Ground,' repeated Casuaban. 'After that, I was lost. I watched Leto Barbaden order the attack and I knew it was wrong, but I didn't say anything, not until it was too late.'

Pascal drained the last of his raquir and placed the glass down on the desk.

'When you and Cardinal Togandis are ministering to the needy of Junktown tomorrow, leave the supplies in the marked Leman Russ. You'll see the signs.'

An awkward silence descended. 'You haven't asked about... him,' said Casuaban.

Pascal licked his lips. 'He's still alive?'

'He is,' confirmed Casuaban. 'Did you even doubt it?'

'Sylvanus Thayer always was a tough bastard,' said Pascal, glancing nervously towards the stairs that led back down to the wards.

'Do you want to see him?'

'No,' said Pascal, 'not even a little bit.'

Casuaban watched as Pascal made the sign of the Aquila across his chest.

He laughed. 'Now that's irony,' he said bitterly.

URIEL LOOKED OUT over the city as it slipped into darkness below. From this height, it looked peaceful, but the ambush this morning had given the lie to that impression. Barbadus was a city at war with itself, held by Imperial forces, but wracked by dissent and insurgents who fought their rightful rulers every step of the way.

Though Uriel did not like Leto Barbaden, he was the rightful ruler of Salinas and no amount of insurgency would change that. Salinas had been won for the Imperium by an army of conquest and the world was theirs to rule in the name of the Emperor.

Yet something nagged at the back of Uriel's mind, a suspicion that all was not as it seemed, that secrets lurked beneath the surface and would radically alter his view of this world's dynamic were he to learn them.

He turned from the shimmering, shielded window and returned to the quarters that had been assigned to them. As far as places of confinement went, it was a great deal more comfortable than some he had been forced to occupy. Two beds, large by any normal measurement, yet small in comparison to a Space Marine, occupied opposite walls and two footlockers sat empty at their ends, though neither he nor Pasanius had anything to put in them.

'You see anything interesting out there?' asked Pasanius.

His friend sat on the floor, idly rubbing the stump of his arm and watching him as he paced the length of the room. Pasanius appeared utterly calm and Uriel envied the sergeant's ability to find a place of stillness within himself, no matter what their circumstances.

'No,' he said, calmed by the very act of watching Pasanius. 'It all looks peaceful now.'

'Then sit down for the Emperor's sake, you'll wear a groove in the carpet,' suggested Pasanius, lifting a bronze ewer from the floor beside him. 'Have some wine. It's not as good as the vintages bottled on Calth, but it's eminently drinkable.'

Uriel lifted a goblet from a table beside the bed and sat on the floor opposite Pasanius. He held out the goblet and Pasanius duly filled it.

He took a long drink, enjoying the taste, despite Pasanius's reservations.

'Not bad,' said Uriel.

'It'll do,' said Pasanius. 'Ah, but do you remember the Calth wines?'

'Some of them,' said Uriel. 'Why the sudden interest in my home planet's wines?'

'A wonderful dialect they spoke in the caverns,' continued Pasanius. 'I remember the first time I spoke to you. I could barely understand a word you said.'

'It had its own character,' admitted Uriel, beginning to see where Pasanius was going.

'I remember it took years for you to shake that accent,' said Pasanius. 'Do you still remember any of it?'

'Some,' said Uriel, switching to the heavily accented dialect of the deep cavern dwellers of Calth. 'It's the kind of thing that never really leaves you.'

Uriel had been six years old the last time he had spoken like this, but his enhanced memory skills allowed him to access the language centres of his brain as though it had been yesterday.

'That's it,' laughed Pasanius, also switching to the same Calthian speech patterns, a dialect that no one outside Ultramar would have any hope of understanding. Certainly any eavesdroppers on this conversation would be lost and even the most sophisticated cogitating machines would struggle with so specific an argot.

'Subtle,' said Uriel, raising his goblet in a mock toast to Pasanius.

'I have my moments,' replied Pasanius.

'I remember the last time we sat with a drink like this,' said Uriel.

Pasanius nodded. 'Aye, on the *Vae Victus*, in the Tarsis Ultra system. A grand victory that was.'

'I suppose,' agreed Uriel, 'but won at a cost, and look where it got us.'

'There you go, always looking for the clouds instead of the silver lining,' said Pasanius. 'Look where it got us? We saved Tarsis Ultra. We saw the daemon creatures of Honsou destroyed and we're on the way home. Think of the good we've done, that we'll go on to do.'

Uriel smiled. 'You're right, as always, my friend. You have a rare gift for cutting through to the heart of things.'

'It's a well known fact that sergeants are the real brains in any army,' said Pasanius.

'Then what's so important that we switch to Calthian dialect?'

'We have things to talk about,' said Pasanius, suddenly serious, 'things best not heard by others, things we need to have clearly stated between us.'

'Very well,' agreed Uriel. 'Things like what?'

'Like the Unfleshed. When are you planning on mentioning them to Barbaden?'

'I don't know,' admitted Uriel. 'I had thought to say something once we'd established our credentials, but having met the man, I'm not sure.'

'I know what you mean,' agreed Pasanius. 'I don't think Leto Barbaden would be too understanding.'

'He'll kill them as soon as look at them.'

'Then what do we do with them?' asked Pasanius. 'You can't just leave them out there. I know you're holding on to the hope that the blood of heroes in their veins will restrain their more animal qualities, but even if it does, it won't be forever. Sooner or later they'll become what they were on Medrengard.'

'Perhaps,' said Uriel, 'but I can't abandon them. They gave everything to help us against Honsou. Most of them died in that fight. We owe them.'

'Aye,' nodded Pasanius, 'that we do, but let's be sure we don't get them killed trying to repay that debt.'

'Perhaps we can make an approach through the cardinal?'

Pasanius looked sceptical. 'The fat man? I don't think Barbaden takes much notice of him. I don't think he takes much notice of anyone, if you know what I mean?'

'I do,' said Uriel, taking another drink. 'I've seen his kind before, commanders who divorce themselves utterly from the fact that they're commanding soldiers of flesh and blood. To men like Barbaden, notions of honour and courage are fanciful things, ephemera. To them war is about numbers, logistics and cause and effect.'

Pasanius nodded. 'Aye. Dangerous men.'

'The most dangerous. That kind of commander doesn't care how many men die to achieve his goals, so long as he gets a victory.'

'So how did a man like that get to be in charge of a planet?'

'The Falcatas were an army of conquest,' said Uriel. 'The right to settle a conquered world is the highest honour the Imperium can bestow upon a Guard regiment that's fought for decades. Barbaden was the colonel of the regiment, so the governorship would naturally be his, and I'd be surprised if the majority of the planet's hierarchy weren't ex-Guard.'

'Soldiers that fought in some of the most horrific warzones in the galaxy year after year, and now they're in charge of a planet.'

'Exactly,' said Uriel, 'all those years of killing and suddenly it's all over.'

'Then you have to try to turn off the instincts that kept you alive all those years.'

'Except you can't,' said Uriel.

Pasanius sighed and shook his head. 'No wonder their planet's a mess.'

Ʊ
EIGHT

BEING ALONE IN his private library normally brought Shavo Togandis comfort and peace, but tonight he found his irritation growing with every page he leafed through. His books had always offered comfort in troubled times, but now they offered nothing beyond vague references to steeling one's soul with something an anonymous, and frustratingly incomplete, text called 'the armour of contempt'.

Quite how one girded one's loins with such armour went unsaid and Togandis pushed the manuscript away. Flickering electro-candles sent dancing shadows around the room, the air in the library stuffy and redolent with the lingering aroma of the sumptuous repast he had consumed barely an hour before, a roasted poultry dish with a spicy sauce and fragrant side plate of steamed vegetables grown in the cathedral gardens.

A hovering skull with glowing green lenses for eyes bobbed at his shoulder, drifting higher into the air as he sat back on his expansive and heavily padded chair. He waved at the skull and said, 'The Sermons of Sebastian Thor, volume thirty-seven.'

The skull scooted over to the sagging shelves, a shimmering green light bathing the gold and silver leafed spines of the books, before a set of suspensor-enabled callipers reached onto the shelf and removed a heavy tome, bound in rich red leather.

Struggling under the weight of the book, the skull deposited it before the cardinal and resumed its position at his right shoulder.

Togandis rubbed his tired eyes and leaned forward to open the book, straining to read the tightly wound, cursive script that filled the pages. The blank book in which he wrote his notes for future sermons sat next to him, and Togandis rested his arm next to it as he scanned the text in the volume that the skull had just brought him.

A delicate arrangement of wires and metal rested on his forearm, and from this sprouted a lightweight, extendable armature of brass. At the end of this armature was a mnemo-quill, its nib twitching as it awaited his commands.

Fine silver wires ran from this attachment to something that resembled a portable vox-caster sitting on the desk before the cardinal. Togandis nodded as he recited lines from the book.

'The strength of the Emperor is humanity, and the strength of Humanity is the Emperor. If one turns from the other we shall all become the Lost and the Damned.'

As the words left his mouth, the mnemo-quill twitched and copied the words onto the blank pages of the book. He had filled page upon page with such words, words which never failed to move him, but which he felt would be precious little use in warding the palace from the intrusions of any malicious entities.

He dreaded the thought of returning to the palace without something concrete to show for his efforts. Of course he could recite entire verses of scripture, but Leto Barbaden would sense the lie in him in a second. Togandis mopped his brow with the edge of his napkin at the thought of Leto Barbaden.

As colonel of the Achaman Falcatas, Barbaden had been a tyrant.

As Imperial Commander of Salinas, he was a monster.

He could still picture Barbaden riding tall in the turret hatch of the Hellhound as it rumbled through the burning streets of Khaturian. The Marauders had been thorough in their attentions and little of the city had been left standing by their bombs.

What was left was being finished off by the Screaming Eagles.

Togandis closed his eyes, remembering the feel of the pistol in his hand as he walked alongside Barbaden's vehicle. The sound of lasguns and the roar of flamers sounded impossibly loud to him, but he had not fired a shot. He remembered looking at the pistol, matt black in his pink, fleshy hand, and thinking it absurd that he of all people should be carrying a weapon at a time like this.

It was the screaming that returned to him the most, the awful, intolerable sound of another human being in agony. It seemed inconceivable that anyone could be in such pain, but these were commonplace noises in Khaturian.

As the Eagles completed the massacre, Togandis had stumbled from the carnage and voided the contents of his stomach over the brittle, tinder-dry ground. In the hours that followed, the Screaming Eagles had walked from the ruins, their cries of victory sounding hollow to the confessor.

In the weeks, months and years that followed, Togandis had seen many of those same soldiers in his cathedral, drawn by feelings that they dared not voice anywhere else, to speak of what they had seen and done on that Killing Ground.

Hanno Merbal had been one such soldier and Togandis vividly recalled the terrible things that had passed between them in the darkness of the confessional: awful sins, aching regret and unbearable guilt.

Hanno Merbal was dead, his brains plastered over the roof of a dingy bar in Junktown. Hard on the heels of Hanno Merbal came thoughts of Daron Nisato, the former commissar of the Falcatas and a man of honour and quiet nobility.

No wonder Leto Barbaden had transferred him out of the Screaming Eagles before the mission to Khaturian.

A guilty flush warmed his skin as he thought of how near he had come to telling Nisato everything about the Killing Ground earlier that day, the things Hanno Merbal had told him and the things he himself had seen.

Togandis knew he was a coward, and the thought of defying Leto Barbaden had so unmanned him that he could not unburden himself of the guilt and allow Nisato to bring the truth of the Killing Ground into the light.

He thought of Nisato's whispered words to him as the enforcer had been dismissed from Barbaden's presence: 'To whom does the confessor confess?'

They were simple words, honestly spoken, but the consequences… Oh the consequences.

Togandis closed his eyes and fought the tears of guilt that threatened to spill unchecked down his face. If he wept now, he didn't think he'd be able to stop: tears for the dead and, selfishly, tears for himself.

He took a deep breath and once again scanned the pages of the book before him, concentrating on the millennia-old words of Sebastian Thor, a man for whom Togandis had nothing but admiration and whose writings had always inspired him.

A simple man, Sebastian Thor had stood against the tyrannies of the insane High Lord of the Administratum, Goge Vandire, and had cast him down in the fiery wars known as the Age of Apostasy. Thor had become Ecclesiarch and his sermons had always been favourites for Togandis to deliver to his congregation.

He wondered what Sebastian Thor would have made of events on Salinas and shuddered as he pictured himself being cast from his cathedral as Thor had cast the preacher from his pulpit on Dimmamar in the middle of a prayer session.

Pushing that image away, Togandis spent the next few hours reading passages aloud for his mnemo-quill to transcribe, steadily filling the pages of his prayer book with inspirational verses and catechisms of watchfulness against the daemon and the impure.

The glow of the electro-candles grew stronger as the light through the high windows dimmed. Togandis heard a noise through the door behind him and blinked in surprise as he looked up and saw the darkness beyond the stained glass.

It was later than he had imagined and he still had duties to attend to. His priests and vergers would be gathering for vespers and it would be unseemly for him not to join them. His library was just off the main body of the temple, and already he could hear insistent voices from the other side of the door.

They seemed to be calling his name, the sound muted by the heavy timbers so that it sounded little louder than a whisper.

As he stood and wiped a hand across his mouth, he realised that the sounds he could hear were altogether too insistent. Shavo Togandis, a master of self-deception in many other regards, was honest enough to know that his sermons, while filled with relevance and poignancy, were hardly ones that people gathered to hear with excitement or called out to him to deliver.

Curious, Togandis slipped the mnemo-quill armature from his forearm and gathered up his prayer book. He made his way towards the door, but as he reached for the handle some unheard timbre in the voices on the other side of the door resonated with that portion of his mind that knew fear.

You were there.

With sudden, awful clarity, Shavo Togandis knew what lay on the other side of the door.

MESIRA BARDHYL FELT the power growing throughout the city, a malevolent vibration in the bones that grated along her nerves like nails down a blackboard. Her room was dark, yet silver threads of light, invisible to those not cursed with psychic abilities, wormed their way inside, pushing between the brickwork, oozing through the mortar and slithering beneath the doorjambs.

Ghostly frost limned the door and her breath feathered the air before her.

She closed her eyes. 'Please, go away. What did I do? I didn't do anything.'

Even as she said the words, she knew that was crime enough.

To stand by while such slaughter was enacted and do nothing about it was almost worse than pulling the trigger or slicing with the falcata. The dead were massing and whatever dreadful, terrifying thing had brought the two Space Marines to this world had forever altered the balance of power on Salinas.

Immaterial energies were part of the fabric of the world now, enmeshed in the very warp and weft of it, and things that had once been incapable of doing more than unleashing nightmares now had a very real, very dangerous wellspring of power to draw upon.

She could feel a dreadful force within the room, a solidity to the air that could only be caused by another presence.

'Please,' she wept. 'No.'

Open your eyes.

Mesira shook her head. 'No, I won't.'

Open your eyes!

Mesira cried out as her eyes were forced open and she saw him: the Mourner, his black outline a stark silhouette against the soft glow from beyond her window.

Shimmering with spectral light, his blazing eyes fixed her in place and held her pinned like a moth in a display case. The stink of smoke and seared skin filled her senses and silver flames roared into life around her, cold and unforgiving.

In the icy light surrounding the Mourner, she saw the burned flesh of his body, the meat and fat of him running in yellow runnels from his bones.

You were there.

Mesira Bardhyl screamed and screamed until her mind detached itself from her senses and spun off into the darkness.

SHAVO TOGANDIS FELT the chill of the door handle before his skin made contact with it. His breath was mist before him and he could feel the sudden cold that engulfed the room through the thickness of his robes.

He could feel them on the other side of the door, willing him to come out, willing him to face them, to face his accountability.

Terror filled him, his legs feeling like they might give out at any moment.

Togandis whispered a prayer to the God-Emperor, closing his eyes and reciting verses that he had learned as a child when he had been afraid of the dark and his mother had told him that the Emperor would protect him.

In that moment, Shavo Togandis was four years old again, wrapped in blankets in the darkness as he rocked back and forth with the simple catechisms of a child spilling from his lips to hold back the monsters.

The words came easily, his terror reaching back over the decades to his youth and plucking the memories from the forgotten corners of his mind. With every word spoken, he felt the terror diminish and his hand gripped the frozen metal of the door's handle.

Togandis turned the handle and pushed, forcing his unsteady legs to carry him through the door. A wave of cold air, like a winter's breath, blew past him, questing around his body like eager hands that pulled him onwards.

He could feel the cold wind's exploration of him, but with each recitation of his childhood prayer, their ministrations grew lighter and less urgent. With his prayer book held outstretched, Shavo Togandis emerged from his library and into the temple proper.

His words faltered as he saw that the temple was full, but that none of those gathered before the magnificent golden statue of the Emperor at the end of the nave were parishioners or worshipers, or were even alive.

Little more than smudges of silver light, like candle flames viewed through misted glass, they had the semblance of human forms, but little more.

'Emperor protect me,' he whispered, unwilling steps carrying him along the transept towards the altar before the towering statue of the Emperor. The fragile courage that had bloomed briefly in the library deserted him, and cold, clammy terror seized his heart once more. His bladder loosened and he felt an almost uncontrollable urge to void his bowels.

With an effort of will, he kept control of his bodily functions, looking past the flickering lights of the intruders towards the altar, seeing his priests, vergers, confessora minoris and attendants huddled before it.

Their faces were alight with awe at the sight before them.

Could they not see that these figures of light were terribly, horribly wrong?

Did they not know that they were in the most terrible danger?

Something of the man Shavo Togandis had been before the horror of the Killing Ground stirred within his breast and he walked towards the great statue and the living people who gathered beneath it.

These were his people and he had a duty to them.

As he walked, he felt the heads of the ghostly intruders turn towards him, their stares accusing and their eyes filled with a newly awakened sense of malice.

One of his priests looked up as he approached. 'Can you see them?' cried the priest. 'Angels, your eminence! Angels of the Emperor!'

Togandis looked towards the spectral figures, horrified that such dreadful things could be mistaken for something as holy and reverent as angels. Though the meat and bone of their faces was obscured by the silver light that billowed outwards from their core, Togandis could see enough to know that these were no angels, but daemons in human form, fiends sent from the blackest pit of the abyss.

'Stay away from them!' shouted Togandis, hurrying his steps towards his priests. The sweat on his brow chilled him to the bone and his breath came in short, hot spikes in his chest. The priests looked at Togandis uncomprehendingly, not seeing what he was seeing, and he interposed himself between them and the figures of light.

Togandis was breathless with fear. He could feel their hunger and anger, knowing now that these were no daemons from the pit, but the vengeful dead, hungry and voracious souls come to take what was theirs by right of blood.

His recitation of the child's prayer seemed foolish in the face of such terrible evil and part of him knew that he should just lay down his prayer book and face the consequences of his actions. Togandis felt his grip loosening on the prayer book.

The Falcata's previous confessor, a waspish old man by the name of Thorne, had given him the book the day before he had been killed, and as Togandis looked down at it he saw the words his mnemo-quill had written there only moments before.

He saw the strength in those words, a strength that fanned the last, defiant embers of his heart.

'Oh Emperor, merciful father that watches over us, send us your light that we might carry it into the dark places,' he said. 'In times of need, send us the courage that fires the hearts of all servants of righteousness. Be our strength and shield, that we might in turn be yours!'

Togandis felt the presence of his clerics gathering behind him, and their closeness gave him strength. He flipped the pages of his prayer book, reading each passage aloud with a power and clarity he had never before displayed in the pulpit.

Though the words he spoke were simple prayers and benediction, they carried his weight of belief and thus had strength. It was a simple revelation, yet a revelation nonetheless, and such things had power.

The cold wind that had pulled him into the temple blew again, stronger this time and without the gentle inquisitiveness it had displayed earlier. A gale blew from the end of the nave, howling and fierce, and Togandis felt his robes billowing around him, the pages of his prayer book flapping and tearing with its force.

His priests cried out as the ghostly shapes of the congregation were swept up in the maelstrom of bone-chilling light. Like wind-blown mist, the spectres dispensed with individuality and became one howling mass of gibbering faces.

'The Emperor protects!' screamed Togandis as the anguished phantoms screamed and wailed. The sourceless wind pulled the glittering, ghostly mass around the interior of the temple, slicing the air and twisting in coils of glittering silver light.

They gathered beneath the rose window at the far end of the nave, above the mighty bronze portals that led to the outside world, a roiling, tumbling, churning mass of light and mist. Silver tongues of cold fire burst into life around the edges of the temple, leaping from pillar to pillar and Togandis's eyes filled with tears at the sudden stench of burning flesh.

Frost was forming on the pews before him and a skim of ice crackled in the font beside him. The priests and vergers were on their knees, hands clasped in prayer. Still their eyes were full of adoration, and Togandis knew that the terror of the visions was meant solely for him.

Only he beheld the true face of the spirits, for they had come for him and him alone.

The mass of spirits shot down the nave towards the altar and Togandis felt their hunger for him in every agonised wail. The hundreds of mouths ran together and the billowing light flared outwards like the wings of some terrible, avenging angel.

'In Your eyes we are but humble servants,' screamed Togandis, the words snatched from his mouth by the cold air. 'Turn your face towards us and banish shadows, shield Your servants and protect them from the iniquities of the warp!'

The spirits were losing cohesion, skins of light peeling back from the angel of retribution as it came towards him. Togandis closed his eyes. He clutched the holy aquila that hung around his neck and lifted his prayer book high.

A blast of silver fire swept over Togandis and he felt the glacial cold of the dead pass through him. The ache of their pain and the horror of their existence suffused every molecule of his being, from his overburdened feet to his sweat-streaked pate, but, finding no purchase, they poured from him with a wail of frustration.

His heart creaked and bulged at the strain placed upon it, the valves and arteries pushed to their limits in keeping Togandis alive. Blood vessels strained and twisted, but whatever reserves of strength the cardinal's flesh possessed were up to the task of keeping him alive for a little longer.

Togandis kept his eyes closed for long moments, knowing that were he to open them he would gaze into the face of something so terrifying it would be the death of him. Sudden, unnerving silence descended on the church, the only sound the heave of his breath and the echoes of the departed.

A hand brushed his shoulder and he cried out, feeling a knot of pain in the depths of his chest and a tingling sensation in the tips of his fingers.

'Cardinal?' said a tentative, awed voice at his ear. Togandis recognised the speaker. It was one of the evening vergers, though he did not know the man's name.

Taking a deep breath to steady his nerves, Togandis opened his eyes.

The temple was as it had always been at night: cool, shadowed and dimly lit by the stuttering glow of candles. No trace remained of the silver flames or the vengeful spirits, but a rime of melting ice dripped from the lip of the font.

Togandis waited until he was sure that his voice would not betray his earlier terror.

'What?' he asked at last.

'Was that an angel?' asked the verger.

Togandis looked beyond the verger to the enraptured faces of his priests. What was he to tell them? The truth? Hardly.

The light of faith was in their eyes and he could not take that away from them.

'Yes,' nodded Togandis. 'That was an angel of the Emperor. Pray you never see another.'

NIGHT IN THE mountains north of Barbadus was absolute.

With the descent of the sun, the Unfleshed had tentatively ventured from the cave, their steps hesitant and wary as though they feared that the sun might return at any moment. Through the course of the long day, the Lord of the Unfleshed had felt his tribe's sense of hurt betrayal as the sunlight hovered on the brink of destroying them.

The cave stank of fear and only when the light ventured no farther did that fear turn to relief. They would be safe, for a time at least.

The Lord of the Unfleshed could taste the tribe's terror, a rank outpouring of chemicals that had once been a scent to be savoured in others, but which only made him angry now.

He was tired of fear, tired of having it as his constant companion.

Though he was powerful and strong, fear had nestled in his heart for as long as he could remember: fear of the Iron Men, fear of the Black Sun, fear of his own monstrous nature and fear of what the Emperor would make of it when he finally stood before Him.

The Lord of the Unfleshed lifted his arm and stared at the raw, pink newness of his flesh. The slick, sheen of his body had faded over the course of the day and as he tentatively explored the surface, he felt the new skin responding to his touch.

Instead of pain, he could feel the texture of his clawed fingers and the roughness of his hands.

Perhaps this place *would* be a new beginning for him and the tribe.

He looked over to where the tribe feasted on yet more of the fleshy creatures that grazed on the mountains. Their meat was rich and tender, and their limbs no match for the ferocious speed of the Unfleshed.

The Lord of the Unfleshed wanted to be away from this place, but did not yet dare lead the tribe far from the cave for fear that the sun would catch them in the open again. Most of the tribe were growing new skin across their bodies, but at wildly differing rates, and those without a thick enough covering would die if the sun found them without shelter.

Eventually they would have skin to match his, but it would take time for their more degenerate bodies to catch up to what his had already achieved. Rippling skirts of flesh took longer to cover than knotty lumps of bone, and fused craniums of meat that pulled and twisted as each mouth fed, tore and healed as their owner took wrenching bites of food.

The Lord of the Unfleshed glanced over his shoulder.

Though the night was dark, the dead city below was bathed in light.

To mortal eyes, the city was as empty and silent as ever, but to eyes fashioned with sorcerous engineering of the darkest realms and a mind grown to maturity within the womb of a creature saturated in chaos magic, the streets were alive with a cavalcade of shapes. Not the shapes of the living, but shapes of… something else.

Before now, the Lord of the Unfleshed had been aware of them as a glimmering presence on the edge of perception, but he saw they were gathering now, drawn to this place of death by the arrival of the Iron Men's machine.

Uriel and his companion had not seen these presences, or even been aware of them, but the dreadful energies washing from the terrifying machine had found common cause in the forgotten streets of the dead city, drawing back those that had once called it home and filling them with borrowed power.

He had kept the tribe away from the gathering strength of their unquenchable rage, knowing on some marrow-deep level that to disturb the pool of anger and pain would be to invite disaster.

As though his observation had given the lights notice of their presence, the Lord of the Unfleshed saw them drifting through the streets towards the metal barrier that surrounded the city. Where such a barrier would prevent creatures of flesh and blood from egress, it provided no such impediment to these beings of light and rage.

They came towards the mountains and the tribe feasting at the mouth of the cave.

The tribe felt them come, baring their fangs and unsheathing their claws.

The Lord of the Unfleshed stood and watched the approach of the light. He did not fear them, for the world of the Black Sun had vomited horrors worse than them from its smoky depths.

The tribe retreated within the cave and the Lord of the Unfleshed stood protectively before them, resplendent and magnificent in his new suit of skin. He felt the burning rage at the core of these strange beings of light, but more than that he sensed their hunger and their desire to wreak harm on those who had wronged them.

As he watched them approach, the mouth-watering flavour of burned flesh arose in the back of his mouth with the forgotten taste of human meat. He moaned and thick saliva gathered in the folds of his jaw.

He shook his head.

Uriel had forbidden them to taste the rich flesh of humans and drink their warm blood.

The Emperor did not want them to eat His subjects.

Behind him, the tribe grunted and worked their fanged mouths as the smell of cooked flesh filled the cave and they too recalled the taste of human meat. The smell was overwhelming and the Lord of the Unfleshed struggled to keep his mind on the approaching beings.

Without seeming to move, they gathered at the cave mouth, a jostling cascade of ghostly, heart-lit shapes. He saw the suggestion of human forms in their depths, men, women and children who looked upon him with expressions that ranged from pity to anticipation.

Their faces were blackened and burned, the flesh seared from bodies, and the Lord of the Unfleshed felt their pain, an eternal agony that could only be ended one way. He knew that these were no living things, but dead things that should not be.

They surged into the cave towards the Unfleshed, but instead of death they craved life.

The Lord of the Unfleshed felt the dead wash over him like a tide, a tumbling cascade of thousands of lives. The cave filled with light, burning, all-consuming light. It pressed against him, oozing into his body by some unknown process of osmosis.

A million thoughts, like a swarm of angry insects, roared in his head and his hands flew to his skull at the deafening noise. Thousands of voices echoed within him, each one clamouring to be heard over the others, each one begging, pleading and demanding to speak.

Pain filled him as he felt his body burning, the blood boiling in his veins, the meat of his body searing and his bones cracking in the fire. The walls of the cave seemed to twist and melt, as though fading away, only to be replaced by walls raised by human hands and cast down by the artifice of man's war machines.

Instead of rock above his head, he saw sky, clear skies filled with cruciform shapes shedding iron canisters that descended on vapour trails and exploded in sheets of white-hot flame. Fire surrounded him, leaping and dancing like a living thing as it consumed everything around it with gleeful abandon.

He knew he was seeing their deaths, these beings of light and anger, but could not force the images from his mind. He heard screaming: deafening, heart-rending screaming.

'No!' bellowed the Lord of the Unfleshed. 'Get out of my head!'

He heard the terrified roars and cries of the tribe and surged to his feet, clawing at the new skin that clothed his face. Yellow talons tore great gouges in his cheeks and the pain was welcome for it was pain. Flaps of sliced skin hung down from his face and fresh blood pattered on the floor of the cave.

His limbs rippled with unnatural motion, convulsing and swelling with the presences that poured into him. His every muscle, fibre and cell was suffused with the energy and fury of the dead.

Only the pain remained his and he clasped his claws across his heart, tearing outwards in an upward fan, scoring a series of bloody grooves across his chest like the wings of an agonised, screaming eagle.

The Lord of the Unfleshed dropped to his knees with his clawed arms upraised as the dead of Khaturian filled him, pressing the last remnants of his pain and fear into a creaking corner of his cranium.

Instead of his own pain, he felt the entirety of theirs.

Their rage and their fury were his.

Only one thing could end it: death.

NINE

URIEL AWOKE FROM a deep slumber, surprised that he had fallen asleep with such ease and that his dreams had been untroubled by visions of blood and death. He had been so long away from the real world that he had quite forgotten what it was to sleep without fear of such things.

Pasanius slept soundly on the bed across the room, his eyes darting beneath his lids. Uriel frowned as a snatched fragment of the dream he had been having returned to him.

He had seen a cave and something bright and malevolent that had emerged from its depths. Uriel could not make out its shape or identity, but he knew that whatever it was, it had been something unutterably dreadful. He shook off the last vestiges of the dream and swung his legs from the bed.

As quietly as he was able, he poured a goblet of water and rinsed his mouth. He tasted ashes and a metallic flavour that reminded him of blood. He caught the tang of something burning nearby and wondered if the quarters they had been assigned were near a kitchen or mess hall.

Uriel rubbed the heels of his palms against his eyes, frowning at the sluggishness that seemed to afflict his limbs and thought processes. A

Space Marine could normally go from sleep to wakefulness in the time it took to draw breath, but ever since arriving on Salinas he had felt a lethargy that seemed to leech his vitality.

Perhaps that explained the perpetually downcast faces he had seen on the streets and among the Falcatas. This was a grim world, but perhaps the melancholy he felt ran through the very fabric of the world and its inhabitants.

Pasanius stirred on his bed and sat up, reaching up to rub his scalp, a scalp that was now shaggier than it had been in a long time. Both arms came up, but only the left was able to make contact with his head.

'Damn, but I can't get used to that,' said Pasanius, looking at the red stump of his right arm. 'I hated it when I had that xeno-tainted arm and now I miss it. How's that for perverse?'

'It's only natural, I suppose,' said Uriel. 'I heard that some men who lose a limb claim they can still feel it itching, as though it's still part of them.'

'Who did you hear that from?'

'It was back on Tarsis Ultra,' explained Uriel. 'Magos Locard told me of an ancient Adept of Mars by the name of Semyon who developed a whole slew of new forms of augmetic implantation. It seemed this Semyon claimed to be able to produce electrographic images of subjects that showed their limbs still in place, even after they had been surgically removed.'

'How could he do that?' asked Pasanius, rubbing at his stump, which Uriel saw was an angry red, with patches of raw scabbing where the skin had been worn down.

'Locard didn't know,' said Uriel, rising from the bed and beginning a series of stretches to loosen the muscles in his arms. 'He said that Semyon was part of something called the Dragon Cult and that no one really knew if he existed at all. His work is like some sort of myth on Mars. The story goes that he died during the Martian schism back at the end of Old Night.'

'Emperor's teeth, that's so long ago, who knows what's true and what's not?' said Pasanius, joining Uriel in stretching.

'That's kind of what Locard said,' replied Uriel. 'He said that so much of Mars was laid waste that any kind of history was as good as legend.'

'Legend is time and rumour,' nodded Pasanius. 'Isn't that what they say?'

'With enough time, everything becomes legend,' agreed Uriel. 'One day you and I might be legends. Perhaps there will be murals in the Temple of Correction.'

'Or statues on the Avenue of Heroes,' smiled Pasanius.

The two friends passed the early hours of the morning, reminiscing over Macragge and the beauty of the world they hoped to see again soon. Within a few hours, both had come to the realisation that it had been a long time since either of them had endured a proper Astartes strength and endurance test. Without their fellow battle-brothers to measure themselves against and to drive them onwards, their powers had waned. It was an unwelcome truth to learn.

As they finished their exercises, there was a polite knock on the door and Eversham entered, looking as dangerous and catlike as ever. The man's face was unreadable, though Uriel had never found it easy to read the emotions of mortals.

'Good morning,' said Uriel.

'Indeed,' said Eversham. 'I trust you rested well?'

'Well enough,' said Pasanius.

'What can we do for you, Mister Eversham?' asked Uriel.

'Governor Barbaden sends you his greetings,' began Eversham, 'and bids me inform you that he has arranged for you to consult with the Janiceps.'

THE SUNLIGHT ON Serj Casuaban's skin was welcome after the cramped, claustrophobic interior of the House of Providence. Though the air in Junktown wasn't exactly fresh, it was certainly better than the stale aroma of death and desperation that saturated every breath he took within its metal corridors and wards.

Junktown was a somewhat obvious name for the largest district of Barbadus, but it was, Casuaban reflected, an apt one. Many of the original dwellings that had stood here were rubble, demolished in the original war of pacification and never rebuilt. Those that remained stood cheek by jowl with the detritus of that war.

A regimental graveyard of fighting vehicles had been abandoned here, the remains of a dozen armoured companies whose crews had mustered out of the Falcatas or which had broken down and could

not be repaired. The ingenuity of the locals in rendering vehicles that
had once borne their enemies into battle was little short of ingenious,
and abandoned squadrons housed entire families, with engines serving as reconditioned heating units and ammo stowage as makeshift
sleeping compartments.

Thousands of people lived here in cramped conditions until the
work klaxons blared to summon them to work in the munitions
forges or promethium refineries. A pall of ash and sullen melancholy
hung over Junktown and Casuaban knew that his presence was only
tolerated due to the medicines he was distributing and the treatment
he was providing.

Casuaban sat behind a metal trestle table, applying a soothing bac-
itracin poultice to the arm of a male worker who had been burned
while processing gel fuels for shipping off-world. The man had been
lucky; a trained corpsman had been on hand to treat the wound at the
site of the accident, yet the scarring was likely to be severe.

With the poultice applied, Casuaban sent the man on his way with
a stern warning to keep his wound clean, even though he knew that
such advice would be hard to follow in a place like Junktown. Behind
him, an idling truck with a bored-looking orderly lounging in the driver's cab was filled with immunisation ampoules, sterilised needles,
gauze, synth-bandages, vitamin supplements, water purification
tablets and a host of other vital medical supplies.

Casuaban rubbed his hands over his face and took a deep breath.
He stood from his trestle table and waved a hand at the people queu-
ing to see him.

'I will be back in a few minutes,' he said, moving over to the truck
and accepting a mug of lukewarm caffeine from the orderly. The drink
was brackish and tepid, but welcome nonetheless.

Casuaban closed his eyes and sat back on the running board that
ran the length of the engine housing of the truck. He let his tired eyes
drift closed, his body exhausted despite the few hours of disturbed
sleep that he had snatched on the cot bed in his office.

He had been working in Junktown since the sun had risen and it
would soon be time to move on to the next temporary medicae station. His eyes flickered to the truck, knowing he would have to find
some way of distracting the orderly when he saw the Leman Russ that
Pascal Blaise was going to mark for the drop of supplies.

'It doesn't get any easier does it?' said a nearby voice.

Casuaban jumped, a guilty jolt of adrenaline sending a shock through his system. Caffeine spilled onto his tunic.

Angry, he looked up to see Shavo Togandis, struggling to emerge from the comfort of an Ecclesiarchal palanquin like some overlarge butterfly from a stubborn chrysalis.

'What?' he snapped, grateful the caffeine was only lukewarm. 'What's not easy?'

'Ministering to the needy,' said Shavo Togandis. 'One feels one has accepted a never-ending task does one not?'

'Correct, Shavo,' agreed Casuaban, leaning back. 'It doesn't get any easier. Nor should it.'

'Quite,' said the cardinal. Togandis was sweating profusely, which wasn't unusual given his bulk, and Casuaban was forced to smile as he saw him use his staff to help propel him from the palanquin.

Free at last, Togandis made his way to the truck and shook hands with Casuaban, who fought the urge to wipe his sweat-slick hand on his trousers.

'Good morning to you, my friend,' said Togandis. 'Another day of serving the Emperor and his people.'

'Another day of putting right the wrongs of the past, eh?' said Casuaban.

Togandis shot him a strange look and nodded, indicating to the priests and servitors that made up his retinue that they should set up his mobile shrine against the hull of a burnt out Griffon mobile artillery piece that was missing its launcher.

Serj Casuaban and Shavo Togandis were an unlikely duo, but the years following Restoration Day had seen them become, if not friends, then at least comrades in shared atonement. They had never openly spoken of what they had witnessed at the Killing Ground, but both had recognised a shared need in the other and, almost without speaking of it, they had set out to repay their debt to Salinas, one person at a time.

Every week, they would tour the worst affected slums of Barbadus, Casuaban offering medical attention and advice to those that needed it, and Togandis preaching the word of the Emperor to those who would hear it. Initially, Casuaban had the busier time on these expeditions, but as time passed and their hardships increased, more and

more people turned to the word of the Emperor to see them through
the years following Restoration Day.

No soldiers travelled with Casuaban, only a driver and a handful
of servitors for lifting and basic security, a situation for which he had
Pascal Blaise to thank. Togandis travelled with a little less austerity,
riding in a palanquin of engraved wood and silver, followed by a
chanting coterie of priests and lobotomised censer bearers.

'You're late getting here today,' said Casuaban without reproach.

'Yes,' said Togandis, 'my somnambulating was plagued with phan-
tasmagoria.'

Casuaban threaded his way through the cardinal's words and
nodded as he said, 'You had a bad dream?'

'That scarcely covers the details, my Hippocratic friend.'

'A nightmare?' asked Casuaban, as casually as he could.

'Indeed. Visions of such repellence to make a man believe he is
going quite mad.'

'What did you dream?'

'I think you know, my dear Serj.'

'How could I possibly know, Shavo?'

Togandis leaned in close, so that no one could hear. 'I dreamed of
the Killing Ground.'

'Oh.'

'An exclamation of one syllable,' said Togandis. 'Well, it will suf-
fice.'

'What did you expect?' hissed Casuaban, taking hold of Togandis's
arm and steering him away from the driver's cab of the truck. 'Keep
your damn voice down. That's not a subject you should mention out
loud, here of all places.'

'Are you saying you do not dream of Khaturian?' said Togandis. 'I
fear you would be lying to me if you did.'

'You're not my confessor, Shavo,' said Casuaban, slipping a
battered silver hip-flask from his jacket and taking a slug.

'Ah, I see now why you do not recall your dreams,' said Togandis.

'Don't you dare judge me,' snapped Casuaban, taking another
drink. 'You of all people.'

'If a man of the cloth may not judge you then who can?'

'Not you,' said Casuaban. 'You don't have the right. You were there
too.'

Togandis nodded and stepped even closer to Casuaban. The medicae could smell the cardinal's last meal and the stale odour of his sweat.

'I was there, yes, and not a rotation of this world goes by that I don't regret that fact.'

'Really?' sneered Casuaban, jabbing his finger into the cardinal's chest. 'Then why do you still wear the medal? Pride?'

Togandis at least had the decency to look uncomfortable. 'No, not pride. I wear it because if I did not then what message would that send to Leto Barbaden? You think he would balk at sending Eversham for us if he thought we were plotting against him?'

Casuaban gripped Togandis's robes. 'Keep your bloody voice down!' he whispered. 'Or are you trying to get us killed?'

Togandis shook his head and reached down to prise Casuaban's hands from his chasuble with a grimace. 'I did not come here to fight with you, Serj,' said Togandis.

'Then why?'

'To warn you.'

'Warn me? Of what?'

'I saw them last night,' said Togandis, 'the dead of Khaturian.'

'In your nightmare?'

'No, in the temple.'

'What are you talking about?'

'They came for me,' said Togandis. 'They came for me, but they didn't take me, although I confess I do not know why. They have power now, Serj, real power. It is only a matter of time before they come for us all.'

Casuaban waved his hip-flask in front of the cardinal's face. 'I don't think it's me you need worry about, Shavo. Perhaps you should take a look at yourself first.'

'This is no joke, Serj,' said Togandis. 'Haven't you felt it? Something has changed, and not for the better. This world is different now. I can feel it in every breath I take.'

Serj Casuaban wanted to argue with Togandis, but the image of the small girl lying in his infirmary and the words she had said to him still haunted him. And hadn't he woken in the middle of the night with a pounding headache in the midst of a terrible dream in which a monster with burning eyes emerged from its cave to devour him?

But the dead?

'You have felt it!' said Togandis, seeing his expression.

'And if I have? What can we do about it? You and I both know what we did, what we allowed to happen. If the dead are coming for us then perhaps we should let them take us.'

'You want to die?' asked Togandis.

'No,' replied Casuaban, his shoulders slumping and looking at the hostile faces that called the wasteland of Junktown home. 'Death would be easy. It's living with what we did that's a punishment.'

'I'm not sure the dead see it that way,' said Togandis.

URIEL AND PASANIUS followed Eversham through the corridors of the palace, their austerity making more sense now that they had met Leto Barbaden. Red-jacketed Falcatas were stationed throughout, their breastplates gleaming and their curved blades shining like silver, though Uriel noticed that none carried a lasgun or so much as a pistol.

Eversham said little along the way, politely and concisely answering any questions put to him, but venturing no information beyond what was necessary. Of the Janiceps, he had said nothing more, simply that Uriel would understand when he saw them.

At last, they emerged on the other side of the palace from which they had entered. High buildings with saw-tooth ramparts stretched away at angles to the main structure to form a triangular courtyard area. Where the palace was constructed of dark, intimidating rock, these wings were fashioned from a smooth pink stone that shone like polished granite. Narrow windows pierced the outer walls of the plain west wing, but no doorways led within and the roofs bristled with antennae.

The eastern wing was of a different character altogether, its age obviously greater than the rest of the palace. The stonework of this wing was more ornate and a tribute to the craftsman's art: a building that celebrated the fulfilment of talent.

Where the rest of Barbaden's dwelling was clean and sharp, this wing had grown old and decrepit, the stonework cracked and weathered like the face of an elderly statesman, its windows grimy with dust and memory. Despite the disrepair, or perhaps because of it, Uriel immediately liked the building, feeling a strange sense of connection to it, or to something within it.

There was a bleak stretch of bare concrete in the space between the two wings, as large as the parade ground before the Fortress of Hera and large enough for the entire Chapter to assemble. Nothing disturbed the blunt uniformity of the space, no statues, no outbuildings and nothing to rescue the eye from the utilitarian nature of the ground save a drum tower that squatted, ugly and threatening, at the far end of the concrete.

'A parade ground?' asked Uriel, as Eversham led them straight across the middle of the open concrete space.

'Indeed,' said Eversham. 'This was the muster field where Restoration Day was declared.'

'Restoration Day?' asked Pasanius.

'When Imperial rule was officially restored to Salinas,' explained Eversham. 'A great day for the regiment.'

'Yet you felt the need to hide it away back here,' said Pasanius.

Eversham glared at Pasanius. 'The regiment died here also.'

Uriel seized upon this uncharacteristic display of emotion and said, 'Died here?'

'We were no longer an army of conquest,' said Eversham, the bitterness in his voice plain to hear. 'We were formally disbanded as a serving regiment and those that remained to bear arms were designated a Planetary Defence Force.'

'That cannot have been easy to bear,' said Uriel, knowing the disdain that most Imperial Guard forces, wrongly, held for PDF regiments. Guardsmen called them toy soldiers, but such bodies of men were often the first line of defence against invasion or uprising. Uriel had met many a courageous PDF trooper in his time, remembering Pavel Leforto of the Erebus Defence Legion on Tarsis Ultra, a man who had saved his life.

Simply because a soldier did not travel beyond the stars to make war did not lessen him in the eyes of the Emperor.

'It wasn't easy,' said Eversham, his pace quickening with remembered anger. 'To be part of something magnificent and then to be nothing; can you imagine what that's like?'

'Actually I can,' said Uriel.

Eversham looked over at him and, realising he had loosened his tongue, simply nodded and resumed his usual guarded expression.

Changing the subject, Uriel indicated the decaying east wing of the palace. 'That building? What is that?'

Eversham said, 'That is the Gallery of Antiquities.'

'A museum?'

'Of sorts,' said Eversham. 'Somewhere between a regimental museum and a repository for items that Curator Urbican believes should be kept and put on display. It's a waste of time. No one will ever see them.'

'That's where our armour is?' asked Pasanius.

'So I believe,' said Eversham.

'I think I should like to see this Gallery of Antiquities,' said Uriel and Eversham shrugged, as though the matter was of no interest to him, which it undoubtedly wasn't, thought Uriel.

There was no further conversation between the three of them and a palpable sense of unease descended upon them. The feeling grew stronger as they approached the brooding grey tower at the far end of the parade ground.

Now that they were closer, Uriel could see that a series of recessed bunkers surrounded it. The flat, featureless walls were unpunctuated by so much as a sliver of a window, though a single portal sat incongruously open at the tower's base.

This was clearly their destination, the lair of the Janiceps, whatever they were.

Uriel did not like the tower and saw that Pasanius felt exactly the same.

An air of dread hung in the air and coils of razor wire surrounded it like thorn patches grown wild around the base of a dead tree stump.

'What is this place?' asked Uriel, the words lingering like dead things long after they were spoken. 'The lair of a psychic?'

'This is the Argiletum,' said Eversham, as though that were explanation enough, 'home of the Janiceps.'

'Nice,' said Pasanius, looking at the grim edifice without enthusiasm.

As they approached, a detachment of Guardsmen emerged from the nearest bunker and ran towards the edge of the razor wire. Now that he looked closer, Uriel saw numerous sheets of metal, which the soldiers manhandled with difficulty to drop over the wire until a clear path was created.

Eversham led the way across the flattened razor wire and Pasanius leaned close to Uriel to whisper. 'I can't help but notice that these Falcatas are armed with more than just blades.'

Uriel nodded. He too had seen the barrels of lasguns poking from the firing slits of the bunkers. The soldiers who had cleared them a path across the razor wire had been equipped with firearms. Was what lurked within this gloomy tower so potentially dangerous that Governor Barbaden felt the need to relax his policy of guns within the palace grounds?

Uriel stepped from the sheet metal bridge and no sooner had they set foot within the circuit of razor wire than the soldiers behind them began to remove it, leaving them trapped at the base of the tower.

Uriel saw it was formed from dark stone blocks inscribed with tightly wound warding script that ran the length, breadth and height of the tower. The portal that led within seemed to gape like the maw of some dreadful gateway to the nether-world, and for a moment, Uriel thought he could feel the breath of something ancient and malicious from within.

'They have that effect on everyone,' said Eversham, sensing Uriel's discomfort.

'Who?'

'The Janiceps,' said Eversham, heading towards the open portal. 'Come, Governor Barbaden is waiting for you.'

INSIDE, THE TOWER was scarcely any less welcoming, its structure hollow and rising into darkness. A single shaft of light descended from the centre of the floor above and a frost-limned screw-stair of dark iron rose within it.

The air was cool, like that of a meat locker, and the walls glistened with moisture. Uriel felt a strange sense of dislocation, for the curve of the walls seemed to stretch far into the distance in defiance of what the outer circumference of the tower should have been able to enclose.

Uriel could feel the bitter, metallic taste of psychic energy in the air, an unmistakable actinic tang that unsettled him to the very core of his being. It was an irony not lost on Uriel that the potential for psychic power should so unsettle humans, yet without it the very fabric of the Imperium would crumble in the face of the vastness of the galaxy's unimaginable scale.

Once again, Eversham led the way, although his stride was a good deal less purposeful as he made his way across the hard, reflective floor towards the stairs. Careful not to touch the handrail, Eversham began his ascent and Uriel followed him. The stairs were narrow and groaned under his weight, but Uriel's thoughts were focused more on what lay at their end than on any risk of them collapsing.

Onwards and upwards the stairs stretched and Uriel knew, knew for a fact, that they had climbed higher than the tower had appeared from the outside. He heard laughter, small and childish, yet old beyond words.

Whispers seemed to echo from the walls, but Uriel kept his mind on putting one foot in front of the other until, at last, there were no more stairs to climb.

Uriel found himself in a gloomy chamber, lit only by the diffuse glow of sunlight that filtered through darkened windows that had been invisible from the outside. The walls of the chamber were cloaked in shadow, although Uriel could make out indistinct forms against the chamber's circumference, hooded figures that muttered nonsensical doggerel.

Uriel's breath misted before him and the cold knifed into his bones. Once again, he wished he were clad in his Mk VII plate instead of this thin robe, which offered scant protection against the unnatural chill.

Eversham strode to the centre of the room, where Governor Leto Barbaden stood before a reclining couch upon which lay something obscured from Uriel's view.

Barbaden was speaking, his voice low and little more than a whisper. He turned at Eversham's approach and impatiently waved Uriel over.

Uriel swallowed his anger once more and marched over to where Barbaden and Eversham stood, feeling the crackling psychic potential that emanated from the centre of the room. Barbaden moved to his left as Eversham stepped behind the reclining couch, and Uriel had his first sight of the Janiceps.

His first thought was that this was some sort of cruel hoax and that he had been brought before some hideous mutant. Uriel's hand clenched as he reached for a weapon he wasn't carrying. He fought down his horror at the... thing before him and looked more closely as he saw a glimmer of a smile on one of the faces that looked up at him from the couch.

She, or rather, they lay at a disturbing angle on the couch, a shapeless knotted mass of human flesh bound together in ways that anatomy had never intended. This was no mutant creature, but something conceived and grown within the womb as twin girls and upon which aberrant nature had played a cruel joke.

Their heads were fused along the rear quarter of the cranium so that neither could look upon the other. The poor, malformed girls had two mouths and two noses; in each face an eye, well conformed and placed above the nose with a third, milky and distended eye in the middle of the forehead common to both girls.

The brain of one girl was quite visible through a thin membrane of bruised skin that glistened and heaved in time with her breath. On the right side of her head was a rudimentary external ear, from which hung a golden earring, and their small, withered bodies lay in the grip of an embrace that their accident of birth had forced them into.

They were wrapped in dark green robes of plush velveteen, and Uriel saw an eagle head badge pinned there, the symbol of the Adeptus Astra Telepathica. Was this the astropath who would transmit their message of return to the Ultramarines?

Uriel was horrified at the pitiful sight of the girls, seeing the light of intelligence in the single eye of each one. The milky eye in the forehead of the conjoined girls swam with patterns like droplets of coloured ink stirred into white paint.

Uriel had seen patterns like that once before, when he had looked through a crystal dome into the seething depths of the warp when the Omphalos Daemonium had seized the *Calth's Pride* in its grip.

'Welcome, Uriel Ventris,' said the left mouth. 'I am Kulla.'

'And I am Lalla,' said the other.

'We are the Janiceps,' they said in unison.

ʊ
TEN

LALLA'S VOICE WAS sweet and sounded like a carefree young girl who knew nothing of the cruelties of the world. Kulla's, on the other hand, was bitter and husky, as though she alone bore the full knowledge of what the vagaries of unthinking nature had wrought upon them.

Uriel stared in uncomfortable fascination at the conjoined girls, unsure of what to say.

Astropaths were often eccentric souls, cursed with the ability to hurl their minds across the vastness of the galaxy and communicate with others of their kind, thus allowing the Imperium to function.

Uriel had seen many astropaths, but none as physically tormented as the Janiceps, none so cursed by birth as to be better off dead than consigned to this fate. On ninety-nine worlds out of a hundred, the girls would have been killed, but whichever world had birthed them had obviously been a more tolerant place.

As much as Uriel felt sorry for them, he couldn't shake the sense that they were dangerous mutants and fought to get past that impression.

'Don't feel sorry for us, Uriel,' said Lalla. 'We like being useful.'

'Be quiet,' snapped Kulla. 'What do you know of useful? I do all the work!'

'Come now, girls,' said Barbaden, his voice unusually soft and yielding. 'You shouldn't argue. You know what happens when you argue.'

'Yes,' sulked Kulla. 'You have your damned warders tighten their noose on us.'

'And it hurts us so!' squealed Lalla.

'This is the astropath?' Uriel asked Barbaden.

'You can speak to them yourself,' said the governor, 'they're right in front of you.'

'He thinks we're mutants, Kulla,' said Lalla pleasantly.

'Well, aren't you?' asked Uriel.

'No more than you, Astartes,' sneered Kulla. 'What are you if not a freak? In fact your gene structure is more removed from humanity than ours.'

Uriel took a deep breath. From the precautions Barbaden had taken with their confinement, Kulla and Lalla were obviously powerful psykers and it would be foolish to needlessly antagonise them.

'Yes, it would,' smiled Kulla.

Uriel started and Lalla sniggered. 'She does that all the time, but don't worry, she can only read your surface thoughts, unless you want her to read more, and then we'll know all your sins.'

'I am a Space Marine of the Emperor, I have no sins,' said Uriel.

'Oh, come now,' said Lalla, laughing 'we all have our secrets.'

'No,' said Uriel, 'we don't.'

'He's got secrets to hide,' said Kulla, laughing with a cackling screech that stretched the membrane across her brain.

'Can we get on with this?' asked Uriel, uncomfortable in the presence of the Janiceps now that he knew they could read minds as well as communicate telepathically with other astropaths.

'Of course,' said Barbaden, amused at Uriel's discomfort. 'Simply kneel before the twins and do as they tell you. It will go much quicker if you do not question everything.'

'Both of us?' asked Pasanius.

'If you'd like to,' said Lalla. 'It wouldn't make any difference.'

'Then I think I'll sit this one out,' said Pasanius, gesturing to Uriel to step up.

'And you have awards for valour,' said Uriel.

'The burden of command is that you sometimes have to lead from the front,' replied Pasanius, 'and she said it wouldn't make a difference.'

'How convenient,' said Uriel, kneeling before the twins.

'Give us your hands,' said Lalla, 'and hold on.'

Uriel nodded, wondering at the necessity of Lalla's last comment, and lifted his hands towards the girls. He took their hands hesitantly, feeling the rapid pulse of blood in their tiny, delicate fingers.

'We're not made of china,' said Kulla. 'I thought you Astartes were supposed to be strong. Grip our hands.'

Lalla giggled and Uriel blushed as he tightened his hold.

'That's better,' said Kulla. 'Now we can control your mind.'

Uriel's eyes widened, but Lalla smiled. 'She's joking. We wouldn't do that, not without asking you first.'

His hands became cold and he felt the chill spread along his arms and into his chest. How much of the twins' banter was playful and how much was truth, he didn't know, but he had the feeling that were they of a mind to do him harm, there would be nothing he could do to prevent them from killing him with a thought.

'So what do I need to do?' asked Uriel, trying not to let his unease show.

'Where are you sending this message?' asked Lalla, her eye drifting shut.

'Who are you sending it to?' demanded Kulla.

'To the Ultramarines,' said Uriel. 'To the world of Macragge.'

'Open your mind, Astartes,' ordered Kulla, her voice rasping and harsh.

Uriel nodded, though the instruction was vague, and closed his eyes, slowing his breathing and awaiting the touch of the twins' mind. He felt nothing and tried not to get impatient.

'Your mind is closed to us,' said Lalla, 'like a fortress preparing to resist an invader.'

'I don't understand,' said Uriel.

'You Astartes, your minds are as rigid and unbending as adamantium,' said Kulla, and Uriel knew that her mouth was not moving. Her voice was arriving directly in his thoughts without recourse to speech. 'You are trained, conditioned and enhanced in so many ways, but your minds are like locked doors to a place of miracles and wonder. All the potential you are trained to access: memory, language, combat analysis, and yet your masters train you to close off the one part of your mind that might actually allow you to soar.'

You do not feel as others do, but we can open that door for you if
you let us.'

'Stop it, Kulla,' said Lalla. 'You know that's not allowed. Leave him
to his blindness.'

'Oh, all right,' sulked Kulla, with a sigh that Uriel heard in his
mind. 'Very well, Astartes, picture your home world: its people, its
mountains and its seas. Smell the earth and taste the air. Feel the
grass beneath your feet and the wind on your face. Remember all
that makes it what it is.'

Pleased to have an instruction he understood, Uriel pictured his
last sight of Macragge, a beautiful blue globe turning slowly in the
depths of space. The vast seas that covered much of its surface shone
with an azure light and spirals of storm clouds, like miniature galaxies, spun lazily in the atmosphere.

Passing through the clouds, Uriel pictured the awesome marble
colossus that was the Fortress of Hera upon the great peninsula. He
saw the soaring fluted columns of its majestic portico, the colon-
nades filled with statues of heroic warriors. His mind soared
onwards, over golden roofs, silver domes and towering spires of glittering light: magnificent libraries, halls of battle honours, and
gilded halls of pilgrims and worshipers come to the Temple of
Correction, where the body of the mighty Roboute Guilliman was
held in stasis.

Beyond the Fortress of Hera, Uriel imagined the wild, untamed
glories of the Valley of Laponis, its white cliffs towering above the
achingly blue river that wound its way through the mountains to the
plains below. As though a bird in flight, Uriel plummeted down
through the valley, speeding towards a thundering waterfall cascading from the heights above.

Billowing clouds of spray boomed into the air, filling it with bit-
ingly cold mist and Uriel laughed aloud as he tasted the crystal clear
waters of his Chapter's home world. He soared from the valley, visualising the mountains and forests of Macragge, the sweeping, rocky
coastlines and vast, depthless oceans.

'Pasanius,' he breathed, 'I'm there.'

'Hold to thoughts of home,' said Kulla. 'Speak of your desire.'

'My desire?' asked Uriel.

'To return home,' said Lalla, a note of strain in her voice.

Uriel nodded in understanding. 'We have completed our Death Oath,' he said. 'It is time to return to our battle-brothers.'

'Show us,' said Kulla, 'all of it.'

Though he hated to return there, even in memory, Uriel summoned images of Medrengard, the ashen plains, the belching continents of manufactorum and the hellish, damned creatures that dwelt there. He pictured the nightmare fortress of Khalan-Ghol, the horrific daemon-wombs of the Daemonculaba and the final victory over Honsou.

Uriel felt the twins' hands shaking and opened his eyes as the awful stench of burning flesh arose in his nostrils. Ghostly flames swelled and billowed around the chamber, but its occupants appeared to be oblivious to them.

The flames bathed everything around him in light and Uriel had the distinct impression of hungry eyes watching him from the darkness.

The cold, heatless fire reflected a strange light from everyone gathered here and Uriel gasped as he saw a measure of what the twins saw.

A shadowy darkness surrounded Eversham, and a nimbus of silver, like a moonlight reflection on a stagnant lake, bathed Barbaden's features with a cold halo. Flickering arcs of golden lightning crackled around the twins' heads and a scarlet bloom like blood in the water surrounded Pasanius's outline. Uriel saw that the red glow extended past the stump of Pasanius's arm and formed the blurred outline of a hand.

Looking down at his own body, he saw that same red glow, like the embers of a smouldering fire, around his arms and torso.

'You are warriors,' said Kulla, her voice sounding as though it came from far away. 'What other colour would you expect your aura to be but that of blood?'

Pasanius said something, but Uriel could not understand the sense of it, his friend's voice sounding as though it came from an impossibly far-off distance. As the sound of Pasanius's voice faded even further, Uriel felt his gaze drawn to the swirling, milky eye in Kulla's and Lalla's cartilage-fused forehead.

Stars wheeled in the eye's depths, planets and the endless gulfs of trackless space that separated them. Uriel cried out as he was carried into that eye, a mote in the void of space. Distances so vast that the human mind simply had not the capacity to imagine them, flew past at the speed of thought. He was part of that thought, everything he had visualised and everything he had sought carried with the psychic beacon of ideas and images that were cast across space by the power of the twins' mind.

The dizzying sense of vertigo was almost unbearable and it was all he could do to hold onto the twins' hands as they passed what he had given them to the void.

Then it was over.

Uriel gasped as the twins released his hands. He blinked rapidly, his normal sight restored, and all the colours he had seen earlier vanished like the fragments of a dream.

'Is it done?' he asked, the breath heaving in his chest.

'Your call will be heard,' said Lalla.

'By any with the wit to listen,' added Kulla.

WHEN EVERSHAM LED Uriel and Pasanius from the Argiletum, the sky was dark and painted with a scattering of stars. The sense of relief at leaving the presence of the Janiceps was total, and as Uriel took a cleansing breath, it tasted as sweet as the crisp mountain air of Macragge.

'How long were we in there?' asked Uriel, staring up at the stars.

'Too long,' answered Pasanius as the soldiers once again flattened the razor wire to allow them to cross. 'You crouched in front of those… girls for hours.'

'I did?' said Uriel. 'It felt like a few minutes at most.'

'Trust me,' said Pasanius, scratching at the raw flesh at the end of his arm. 'It wasn't. Barbaden left almost as soon as you started.'

'Is your arm hurting?' asked Uriel, following Eversham over the bridge of sheet metal.

'A little,' admitted Pasanius. 'It wasn't exactly removed with surgical precision.'

Uriel caught the anxiety in Pasanius's tone and knew that his friend was worried. Pasanius had lost his arm fighting an ancient star god beneath the surface of Pavonis, and microscopic slivers of the living metal of its blade had entered his bloodstream and incorporated its structure into the augmetic the adepts of that world had grafted to him.

The augmetic had developed regenerative powers and Pasanius had struggled with the guilt of that for long months until he had been forced to confess the truth to Uriel. The Savage Morticians, horrific torturer-surgeons of the Iron Warriors, had later amputated the arm and presented it to the Warsmith Honsou, but the guilt was still there.

'You are free of the xenos taint,' said Uriel, keeping his voice low. 'I am sure of it.'

'What if something from Medrengard got into me?'

'You'd know if it had,' said Uriel. 'If the Ruinous Powers had corrupted your flesh, you would not be speaking to me like this. You would have turned that bolt pistol on me when we were in battle yesterday.'

'Would it be that quick? Maybe I've only taken the first steps on the path to evil.'

'I don't know for sure,' replied Uriel, hearing the fear in his friend's voice, 'but I believe that to question whether you are evil tells me that you are not. Those who have fallen to evil never question, never believe they are wrong and cannot see the truth of their actions. If you were on that path, I would see it.'

'I hope you're right,' said Pasanius.

'If you want to be sure, I will ask Governor Barbaden for a medicae scan.'

'You think that would find anything?'

'It would at least show any infection,' said Uriel.

Pasanius smiled in gratitude. 'Thank you, Uriel. Your friendship means a lot to me.'

'In these times, it's all we have, my friend,' said Uriel.

RYKARD USTEL WAS going to die, as sure as day turned to night. Pascal Blaise could see it in the boy's eyes, the look that said his body had already given up the fight to live and that it was just a matter of time before the biological machinery shut down. They had done what they could for him, but none of them were trained medics and their imperfect knowledge of how to treat battlefield injuries had been learned by seeing others die.

Serj Casuaban had delivered the medical supplies as promised and many of those who had been wounded in the attack on the Screaming Eagles would live: many, but not all.

Unfortunately for Rykard Ustel, he was not one of the lucky ones.

Cawlen Hurq sat by the boy's bed, holding his hand and speaking softly to him, the light from the two oil burners casting a warm, healthy glow over Rykard's pale face that belied his prognosis.

Pascal rubbed the las-burn on the side of his head and took another drink of raquir, suddenly wishing that he could drain the bottle and fall into dreamless oblivion. He knew he couldn't; there were people who depended on him and he was grimly aware that the Sons of Salinas could not continue in this way.

He had known that stark fact for years, but his hatred of Leto Barbaden had blinded him to the simple reality of it. This was a war that could not be won with violence, and the futility of the fighting and killing he had taken part in sickened him. Had it all been for nothing?

Pascal heard a soft curse and looked up.

'He's gone,' said Cawlen, his face a mask of anger as he slumped into the chair opposite Pascal. 'Rykard, he's dead.'

Pascal nodded and slid the bottle over the table to Cawlen, who took a long swallow of the powerful spirit.

'What did he die for, Cawlen?' asked Pascal. 'Tell me why he died.'

'He died for Salinas,' replied Cawlen, 'to defeat the Imperium.'

Pascal shook his head. 'No, he died for nothing.'

'How can you say that?' snarled Cawlen. 'He died fighting the oppressors. How can that be for nothing?'

'Because the idea of defeating the Imperium is ludicrous,' said Pascal sadly. 'I think I always knew that, but I just wouldn't admit it to myself. I mean, what can we do? Really? We fight with stolen weapons that are so old they're probably more dangerous to us than anyone we actually point them at. They have tanks and aircraft and now they have Space Marines.'

'Only two of them,' said Cawlen, 'and one of them is missing an arm.'

'Doesn't that tell you something? That we only merit the attention of two Space Marines? It tells me plenty.'

'So we can't win? Is that what you're saying?' demanded Cawlen.

'No. Yes… Maybe. I don't know any more,' said Pascal.

'Sylvanus Thayer would never have given up!'

'Sylvanus Thayer led the Sons of Salinas into a suicidal battle without hope of victory and I won't do that, Cawlen. I won't.'

'He died a hero,' Cawlen said defiantly.

For a brief moment, Pascal wanted to tell Cawlen the truth, that Sylvanus Thayer lay burned and horribly mutilated in the House of Providence, but fate had cast the former leader of the Sons of Salinas in the role of martyr and it seemed churlish to deny him that honour.

'Yes,' said Pascal, 'he did, but I don't want any more martyrs. I want people to live their lives. I want peace.'

'That's what we're fighting for.'

Pascal laughed, but the sound was bitter and harsh. 'Fighting for peace with acts of war?'

'If that's what it takes.'

'Thinking like that will get us all killed,' promised Pascal.

THREE FIGURES WERE arranged in a triangular pattern in a cramped chamber of heat-resistant tiles, each facing the centre of the room. The first of the figures was a young man who lay strapped to an upright restraint couch, his limbs bound by silver chains and his head held fast with clamps that prevented it from moving so much as a millimetre.

Hissing atomisers moistened gaping, empty eye sockets, the lids of which were held permanently open by ocular speculums, and gently swaying pipes fed him nutrients while others disposed of his bodily waste. Behind him, a clicking, whirring bank of machines monitored his vital signs, the rhythmic pulse and bleep the only signs that he lived at all, so shallow was the rise and fall of his chest.

A meshed vox-capture unit was fitted over his mouth, connected to a series of golden wires that coiled and looped across the floor before arriving at the second occupant of the room.

This figure was likewise restrained, though there was precious little need for it as every limb save his right arm had been surgically removed. He sat in a mechanical cradle of brass armatures and pulsating cables, and, like his opposite number, matter was delivered and retrieved through gurgling pipes. The golden wires from the room's first occupant ran across the room's floor and up over the back of his skull before dividing and plugging into iron sockets grafted where his ears had once been. His eyes had been sewn together and tiny script had been tattooed over the withered, sunken lids.

A wooden lectern sat to one side of this individual, upon which rested a sheet of yellowing parchment dispensed from a roll that sat below a glowing pict recorder. The figure's only remaining limb lay unmoving beside the parchment, a long, feathered quill held tightly between the forefinger and thumb of its spindly hand.

The room's final occupant was also a meld of flesh and machine, but where its fellows were bound to their task through restraints and wards, he was simply obeying orders hardwired into his brain through lobotomy and instruction wafers fed to him by his masters.

A gun-servitor, he had no mind left to call his own and was simply a living weapon-bearer with no will to perform any task other than that which was ordered. Though more humanoid in form than the other two occupants of the room, his body had been enhanced with bionics, muscle stimulants, balance compensators and targeting hardware to allow him to bear the weight of the enormous incinerator unit that replaced his left arm.

The weapon alternately tracked between the room's other occupants, the gun-servitor's brain primed for any of the warning signs that would trigger its attack response and fill this chamber with blessed fire and immolate everything in it, including itself.

The incinerator swung to aim at the figure in the restraint couch as his chest began to heave with effort. The bleeping noises from the machine behind him increased in frequency, becoming shrill and warning.

A hissing blue flame sparked to life at the mouth of the incinerator's enormous muzzle.

The first restrained figure, though bound at every portion of his body capable of movement, stiffened, as though an electric current was discharging through him. His jaw worked up and down, although the vox-capture unit prevented any of the sounds from issuing into the air.

No sooner had this begun, than the quill-bearing figure jerked to life like a machine freshly supplied with power. The quill began scratching across the page, filling it with spidery script, the wiry limb snatching back and forth across the parchment. The glow from the pict reader flickered as the words passed beneath it, carried off to yet another secure room within the facility.

The incinerator filled the room with the hot hissing of its pilot flame, but the gun-servitor's parameters of action had not been fulfilled, and so it sat immobile as the process went on before it.

At last the restrained young man with the burned out eye sockets relaxed, the tension flooding from his body and an inaudible, yet wholly felt sigh escaped him. His colleague also relaxed, the withered arm returning to its place beside the now filled section of parchment.

Silence descended upon the room as the incinerator's blue flame was extinguished and the gun-servitor returned to its monitoring repose.

A recessed door opened in the wall, invisible from the interior of the room, and a series of robed thurifers entered. Each carried a smoking incense burner and their hooded faces were blind to the room's occupants. They made a number of circuits of the chamber, guided by questing hands on the wall while gently swinging their censers of blessed oils and fragrant smoke.

Mist like a morning fog filled the room, but this did not trouble the giant, armoured figure that followed the thurifers into the room. Enormous to the point of gigantic, the burnished, blue-steel silver of his armour seemed to fill the room. The smoke would have blinded any normal man, but this warrior made his way to the lectern table without difficulty.

A huge, gauntleted hand reached down and tore the parchment from the dispenser, holding it up to his helmeted head as he read the words written there.

He had heard them recited through the mouth of a vat-grown cherub, but he needed to see the words for himself, to know them and feel their truth with his own eyes.

The signs were unmistakable.

The Great Eye had opened and the portents of the haruspex were coming to pass.

He heard heavy footfalls behind him as a figure clad in enormous plate armour, the equal of his own, entered the chamber. He clutched a heavy bladed polearm in one fist.

'Is it true?' asked the newcomer. 'A power stirs on Salinas once more?'

'It is true,' confirmed the warrior. 'Begin our deployment, Cheiron.'

'I already have.'

The warrior nodded. He had expected no less. 'Projected flight time to Salinas?'

'The planet's orbit closes with us. Five days at the most.'

'Good,' said the warrior. 'I want to get there while there is something worth saving.'

'That may not be possible,' said Cheiron.

'Then we must make it so,' said the warrior. 'I grow tired of extermination.'

PART THREE
NEMESIS

'On wrongs swift vengeance waits.'

⊍
ELEVEN

Dust LAY THICK on hundreds of glass cabinets and the air within the Gallery of Antiquities was ripe with musty neglect and forgotten history. Of all the places he had seen on Salinas, this was the one that truly spoke to Uriel. The legacy of the past and sense of belonging to something bigger was strong and he was reminded of the many halls of ancient banners and honour trophies that filled the Fortress of Hera.

It was the day after their meeting with the Janiceps and the guilty taste of psychic contact had not yet left Uriel's mind. As dawn had spread its sour light over Salinas, Uriel sent a request to Governor Barbaden, via their ubiquitous shadow, Eversham, that they needed a trained medicae to examine Pasanius.

No reply was immediately forthcoming, and rather than simply sit and wait for a response, Uriel had decided they would use the time before their battle-brothers made contact to better acquaint themselves with this world.

The best way to do that, decided Uriel, was to learn of its past.

Having travelled through the palace corridors to the parade ground once before, the route was embedded in Uriel's memory and they found their way to the outer doors of the palace with ease.

The bare concrete esplanade and grey tower at its far end were no less depressing than they had been the day before and as he made his way towards the decrepit Gallery of Antiquities, Uriel couldn't help but feel as though he was being drawn to this place, that somehow this journey was *necessary*.

'Doesn't look like much,' Pasanius had said, looking at the neglected wing of the palace. Despite feeling that great things awaited in the gallery, Uriel had been forced to agree with him.

That feared disappointment was dispelled as soon as they had entered and seen the vast array of cabinets, packing cases and curios that filled the wing. Much of its depths were shrouded in darkness, and who knew what treasures awaited discovery farther in, for a planet's worth of battle honours and history filled the Gallery of Antiquities.

In charge of imposing order on this haphazardly collected memorabilia was Curator Lukas Urbican, a meticulous and proud man, who Uriel had immediately warmed to upon meeting.

'Ah,' said Urbican, looking up over his spectacles as they had pushed open the doors to the gallery. 'I was hoping you would feel compelled to visit my humble gallery, although I must apologise in advance for the somewhat… random nature of the exhibits.'

Urbican was of average height and from his bearing he had once been a soldier. Though he wore the dark robe of an adept instead of a uniform, it was clear that he kept fit and healthy. Uriel guessed he was in his early sixties, his face lined and hard, and what little remained of his hair was shorn close to his skull and as white as powdered snow.

Urbican beckoned them in and marched over with a liver-spotted hand extended in welcome. Uriel took Urbican's proffered hand, the old man's grip strong and rough textured.

'Curator Urbican I presume?' said Uriel.

'None other, my friend, none other,' said Urbican with a disarming smile, 'but call me Lukas. I'm guessing you would be Captain Uriel Ventris, which, if I'm not mistaken, would make your one-armed friend, Sergeant Pasanius.'

'You're not mistaken,' said Pasanius. 'The arm is a bit of a giveaway.'

'You have heard of us?' asked Uriel.

'I shouldn't think there are many on Salinas who haven't,' said Urbican. 'News of the arrival of Adeptus Astartes travels fast, though I must confess I was afraid that Leto would keep you all to himself. Our vaunted governor doesn't have much time for me, or the dusty old relics of the past. A waste of time, he'd say.'

'Actually, Governor Barbaden appears to want little to do with us,' said Uriel, surprised at his candour.

'Well, he has a lot on his plate, I suppose,' conceded Urbican, 'what with all the trouble the Sons of Salinas are causing.'

'Exactly,' said Uriel, sensing that he could learn much from Lukas Urbican. 'Thus, we find we have time on our hands.'

'And you use that time to visit my poor gallery of antiquities? I'm honoured,' said Urbican, beaming. 'I know how rare it is for a soldier such as yourself to have time on his hands, or any man of war for that matter. Of course, it has been some time since I could call myself a soldier of the Emperor.'

'You served with the Falcatas?' asked Pasanius.

'For my sins,' said Urbican, smiling, although the smile faltered for the briefest second. He waved a dismissive hand. 'Of course, that was many years ago. I mustered out after Restoration Day, though I think Colonel Kain would have retired me had I not. War is a young man's game, eh?'

Urbican suddenly paused and raised his hand with his middle finger exposed. 'Of course! Where are my manners? I know what you've come for, how silly of me.'

Uriel smiled as the aged curator bustled off into a chamber just off the main hallway.

The interior of this wing of the palace had seen better days. The paint was peeling from the walls and spreading patches of damp rose from the floor and spread across the arched ceiling. Banners hung on the walls, red and gold guidons and rectangular standards emblazoned with a golden warrior with the head of an eagle bearing twin falcatas.

A long row of glass-topped display tables ran down the centre of the hall and the walls were stacked high with crates. Some of these were open and scrawled with illegible notations, with portions of uniform jackets and assorted pieces of battle dress hanging from them. Cracked glass cabinets stood between the packing crates and lifeless mannequins dressed in what looked like mismatched pieces of uniform and armour carried rusted lasguns that looked about ready to fall apart.

There appeared to be no order to the collection, and yet Uriel found it incredibly reassuring to know that at least one man of Salinas cared for the memory of those who had served in the regiment and who honoured the people of the planet they had claimed.

'How many years of service must be gathered here?' Uriel asked Pasanius, peering into a cabinet filled with medals and a variety of bayonets.

'Decades,' said Pasanius, lifting a falcata with a rusted blade, 'if not centuries.'

While Urbican rooted around for whatever it was he sought, Uriel wandered along one of the aisles between the display cabinets. The first cabinet he stopped at was filled with battered leather notebooks bound with rotted cord. Most were rotted to illegibility, but one was arranged proudly in the centre of the cabinet.

The gold leaf on its cover was faded, but Uriel could make out enough of the lettering to know that it was a copy of the Tactica Imperium, the mighty work by which the Imperium's armies made war. The date was worn away, but the edition number appeared to be in the low hundreds, making the book well over a thousand years old.

'Ah, I see you've found Old Serenity's copy of the Tactica,' said Urbican, his head poking from the doorway. 'Very rare piece, and said to have a personal note from Lord Solar Macharius on its inner cover, but the book's so fragile I don't dare open it.'

'Who was Old Serenity?' asked Pasanius.

'The Colonel of the Falcatas before Leto Barbaden,' shouted Urbican, 'a grand old man indeed, a gentleman. Never lost his cool in battle, even when things went awry. When we were set to be overrun at Koreda Gorge he turned to his adjutant and said, "I shall never sound the retreat, never. Warn the men that if they hear it, it is only a ruse on the part of the enemy." Stirring stuff, eh?'

'Is that true?'

'I have no idea,' said Urbican. 'Old Serenity was killed an hour later, but it sounds good, eh? Ah! Here we are.'

Urbican emerged from the back room, carrying a long, cloth-wrapped bundle, which he reverently laid on the table before Uriel.

Even before Urbican unwrapped it, Uriel knew what it was and felt his pulse quicken as the sheathed sword of Captain Idaeus was revealed.

'Eversham brought your sword here, Captain Ventris,' said Urbican, 'and I have kept it safe for you.'

Uriel drew the golden-hilted sword from its scabbard, his fingers naturally slipping around the wire-wound hilt and the quillons fitting neatly against the top of his fist. To hold his blade once more and feel the connection to his heritage as a Space Marine was a sublime sensation, another sign that their exile from the Chapter was almost at an end.

He turned the blade in his hand, the pale light of the gallery reflecting along its gleaming, unblemished surface. 'Thank you,' he said. 'This blade means a lot to me.'

'A fine piece,' said Urbican, 'although I feel the blade is perhaps not the original.'

'You have a good eye, Lukas,' said Uriel. 'The blade was broken on the world of Pavonis. I forged a new one on Macragge.'

'Ah, that explains it. Still, it is a fine weapon,' said Urbican. 'Perhaps you could tell me of its illustrious history sometime?'

'I would be proud to,' nodded Uriel, attempting to buckle the sword around his waist, but finding that without the bulk of Astartes plate, the belt was too large. Seeing the difficulty Uriel was having, Pasanius said, 'Is my armour here also, curator?'

Urbican smiled. 'Indeed it is, sergeant, Mk VII if I'm not mistaken, Aquila pattern?'

'That it is,' confirmed Pasanius. 'You know Astartes armour?'

'Only a very little,' admitted Urbican. 'It is a passion of mine to study the battle gear of our most heroic protectors, although I confess I have only ever had the chance to study armour and weapons of a far greater age than yours.'

'You have studied Space Marine armour?' asked Uriel. 'Where?'

'Well, here of course,' replied the curator, with an expression of puzzlement, which suddenly turned to one of unalloyed joy.

'Ah, I see! Oh, you must come with me,' said Urbican, setting off down an aisle leading deeper into the gallery.

'My friends,' said Urbican, 'you are not the first Astartes to come to Salinas.'

* * *

FOR SOMEONE WHO had faithfully served Leto Barbaden in the Achaman Falcatas, Mesira Bardhyl had fared particularly poorly in the years following Restoration Day, thought Daron Nisato. Many times while the regiment had fought through some tough campaigns, Nisato had seen the shivering form of Mesira next to the colonel, her stooped form lost in the Guard-issue greatcoat, and felt a stab of sympathy for her.

He'd known it was wrong to feel like that, for, as a company commissar, it could easily have fallen to him to put a bullet through her brain in the event of her psychic powers becoming dangerous.

For all her apparent frailty, however, Mesira had served the regiment and never once faltered in her duty.

And this was her reward upon mustering out: a roughly built, brick and timber structure on the outskirts of Junktown; anti-Imperial slogans painted over the walls and crude representations of horned monsters on the door. The street was empty in both directions, but that was no surprise; the arrival of a growling Chimera in the black and steel livery of the Barbadus Enforcers had a way of emptying streets like no other.

Nisato pulled himself up from the commander's hatch of the vehicle and slid down the armoured glacis to drop to the hard-packed, sandy ground. His armour weighed heavily on him, but it would be foolish to come this close to Junktown without it. He scanned the street again, his eyes flicking from rooftops and windows to recessed doorways where an opportunistic gunman might wait.

He turned back to the growling vehicle and said, 'I'm going inside.'

'You want backup?' asked a voice in his helmet: Lieutenant Poulsen.

'No, wait here, I'll only be a few minutes.'

'We'll be ready if you need us,' said Poulsen and Nisato heard the man's eagerness. Poulsen had been a junior commissar at the outset of the Salinas campaign and took Nisato's lead in all things, following him into the Enforcers after the muster out after Restoration Day.

It hadn't offered much in the way of advancement, but at least they were not as hated as the men and women who had chosen to remain with the Falcatas. At least as keepers of the peace and upholders of the law, they could be seen to be doing some good.

At least that was what Daron Nisato told himself before he went to sleep each night.

'Stay alert,' ordered Nisato, 'and if I'm not out in ten minutes, come in and get me.'

'Understood, sir.'

A squad of five enforcers sat in the baking confines of the Chimera, armed and armoured for combat, but Nisato did not think he would need them. Mesira was a lonely, afflicted woman, but she wasn't dangerous. When he had seen her at the palace, he had seen the desperation etched into her face and although it fell somewhat beyond his remit of upholding the law to check on her like this, he felt he owed her a duty of care.

For, if not him, then who?

Nisato rapped his gauntlet against her door, hearing the empty echoes of it up the stairs and feeling the give in it that told him it wasn't locked. He pushed the door open, not liking the stale, abandoned air he felt from the dwelling. Dozens could live in a place like this, but fear of Mesira's abilities had kept her isolated, for who wanted to live with a witch?

His hand went to his bolt pistol as he slid through the door, keeping his steps as light as he was able. Inside the door was a narrow vestibule with boarded up doors and a staircase that led up to a landing. Weak light filtered down the stairs from a skylight above and dust motes spun in the air where his opening of the door had disturbed them.

'Mesira?' he called, deciding that there was no need for stealth after having knocked. 'Are you in here?'

There was no answer. Nisato drew his pistol, his instinct for trouble warning him that all was not right. Carefully, knowing that Mesira lived on the first floor, Nisato climbed the stairs, keeping his pistol trained on the space above him. Keeping his breathing even, he eased onto the landing, seeing an open door along a wooden floored corridor with flakboard laid along its length in lieu of carpet or tiles. The reek of *khat* leaves was strong, telling him that this was Mesira's home; many psychics turned to narcotics to allow them to sleep without dreaming.

Checking both ways along the corridor, Nisato called Mesira's name once more, again receiving no response. He swept along the corridor until he reached the door and pressed himself against the wall beside it. Reaching up, Nisato snapped his helmet's visor down and reached up to amplify the aural gain on its auto-senses.

Amid the crackling static, he listened for the tread of footsteps, the rasp of frightened breath or the sound of metal as a pistol was cocked. Nisato remained motionless for several minutes until he was sure there was no immediate threat.

Taking a deep breath, he spun around and kicked the door inwards, moving swiftly inside, twisting this way and that to cover his blind spots and check the dead zones where an assailant might be lurking.

With quick, professional skill, Nisato moved from room to room, seeing no evidence of a struggle or any sign of Mesira.

He did, however, see plenty of evidence of a lost, desperate soul in need of a friend. Rumpled, dirty sheets covered a threadbare mattress in the corner of one room. Empty bottles of raquir lay scattered everywhere and the air reeked of *khat* leaves. Food wrappers lay where they had been thrown and Daron Nisato felt a terrible regret at not reaching out to Mesira.

Something told him that, as was often the case, regret only came when it was too late to do something about it. The place was empty and he lowered his pistol, saddened at the waste of a life that was laid out before him.

Nisato moved into the main room and walked over to the grimy window that looked out over the city of Barbadus. Sprawling and ugly, it simmered in the heat of the day, fumes and smudges of smoke staining the sky from the distant manufactories. Enforcing Imperial Law in a place like this wasn't how Daron Nisato had imagined ending his career with the Achaman Falcatas, but then life very rarely took you down the paths you imagined when you were young.

He remembered leaving the Schola Progenium on Ophelia VII, thinking of the plum assignments that would be his and the great things he would achieve in the service of the Emperor. For a time, it had been as he'd imagined. His service in the Falcatas had been honourable and he was, if not liked, (what commissar was ever really liked?) respected.

Then Colonel Landon, Old Serenity the men called him, had been killed at Koreda Gorge along with his senior officers and Leto Barbaden had assumed command. Nisato had met Barbaden only once before then and had not been impressed. The man was a quartermaster and regimental logistician, a man who dealt with absolutes and to whom men were simply numbers in a ledger.

Nisato shook off such thoughts, not liking where they were leading, and turned to face the room, seeing scattered papers on a leaning desk, a dark pile of clothing and a rumpled greatcoat.

Even as he took in the details, his attention snapped towards the wall opposite the window, where five words had been daubed in what he knew instantly was blood.

Help me... I was there.

Below that was a gleaming medal depicting a screaming eagle.

THEY WERE BEAUTIFUL.

Uriel had scarce seen anything that had filled him with such a welcome sense of return. Hidden at the back of the Gallery of Antiquities, they stood in serried ranks and gleamed in the dim light. The blue and white paint of their elongated helmet muzzles was scraped and every breastplate was dented or cracked from long ago impacts.

Under normal circumstances, they would be considered horrifically damaged or, at the very least, grossly neglected, but to Uriel's eyes, these suits of armour were the most perfect things he had ever seen.

There were nineteen of them, each painted in quartered blue and white, the left shoulder guard a studded auto-reactive plate, the right stamped with a golden 'U' over a pair of white wings. In each fist was clutched a bolter, some damaged, some gleaming as though fresh from the armoury.

'You recognise the Chapter symbol?' asked Uriel.

Pasanius nodded. 'The Sons of Guilliman,' he whispered, 'a founding of the thirty-third millennium. Unbelievable.'

'I know,' said Uriel, reaching to run a hand over the eagle emblazoned upon the nearest suit's breastplate. 'Mk VI, Corvus-pattern power armour.'

Uriel turned to Lukas Urbican, and the curator took a step back as he saw the anger in his face. 'How did this armour come to be here? How did the Falcatas come to be in possession of Astartes power armour? These should have been returned to their Chapter!'

'Oh no!' said Urbican quickly. 'These aren't battle trophies or spoils of war. These suits of armour were here in the gallery when I took on its upkeep, I assure you.'

Uriel saw the truth in the curator's fear and raised his hands in apology. 'I am sorry, I should have thought before I spoke, but to see

Astartes armour paraded by mortals like this is… unusual. No Chapter would willingly leave such a precious legacy of their history behind.'

'I understand,' said Urbican, but Uriel saw that he did not and the curator was still shaken by his earlier anger. Uriel took a deep breath and said, 'Allow me to explain, Lukas. To a Space Marine, his armour is more than just plates of ceramite and fibre-bundle muscles, more than simply what shields him from the bullets and blades of his enemies. The armour becomes part of the warrior who dons it. Heroes have fought the enemies of mankind wearing this armour and upon their death, it is repaired and given to another warrior to fight in the name of the Emperor. Each warrior strives to be worthy of the hero before him and earn his own legend to pass on.'

'I think I understand, Uriel,' said Urbican, moving forward to place his hand on the scarred vambrace. 'You're saying that it is more than just a functional piece of battle gear, that there's living history in every plate. Legends are carved in every scar upon its surface and a life of battle encapsulated in its very existence. Yes, I see that now.'

'So how did they come to be here?' asked Uriel again.

'Well, as I said, you are not the first Astartes to come to this world,' said Urbican, 'although I believe it was many centuries before the Falcatas arrived that these warriors fought here.'

'Who were they fighting?'

'Ah, well, there things tend to get a bit hazy. The record keepers of Salinas were somewhat vague on that account, although there are veiled references to great beasts without skin, red-fleshed hounds that could swallow a man whole, and armoured warriors who could bend the very nature of reality. All lurid stuff, to be sure, and no doubt magnified by the writer, but whatever they were they were serious enough to warrant the attentions of Space Marines.'

Uriel recognised warriors of the Ruinous Powers from Urbican's description and shared an uneasy glance with Pasanius at the mention of great beasts without skin as the curator continued with his tale. Uriel had not forgotten that the Unfleshed still roamed the hills around Khaturian and knew he could not afford to leave them alone for much longer.

'There was talk of a great battle near an abandoned city in the foothills of the northern mountains.'

'I think we know that city,' said Pasanius. 'Khaturian isn't it?'

'Ah, yes, I believe that was its name,' said Urbican. 'Anyway, these Sons of Guilliman, as you call them, fought the enemy, but were, unfortunately, wiped out.'

'So where are the rest of the suits of armour?' asked Uriel.

'These are the only ones we have. The texts of the time talk of other Astartes coming to Salinas in the aftermath of the battle, warriors who were able to defeat these beasts.'

'Do your texts say who these warriors were?'

'No, although they were described as "giants in silver armour who smote the vile foe with lightning and faith". Apparently, they defeated the enemy and left immediately after the victory was won. I have always presumed they took whatever armour the Sons of Guilliman left behind.'

'Then why did they not take these?'

'According to the archive labels, they were discovered buried in the ruins of a collapsed building in Khaturian many decades later, by servitors hauling stone to build the new temple by all accounts. I suppose these silver giants must have missed them when they left.'

'What of the bones?' asked Pasanius. 'The warriors who wore this armour.'

'I'm sorry, I don't know. There was no mention of bones, just the armour.'

Uriel turned back to the silent warriors and walked along the line of Mk VI plate, now knowing that brother Space Marines had died fighting the great enemy of mankind on this world in ages past. The dim light of the gallery seemed to shine in the depths of the eye lenses of the helmets, as though some flickering ember of the warriors who had worn this armour remained within.

'They were waiting,' said Uriel, and no sooner had he spoken the words than he felt the rightness of them on a deep, instinctual level.

'Waiting for what?' asked Pasanius.

'For someone to find them and reawaken their glory,' said Uriel, the words leaping unbidden to his lips, as though spoken by another, 'to fight their enemies once more, and to bring them home.'

He stopped before a suit that had been punctured through the gorget by some unknown weapon, the plates, seals and inner linings of the armour buckled inwards. Dark stains striated the inner surfaces and, although centuries old, Uriel could smell the ancient hero's blood.

As he stared at the blood, Uriel felt the kinship he shared with this warrior on a level he could not articulate. This was a legacy of heroism that stretched back thousands of years, and even over the aeons of time and distance that separated them Uriel knew that this armour had not just been waiting: it had been waiting for *him*.

No word was forthcoming from Governor Barbaden regarding the possibility of a medicae examining Pasanius's arm, so Uriel spent the next two days working on his suit of armour, working with craftsmen from the palace forges to restore it to functionality.

Pasanius had been reunited with his own armour, and soon Uriel no longer thought of this armour as belonging to another warrior.

It was his, though he knew that it would be his for only a limited time.

The armour belonged to the Sons of Guilliman and it would dishonour their warriors to wear it for any longer than was necessary. After a thorough inspection, it was clear that the damage was largely superficial, but with broken parts replaced with components from other suits, it was not long before Uriel stood before a fully restored suit of Mk VI plate.

Palace artificers were already attempting to modify the cable heads of their generators in an attempt to recharge the internal power of the armour, and they confidently predicted that they would have the armour fully functional within the day.

In the meantime, Uriel and Pasanius explored the Gallery of Antiquities with Curator Urbican. The gallery held many fascinating treasures, although none was as magnificent as the nineteen suits of Corvus-pattern power armour they had discovered on their first visit.

Urbican was a genial host and a garrulous orator, endlessly pleased to have someone to whom he could hold forth on the history of the Falcatas and the world they had conquered.

On the eastern edge of the Paragonus sub-sector, a lynchpin of Imperial defences of the coreward approach to Segmentum Solar, the Salinas system was one of a dozen that had felt the wrath of an Imperial Crusade some thirty-five years ago. The core worlds of the sub-sector had fallen prey to agents of the Archenemy, and the forces of Warlord Crozus Regaur had begun to swallow up the outlying systems, one by one.

Before the enemy forces had gained an unbreakable hold on the sub-sector, the Imperium had retaliated, raising regiments from the outlying systems to fight the threat. Such measures held the enemy in check, but had not the strength to dislodge him from the sub-sector, and thus regiments from beyond the immediate sphere of the conflict were dragged into it.

The Falcatas had been one such regiment and had been tasked with cleansing the outer systems of taint. For the first planets of the Salinas system, it had already been too late, their governors overthrown and their populace in thrall to the enemy.

Along with a dozen other regiments and a demi-legion of titans from the Legio Destructor, the Falcatas had fought for two decades upon the blasted surfaces of these planets to drive Regaur's forces off-world. Urbican's voice choked as he told of the campaigns, and Uriel could only guess at the horrors and bloodshed he had seen in the liberation of the planets.

Salinas had been the third world in the system and when the Achaman Falcatas had made planet-fall, they had come as an army of conquest. Despite pleas of loyalty to the God-Emperor from the populace, the battle-hardened veterans of the Guard, men and women who had waded through blood and the dead for most of their adult lives, were in no mood for half measures.

The planetary governor had been executed and when his forces had taken arms in response to this, Barbaden had unleashed the full horror of the Falcatas' experiences of the last two decades.

Men and women who had desperately tried to minimise civilian casualties in their first months as soldiers, soon cared little for the collateral damage caused by their assaults and the local PDF regiments had been obliterated within months of planet-fall.

Although organised forces had been defeated, there remained a powerful core of resistance and, for many years, the Falcatas had fought a dedicated and utterly ruthless insurgent army named the Sons of Salinas that murdered Imperial soldiers and bombed their bases.

All that had come to an end with the Khaturian Massacre.

Uriel saw that Urbican was reluctant to speak of this, but gently pressed the old curator over the course of their second day of exploration of the galleries.

'It was close to the fourth year after we arrived,' said Urbican. 'I wasn't there, of course, so I have this only secondhand. Well, the insurgents were getting out of hand and not a day went by without a bomb going off or a patrol being ambushed and slaughtered. We couldn't keep the peace; we were too few and our equipment was beginning to fail. Without re-supply and a corps of trained enginseers, tanks were getting a bit thin on the ground. We were getting weaker and they seemed to be getting stronger.'

'So what did Barbaden do about it?' asked Pasanius. 'He was still colonel then wasn't he?'

'He was,' agreed Urbican. 'He said that Khaturian was a base of operations of the Sons of Salinas and led the Screaming Eagles to surround it. Apparently, Barbaden gave the city fathers two hours to hand over the leader of the insurgents, a man named Sylvanus Thayer, or else he would order his men to attack.'

'I'm guessing they didn't hand him over,' said Uriel.

'They said they couldn't,' explained Urbican. 'They said he wasn't there, that he never had been. They begged Barbaden to call off his attack, but once Leto has his mind set on something, there's nothing anyone can do to dissuade him.'

'So what happened?'

Urbican shook his head. 'You must understand, Uriel, this is hard for me. The Killing Ground Massacre is not something I am proud to have associated with my regiment. All the good we did, all our honour and our glory died that day.'

'I know this is hard for you,' said Uriel. 'You do not have to go on if you do not wish to.'

'No,' said Urbican, 'some shames need to be told.'

The curator drew a breath and smoothed down his robes before he continued. 'Well, the deadline for the people of Khaturian to hand over Thayer came and went, and for a time they thought that Barbaden's threat had been a bluff.'

'But it wasn't, was it?'

Urbican shook his head. 'No,' he said, 'it wasn't. Marauder bombers flew in over the mountains and dropped a dreadful amount of bombs. They blew the city apart. You could see the fires from Barbadus. It was as if the whole sky was aflame, a terrible sight, just terrible, and, well, after that reports are somewhat confused.'

'Confused how?' asked Pasanius, scratching at his arm.

'No one I've spoken to seems to be able to agree on exactly what happened next or even how it happened, but Colonel Barbaden ordered the Falcatas into the ruins of Khaturian and when they came out six hours later, there wasn't a single soul left alive in the city.'

'He killed the entire city?'

'Yes,' nodded Urbican, 'seventeen thousand people in six hours.'

'What happened after the attack?' asked Uriel. The sheer scale of the dead was staggering.

'The Sons of Salinas, what was left of them, came down from the mountains,' said Urbican, shaking his head. 'Supposedly Sylvanus Thayer and many of his followers' families lived in Khaturian and, mad with grief and rage, he led them in one last glorious charge.'

'And they were destroyed,' said Uriel, guessing the outcome of that charge.

'They were, but what a magnificent, if futile, way to die: fighting the enemy with the green and gold of their cloaks flying out behind them as they charged,' said Urbican. 'But what chance did they have? They were guerrillas, not an army. Thayer and his men were pounded to ruin by artillery and then shot to pieces before noon. And that was the end of the resistance of Salinas. By the end of the week, we'd had Restoration Day over on the esplanade and that was that.'

'Except that wasn't the end of the resistance, was it?' asked Uriel, remembering the graffiti he had seen that said the Sons of Salinas would rise again.

'No, would that it had been,' said Urbican. 'The brutality of the Falcatas subjugation of Salinas is a matter of great shame to many of its former soldiers and the scars of that war are far from healed, Uriel. Thayer's second-in-command, a man named Pascal Blaise, took up where his friend had left off, although he doesn't have the weapons or training to be anything like as dangerous as Sylvanus Thayer.'

'Pascal Blaise?' asked Uriel. 'What does he look like?'

Urbican shrugged. 'I don't know, I've never seen him, but I'm told he's a shaven-headed man with a forked beard. Why do you ask?'

'I think I saw him during the attack on Colonel Kain's force when we arrived.'

'That wouldn't surprise me. The Sons of Salinas have an especial hatred for Verena Kain.'

'Why?'

'Well, she led the Falcatas into Khaturian,' said Urbican. 'Barbaden gave the order, but I believe it was her that went into the flames and carried it out.'

TWELVE

THE BAR WAS busy tonight. Cawlen Hurq had made sure of it. The buzz of conversation filled it and the smell of sweat and stale alcohol was powerful. Almost a hundred people filled the bar with noise, their conversations blurred into a raucous babble. Cawlen had six men with guns among the patrons and, as far as any place in Barbadus could be called safe, this place was safe. Pascal Blaise sat in a booth at the back, nursing a glass of raquir and wondering what had made him think this was a good idea.

'He won't come,' said Cawlen, 'not if he's got an ounce of sense.'

'He'll come,' replied Pascal. 'We have something he wants.'

'What makes you think he has any interest in her?'

'He was at her house,' said Pascal, taking a drink. 'He was looking for her.'

'So? That doesn't mean anything.'

Pascal knew Cawlen was right. There was no reason to think that Daron Nisato would come to the bar, except Pascal knew that he would. Daron Nisato, out all the men and women who had mustered out of the Falcatas, was the one person he credited with a shred of honour. He knew for a fact that Nisato had not been present at the Killing Ground massacre and had done all he could to learn the truth behind it.

Pascal scanned the faces that filled the bar, remembering the last time he had come here and the soldier of the Achaman Falcatas who had eaten the barrel of his pistol. The bloodstains had been cleaned from the roof, but Pascal could still see the impact the bullet had made on the roof beam.

'Guilt can be a great motivator,' he whispered.

'What?' asked Cawlen. 'Did you say something?'

'No, just thinking aloud,' replied Pascal.

Cawlen looked around the bar, his nerves jangling on the surface of his skin. 'I don't like it. What if Nisato comes here with a dozen enforcers? Everything we've done over the last ten years would be for nothing.'

'He won't.'

'You don't know that,' said Cawlen. 'It's too much of a risk.'

Cawlen was right, this was risky. He was exposed here. There was an undercurrent of fear and resentment in the bar; he could hear it in the too boisterous conversation and ever so slightly forced laughter. He could feel the peoples' fear and knew that part of that fear was thanks to him.

They were afraid of what might happen because of him being there.

Time was, these people would have done anything for him: helped his freedom fighters, provided them with food, shelter and information, but times had changed and ten years of misery and hardship had hardened a lot of hearts and eroded a lot of the goodwill he'd inherited from Sylvanus Thayer.

People were tired of war and he didn't blame them.

He was tired of it too.

The ironic thing was that he didn't hate the Imperium. For most of his adult life he had faithfully served the Golden Throne, making his own small contribution to the welfare of mankind. Then the Falcatas had come with anger in their hearts and blood on their blades and cut themselves into the flesh of the world.

A decade later, Pascal Blaise had lost the best years of his life fighting soldiers of an Emperor he had sworn to serve, but he was fighting them, not what they represented.

Pascal was not naïve enough to think he could win, but he had come to realise that his fight had nothing to do with winning, and everything to do with justice. The guilty had to pay. It was as simple as that. The guilty had to pay and the natural order of justice had to be restored. He realised that none of the killing had been about anything other than that.

Yes, Cawlen was right, this was risky, but he was tired of killing and if this gesture could be the beginnings of an end to it, then it was worth a little risk.

'There he is,' said Cawlen, stiffening in his seat, his hand sliding to the pistol concealed beneath his storm cape.

'Ease up, soldier,' warned Pascal. 'We're not here for violence, and by the looks of it, neither is he.'

Daron Nisato had just entered the bar, his expression guarded and wary. The conversation dipped in volume as he ducked under the iron girder that served as a lintel and approached the bar. Pascal watched as the enforcer's eyes scanned the patrons with a lawman's gaze, sorting the threats from the chaff.

The enforcer could not know for sure what Pascal looked like, but his eyes settled on him and stayed there.

'He's good,' said Pascal as Nisato began to thread his way through the bar towards the booth. 'You've got to give him that.'

Cawlen grunted and rose from the booth as Nisato approached. The enforcer stopped at the table and said, 'I'm presuming it was you that sent the message to me.'

'It was,' confirmed Pascal. 'Sit down.'

Nisato glanced at Cawlen. 'Maybe I will, if you send your goon away. He's making me itchy and if his hand moves any closer to the weapon he's got under his cloak, I'll break it off.'

'You can try,' growled Cawlen.

'Just give me a reason,' responded Nisato, squaring off against the big man.

Pascal clinked his glass against the bottle on the table. 'Can we just assume that we've passed through the pointless threats stage of this conversation please? Cawlen, back off. Mister Nisato, sit.'

Reluctantly, Cawlen Hurq backed away from the booth and Nisato slid onto the bench seat opposite Pascal. The enforcer stared at him and Pascal couldn't decide which emotion was uppermost in the man's features. Nisato was a handsome man, dark-skinned and with a prominent nose. His eyes were old, decided Pascal, but who on Salinas could say otherwise?

'Finished your inspection?' asked Nisato and Pascal smiled.

'My apologies,' said Pascal. 'It's not often I sit this close to a man who'd like nothing better than to put a bullet in me.'

'Is that what you think?'

'Don't you?'

'Not at the moment, but the night is young.'

Pascal poured a glass of raquir for Nisato and slid it across the beaten metal table.

'I wasn't sure if you'd come,' said Pascal.

'I didn't think I would.'

'So why did you?'

'Because…' began Nisato and Pascal saw that he was struggling to rationalise to himself why he had come. 'Because someone had to. Mesira's got no one else.'

'Mesira? Is that her name?'

'Yes. You didn't know?'

'No,' said Pascal. 'She hasn't said much that's made sense since we found her.'

'Found her? You didn't take her from her house?'

'No, she was wandering the streets of Junktown, screaming and tearing at her body.'

Nisato frowned, clearly not having considered the possibility that the woman had wandered off by herself. His first thoughts had been of kidnap.

'Her mind's gone if you ask me,' offered Pascal.

'If you've hurt her…'

Pascal waved a placatory hand. 'Of course we didn't hurt her. Any hurt that's been done, she did to herself.'

'What do you mean?'

'Just what I say,' replied Pascal. 'She was in a pretty bad way when we found her.'

Nisato leaned back and took a drink of his raquir. 'How did you know I was looking for her? Your message was pretty specific.'

'Come on, this was my city before it was yours. People tell me things. The head of the enforcers going to visit the witch woman doesn't go unnoticed. Why were you looking for her?'

'None of your business.'

'Is she your woman?' asked Pascal. 'Does the chief enforcer like getting his ya-yas from dangerous women?'

Nisato sneered. 'I told you, it's none of your business.'

'Fair enough,' said Pascal, holding up his hands.

The enforcer was visibly struggling to hold onto his cool and Pascal decided it was time to end this period of baiting. He took a deep breath and said, 'You want the truth? The woman means nothing to me. On any other day, I'd have left her in the street to die, but I knew she meant something to you.'

'So you want a favour, is that it? Blackmail?'

'No, nothing like that,' said Pascal.

'Then what?'

Pascal leaned over the table and placed his hand on Nisato's arm. The enforcer looked down at his hand as though it was a poisonous viper.

'I want the killing to end,' Pascal said. 'I want to end this grubby, dirty war with honour and if helping you out buys me a little goodwill, then it's a trade I'm willing to make.'

Nisato tried and failed to hide his surprise. 'This is a gesture of goodwill?'

'Exactly,' said Pascal, leaning back.

Nisato took a moment to consider what he had heard and Pascal could see that the idea was appealing to him. He remained silent, sensing that to intrude on the enforcer's thought processes would be a mistake.

At last Nisato leaned forward and said, 'Take me to her.'

'I DON'T LIKE this,' said Verena Kain. 'Not one bit.'

'Governor Barbaden does not share your misgivings,' said Uriel.

'Governor Barbaden,' she said, placing undue emphasis on his title, 'no longer commands the Achaman Falcatas. The regiment is mine to command and it is my right to decide what is acceptable and what is not.'

'It was my understanding that the Achaman Falcatas were no longer a serving regiment, that they were now designated a Planetary Defence Force,' said Uriel, unable to resist the barbed comment. 'As such, they are Governor Barbaden's to command.'

Kain glared at him and Uriel felt a guilty satisfaction at her anger. Beside him, he could feel Pasanius's grim amusement at Colonel Kain's discomfort.

'It is *my* understanding that you were exiled from your Chapter.'

'Ah, but we are going home,' said Pasanius. 'The Falcatas will always be PDF.'

Uriel tried, unsuccessfully, to hide a smile as Kain angrily turned on her heel and stalked away to join her adjutant, a put-upon looking man named Bascome. Ever since Uriel had met Verena Kain, she had been bitter and spiteful, as though he somehow wronged her by his very existence. Since hearing of the slaughter that had taken place at Khaturian, the Killing Ground as it was known, he had little time for Kain or her ill-temper.

Uriel put Kain from his mind as he watched a number of servitors and the few remaining enginseers of the Falcatas prepare the coupling heads of the generators.

The air in the Screaming Eagles' vehicle hangar was cool and stank of metal and electricity. A pair of parked Leman Russ battle tanks sweated oil and fumes, with coiled and ribbed cables snaking from beneath their hulls to a coughing generator.

Uriel paid no heed to the powerful war machines, his attention firmly fixed on the suit of armour that stood in the centre of the hangar. Its surfaces had been cleansed and returned to their former glory by Leto Barbaden's craftsmen and, like the last warrior standing after a battle, the armour stood immobile, its joints locked and its strength existing only as potential.

The armour's backpack was bereft of power and no solution the palace adepts could devise would restore it. Pasanius had suggested that perhaps the military grade generators and couplings might have a better chance and, after a petition to Governor Barbaden, a convoy of vehicles had traversed the city to the Screaming Eagles' barrack compound.

The enginseers there had jumped at the chance to work on the problem and their solution had been elegantly ingenious. The chargers for the onboard electrics of a Leman Russ had been adapted to run a powerful generator's output through a manually calibrated transformer, which would allow an enginseer to adjust the power supply to a level that the armour's backpack could use.

At least that was the theory. Whether or not it would work, was another matter entirely.

Uriel forced himself to be calm as he watched the enginseers work, taking solace in their apparent relish for the task. He could only hope that their competence matched their enthusiasm.

Pasanius stood beside him, resplendent and towering in his cleaned and polished armour, a bolter held tightly in his gauntlets like a talisman. The palace artificers had done a magnificent job in undoing the damage that had been done on Medrengard and Uriel felt a surge of pride as he looked at the gleaming plates of his friend's armour.

His left shoulder guard had been repainted with the symbol of the Ultramarines and a laurel wreath. He looked every inch the Ultramarines hero he was.

The armour in the centre of the hangar had also been repainted in the colours of the Ultramarines, although Uriel had been careful to leave the helmet in the original colours of the Sons of Guilliman. To do otherwise would insult the heritage of the warriors who had worn it before him and Uriel had no wish for the armour to fail him in battle through any lack of respect done to it.

'You think this will work?' asked Pasanius.

Uriel considered the question before answering. 'It will,' he said.

'You sound awfully sure.'

'I know, but I can't believe the armour would have drawn us to it if this wasn't going to work.'

Pasanius simply nodded and Uriel could tell that his friend had felt a similar pull towards the armour in the Gallery of Antiquities. Some things were just felt in the bones and although it went against Uriel's training to believe in things he could not see and touch and know were real, he felt sure that he was meant to wear this armour.

'We are ready to begin,' called Imerian, one of the enginseers, a hybrid being of flesh and metal who was swathed in red robes and whose arms were partially augmetic. Uriel felt his muscles tense and walked over to the armour, placing his hand in the centre of the golden eagle upon the breastplate.

'You will live again,' he said.

'Captain Ventris,' said Imerian, 'you might want to step away from the armour. If we are unable to calibrate the energy flows correctly then it would be advisable to be some distance from the backpack. Ceramite makes for deadly shrapnel.'

Uriel nodded and stepped away from the armour, moving to join the rest of the personnel within the vehicle hangar behind a hastily erected bulwark of sandbags. Imerian unspooled a length of cable from a heavy, brass-rimmed wooden box carried by a serious-faced servitor and made a number of complex, last minute adjustments to the dials on the front of the box.

At last he appeared to be satisfied with the arrangements and his finger hovered over a chunky black dial in the centre of the transformer.

'Colonel Kain?' asked Imerian. 'We are ready.'

Kain shot Uriel a bitter look of resignation and nodded curtly, saying, 'Proceed.'

The enginseer waved his hand at a crewman who sat upon the upper hull of one of the Leman Russ tanks and its engine roared to life with a thumping bass note that shook the dust from the roof of the hangar.

A crackling, electric sensation danced on the air and a rising hum, like the throbbing beat that filled the heart of a starship built from the box carried by the servitor.

Imerian furiously worked the dials as needles jumped, snapping into the red sections on the far right of the displays.

Arcs of lightning sparked from the transformer and Imerian flinched. The hum from the box became a whine and Uriel felt a moment's fear as he wondered if something had gone horribly wrong with the process.

He looked around the edge of the sandbag barrier, seeing the red lenses of the helmet glowing brightly with power.

'It's working!' he cried.

A subtle vibration was passing through the armour, a miraculous sense of reawakening that made Uriel's heart sing. He stepped from behind the sandbags and marched across the hangar over the warning shouts of Imerian.

Uriel knew he had nothing to fear from this armour's rebirth, for it mirrored his own.

In the time he had spent away from the Ultramarines, he had been less than whole, a shadow of his former self, but as the armour was reborn to its sacred purpose, so too was he.

Uriel smiled, and the glow in the helmet's lenses was mirrored in his own.

Daron Nisato followed Pascal Blaise up a set of metal stairs towards the bar's upper rooms. His footsteps echoed loudly on the metal and he found himself wondering at the strangeness of fate that found him breathing the same air as Pascal Blaise and not hauling him back to the enforcer's precinct house.

If Blaise was serious about opening a dialogue between the Sons of Salinas and the Imperial authorities, it could signal an end to the bloodshed that plagued the streets of Barbadus and a new beginning for Salinas.

Blaise pushed open a rusting iron door and beckoned Nisato into a long room with a handful of beds along one wall and a desk on the other. A single window looked out over the city of Barbadus. Mesira Bardhyl was sitting on one of the beds, her knees drawn up to her chest and her arms hugged around her shins. She wore a shapeless, white robe and her arms were bound with bandages.

Nisato took a seat next to Mesira on the bed and lifted her chin, seeing that her eyes were glassy and far away.

'Emperor's blood, what happened to her?' he asked.

'That's pretty much how we found her,' said Pascal Blaise, 'except that she was naked.'

'Naked?'

'Like I said, I think her mind's gone.'

Nisato had seen the same blank look in many a soldier's face, the shattered mind behind the eyes no longer capable of dealing with whatever trauma had broken it open, and was forced to agree.

'Mesira?' he said. 'Can you hear me? It's Daron Nisato. I'm here to take you home.'

She rocked back and forth, shaking her head. 'No,' she said. 'Can't go home. No home to go back to. We burned it. We burned it all. He's coming for us. Won't let us go. Must punish us for what we did.'

'Mesira, what are you talking about?'

'The Mourner... He's coming for us,' sobbed Mesira, tears spilling down her cheeks, 'for all of us who were there.'

Nisato looked helplessly at Pascal Blaise. The man was pale and his eyes were wide.

'Do you know what she's talking about?' demanded Nisato. 'Who's this Mourner?'

'The Mourner,' said Mesira. 'I see him all the time... He's burnt, black and dead. His eyes though... His eyes are fire and he burns. No! Not with fire, no, not with fire, but with rage.'

'Damn you, Blaise,' snapped Nisato, rising from the bed and moving towards the leader of the Sons of Salinas. 'Tell me what you know. Who is the Mourner?'

Pascal Blaise swallowed heavily, looking over at Cawlen Hurq who stood at the doorway.

'It's what we used to call the old man,' said Blaise, 'Sylvanus Thayer.'

'The leader of the Sons of Salinas before you?'

'Yes,' said Blaise, nodding.

'But he's dead isn't he?' said Nisato. 'He was killed after the Khaturian massacre.'

Blaise didn't answer immediately and Nisato said, 'Wasn't he?'

'No,' said Pascal, 'he wasn't.'

Sergeant Tremain paced the walls of the Screaming Eagles' compound, nodding and passing a word with the sentries as he went. His rifle hung loosely over his shoulder and his falcata was a reassuring presence at his hip, the sheath slapping against his thigh with every long stride he took. It felt good to be armed like an ordinary soldier, the familiar weight of the weapon he had first been issued with back on the old home world of Achaman.

The old home world...

Tremain could barely remember the world of his birth, save that it was more temperate, more beautiful and more interesting than this ugly rock. His memories were rose-tinted, he knew. Every soldier's memory of home was, but even allowing for that, he still missed the spiced hint in the air and the golden sunsets in the russet skies.

He smiled at his unusually poetic turn of thought and paused beside a corner turret, a boxy construction of reinforced concrete, further protected by a layer of steel mesh to defeat shaped warheads. The turret scanned across the dead ground before the compound, twin autocannon protruding from the firing slit to cover the roadway that led from the urban sprawl of Barbadus.

The night was quiet, although the rumble of engines and a teeth-numbing hum of electrics coming from one of the vehicle hangars against the far wall was an unaccustomed disturbance. The two Space Marines they had found, Tremain didn't like to use the word detained, were in there with Colonel Kain. There was something about recharging a suit of armour, although he didn't really understand what was going on.

All he knew was that he didn't like it. Sergeant Tremain didn't like anything that upset the status quo and he'd suspected those two warriors were trouble the moment he laid eyes on them within the fenced off area of the Killing Ground.

He'd known for certain when Uriel Ventris lied to him in the back of the Chimera.

Tremain shifted the rifle's weight on his shoulder and leaned out over the parapet to look at the smoky outline of Barbadus, squatting like a diseased tumour on the landscape. Of all the worlds they had been given to conquer, why did it have to be this one?

It was foolish to expose himself like this, but it enhanced his reputation amongst the men as a man who didn't care overmuch for the threat posed by the Sons of Salinas.

'Better watch out, sergeant,' said one of the wall sentries. 'You don't want to get your head shot off by a sniper.'

Tremain shook his head. 'Don't you worry about me, lad,' he said. 'The Sons of Salinas might be hard fighters, but they're not soldiers and they don't have a marksman worthy of the name to worry about.'

The sentry smiled and continued on his rounds, and once Tremain was satisfied that he had waited long enough, he leaned back. It was all very well being blasé about the Sons of Salinas, but fate had a strange sense of humour when it came to hubris, and it would be just his luck to make a crack like that and have a sniper blow his head off.

Tremain continued his rounds, finding that his gaze was continually drawn to the mountains that were little more than a jagged dark line on the horizon. He remembered the same mountains lit by the flames of Khaturian and shivered. He hadn't thought of the Killing Ground in many years. He tried to keep his thoughts away from that day as far as possible, but there was a strange sense of unease in the air tonight, an unease that made him think of past shames and which had driven him from the warmth of the barracks to wander the walls of the compound.

Perhaps it was simply the presence of the Space Marines that was unnerving him, for there could be no doubt that Sons of Salinas

informers would have passed word of their arrival to enemy com-
batants, but something told him that whatever he was feeling had
more to do with the past than what was transpiring here tonight.

Tremain paused on his rounds, looking up at the flag that billowed
and snapped high above the walls, the golden screaming eagle,
resplendent against a crimson field. The sight of the fiery eagle used to
fill Tremain with pride, but every time he looked at it now, he felt a
curious mix of sadness and regret.

The turret at the north corner of the compound wheezed as its
hydraulics moved it around and Tremain slung his rifle about and
quickly checked the charge. He set off at a casual pace, not wanting to
seem too concerned, but anxious to know what had alerted the gunners.

The back of the turret was supposed to be sealed, but parts had been
cannibalised to repair a damaged Leman Russ and thus Tremain was
able to lean inside. Two gunners sat in uncomfortable metal seats
before a chunky fire-control console and flickering pict screen. Waves
of static rippled over the screen, intermittently spiking with a judder-
ing image of the weapons' killing zone.

'What have you got?' he asked. 'Something moving?'

One gunner remained hunched over the screen, while the other
turned to face him, a look of confusion plastered across his features.

'We're not sure, sergeant,' said the gunner. 'It looked like there was a
crowd gathering at the edge of our range, but then…'

The man's words trailed off and when he didn't continue Tremain
said, 'But then what?'

'Then they vanished,' said the gunner helplessly. 'One minute they
seemed to be there, the next they were gone, and then the targeters
went to hell.'

That was certainly true. The pict screen was a hash of grainy nonsense, the speakers buzzing with static howls that sounded like a
wounded animal.

'Probably a surveyor malfunction,' said the other gunner. 'They're
getting worse every day.'

The soldier's sense for danger that had kept Tremain alive all these
years was yelling in his ear that this was not some equipment malfunction, but something far, far worse.

'Keep at it,' he said, 'and sing out the moment you get a solid return.'

The gunner nodded and Tremain ducked back out of the turret and waved over a number of wall sentries. He toyed with ordering an alert, but Colonel Kain would have his balls in a sling if he took such drastic action without proof that something was really wrong.

Half a dozen soldiers joined him, their weapons at the ready, and bolstered by their presence, Tremain leaned over the wall again, sliding down his helmet's visor and allowing the optical augmetics to adjust to the darkness.

The lurid green of the night vision made everything blurry and ghost-like, and at first he wasn't sure what he was seeing, for it seemed too ridiculous to be true.

The ground before the walls was filled with people, thousands of shining, glowing people that drifted like wisps of wind-blown cloud. They fled in and out of focus, as though they weren't really there, but were simply impressions on the surface of the world.

There were things moving amongst them, though, horribly fast things that used the shifting, glowing mass as a shroud by which to approach. Tremain blinked as he caught a glimpse of one of the things moving below him, the breath catching in his throat at the horror of it.

He reeled back from the wall, tripping and falling on his backside as it leapt upwards.

Something slashed past Tremain. He heard a muffled grunt and his visor suddenly flared with brightness as something hot and wet splashed his face. Blinded, he staggered against the wall and wrenched the visor up in time to see a hulking monster squatting on the wall. It held the head of one his soldiers in its hands. The body this trophy had once belonged to was on its knees, jetting a vigourous fountain of arterial blood into the air.

The killer glistened in the reflected light of the compound, its flesh the hideous, slick blue and pink of a stillborn child. Its head was an elongated, twisted mass of molten flesh and bone, the eyes like hot coals placed in two wounds gouged in the meat of its face. Chisel-like teeth unsheathed from its jaws and Tremain scrambled back on his rump, desperate to be away from this abomination.

More were joining it, half a dozen and more, their elastic limbs hauling their vile bulks easily onto the walls. Tremain's terror soared and threatened to unman him as he saw their unnatural bodies, the nightmarish creations of a demented anatomist, all knotted masses of bone, flesh and muscle combined in unreasoning, lethal forms.

Shots were fired, bright in the half-light, and screams soon followed them.

Claws and teeth flashed. Blood squirted and men died.

Tremain scrambled for his rifle, but it was already too late.

The Lord of the Unfleshed reached down and tore him in two before his finger even slid through the trigger guard.

THIRTEEN

THE ARMOUR WAS coming alive before him. Uriel could feel the power coursing around its ancient machinery as surely as he could feel the blood in his veins. The subtle vibration of life was returning to the armour and the sense of approbation he felt from this rebirth was palpable.

Uriel could almost see the lighting running through the armour, strength returning to the long-dormant muscles that would give the wearer the power to smite his enemies and the protection to suffer their violence. To wear such armour was an honour few were worthy of and one Uriel knew he would have to earn.

Pasanius had joined him standing before the armour, and Uriel was again thankful for the loyalty and friendship his comrade offered him.

'How long now, Enginseer Imerian?' called Uriel, raising his voice to be heard over the threatening roar of the Leman Russ's engines and the throb of power.

Imerian risked sticking his head out from behind the sandbag barrier. 'I have the correct frequency, Captain Ventris, so it should only take another few hours for the backpack to become fully charged.'

Uriel did not reply, for he had seen the mask of battle drop over Pasanius's face. A second later, he knew why. Over the rumble of tank engines, his enhanced hearing picked out the sounds of gunfire.

'Colonel Kain!' he shouted, pinpointing the sound. 'Weapons' fire! At your perimeter.'

Verena Kain emerged from the sandbagged barrier and placed her hand to the side of her head. Uriel saw her expression transform from one of irritation to one of cold, hard anger.

'Shut this down,' she ordered Imerian, before turning to draw her pistol and falcata, which she pointed at the Leman Russ, 'and fire up those tanks.'

'Let's go,' said Uriel, drawing his sword from its sheath.

Pasanius followed him, the borrowed boltgun clutched in his left fist, as a detachment of soldiers formed up on Colonel Kain. The commander of the Falcatas jogged over to the main doors of the hangar as they began to rumble open.

Uriel reached the doors at the same time and Kain favoured him with a withering expression of scorn.

'If this has something to do with you…' She left the threat unfinished.

'Then you can berate me for it later,' said Uriel.

The doors opened wide enough to allow egress from the hangar and Colonel Kain slipped through, her soldiers swiftly following her outside. Uriel let her go first; this was her command after all, but he made sure he caught up to her quickly.

No sooner had he emerged onto the open ground in the centre of the compound than a screaming siren split the night open. With a snap and an actinic clash of circuits, blinding arc lights flared to life, dispelling the night's darkness and bathing everything in bleaching brightness.

'Oh no,' said Uriel as he saw the carnage at the walls.

Monsters were loose in the compound.

The Unfleshed ran rampant through the soldiers of the Screaming Eagles, tearing limbs from torsos and undoing human forms with crushing blows or snapping bites. Their forms were huge and swollen, their previously exposed organs and meat now sheathed in slimy layers of new skin.

The Lord of the Unfleshed roared as the lights came on, towering, magnificent and unspeakable, as though his veins ran with light instead of blood. His tribe poured into the compound like an army, although less than a dozen of them remained alive. Men fled before them, only to be plucked into the air and casually dismembered. Las-bolts flashed and burned the air, but the flesh of these monsters was impervious to such inconsequential energies.

'What are they doing?' hissed Uriel.

'Killing,' replied Pasanius, reproach heavy in his voice.

Colonel Kain and the Falcatas that surrounded her watched in dumbfounded horror at the bloodshed being unleashed within their sanctum. Soldiers were beginning to emerge from one of the barracks, but a grotesque beast with reverse jointed legs and a hideously curved spine of knotted cartilage, hacked them down as they emerged. A sandbagged gun position opened up on the walls, the gunners knowing that killing their own men would be a kindness. Heavy calibre rounds hammered the inner face of the concrete walls, tore through the bloodied flesh of the dead soldiers and smacked wetly into the bodies of the Unfleshed.

The Lord of the Unfleshed leapt from the wall, his strength and power carrying him through the air to land on the roof of the second barracks building. His enormous weight smashed through the corrugated tin roof and he vanished from view, although his bellows of rage could still be heard.

Uriel ran towards the violated building, Pasanius hot on his heels as Colonel Kain fought to impose some kind of order upon her command. Screams and roars filled the air, the Unfleshed bludgeoning their way through the Screaming Eagles without mercy.

A beast with two fused heads and elongated arms that ended in stump-like claws sawed its way through the red-armoured soldiers, its flesh peppered with bullets and scorched by las-bolts.

One with a monstrous twin bulging from its flesh, slaughtered men and women and fed them to the ravenous growth, its lunatic hunger uncaring whether the meat was alive or dead.

Uriel tried to ignore the horrors around him, vaulting a metal girder fallen from the roof of the barracks. Inside, he could hear frantic screams, random bursts of las-fire and a terrible roar of pure hatred. He kicked aside the buckled door and pushed his way inside.

The interior of the barracks was an abattoir, worse than anything Uriel had dreamed while in the depths of the Omphalos Daemonium. Blood sprays coated every wall, broken bodies and shredded limbs lay scattered like debris from an explosion in a mortuary, and it seemed impossible that so many men could have died in so short a time.

'Emperor's blood!' he swore as he saw the Lord of the Unfleshed bend a man in half until his spine snapped and jagged bone erupted from his belly. Blood sprayed the giant creature and Uriel felt an almost physical hurt at this betrayal.

'Stop!' he shouted, raising his sword before him. He knew the weapon was scant defence against so colossal a creature. Had this weapon not been wrested from his hands in the belly of a lesser member of the tribe than its master?

'What in the Emperor's name are you doing?' demanded Uriel.

The Lord of the Unfleshed's head swung towards him, ponderous and dripping with blood. Scraps of meat and cloth hung from his jaws and Uriel saw a dull light in his eyes, a light that spoke of a thousand minds behind it.

'These men deserve to die,' said the Lord of the Unfleshed. 'They were there.'

Uriel knew something of the history of the world and of the regiment that had claimed it, but how could the Lord of the Unfleshed?

'That is not for you to decide,' he yelled. 'Why are you doing this?'

'Because someone must,' said the Lord of the Unfleshed. 'The dead must be avenged.'

Uriel took a slow step towards the towering creature as it scooped up a weeping soldier, his red uniform torn and dark with blood. Whatever forces were abroad in this compound, they were privy to the secrets of the Falcatas and had taken the Unfleshed for their own.

Screams and the rattling bark of gunfire sounded from beyond the walls of the barracks, although a curious peace reigned within.

'Put that man down,' ordered Uriel. 'The Emperor will be angry if you hurt him.'

The Lord of the Unfleshed threw his head back and let loose a terrifying roar that encompassed a lifetime's worth of anger, hurt and self-loathing.

'The Emperor does not care for him,' said the Lord of the Unfleshed, displaying an eloquence that belied his previous utterances. 'He forsook this vessel a long time ago, just as he forsook us.'

The words were spoken with a human mind, but a monster's mouth, and they came out sopping and malformed, cruel and bitter. Uriel heard the ache of loss in every mangled syllable and felt the pain behind the words, but whoever he spoke to was not the being whose flesh he addressed. Whatever intelligence dwelled behind those burning eyes was not the creature that had set foot on Salinas with him.

'Enough,' said Uriel, turning and nodding to Pasanius, who aimed his bolter towards the Lord of the Unfleshed. 'You have to stop this, now!'

Seeing the weapon raised, the Lord of the Unfleshed lifted the weeping soldier high and plunged him, head first, into his enormous maw.

'Imperator, no!' cried Uriel. 'Pasanius, shoot!'

The air was filled with the distinctive bangs of bolter fire and mass-reactive shells stitched a path across the Lord of the Unfleshed, each one detonating within his body. New skin and old meat erupted from him, but not before the soldier was bitten in two. Uriel leapt forward, but the lower half of the dead man was hurled into him and he crashed to the ground.

More bolter shots ripped out, but the Lord of the Unfleshed was on the move once again. Uriel rolled to his feet as he saw the Lord of the Unfleshed crash through the outer wall of the barracks, smashing the cinderblock walls to powder as he went.

Pasanius was already outside, following the creature with barks of bolter fire, and Uriel clambered over the rubble to reach the inner compound.

Uriel saw that Pasanius was as accurate as ever, but that his bolts were having little effect on the Lord of the Unfleshed beyond the cosmetic. Blood and light streamed from the Lord of the Unfleshed, but what, if any, harm these wounds were causing was hard to tell.

Soldiers fought in tight groups, overlapping fields of fire spraying the Unfleshed with controlled volleys. Heavy weapon teams were setting up their guns to support their quicker comrades. As she had when the Sons of Salinas had ambushed her forces, Verena Kain was rallying her soldiers quickly and effectively.

It wasn't nearly enough.

Against other men, even other soldiers, her masterful leadership and the courage of the Screaming Eagles would easily have won the day, but they were fighting a foe beyond any they had fought before. Explosions burst among the Unfleshed, but neither fire nor shrapnel nor bullets could bring them low.

They shrugged off wounds that would have killed even the largest tyrannic beast thrice over, smashing through entire platoons and killing every soldier in the time it took to scream. Wounded light flowed from them as they were hit, the glow knitting solid over the wound like a bandage.

The monsters were unstoppable, killing with a demented frenzy of rage.

Uriel's heart turned to ice as he saw the savage joy in the faces of the Unfleshed.

Whatever hopes he had held of their redemption, or for a new life, were being dashed before his eyes. There could be no atonement or forgiveness for relish taken in wanton slaughter.

Even as he ran to join the battle, a missile skewed in flight as its firer was disembowelled by a hooking punch from a clawed fist. It slashed through the air in a wild, spiral pattern before impacting on the compound's main generator building.

Uriel dived forward as the warhead punched through the lightly armoured door of the building and exploded, destroying the generator in a mighty blast that lifted the roof hundreds of feet into the air on a column of fire and demolished a portion of the outer wall.

The compound was plunged into darkness.

'WHAT DO YOU mean, Sylvanus Thayer's still alive?' demanded Cawlen Hurq.

'Just what I said, Cawlen,' said Pascal. 'Although he might as well be dead.'

Daron Nisato was as shocked as Hurq at the revelation that the old leader of the Sons of Salinas was alive, but the anger in Pascal's bodyguard was raw and in need of venting.

'You told us he was dead!' said Hurq, and Mesira put her hands over her ears at the noise. Nisato put an arm around her, but she flinched at his touch, moaning in anguish.

'And he was, to all intents and purposes,' said Pascal, trying to defuse Cawlen's anger. 'I found him on the battlefield the day after the fighting. There was almost nothing left of him, Cawlen, just scraps of flesh and blood. I don't know how he was still alive, but he was. I couldn't help him, so I took him to Serj Casuaban at the House of Providence.'

'To Casuaban?' said Cawlen. 'He's a Falcata!'

Pascal shook his head. 'No, he's been helping us since the Killing Ground Massacre.'

'He's been helping us? How?'

'Where did you think our medical supplies were coming from?'

Daron Nisato tried to concentrate on what the two men were saying, but Mesira was rocking back and forth with ever greater urgency.

'Why didn't you tell us?' asked Cawlen. 'We could have let the people know?'

'What good would it have done? Sylvanus was already a martyr. He had done more for us by dying than he ever could again,' said Pascal. 'Besides... He's...He's not the same man he was before.'

Nisato caught the strangeness of Pascal's tone and looked up from the weeping Mesira Bardhyl. 'What do you mean? How is he different?'

Cawlen Hurq glanced around at him and said, 'Stay out of this, enforcer. This doesn't concern you.'

Nisato stood and spun Hurq around. The big man looked set to go for his gun, but Nisato deftly plucked the weapon from the man's holster. He jammed the barrel in Hurq's belly and said, 'Sit down and shut up.'

Reluctantly, Hurq did as he was ordered and Nisato turned to Pascal Blaise. 'What did you mean he's not the same man? I've had to shoot men who woke from comas or serious injuries with latent abilities that they did not possess before. Is that what you mean?'

'Something like that,' agreed Pascal. 'He couldn't speak or move. There wasn't enough left of him to do either, but... you could feel it when you were around him.'

'Feel what?'

'His anger,' said Pascal, 'his unquenchable anger.'

A scream made both men flinch and Nisato turned to see Mesira Bardhyl standing by the window, looking out into the night's darkness with her arm extended. Her face was lit by the soft glow of the city beyond, but as they watched a brighter glow from beyond the glass illuminated her face with hot, orange light.

Nisato rushed to her side. 'What is it?' he asked.

'The Mourner,' hissed Mesira.

Daron Nisato and Pascal Blaise watched as a blooming pillar of fire lifted from beyond the edges of the city. Seconds later, the rumble of the explosion rolled over them, accompanied by the popping crack of small-arms fire.

'That's the Screaming Eagles' compound,' said Nisato. 'Your handiwork, Blaise?'

'No,' said Pascal, and Nisato believed him, 'not mine, I swear.'

'It's the Mourner,' said Mesira Bardhyl. 'He's found one. He's killing them all to get to her.'

She turned to face him and Nisato saw that she was smiling with calm serenity.

'He's coming for me next.'

URIEL HAD NO weapon but his sword, and this he put to good use as he fought his way into the mass of struggling bodies. The Unfleshed were stronger than ever, their bodies filled with a power they had not possessed before, and they had been horrifically powerful then.

A towering shape rose up before him, a monster with lumpy stumps for legs and a frill of flesh that hung from its chest and rippled with life. Unnatural bone structures beneath the skin lashed out at Uriel, but he parried desperately as taloned hooks sought the soft meat of his throat.

He rolled beneath a lashing bone hook and slashed his sword through the beast's flesh. The blade cleaved through its body, but no sooner had it torn clear than the strange light that filled the beast restored the flesh whole.

The creature howled, despite the healing effect of the light, and it backed away from him, seeking easier prey among the Screaming Eagles. Uriel let it go as he sought out Colonel Kain in the confusion of the battle.

With the generator destroyed, the conflict was being fought in the strobing darkness of muzzle flashes, las-bolts and the diffuse glow of reflected starlight. Struggling knots of soldiers ran from cover to cover as the Unfleshed tore through the compound, demolishing barricades, gun emplacements and buildings as they went.

The fuel store erupted in a great mushroom-cloud of fire as a stray round punctured its skin and the reek of promethium filled the air. Burning clouds billowed upwards and burning streams of promethium spilled through the compound.

Uriel ran through the chaos of the battle to join Pasanius, his friend firing the last of his bolt rounds at a monster with swollen arms that pounded its way through the medicae building and butchered the wounded with great, clubbing sweeps of its iron-hard fists.

'How many rounds do you have?' shouted Uriel over the din of battle.

'One magazine left,' said Pasanius, 'but it's tricky to reload.'

Uriel swapped his sword for the bolter, ducking behind the cover of an avalanche of sandbags as he quickly and expertly reloaded the weapon.

'Thanks,' said Pasanius, as Uriel returned the weapon and took his sword back. 'Now what? What in the name of the Emperor is going on? Why are they doing this?'

'They're not,' said Uriel, finally catching sight of Colonel Kain.

The bark of heavy weapons joined the fight as soldiers clambered up to the hatches of parked Chimeras and unleashed torrents of lasfire from multi-lasers or hails of shells from heavy bolters.

'What do you mean?' demanded Pasanius, firing over the sandbags into the monster attacking the medicae building. 'I'd say they are.'

'This isn't them,' persisted Uriel. 'I don't know what, but there's something controlling them, I'm sure of it.'

Pasanius shrugged, and Uriel realised that, at this moment, it didn't matter why the Unfleshed were attacking the Screaming Eagles, just that they were. The Lord of the Unfleshed was killing men by the dozen with every roar and swing of his massive fists, his flesh an impregnable fortress and proof against all weapons.

'Then I hope you have a plan,' said Pasanius. 'Otherwise they're going to kill everyone here, including us.'

Uriel had no answer for Pasanius, but then the roar of engines sounded from the hangars as a trio of Leman Russ battle tanks rumbled from within. The main guns would be useless within the compound, but each vehicle carried a host of support weapons and their bulk alone could turn the tide of the battle.

A great cheer went up from the Screaming Eagles as the tanks emerged, and Colonel Kain lifted her sword high for all to see. A soldier unfurled a banner and the sight of the crimson emblem of the Achaman Falcatas gave the soldiers heart.

Uriel watched the lead tank, the vehicle that had begun to power his armour, split the night with an incandescent spear of light from the lascannon mounted on its hull. A beast with scything limbs fell, sheared in two by the beam, its entrails cooked and its blood boiled to steam. The other tanks sawed the bullets of their sponson weapons across the Unfleshed, the creatures driven back from the fight by the sheer weight of fire.

The great metal beasts did not cow the Lord of the Unfleshed, however. He cast aside the body of the soldier he had just killed and charged the tank with his head lowered and his fists balled at his side.

Just as it seemed he would run headlong into the vehicle, the Lord of the Unfleshed leapt into the air and landed on the tank's frontal section. Bullets ripped across his body, but slowed him not at all. Monstrously powerful hands closed on the foreshortened barrel of the tank's main gun and inhumanly strong arms ripped upwards.

With a screech of tortured metal and a fountain of sparks the entire turret was wrenched clear. The turret gunner fell from the ruin of the main gun's housing, only to be crushed by the treads of his tank. The Lord of the Unfleshed slammed the twisted wreckage into the side of the tank, crushing the side guns and buckling the hull inwards with tremendous booms of metal.

The tank's engine howled in protest, jetting filthy blue oil-smoke as it seized and died. Flames erupted across its rear quarter and with his foe defeated, the Lord of the Unfleshed hurled the buckled and twisted mass of the turret across the compound and vaulted to the ground.

With a rousing battle cry, Colonel Kain led the charge of the Screaming Eagles.

Uriel rose from cover as they charged, admiring their courage while cursing the futility of the gesture. These men could not triumph against the Unfleshed, not while some dark power worked their bodies like marionettes and healed killing wounds.

'Come on!' he shouted, and Pasanius rose with him.

He charged through the blazing compound, the reek of burning promethium filling his senses and the thick pall of black smoke making his eyes water and his throat burn. The heat was incredible, leaping flames devouring the compound with a furious appetite.

The Unfleshed and the Screaming Eagles clashed in the centre of the compound, a battle fought in the bright heat of the fires. It was a battle that could only end one way, but the Screaming Eagles fought with a fatalistic fervour that spoke volumes of their involvement in the Killing Ground Massacre.

Uriel swept his sword out as a beast with arms like pistons and a hunched spine loped towards him through the smoke and flames. Its mouth was a lopsided horror of broken teeth and rotted gums, its eyes a gelatinous mess of run-together pupils and milky irises. Its flesh was glistening and new, but rotten and slick, as though grown from diseased cultures.

It spat a mouthful of obscenities, its fist thundering towards him as it screamed. Uriel turned the blow aside and spun around the creature, driving his sword down into its back. The blade grated on a malformed spine and Uriel twisted the sword as he thrust it deep into the monster's body.

It shrieked and dropped to its knees as Pasanius ran up and hammered his armoured boot into its face. Fangs snapped and bloody phlegm sprayed the air. Uriel wrenched his sword free in a wash of light and frothing blood. Pasanius jammed his bolter into the beast's mouth and pulled the trigger. Light exploded in its skull and the back of its head mushroomed outwards.

The monster collapsed, steaming brain matter leaking from the opened lid of its skull, and Uriel saw a mist of light follow it into the air. He cried out as he felt the enraged frustration within the light and dropped to his knees as the force of it threatened to overwhelm him.

Uriel dropped his sword as his vision blurred and he saw the compound and the walls surrounding it thronged with observers, spectral figures who watched the carnage enacted in their name dispassionately. Hundreds of figures jostled for position on the walls and Uriel shook his head as he fought to free his thoughts from their desire for vengeance.

'Uriel!' cried Pasanius, and the spell was broken.

The creature they had fought was dead, the healing light having fled at its demise, but Uriel saw that this was the only triumph in the battle so far.

Flames had claimed those the Unfleshed had not. Men of fire screamed as they were consumed and Uriel felt a horrible sense of vindication from the invisible voyeurs who had set this slaughter in motion.

'We have to get out of here,' said Pasanius. 'We can't win this.'

Uriel nodded, sweeping up his sword. 'I'll try to reach Kain.'

He rose to his feet and sought the banner of the Screaming Eagles, catching sight of it through the flames as Colonel Kain fought a losing battle against the monsters butchering her soldiers.

'Over there!' said Uriel. 'Come on.'

They set off through the flames towards the beleaguered warriors, and Uriel could feel his skin blistering from the heat. He could only imagine the pain the mortal soldiers must be feeling.

Uriel saw Verena Kain fall, bleeding from a deep wound to her shoulder. The creature closed on her for the kill, but her men valiantly formed a line before her, guns rippling with fire and curved swords ready to defend their colonel.

In the face of their firepower, the beast fell back and Uriel skidded to a halt beside Kain.

The woman was tough, Uriel had to give her that. Her left arm hung uselessly at her side and her face was a fire-lit mask of blood. She looked up at Uriel and her face was wretched with anger.

'My men are dying because of you!' she shouted over the gunfire and roar of flames. 'I don't know how, but I know this has something to do with you.'

'Colonel Kain,' began Uriel, 'you're right, but deal with it later. We have to get out of here, now. This isn't a fight we can win.'

'Never!' said Kain. 'The Screaming Eagles never sound the retreat.'

'I know,' snapped Uriel. 'I heard Old Serenity's saying, but he died, and so will you if we stay here.'

He thought she was going to refuse, but saw the spark of anger fade from her eyes to be replaced by the weary resignation of acceptance. Uriel nodded and turned to Pasanius as an enormous shadow blotted out the light of the fires. The bearer of the Screaming Eagles' banner was killed as his head was ripped from his shoulders and a steaming pillar of blood erupted from his shorn neck.

Uriel spun around as the banner fell. The Lord of the Unfleshed towered over him, his form impossibly massive and swollen since Uriel had last laid eyes upon him. Light shone beneath his skin, too bright to look upon where it oozed from his wounds, and his muscles were aflame with borrowed power.

A fist like a boulder slammed into Uriel, hurling him through the air to land in an ungainly heap against the hull of the wrecked Leman Russ. Bright lights danced before his eyes and he fought for breath, hearing the bark of bolter fire as Pasanius opened fire.

The Lord of the Unfleshed smote Pasanius with a terrible blow that crushed him to the ground, and then reached for Verena Kain. The colonel of the Screaming Eagles had lifted her regiment's banner from the earth and the rippling silk of the flag was on fire. Uriel cried out and pushed himself to his feet, swaying as he lurched towards the Lord of the Unfleshed.

Colonel Kain hacked at the Lord of the Unfleshed with her falcata as she was lifted from the ground in his enormous fist. Blood and light seeped from the wounds, but she could not break the hold the enormous creature had on her.

Uriel saw the anger on the Lord of the Unfleshed's face, an anger that was so distilled and overwhelming that it halted him in its tracks, so singular was it. This was no anger the Unfleshed possessed, this was the anger of those without voice, the anger of those who had only this last revenge left to them.

The Lord of the Unfleshed carried the struggling colonel over to the blazing plume of promethium that was all that remained of the fuel store. Uriel tried to keep up, but his limbs were leaden and the breath burned in his lungs.

'No,' he hissed through gritted teeth as he realised what must come next.

The Lord of the Unfleshed paused, as though to relish what he was about to do. He leaned in close to Verena Kain and though he whispered the words, they echoed in the skulls of everyone within the compound.

'You were there.'

Then he hurled her into the white heat of the flames.

Uriel cried out, a wordless exclamation at the horror of this murder, and the Lord of the Unfleshed tipped back his head to let loose a terrible, roaring howl of desperation. The creature turned his wounded, blistered face to Uriel and the look that passed between them was intimate, a moment of shared repulsion.

The Lord of the Unfleshed dropped its face and the moment of connection was over as the multitude of minds that had taken over the workings of the Unfleshed tightened their grip.

There was no gunfire anymore. The compound was silent, but for the anguished cries of dying soldiers. The Lord of the Unfleshed roared and called his tribe to him as Uriel staggered through the bloody debris of the battle.

'Why?' he shouted. 'Why did you need to do this?'

The Lord of the Unfleshed looked up and the white light of vengeance burned there like fiery comets in his eyes.

'Because they were there,' he said. 'All must be punished.'

With that dreadful pronouncement, he turned away, leaping through the gap in the wall blown by the explosion of the generator building. The remaining Unfleshed swiftly followed him, and Uriel saw that they were moving towards the simmering city of Barbadus.

With awful certainty, Uriel knew that this night's bloodshed was not over.

♈ FOURTEEN

LETO BARBADEN WATCHED the fires raging to the north of his city from the highest garret of his private library. He knew the source was the Screaming Eagles' compound, but he felt nothing for the men and women he knew must be dying beneath the pall of smoke, a dark smudge against the night sky.

He knew the reasons for the attack, but cared little for them. The people of Barbadus were venting their aggression against their conquerors. It was the only reaction the corpse of a beaten populace could make against their rulers, the last, spastic, gasps of a body that did not yet know it was dead.

That it was only natural was no excuse, however, and he had already ordered more units onto the streets to keep the peace, with force if need be. He would have order, even though blood would be spilt and lives lost to enforce it.

Barbaden turned away from the shielded window and laced his hands behind his back as he descended the iron screw-stair to the main floor of the library. He had known that the early years of his governorship would be difficult; it was the lot of great men to deal with difficult times, but it was a measure of their greatness how they dealt with them.

He reached the bottom of the stairs and crossed the marble floor of the library, taking a deep breath of the musty odour of his books, papers and manuscripts. He had painstakingly assembled the books over decades of war, transporting them from campaign to campaign. The solid, reassuring feel of the facts and figures bound to their pages were a constant comfort to him and he slid a gold-spined volume from the shelf, a biography of Solar Macharius, as he made his way to his drinks cabinet.

He had always admired the great Lord Solar, a man of singular vision and determination who was only undone by the cowardice of lesser men. It was the curse of genius that, so often, their greatness was thwarted by the shortcomings of their contemporaries. Lord Solar Macharius had reached the edge of known space, had stood at the very edge of the galaxy, and had dared to meet the gaze of the halo stars.

Only tremulous men who laughingly called themselves warriors had prevented him from conquering those stars for the Emperor. Only the weakness of spirit of his followers had prevented Macharius from achieving his true potential. Leto Barbaden had long ago decided that no such weakness, in him or others, would hold him back from achieving his greatness.

He poured a generous measure of raquir before sitting in the room's only chair and opening the smooth, vellum pages of the book. His beloved words stared out at him, their beauty containing immutable facts and the course of history in every cursive line and illuminated letter.

Leto Barbaden loved to read volumes of history, the more detailed the better, for he was a man to whom the minutiae of history were the choicest sweetmeats. History was written by the victors, an aphorism as old as time, and thus Leto Barbaden knew that his position in history was assured, at least on this world.

Where others might see cruelty, he saw strength of will.

Where others saw coldness and lack of emotion, he saw resolve.

Leto Barbaden knew he was humanity without the drag of conscience or emotion.

He embodied reason and logic uncluttered by emotion, for emotion was a failing of those without the courage of their convictions.

Some might call him a monster, but they were fools.

This was a harsh, grim galaxy and only those who could detach themselves from the ballast of emotion could rise above such petty concerns as morality or right and wrong to do what needed to be done.

He had known that since Colonel Landon had been killed at Koreda Gorge along with his senior officers. The men had called him Old Serenity, a name Barbaden found absurd. How could a name like that be suitable for a man who made war his profession?

Landon would not have had the stomach for the conquest of Salinas. His passions were too close to the surface and he cared too deeply for his men to have succeeded. To Landon, bringing his men back alive in the face of the steel teeth of war was all important, but Leto Barbaden knew that if there was one resource the Imperium was not short of, it was manpower. Machines and weapons were precious commodities, but soldiers could always be replaced, and so too could populations.

It was a truth Barbaden had come to early in the war against the Sons of Salinas, realising that no matter how many people he killed, there would always be more. People were ugly, brutish confections of meat, bone and desires, living sordid little lives and breeding like flies as they went about their pointless lives.

It seemed inconceivable that no one else was able to see this, that life was nothing to be valued so highly.

He alone had understood this stark fact when he had ordered the destruction of Khaturian, knowing that the scale of such killing would so inflame his enemy's passions that they would have no choice but to meet him in battle.

Sylvanus Thayer, who had proved to be a worthy adversary until the death of his family, had led his warriors into an unwinnable battle, and Barbaden smiled as he remembered the sight of the scorched battlefield that had seen the Sons of Salinas destroyed.

Once again, emotion had destroyed a potentially great general.

He read for another hour, sipping his raquir and flipping to quotes from Solar Macharius that he had long ago memorised. His finger trailed down the page until he found his favourite.

'There can be no bystanders in the battle for survival,' he read aloud. 'Anyone who will not fight by your side is an enemy you must crush.'

Barbaden smiled as he read the quote, recognising the genius inherent in those few words.

Brevity and clarity were traits he admired and attempted to emulate.

A knock came at the door and he said, 'Enter.'

The doors opened and the frock-coated Eversham entered, his face pale and his steps hurried. Barbaden lifted his head from his book, seeing that his equerry carried an encrypted data-slate and noting his unkempt appearance.

'Your formal attire is somewhat dishevelled, Eversham,' said Barbaden. 'Smarten up before I have you broken down to kitchen scrubber.'

Eversham looked set to speak without smartening up, but had the sense to pause and fasten his collar and straighten his coat first. As the man opened his mouth to speak, Barbaden cut him off.

'Are you familiar with the works of Lord Solar Macharius?' he asked.

Eversham shook his head, and Barbaden saw that it was taking all his iron control not to speak out of turn. 'No, my lord. I regret I am not.'

'This is one of my favourite quotes, "The meaning of victory is not to defeat your enemy but to destroy him, to eradicate him from living memory, to leave no remnant of his endeavours, to crush utterly his every achievement and remove from all record his every trace of existence. From that defeat no enemy can ever recover. That is the meaning of victory". Rather inspiring isn't it?'

'Yes, my lord,' said Eversham, 'very.'

'You are sweating, Eversham,' noted Barbaden. 'Are you unwell?'

'No, governor,' replied his equerry, holding out the data-slate, as though anxious to be rid of it.

'Tell me,' began Barbaden, ignoring the slate, 'what is the nature of the trouble at the Screaming Eagles' barracks?'

'We don't know yet, my lord. There are reports of gunfire and several explosions, but we have been unable to make contact with Colonel Kain or any of her staff.'

'Very well, order two companies of palace guard to find out what is happening and to secure the site.'

'Of course,' said Eversham, once more offering him the data-slate.

'What is this?' asked Barbaden.

'An astropathic communication,' said Eversham. 'The Janiceps received it earlier this evening and the Diviner Primaris has just finished his interpretation.'

'A communication from whom?'

'I don't know, my lord,' replied Eversham. 'It came in with the highest priority prefix. It is evidently for your eyes only. No sooner did the diviner transcribe the words than a telepathic mnemo-virus implanted within the message erased his mind, completely.'

Curious, Barbaden took the proffered slate and slid his finger into the reader, wincing at the pinprick of the gene-sampler. With his identity confirmed, the slate flickered into life and the words of the brain-dead diviner scrolled down the screen in silver letters.

He read the body of the message and his eyes widened in surprise.

Slowly, and with deliberate care, Barbaden handed the slate back to Eversham. He closed his book and laid it on the table next to the chair. He rose to his feet and smoothed the front of his tunic, struggling to control a rising panic that stirred in his breast.

'Prepare my private embarkation deck on the upper spires,' he said. 'We are about to receive some important visitors.'

THE TRAIL OF the Unfleshed was not difficult to follow, for they had not been careful in their passage. Their tracks were easy to see, but even had they moved without leaving imprints on the ground, the debris of their course would have been easy to recognise.

Uriel rode in the commander's hatch of a Chimera, its width only barely able to accommodate his genhanced girth. He had been forced to leave his armour in the care of Enginseer Imerian back at the compound, for there was no time to encase himself within it and no telling how long the charge in the backpack would last. If he survived the night, he would return for it in the morning.

Beneath him, Pasanius and five soldiers rode in the Chimera's troop compartment, bloody and in shock at the ease with which their fastness had been breached and their colonel slain.

Two more Chimeras, laden with those soldiers still fit enough to fight, followed behind Uriel's, racing through the dim light of the city's outskirts as they followed the trail of destruction unleashed by their quarry.

In truth, Uriel didn't know exactly what he hoped to achieve by following the Unfleshed. If the entire company of Screaming Eagles could not defeat them, what chance did this ragtag assembly of force have?

He only knew that he had to catch them, if for no other reason than to salve his own conscience. The destruction wrought at the Screaming Eagles' compound was his fault, and the guilt of what his foolish trust had allowed to happen weighed heavily on his soul.

How could he have been so blind to the bestial core of the Unfleshed? Yes, their outward appearance was that of monsters, but Uriel had seen past that to what he had believed was the human nobility at their heart.

Though he felt sure that some darker power was at work within them, he knew it would have found no purchase in souls that were pure. Some rotten canker must have lurked at the heart of the Unfleshed for this power to latch onto, and Uriel cursed himself for a fool for not seeing it.

The deaths of these soldiers were on his conscience, no matter what they might have done in the past to be deserving of retribution. Uriel pushed such thoughts from his mind, forcing himself to concentrate on the task at hand.

The Chimeras rumbled through the streets of the city, the buildings around them tall and metallic, squat and brick-built. The variegated architecture of Barbadus sped past them, flickering faces at shuttered, windowless openings watching them fearfully as they passed. That death was abroad on the streets of Barbadus was common knowledge, the breath of its passing emptying the streets of all but the most curious. Even those few lingering pedestrians quickly abandoned whatever task they were about to be clear of the streets as Uriel's desperate procession sped past.

Death was hunting tonight and it would take whoever called its name.

THOUGH IT WAS too far away and too dark to make out any details, it was clear that a tremendous battle was underway at the Screaming Eagles' compound. Flames licked the sky and the rattle of gunfire had ceased.

'Whatever was going on over there's over now,' observed Pascal.

Nisato did not reply, staring into the distant flames as if to discern some answer from the darkness. Pascal Blaise claimed not to have any knowledge of what had happened, and, much as Nisato wanted to disbelieve him, he knew in his gut that the man was telling the truth.

This had nothing to do with the Sons of Salinas, but if not them, then who?

'We should get out of here,' said Pascal Blaise. 'If she's right and whatever hit the Screaming Eagles is coming here...'

Nisato nodded and turned back to Mesira. She had resumed her earlier position on the bed, knees drawn up to her chest and arms wrapped around them.

'Mesira?' he said. She looked up, her tear-streaked face no longer drawn into the scrunched expression of fear and guilt it perpetually wore. 'What happened out there tonight? Do you know?'

'It's the Mourner,' she replied. 'He's killed her and now it's my turn.'

'Killed who?'

'Colonel Kain. I felt her die. It was painful.'

'For you?' asked Nisato.

'For both of us.'

Pascal Blaise joined him at Mesira's side. 'Kain's dead? You're sure?'

Mesira nodded and Nisato saw the hollow satisfaction in Blaise's eyes.

The leader of the Sons of Salinas looked up and met his gaze. 'Don't expect me to shed any tears for that bitch,' he said. 'Kain led the Screaming Eagles into Khaturian. She had the blood of thousands on her hands. She got what she deserved.'

'And what do you deserve, Pascal?' said Nisato. 'What do any of us deserve? Haven't we all got blood on our hands? Do we all deserve to die?'

'Maybe,' shrugged Blaise. 'Maybe we do. I've killed men, yes. I've shot them and blown them up, but I don't feel any remorse. The men I killed came as invaders to my homeland. What else could I have done? If soldiers with guns attack the people you love, you'd fight them, wouldn't you?'

'I suppose,' said Nisato, 'but–'

'But nothing,' snapped Pascal. 'This was our world. We were loyal to the Golden Throne, but Barbaden wouldn't listen to us. He killed our leaders and butchered our soldiers. What kind of people would we have been if we hadn't resisted? And don't pretend you're better than me, enforcer. I can't imagine that your hands are any less bloody than mine. How many terrified soldiers have knelt before you, begging for their lives before you shot them in the name of the Emperor? Dozens? Hundreds? Thousands even?'

Nisato rounded on Pascal Blaise, his anger rising with every accusation hurled in his face.

'Yes, I've killed men too,' he snarled, 'and every one of them deserved his fate. They had faltered in their service to the Emperor.'

'Then perhaps we are not so different after all,' said Pascal. 'Perhaps right and wrong are just matters of perspective.'

Nisato sighed, the anger draining from him as the truth of Pascal Blaise's words sank in. He sighed and sat next to Mesira, running a protective hand through her hair.

'There is no right or wrong in our professions,' said Nisato. 'The present changes the past from moment to moment. We can only pray for the future to vindicate our actions.'

Mesira looked up at him, smiling. 'I'm not afraid any more,' she said.

'No?'

She shook her head. 'No. All these years I've lived with what I saw, what I allowed to happen. Now it's over. He's coming for me and I'll be at peace.'

'I won't let anyone harm you,' said Nisato, 'I promise.'

Mesira smiled and Daron Nisato had never seen her more beautiful. The cares and troubles she had worn like a second skin fell away, leaving her luminous, as though a gentle light shone within her bones.

'You don't have to worry about me, Daron,' said Mesira. 'It's going to be all right.'

'I hope so.'

She leaned over and kissed his cheek, the touch of her lips on his skin electric, sending a pleasurable, warm sense of peace through him. 'You are a good man, Daron, better than you know.'

Mesira Bardhyl stood, taking his hand, and he allowed himself to be pulled to his feet. She reached out to take the hand of Pascal Blaise and said, 'If this world is to survive, then it will be men like you that will save it. You have both done terrible things in your lives, but they are in the past. All that matters now is the future. Old hatreds must be put aside and new bonds forged between the people of this world. Do you understand?'

Nisato looked from Mesira to Pascal. Her words were like a cool stream that washed him from his decaying suit of skin to the very core of his marrow. Was this some psyker magic? Had whatever madness possessed her to wander naked from her home unlocked yet more powers within her?

Whatever flowed from Mesira, he could feel no evil within it and let its healing light bathe him with its restorative powers.

'I understand,' he said, seeing the same illumination within Pascal Blaise. Without knowing how, he knew that they would both be changed forever by this contact.

Mesira released their hands and Nisato felt a sting of disappointment at the withdrawal of her touch.

The door opened behind her and Cawlen Hurq re-entered the room, a rifle slung over his shoulder, and the pistol, which Nisato had returned to him before he'd left, clutched in his fist. Nisato felt nothing for Hurq; not hate, not fear, nothing. It was as if all the rancour and posturing that had passed between them had been erased.

'Cawlen,' said Pascal, taking a moment to recover from the contact with Mesira. 'How many men have we got here?'

'Including us, eight,' said Hurq, 'but I've sent the word out and there'll be others arriving soon. What are we expecting? Falcatas?' The man's tone was eager and Nisato felt pity for him, so caught up in his hatred was he.

'No, I don't think so,' said Pascal. 'I'm not sure exactly, but stay alert.'

Nisato took Mesira's hand and followed Pascal Blaise as he made his way towards the door. She took his hand willingly and together they descended the stairs he had climbed earlier that evening.

Cawlen Hurq pushed open the door to the bar and they entered the smoky, sweat-pit of the common area. The heat and stench of the place took Nisato's breath away, despite him only having left it recently.

Heads rose from drinks as they entered the room, and Nisato felt acutely vulnerable, more than he had when he'd first arrived. Then he only had his own safety to worry about, but now he had to keep

Mesira safe from whatever force she believed was coming to claim her. Beyond that, he now felt responsible for Pascal Blaise's safety, which was stupid, for he had armed men in the bar and, if Hurq was to be believed, there were more on the way.

The armed men he had spotted on his arrival made their way through the bar towards them, and the crowded drinkers made way for them without complaint. Nisato caught snatches of conversation as they made their way through the throng.

News of the attack on the Screaming Eagles' compound had reached the bar and Nisato was surprised to see fearful looks being cast towards Pascal Blaise.

'What's going on?' he said, drawing level with Blaise. 'Why do I get the feeling these people would as soon lynch you as look at you?'

'They're afraid,' said Pascal over his shoulder.

'Of what?'

'Reprisals,' replied Pascal. 'They think we hit the Screaming Eagles and they're afraid of what Barbaden will do in response. I told you I was tired of the killing. Well, I'm not the only one.'

Nisato saw it now, the fear and tiredness in every face. It was a tiredness he could understand. He looked back into Mesira's face and smiled. She moved gracefully through the crowded bar and all who looked upon her seemed touched by the same balm that had eased their troubled souls upstairs.

She was a calming ripple in a pond, the soothing wind that cools the day.

Nisato reluctantly tore his gaze from her as Pascal Blaise placed a hand on his shoulder.

'Wait. Let Cawlen's men check outside first.'

Nisato nodded and pulled Mesira close. Over the hushed babble of conversation, he could hear strange sounds from beyond the steel door of the bar, a mingled din of distant rumbling engines and heavy thuds.

He started as he heard the unmistakable sound of gunfire and an awful, blood-chilling roar of animal hunger. The sound echoed inside the bar and every head turned towards them.

'What the hell was that?' said Cawlen Hurq. More gunfire sounded, followed by shrieks: horrible, agonising shrieks and bellowing roars, and wet sounds like tearing cloth and snapping wood.

Hurq backed away from the door, his face fearful. That fear was contagious. People began to shout and, as yet another monstrous roar echoed within the bar, panic took hold. Men and women pushed one another aside in their haste to escape the bar, heading for back doors or windows that led away from the source of the terrible roars.

Nisato drew his pistol as another roar sounded, this time from right on the other side of the door. The noise was deafening and a sickening, rotten meat smell was forced inside the bar by a heaving, noxious breath.

'Let's find another way out of here,' hissed Pascal.

'Yes,' agreed Nisato, pulling Mesira with him.

Cawlen Hurq followed them and as Nisato risked a glance over his shoulder, the front of the bar was ripped upwards. Corrugated sheets of metal flew off into the night and the door crumpled inwards under a terrifyingly powerful impact. Metal screamed and buckled, and the iron girder that served as a lintel was ripped upward and tossed away as easily as a dog would discard a chewed bone.

Hot air blasted into the bar and the animal reek of spoiled meat became unbearable.

Nisato looked up into the face of a nightmare.

It was a monster, a bloodied, burnt and fanged nightmare with sick coals for eyes. Its monstrous proportions were beyond any measure of sanity or belief, its appearance that of a malformed giant that had suffered unimaginable torments.

'Emperor save us!' cried Pascal Blaise, his face slack with horror as he saw that the beast had not come alone, but with a pack of equally horrific monsters at its heels. The panic that had seized the crowds exploded in a stampede of utter terror. Bodies slammed into Nisato and he fought to hold onto Mesira as the tide of screaming people sought to part them.

Cawlen Hurq raised his rifle and Nisato wanted to laugh at the absurdity of fighting beasts of such terrible appearance with so paltry a weapon. The man screamed an oath as he opened fire, bright bolts of energy spitting from the barrel to explode harmlessly on the creature's chest.

Casually, as though swatting an irritant, the beast batted Cawlen Hurq across the room. The man slammed head first into the beaten iron bar top and even over the sound of tearing metal and screaming crowds, Daron Nisato heard his neck snap with an awful, brittle crack.

Nisato tried to drag Mesira away from the ripped open entrance to the bar, but she released his hand and he was carried away from her, watching helplessly as the monsters tore their way inside the bar.

'It is time,' she said, her voice sounding like a clear bell in his head, 'time to die.'

FIFTEEN

URIEL HEARD THE screams and the sound of tearing metal. The rumble of the trio of Chimeras echoed from the ramshackle walls of the street and curious onlookers were beginning to spill from their homes to see what drama was being played out on their doorstep.

From his vantage point in the commander's hatch, Uriel could see light spilling into the sky and could hear screams that were issued in terror of the monstrous. Whatever bloody task the Unfleshed were about was in full swing by the sounds of it.

A smashed building on the corner of the street provided another sign as to the passing of the Unfleshed and the Chimera's driver expertly guided the heavy vehicle around the cascaded tumble of timber, stone and steel.

Beyond the corner, the street widened out into a stone-paved square, and the few onlookers that had been driven into the street by the noise, sensibly retreated into their homes at the sight that greeted them.

'Guilliman's oath!' swore Uriel as he saw the spectacle before him.

It looked like a brightly lit pyramid of wrecked tanks, their innards hollowed out and reshaped by hammer and welding torch to form a structure with internal spaces, rooms, corridors and low-ceilinged chambers. Light and people spilled from the shuddering building, its structure and fabric under siege by the Unfleshed.

The Lord of the Unfleshed led the attack, his massively muscled arms peeling back steel as he forced his way into the structure. Myriad neon lights spat fat sparks and bathed the square before the building, surely some kind of drinking den, as well as the monsters in lurid greens, shocking pinks and deathly blues. They capered and howled as the leader of their tribe smashed a path through steel and timber like an animal breaking open a nest to devour the prey within. If the Lord of the Unfleshed was aware of their arrival, he gave no sign, but continued with his destruction of the building's frontage.

Fleeing people were snatched up by the Unfleshed and snapped and twisted until they broke, and their agonised screams ceased. Uriel heard gunfire from inside the building and wondered what the Lord of the Unfleshed could want in a place like this.

The Chimeras slowed as they entered the square, but Uriel yelled down to the driver. 'No! More speed. Use the vehicle!'

Understanding Uriel's order, the driver opened up the throttle and the Chimera roared as its speed increased. Uriel braced himself as one of the Unfleshed turned at the sound of the madly revving engine, its face seeming to split in two, such was the width of its fanged jaws.

Its skeleton was visible through the sickly, pallid skin that draped it, yet this new covering could only hope to cover a portion of its malformed anatomy. Long limbs, spidery and clawed, dragged on the ground and short, muscular legs drove it forwards with an ape-like gait.

Beast and machine charged towards one another until they met in a howl of flesh and machinery. The Chimera ploughed into the creature, its understanding of the power and momentum of the tank existing only for the fraction of a second before it was crushed beneath the tracks. Liquid light spurted from its pulverised carcass, blood, meat and bone ground to a paste on the paved square.

The vehicle skidded on the square as the driver instinctively feathered the throttle and applied the brakes. The engine revved one last time and died, mushrooming clouds of stinking, acrid smoke belching from the exhausts as the driver fought to restart the engine.

'Pasanius! With me!' shouted Uriel, pulling himself up from the commander's hatch. He vaulted to the hard ground as the assault door on the back of the vehicle opened and Pasanius led the warriors out onto the strangely lit battlefield.

Uriel's other two Chimeras screamed to a halt on either side of his and the warriors disembarked with practiced efficiency. No matter the losses they had taken and no matter what they may have done in the past, these men and women were soldiers first and foremost, and had learned their lessons well.

They formed up in squads and Uriel felt a forgotten sense of pride at the idea of leading men into battle once more. No matter that these soldiers were not Ultramarines of the Fourth Company, they were warriors of the Emperor and that made them mighty.

'Together! We finish this together! Are you with me?' yelled Uriel, holding his golden-hilted sword up for all to see.

The soldiers unsheathed their falcatas and roared their affirmation as Uriel turned and charged towards the devastated bar.

THE MONSTER'S THICK, veined arm reached into the bar, questing for Mesira. She seemed to welcome the creature's attentions, for she ignored Daron Nisato's shouted pleas to flee from it and make her way through the mob towards him.

Blinded by panic, many of the bar's patrons stumbled into the path of the enormous creature. The lucky ones blundered past it into the night and safety, the less fortunate were torn to fleshy rags or bitten in two.

The press of the crowd was preventing Mesira from approaching the monster any closer, for it seemed that such was her goal. The terrifying creature was utterly fixated upon her, only prevented from reaching her by what strength remained in the collapsed frontage of the bar. For once, Nisato had cause to be thankful that this part of Junktown was comprised of the debris of his old regiment, for it was all that was preventing the creature from gaining access.

Had the bar been constructed from traditional building materials, the beast would even now be feasting on Mesira's bones and wrapping her entrails around its neck. Only the steel girders and beams looted from abandoned tanks had thus far prevented it from simply bludgeoning its way inside and devouring her and everyone else inside.

The structure of the bar groaned and heaved as load bearing members were smashed asunder. Metal ground on metal as lintels were compressed and weight was redistributed to portions of the structure never meant to carry such loads.

The gunmen that the late Cawlen Hurq had placed in the bar fired on the monster with their pistols, emptying magazines' worth of rounds to little or no effect. Where punctured by a bullet, the beast dribbled light and a syrupy ichor, but such wounds troubled it not at all.

The monster howled in frustration, a searing, hungry light roasting in the gouges of its eye sockets. Daron Nisato was paralysed by his fear of it, seeing a primal hunger and anger such as he could barely contemplate existing in any sane universe.

'What in the name of the warp is it?' cried Pascal Blaise, shouting to be heard over the din of the creature's assault on the building.

'I have no idea,' said Nisato. 'We have to reach Mesira and get out of here!'

'You think?' snapped Pascal Blaise, looking in every direction for a means of escape. The press of bodies was too tight and the settling of the structure had wedged many of the doors fast in their frames. Grunting men heaved their shoulders against them, but no amount of human force could overcome the incredible weight keeping the doors shut.

Nisato saw the girder trapping the beast's shoulder twist and buckle until the weld holding it fixed to the upturned chassis of a Chimera finally gave in to the pressure and snapped. The monster roared in triumph and hauled a portion of its vast bulk into the bar.

Its roar galvanised Nisato, and his limbs found strength.

'I've got to get Mesira!' he shouted.

Blaise nodded and said, 'I'm right behind you. Go!'

Nisato lowered his shoulder and began pushing his way through the trapped, terrified crowd, using skills honed in a dozen riots to force himself a path with fist, foot and gun butt.

His progress was slow, but steady, and he could distinguish Mesira easily enough from the grimy, unwashed faces of the factory workers. Her face was serene amongst a sea of panic, beatific and calming those nearest her.

Nisato finally reached Mesira, his powerful grip closing on her thin upper arm.

'Mesira!' he yelled. 'We have to get out of here!'

She turned to face him at his touch.

'No, Daron,' she cried in alarm, '*you* have to get out of here.'

Then the frontage of the bar finally gave way with a tortured scream of metal.

URIEL HEARD THE bar front collapse and thumbed the activation stud on the hilt of his sword. The blade leapt to life with crackling energies and he felt the power of the weapon travel up his arm. The Unfleshed had turned to face them and six of the enormous creatures stood between him and the bar.

Pasanius stood next to him, his bolter held at his side.

'So what's the plan?' asked Pasanius.

'I need you to lead the soldiers,' said Uriel. 'Protect the innocent.'

'What are you going to do?'

'I'm going inside,' said Uriel. 'I've got a feeling there are answers within.'

'There you go again,' groaned Pasanius as a beast with elongated jaws and a distended belly that glistened with writhing motion broke from the pack of beasts towards them. 'You and your damn feelings.'

A volley of las-fire peppered the creature and it screeched in pain. Hissing, steaming light erupted from its swollen limbs and gut.

'Go,' said Uriel, slapping a palm on Pasanius's shoulder guard. 'Lead them.'

Pasanius nodded and marched to join the red-jacketed soldiers, who advanced with their rifles blazing. Individually, lasguns were a poor man's weapon, but gathered en masse, they were formidable and only a fool would underestimate the effect of a massed volley of fire.

The Unfleshed roused themselves from the wanton slaughter of the bar's patrons at these attacks, their howls of anguish at odds with the purposeful light that surrounded them. The creatures writhed in the glow that spilled from their wounds, as though their own ambitions were at odds with the purpose to which they were being driven.

The Lord of the Unfleshed pushed his way inside the bar and Uriel ran towards him, leaving Pasanius to lead the Falcatas in battle. His friend could inspire warriors of the Astartes to undreamed of valour and these soldiers had the honour of being commanded by one of the Ultramarines' finest.

If they survived this night, they would be feted for the rest of their lives.

Uriel quickly made his way around the fighting, heading for the frenzied fury of the Lord of the Unfleshed. The creature had torn its way into the bar. Screams and the bark of pistols sounded from within.

Portions of the structure were beginning to buckle and groan, and it wouldn't take much for the whole thing to come crashing down. Whatever he could do here, he would have to do fast.

The Lord of the Unfleshed pushed his way fully into the bar and Uriel vaulted a fallen piece of masonry as he found an open section of wall where iron panelling had come away from the structure.

Even without his armour, his physique was almost too broad to fit and he felt the metal tear at his tunic. He ducked his head and the smell of the bar hit him. It stank of sweat, raw meat and strong liquor, but most of all it stank of fear.

The Lord of the Unfleshed towered at one end of the bar, his form monstrous and swollen. Whatever had happened to him in the mountains had seen him become more terrible than Uriel could ever have imagined, for mixed with the terrifying power that surged through him, Uriel saw the humanity of him, the skin, the anger and the fear.

All the things that made a person human were distilled and magnified within his breast, but whatever daemons drove the Lord of the Unfleshed to this killing rage were of an order of magnitude greater than any human could ever aspire to.

A woman in a pale robe stood before the Lord of the Unfleshed, her expression serene, in complete contrast to the horror on every other face in the bar. Uriel's memory quickly cast up her name: Mesira Bardhyl, Governor Barbaden's psychic truth-seeker.

In the space of a heartbeat, Uriel also saw the enforcer, Daron Nisato and a man who must surely be Pascal Blaise. Both men fought to reach Mesira, but he could see they would be too late.

'Over here!' he shouted, his voice easily cutting through the din of the bar's collapse. Glass smashed, timber cracked and metal groaned, but every head in the bar turned towards him.

The Lord of the Unfleshed looked up and its eyes burned with a mixture of anger and loathing. The light that bathed him spilled from its mouth like droplets of molten gold and Uriel felt a wave of pity for him. The core of the Lord of the Unfleshed remained his own, but was goaded to slaughter by some outside presence.

Uriel dropped into the bar, its terrified patrons backing away from him as much as they did the Lord of the Unfleshed. The creature seemed momentarily confused, as though it was fighting a battle within itself.

Its confusion gave Daron Nisato the time he needed, and he wrapped his hand around Mesira Bardhyl's arm, pulling her away from the hulking monster. Her cry broke the deadlock within the Lord of the Unfleshed's body and it reached towards her with a clawed hand extended.

Pascal Blaise fired his pistol at the Lord of the Unfleshed, one bullet finding its mark in the creature's eye. Viscous fluid spurted and the Lord of the Unfleshed howled, not even the healing light that filled him able to blot out the pain of the wound.

The Lord of the Unfleshed snatched for Mesira again and Uriel leapt to intercept him. Knowing he had no choice, he swung his sword down on the Lord of the Unfleshed's arm. The blade's energies bit through the meat of the arm, but juddered to a halt and slid clear on the creature's bone.

The Lord of the Unfleshed roared and snatched the arm back, lashing out with his other. Uriel ducked and another portion of the bar was destroyed, bottles and mirrored glass crashing to the floor.

Uriel rose to his feet and the Lord of the Unfleshed followed him as he backed away to the tear in the wall through which he had entered the bar.

'Go!' he shouted. 'Nisato, get these people out of here!'

The enforcer nodded, still holding Mesira to him. Her face was twisted in anguish, but in the brief moment Uriel had before the Lord of the Unfleshed came at him, it seemed as though it was due to her rescue rather than the danger.

As the Lord of the Unfleshed followed Uriel, the panicked crowds pressed into the back wall of the bar broke for freedom, fleeing through the enormous hole the monster had torn in the bar's outer wall.

Uriel continued backing away from the Lord of the Unfleshed, giving Nisato enough time to get the people clear. The enforcer handed off Mesira Bardhyl to Pascal Blaise just as the Lord of the Unfleshed grew tired of his prey backing away and charged.

The Lord of the Unfleshed's bulk was too enormous to dodge, so Uriel leapt towards him. His sword slashed at his foe's chest, the blade easily parting skin and flesh, but unable to work deeper into the meat of the body. A thunderous fist slammed into Uriel's side and he was hurled backwards.

He slammed into a steel column, his body flaring in pain at the impact. Uriel fought for breath and staggered upright as he saw the Lord of the Unfleshed turn from him and haul his bulk across the bar with horrifying speed.

Once again the creature was fixated on Mesira Bardhyl and Uriel watched as Pascal Blaise attempted to protect her. He fired his pistol, but it was wasted effort and the Lord of the Unfleshed hurled the leader of the Sons of Salinas aside with contemptuous ease.

Uriel pushed himself across the wrecked bar and Daron Nisato cried out as he saw what was happening. Once again, Mesira stood before the Lord of the Unfleshed and this time there was no one to save her.

The mighty creature reached down and his hand closed on her skull.

'No!' screamed Daron Nisato, but the Lord of the Unfleshed cared nothing for his plea.

One quick squeeze and Mesira Bardhyl was dead, her corpse flopping to the floor as the Lord of the Unfleshed released her limp body.

With his murder done, the Lord of the Unfleshed turned from the carnage in the bar and made his way quickly to the hole torn in the structure's frontage. Uriel limped after the towering engine of flesh and blood, horrified at the casual ease with which the Lord of the Unfleshed had snuffed out Mesira Bardhyl's life.

'That was not punishment!' shouted Uriel. 'That was murder!'

Daron Nisato rushed to Mesira's body, weeping as he cradled her lifeless form. Pascal Blaise fought to stand as he saw what had been done to his charge, but the Lord of the Unfleshed ignored them all as he clambered over the rubble of the bar's destruction and fled the scene of the crime.

From outside, Uriel could hear gunfire: the hard, heavy bangs of bolters and the snap of lasguns. Roaring jets and the scream of powerful down-draughts billowed choking clouds of dust into the air, and Uriel could see stabbing beams of light from the skies.

Had Pasanius managed to call in air support?

He heard more gunfire and bellowing roars, but beyond that, he could hear the screech of buckling steel and the groans of a structure no longer able to support the weight settling upon it. Uriel looked up as a snaking line of cracks burst across the ceiling, ripping their way from left to right and back to front.

'Run!' he shouted.

Pascal Blaise dragged the protesting Daron Nisato from the bar and Uriel struggled to reach the front of the collapsing building. Lumps of plaster and splintered timber crashed down around him and long spars of metal clanged together as portions of the roof caved in.

Uriel fell as a roof beam crashed into his shoulder and he sprawled onto his front as the rear portion of the bar collapsed entirely. More metal broke and twisted, and he scrambled forwards as the building started to collapse in earnest.

Choking clouds of dust and ash obscured Uriel's vision, but he was guided by the blinding beams of light that came from outside. Half running, half crawling, Uriel forced his way onwards. Torn chunks of concrete struck him and he staggered as an enormous, final groan shook the structure of abandoned tanks.

Uriel dived clear of the bar as the entire assembly of tanks, plaster and timber slammed down, the lowest regions of the structure crushed beneath thousands of tonnes of iron. He rolled as enormous pieces of tanks fell from the building: turrets, doors, iron wheels and lengths of track.

A girder the length of his body slammed down next to him and he scrambled away as it toppled onto its side. Debris and rubble fell in an avalanche of metal and Uriel cried out as more and more of it struck him.

He was forced to his knees by the impact of something heavy and metal. A twirling shard of glass sliced his cheek and a panel of sheet metal slammed into his side, driving the breath from him and pinning him to the ground with its weight.

Dust blinded him and the roar of the building's collapse was deafening.

Uriel struggled against the weight of the metal as yet more debris spilled down from the building's demise. The metal was groaning and heaving and Uriel coughed as he felt the weight pinning him to the ground grow heavier.

He tried to bend his legs beneath the metal to gain some leverage, but his body was wedged solid. The strength of the Adeptus Astartes, normally so prodigious and able to meet any challenge, was powerless to prevent the weight of iron from crushing him to death.

With his armour, he could have escaped, but without it...

Suddenly the weight lessened and through the swirling clouds of blinding dust, Uriel saw huge shapes around him, silver light reflecting from their outlines.

Uriel heard the click of vox units and the tread of heavy feet around him.

He smelled the distinct and wholly welcome scent of oils and lapping powder that could mean only one thing: Astartes armour.

He saw gauntleted hands heave the sheet metal, and the debris that held him pinned to the ground was lifted clear as though it weighed nothing at all. Hands dragged him from the ground and he heard chanting behind the warriors who had saved him. Amongst the smells he associated with Space Marines, he smelled strong, choking smoke, cloying and reeking of the interior of temples.

'Who–' was all he managed before a heavy silver gauntlet fastened around his throat with a grip of unbreakable iron. Uriel was hauled from the ground, his feet dangling in the air as he was brought before an oversized silver helmet with an angular visor and blazing red lenses.

A high gorget protected the warrior's neck and the plates of his armour were massively exaggerated, thick and awesome in their intricacy. A heraldic shield was fitted in the crease between the warrior's enormous shoulder guard and carved breastplate, half in crimson and half in white. The colours were divided down the middle with the image of a black sword, its tip pointing downward.

Uriel knew that this was no ordinary warrior, this was a Terminator, one of the elite, a veteran. No finer warriors than those deemed skilful enough to wear such armour existed in a Chapter.

The Chapter symbol on the warrior's left shoulder guard was a mighty tome, its pages pierced by a sword and set among golden scrollwork. Uriel's eyes widened at the sight of the symbol, for it was an ancient device worn only by humanity's greatest protectors, greater even than the Adeptus Astartes.

The giant who held him helpless leaned in close.

'I am Leodegarius of the Grey Knights,' he said, 'and you are my prisoner.'

PART FOUR
DISSOLUTION

'Yet from those flames, no light, but rather darkness visible.'

SIXTEEN

URIEL'S ARMS BURNED with pain and his wrists were chafed bloody by the silver manacles that held him suspended above the cold, hard floor of the darkened chamber. Its exact dimensions were unknown to him, but he had formed a mental map of the chamber from the echoes of his shouts for answers.

It had been days since the battle with the Unfleshed, but how many he could not say with any certainty, for the darkness was unchanging and his captors had given him no clue as to the passage of time.

His captors... The Grey Knights...

These warriors of legend were spoken of in hushed whispers, for the foes they faced in battle were the most terrifying of all: daemons and unclean creatures from beyond the gates of the Empyrean. Of all the Emperor's servants, they were the most honoured, the most revered, and the most deadly.

Now, their attentions were turned upon Uriel.

It seemed inconceivable to Uriel that he should suffer like this; that fellow warriors of the Adeptus Astartes should inflict such punishments upon him. Yet he could not find it in his heart to blame them, for had he and Pasanius not returned from the most dreaded place in the galaxy, a lair of abominations and monsters?

As much as he railed against what was happening to him, he knew he could have expected no less. From here on out, Uriel was at the mercy of those who knew the threat of the daemonic better than he.

In the time since the Grey Knights had taken him, he had known only darkness. No sooner had Leodegarius hauled him from the rubble of the collapsed bar than a host of powerfully muscled servitors had closed in, carrying extendable poles that terminated in thick metal collars with inward pointing blades.

The restraint collars had fastened on his neck and Uriel knew that to resist would open his throat on the razor-sharp spikes. A robed acolyte had lifted a hood, fashioned from what appeared to be coarse sackcloth weave. Just before it had been fastened over his head, Uriel saw another Grey Knight with Pasanius similarly restrained before the open ramp of a silver Thunderhawk gunship.

The hood had been more than simply fabric, for it had utterly blocked Uriel's perception of the world around him. His five senses were rendered useless and he felt a curious deadness to everything, as though suddenly and completely cut off from the realm of perception.

He had been guided to the interior of the Thunderhawk and flown to the gaol that currently confined him. Uriel had no idea where he was, and what was to happen next was similarly a mystery. Unkind hands had manacled him and then removed the perception-deadening hood before his skull had been shaved and he had been hauled from the ground and left suspended in the darkness.

A murmur of chanting drifted on the incense-scented air, a maddeningly constant refrain that lurked just beyond the range of comprehension. Uriel could see no source for the voices, but he could sense figures moving through the darkness, darkness so impenetrable that not even his genhanced sight could penetrate its depths.

He knew he was being observed and he had spoken aloud of his innocence and his loyalty to the Emperor, but they would have heard such things a hundred times or more, most often from the mouths of heretics and those who consorted with daemons. After a while, he gave up and concentrated on blocking out the pain in his shoulders.

His weight was pulling his arms from their sockets and the sinews were straining and twisting as he hung in the darkness. The metal of the silver manacles bit into the meat of his wrists and congealed blood clotted on his forearms.

Uriel heard heavy footsteps coming towards him through the darkness. A flaming torch sprang to life and the silver giant that had pulled him from the wreckage of the bar approached.

Firelight reflected from the burnished plates of his incredible armour, the vast plates indestructible and magnificent.

Terminators were warriors capable of awesome destruction, trained to be masters of the killing art and unstoppable human tanks. Astartes in Mk VII plate were well-armoured and retained their lethal speed, whereas a warrior clad in Terminator armour sacrificed that mobility for almost complete invulnerability.

As the Terminators of the Veteran company were above Uriel in skill and lethality, so too was this warrior above even them. To be in such a warrior's presence, even as a prisoner, was an honour.

Leodegarius had removed his helmet and Uriel saw that his face was finely sculpted and almost angelic in its symmetry. Silver eyebrows framed clear blue eyes and his white hair was pulled back in a short scalp lock. The warrior's physical perfection matched his assuredly perfect soul, and Uriel was put in mind of warriors from the Blood Angels Chapter of the Adeptus Astartes, such was his beauty.

A group of hooded acolytes followed Leodegarius, one reading from a heavy book supported on the back of a hunched dwarf with a golden lectern fused to its exposed spine, and another carrying a silver aquila, from which issued puffs of scented smoke. Others carried a variety of items on plush velvet cushions, some of which were clearly items of excruciation, while others were devices beyond Uriel's understanding.

Another Grey Knight, clad in gleaming silver power armour, stood at Leodegarius's shoulder and carried the awesome warrior's helmet. Behind him, a pair of sweating servitors dragged a smoking brazier, from which protruded a number of glowing irons.

Uriel felt the chains supporting him go slack and he descended to the floor. The loosening of the chains continued until he was able to lower his arms to his sides.

He rolled his shoulders to flex the muscles there and work the balls of his joints back into their sockets. None of his captors made any move to remove or loosen the manacles that still bound his wrists.

'Tell me why I should not kill you,' said the Grey Knight.

For a moment, Uriel was dumbfounded. The bluntness of the question was such that he had no immediate answer.

'I am a loyal servant of the Emperor,' he said at last.

'I have heard that before,' replied Leodegarius, his disbelief plain, 'so I am going to open you up and examine the farthest reaches of your soul. I will know everything about you, Uriel Ventris, and if I find you to be pure you may yet earn the Emperor's forgiveness, but if I find any hint of corruption or filthy secrets, your body will be purged with fire.'

'I understand,' said Uriel. 'I have nothing to hide.'

'A common declaration of the corrupted,' said Leodegarius. 'You would be surprised how many times I hear it from the mouths of those with a great deal to hide.'

'I am a servant of the Emperor,' repeated Uriel. 'I am not corrupt.'

'That is for me to decide,' said Leodegarius. 'Now be silent.'

Uriel nodded, fully aware that his life was in the hands of the warrior. With a gesture he could end him and erase him from the Imperium. All that he had ever done, all the heroic deeds he had accomplished in his life, would be expunged as surely as if he had never existed.

'State your name and rank,' said Leodegarius, 'for the record.'

'I am Uriel Ventris, former captain of the Fourth Company of the Ultramarines Chapter of the Adeptus Astartes.'

As Uriel spoke, a clattering stenolyte behind Leodegarius scrawled his words on a leaf of parchment, each of his fingers ending in an inky quill-tip. This would either be his vindication or his valediction.

Leodegarius nodded and reached out to twist Uriel's shoulder towards him. Uriel gritted his teeth, the bones of his shoulder twisting painfully in the socket.

'Your Chapter and company tattoos have been burned from your body.'

'Yes,' said Uriel. 'Our Chapter and company markings were removed before we left Macragge on a Death Oath. For all intents and purposes, we were exiled. It would not have been fitting to continue to bear our Chapter's heraldry.'

'Why were you sent on this Death Oath?' asked Leodegarius, and Uriel saw a servitor remove one of the irons in the fire with thick, insulated gloves. The brand was held out towards Leodegarius, but the Grey Knight ignored it for the time being.

'For breaking with the Codex Astartes.'

Leodegarius nodded, as though he was aware of this. Had Pasanius already been interrogated for this information?

Thinking of his friend, Uriel decided to risk a question of his own. 'Where is Pasanius?'

A silver gauntlet seized Uriel's throat and Leodegarius reached back to take hold of the glowing branding iron, its head in the shape of a haloed skull. With a fluid economy of motion he reversed the brand and stamped it down over the place where an Imperial aquila had once been tattooed on Uriel's shoulder.

Agonising pain coursed through Uriel's body as the red-hot iron seared his flesh. His knees buckled and he bit back a cry as Leodegarius kept the burning metal pressed against his skin. Smoke and the horrific smell of blackened, charred flesh filled the air. The pain was intense, but Uriel closed his eyes and focused his mind on blocking it out.

At last the brand was removed and Uriel gasped. The pain was still there, raw, hot and intense, but compared to the agony of the continued burning, it was as though his upper arm were bathed in cool water.

A pair of robed chirurgeons stepped from the darkness behind him and the pain was replaced by a cool, clear sensation of relief as counterseptic was applied to the wound and burn gauze bound to his shoulder.

'That is the first lesson,' said Leodegarius, handing the brand back to the servitor. 'When we begin, you are to speak only when I permit you to speak. Do you understand?'

'Yes,' said Uriel, nodding, 'I understand.'

'Then you are ready for the first ordeal,' said Leodegarius, 'the Ordeal of Inquisition.'

'What are you going to ask me?'

'Ask?' said the Grey Knight. 'I am not going to *ask* you anything.'

CONCENTRIC CIRCLES WERE inscribed on the floor around Uriel and Leodegarius, cut by hooded servitors with acetylene torches for arms, and the grooves filled with bubbling lines of molten silver dispensed from golden urns upon their backs. Strange sigils that were incomprehensible to Uriel were cut in the space between the two circles, which were likewise filled with silver.

Steam billowed from the design as the servitors finished the last of the silver sigils.

'The Ordeal of Inquisition,' said Leodegarius, 'is as old as my order. My mind's eye will see into every darkened corner of your soul. I will know your every thought. You will be able to hide nothing from me. Understand that and you may save yourself a great deal of pain. If you have evil within you, confess it and your death will be swift. Deny it, and if I find any trace of corruption, your death will be agonising and long.'

'I have nothing to confess,' said Uriel. 'I am not corrupt.'

Leodegarius nodded, as though playing out a familiar drama. 'We shall see.'

At last the design on the floor was complete, and the servitors vanished into the darkness, leaving Uriel and Leodegarius alone. As the servitors withdrew, seven other acolytes approached, each carrying a torch, their hoods drawn back. The firelight danced on their faces, and the withered horror of their hairless heads made Uriel long for the darkness again.

Their faces were those of corpses found in the desert, drawn and desiccated as though drained of all vitality and animation. Their eyes had been burned from their sockets, although whether by deliberate artifice or by nightmarish sights, Uriel could not say.

As a Space Marine in the service of the Emperor, Uriel had seen his share of terrors: ancient star gods, the face of the Great Devourer and the abode of daemons, but to see these pitiful beings was to know that there were more terrible things still in the galaxy.

The dreadful acolytes took up positions around them, forming a protective circle, and began to chant with a barely audible, static-like screech. Their low voices set up an atonal wall of sound without rhythm and Uriel felt the same deadening of the senses that he had felt when hooded.

'The Null-Servitors create a barrier of psychic feedback,' explained Leodegarius. 'Together with the lines of power inscribed in the floor, it will prevent any corruption from leaving this circle should I falter in my inquisition of your body and soul.'

'I understand the precaution,' said Uriel, 'but I keep telling you it is unnecessary.'

'Be silent,' instructed Leodegarius, stepping forward and placing his hands on either side of Uriel's face. 'The Ordeal of Inquisition has begun.'

The metal of the gauntlets was cold and Uriel felt their chill spread down through his skin, into the muscles of his face and past the bone of his skull. Cold, questing fingers prised open the lid of his mind and delved inside.

Uriel's immediate inclination was to resist and the mental barriers of his will began to erect in response to the invasion. He looked into Leodegarius's icy blue eyes and the world seemed to contract until all he could see were those glacial orbs, as though crackling lines of power that could never be broken connected them.

Uriel felt his entire body grow numb as the Grey Knight's psychic essence forced its way through his defences and into his thoughts.

'Why do you resist?' asked Leodegarius, the implacable force of his mind pressing on Uriel's thoughts. 'Do you have something to hide after all?'

Uriel tried to reply, but his tongue would not obey him. He tried to lower his defences and allow his interrogator access to his thoughts, but the natural reaction of a human mind is to protect its secrets and internal workings.

Yet even as the defensive architecture of his brain buckled under the strain of resistance, Uriel knew that such a struggle would be futile in the face of the Grey Knight's power. With that realisation came the will to allow another being access to the hidden fortress of his mind: the guarded place where he kept his doubts, his fears, his hopes and his ambitions.

Everything that made him Uriel Ventris would be laid bare for Leodegarius to see, to know and to understand. Every virtue and every vice was open to scrutiny and if Uriel were found wanting in any regard, his life would be forfeit. Curiously, he felt no fear, now that the last barrier between him and Leodegarius was removed.

He felt the Grey Knight's colossal presence within his skull, the warrior's essence blending with Uriel's and learning in a moment what had forged him into a warrior of the Ultramarines. Everything from the blue-lit caverns of Calth of his earliest childhood memories to the fight with the Lord of the Unfleshed became part of the Grey Knight's understanding and in the space of a breath, it was as though they had become one soul.

As Leodegarius learned of Uriel, so too did Uriel learn of Leodegarius, or at least as much as the Grey Knight wanted him to know. He saw the decades of battle, the years of study and solitude, and the complete and utter devotion to his sacred duty.

Leodegarius was a hero in the truest sense of the word, a warrior who fought for no reward, no acclaim and no reason other than that he knew he was one of a select brotherhood that was all that stood between humanity and destruction. Uriel saw unnumbered and unknown battles where the fate of worlds hung in the balance.

He saw triumphs and he saw losses. He saw victories and unimaginable sacrifice.

This was what it took to be a defender of the Imperium and Uriel's own achievements paled in comparison to what this great hero had accomplished.

Their lives intertwined in the space of a moment and the connection was so profound that Uriel began to panic as his sense of self was swallowed by the overwhelming presence of the Grey Knight's mind.

Then it was gone.

Like a sword pulled from a wound, the Grey Knight's power withdrew from Uriel's mind and he sagged against the chains that supported him. He dropped to his knees, suddenly feeling alone, so very alone, within his skull, as if a vital piece of him had been torn out.

In the face of the horrors Leodegarius had defeated, what did the life of a pair of Ultramarines matter? In the grand tapestry of the galaxy, Uriel's life was meaningless and he would welcome Leodegarius ending him now.

'Be at peace, Uriel Ventris,' said Leodegarius. 'A mind will always quail before its insignificance following union with a power greater than itself. Your warrior's pride will restore your sense of self-worth soon enough.'

Uriel looked up into Leodegarius's face, his handsome, perfect and magnificent face. The look of a great hero of mankind was etched into every shimmering line and curve of his skull.

'You saw inside me,' gasped Uriel, every word an effort. 'You know I am not corrupt.'

'You are not knowingly corrupt,' agreed Leodegarius. 'I sense no evil in you, but there are many forms of corruption. You may yet be a herald of wickedness and know it not.'

'I don't understand,' said Uriel, painfully lifting himself to his feet.

'The strands destiny weaves around you are soaked in blood, Uriel Ventris, and times of great danger will forever shadow your life. Your arrival on Salinas is but the latest in a chain of events that may doom this world to exterminatus. Where you walk, it is dangerous to follow.'

'Dangerous for my enemies,' snarled Uriel.

Leodegarius smiled. 'Your spirit is returning, I see. That is good.'

'It is?' said Uriel.

'Of course,' said Leodegarius. 'It means you are ready for the second ordeal.'

ACRID FUMES BILLOWED upwards from the iron cauldron, its contents bubbling and popping as Uriel was led before it. The sides were embossed with a ring of linked eagles and the smell of the boiling oils made Uriel's gorge rise as he suspected what might be asked of him.

The manacles had been removed and he had been permitted to clean the blood from his arms before being marched through the darkness of the chamber to the cauldron. By the light of the burning torch, Uriel was able to make out more of his surroundings: a great open space of soaring arches and thick pillars. The air was thick and cold, leading him to believe that he was below a great building, possibly the palace or the cathedral.

Leodegarius turned to Uriel and said, 'Since earliest times we have used the Ordeal of the Holy Oils to test the flesh of those brought before us. Too often the question of guilt is unnecessary, for actions speak louder than words, but you are a curiosity to me, Uriel Ventris. This ordeal will be painful, but if you have the light of the Emperor within your body you will not falter and you will be borne up by His glory.'

Leodegarius moved to stand opposite Uriel, with the cauldron between them. 'Should your flesh prove true and you pass through this ordeal, you will stand before me at the end and face the *Judicium Imperator*. Only then will your soul be deemed pure.'

'But the Ordeal of Inquisition?' said Uriel. 'I thought you sensed no evil in me?'

'Nor do I,' said Leodegarius, 'but you have travelled to a realm where nothing that is good or pure can live, and your soul has been exposed to corruption that would burn the flesh from your bones were you to know but a fragment of its true horror. You have walked in that world and it falls to me to determine whether any of its corruption has returned with you, hidden within the meat and bones of your flesh. Do you have anything to say before this ordeal?'

Uriel considered his words carefully. 'I ask the same question I asked before. Where is Pasanius?'

'He undergoes ordeals as you do. His fate is his own and he will stand or fall as you will stand or fall: alone.'

'Then I am ready,' said Uriel. 'Yes, we have walked in the realm of the damned, but we faced its temptations and resisted them.'

'Do you think that is enough?'

'I do not know whether it is enough,' admitted Uriel, 'but it must count for something, for only those who try to resist temptation know how strong it is. You measure the strength of an enemy by fighting against him, not by giving in. You find out the strength of the wind by walking against it, not by lying down.'

Leodegarius nodded. 'There is truth in that. A man will never discover the strength of the evil impulse inside him until he tries to fight it. The Emperor is the only being who never yielded to temptation, and thus he is also the only man who knows to the full what giving in to that temptation means.'

'Then by any measure of reckoning, Pasanius and I have matched our strength against the foulest beings imaginable.'

'Then this ordeal should be no ordeal at all,' said Leodegarius, pointing to the bubbling cauldron. 'Have you heard of Saint De Haan of the Donorian sector?'

Uriel shook his head. 'No. Who was he?'

'He was an inquisitor who served the Emperor for over two centuries,' explained Leodegarius, 'a man who rooted out heresy and corruption on over a thousand worlds. Tens of thousands of heretics and evildoers perished before him, and his shining vision of a pure Imperium was a beacon to all whose loyalty to the Golden Throne was unwavering.'

'What happened to him?' asked Uriel.

'He was martyred at the battle of Kostiashak,' said Leodegarius. 'Warriors of the Ruinous Powers captured him and portions of his anatomy were nailed to the defiled cathedral of Trebian. De Haan's loyal acolytes recovered their master's remains and many of the relics are stored in scented rosewood boxes on the worlds he cleansed.'

'Many, but not all?' asked Uriel.

'Correct.'

Uriel looked into the bubbling, viscous liquid. At the bottom of the hissing, spitting oil he could make out the wavering outline of what looked like a dagger.

'You will reach in and lift out the dagger,' said Leodegarius.

'What will that prove apart from the fact that my flesh will burn?'

'Shards of the armour belonging to Saint De Haan are worked into the metal of its handle and only those whose flesh is unsullied by the taint of the great enemy may grip it.'

Uriel took a deep breath and nodded. 'Then I have nothing to fear.'

'I hope that is true,' said Leodegarius, and Uriel was surprised to hear sincerity in the Grey Knight's voice. 'Now, take the dagger.'

Before he could picture images of seared flesh and the skin boiled from his bones, Uriel closed his eyes and plunged his left hand into the cauldron. White-hot agony engulfed his forearm. He gritted his teeth against the pain, an all-consuming fire that sent bolts of screaming white light bursting behind his eyelids.

His legs buckled and he reached out to steady himself with his free hand. His other palm hissed as it came into contact with the cauldron's side and Uriel bit back a scream of agony. He could feel his skin blistering and melting in the oil as his fingers sought out the hilt of the dagger. The pain was unbelievable, almost too much for him to stand. It felt as though his arm was dipped into the heart of a volcano and he almost wished for the oblivion of unconsciousness to spare him from enduring it for a second longer.

But then, wasn't that as much part of the ordeal as being able to grasp the weapon?

Wasn't his ability to overcome such pain further proof of his innocence?

Uriel fought through the pain, embracing it, welcoming it, and he opened his eyes to see Leodegarius staring at him. He felt the Grey Knight's approval and knew with utter certainty that Leodegarius *wanted* him to succeed in this ordeal. He *wanted* to find a reason not to kill him.

His fingers brushed metal and Uriel closed his grip on the wire wound hilt of the dagger. Though he could barely feel the apparatus of his hand any longer, the tendons and muscles of his wrist obeyed him enough to hold the weapon firm.

With his grip secure, Uriel lifted the dagger from the oil and held it before him, his breath coming in hot spurts from the heart of his chest. His hand was a raw, red thing, the meat boiled and layers of oily skin dripping from him in glistening, jellied strings. The pain was like nothing he had known before and the sight of his ruined flesh made it even worse.

Though every nerve in his body told him to release the burning weapon, Uriel held it out towards Leodegarius.

'There,' hissed Uriel. 'Is this what you wanted?'

Leodegarius nodded and took the weapon, his armoured gauntlets protecting him from the blazing heat of the dagger.

'It is indeed,' said Leodegarius, sheathing the weapon at his side and taking Uriel's wrist.

Leodegarius examined the wound and Uriel flinched, gritting his teeth against the pain, but willing himself to remain standing.

'So?' asked Uriel. 'Is my flesh pure?'

'Maybe,' said Leodegarius, releasing Uriel's hand. 'In three days I shall return and we will examine your wound. A warrior whose flesh is pure will have begun to heal, whereas one whose flesh is unclean will have begun to fester. We will know then whether you are ready to face the final ordeal.'

'The final ordeal?' asked Uriel, wondering what could be worse than the ordeals he had already endured.

'Your mind is free of taint and I believe your flesh to be pure,' said Leodegarius, 'but ordeals devised by Man can tell us only so much, so we must now allow the Emperor to judge the strength of your soul.'

'How do we do that?'

'In the *Judicium Imperator*,' said Leodegarius. 'In three days you will fight me, and on the outcome of that shall final judgement be made upon you.'

U
SEVENTEEN

OVER THE NEXT three days, the pain in Uriel's hand pulsed steadily at the edge of endurance. With the Ordeal of the Holy Oils complete, he had been returned to the darkness and isolation of the cold, underground space.

Except, it wasn't really isolation, not when the maddening chants and low level buzzing that kept him from sleep were his continual companions. He had been left alone, as far as he could tell, though he knew there must be weapons trained upon him and armed gaolers standing ready to obliterate him should he make any attempt to escape.

Escape was not on Uriel's mind, however, not when his loyalty and faith were in question.

Time passed slowly in the darkness, and Uriel's thoughts turned from his own predicament to that of Pasanius and events in the world at large. What had become of his friend? Had he suffered through the two previous ordeals as Uriel had?

Uriel had no reason to suspect that Pasanius would fail the ordeals. He only hoped that when the dark surgeons of Medrengard had taken the xeno-infected arm from his body, they had taken the full extent of its taint.

251

If any lingering trace of the Nightbringer's essence remained within him, would that be enough to condemn Pasanius in the eyes of the Grey Knights?

He tried to put such doubts and worries from his mind, wondering what was happening on the streets of Barbadus. His chronology of events from the bar's collapse onwards was piecemeal and he could not say for certain what had occurred. Had the Grey Knights killed the Unfleshed or were they still at large?

Barbadus was such a warren of twisted paths and darkened hiding places that it was entirely likely that the Lord of the Unfleshed and his tribe could have evaded capture or destruction. If that were the case what would their next move be? To hide and lie low? To kill again?

In the space of a single night, the Unfleshed had butchered most of the Screaming Eagles, Colonel Verena Kain and Mesira Bardhyl. Who would be next to die?

It all came back to the Killing Ground.

Those who had taken part in the massacre of the people of Khaturian were being killed and a chain of events had been set in motion that might see Salinas engulfed in flames of battle. Worse, Leodegarius obviously thought that whatever had possessed the Unfleshed might be serious enough to warrant the destruction of Salinas.

Uriel had watched one world burn at the hands of the Inquisition and was in no mood to see another die. Whatever the truth of what was happening on Salinas, he would fight alongside the Grey Knights to prevent further death, assuming he passed the *Judicium Imperator*.

His very soul rebelled at the idea of fighting Leodegarius, but what choice did he have? To refuse to fight would condemn him, but to take arms against a fellow warrior of the Imperium was anathema to him.

To even fight such a sublime warrior was galling, but the idea of besting him seemed inconceivable, ludicrous even. Uriel was wounded, battered and drained, where Leodegarius was in peak condition. It would not be a fight; it would be a shaming defeat.

Uriel Ventris, however, was not a warrior who gave up easily.

On Pavonis, when faced with the awesome, star-destroying, power of the Nightbringer, he had stood against it and denied it a vessel that would have magnified its powers a hundredfold. He had faced the might of a Norn Queen in the depths of a hive ship and defeated her. He had marched into battle on the blasted surface of a daemon world and defeated the daemons and devils that populated its blasted hinterlands.

He would face this challenge and meet it head on.

It was the only way he knew.

Questions of the outside world were irrelevant, for he could do nothing to alter the outcome of what was happening beyond these walls. He could do little enough to alter his own circumstances, but he settled himself upon the cold stone floor and began to prepare for the coming fight.

Uriel closed his eyes and controlled his breathing, directing his body's energies into healing and restoration. Time slowed to a crawl and Uriel felt every muscle, bone and hair on his body as his awareness turned inwards.

He could not actually heal his wounded flesh in the manner of some psykers, but the mental energies of a Space Marine were such that with carefully directed thought patterns, learned over decades of study and application, he was able to focus his energies in replenishment.

Uriel's throat ached where a blade had pierced it on Medrengard, the wound long since healed, but the scar and memory of it remaining. The burning ache in his hand where the holy oils had scalded him terribly faded to a dull ache. His chest tightened where a vengeful spine of the Norn Queen had pierced his flat, ribless torso, and amongst all these hurts, he recalled the memory of a hundred others.

Each would have killed a mortal, but his Astartes frame was proof against such injuries and he had survived them all, coming back stronger from each one. He would come back stronger from this as well.

Uriel knew in his heart that he was no traitor and that his flesh was not corrupt. This was not hubris or overweening pride; it was something he just knew deep in his soul. The very idea that he could be corrupt was intolerable and even had Leodegarius not required this final test, Uriel would have demanded it, for how else could all others know for certain that he had returned from the Eye of Terror with his soul still his own?

Only approbation by a body as august and respected as the Grey Knights would erase any doubt as to his fidelity in the minds of his battle-brothers.

To return to Macragge without such a seal of approval would be unthinkable, and Uriel suddenly saw how naïve he had been to think he could just walk through the gates of the Fortress of Hera without it. While his fellow battle-brothers would accept his word as true, (for what Ultramarine would ever countenance lying to his fellows?) Uriel knew that he would be forever suspect in the eyes of others without the Grey Knights' acceptance of his purity.

Yet, how could he hope to prevail against the might of Leodegarius?

Uriel allowed himself a moment of martial pride as he saw again the mighty foes he had bested in combat, the enemies who were dust in the wind while he was still alive and able to fight.

So long as there was life, there was hope, and while there was hope, Uriel Ventris would fight.

TIME PASSED, THE darkness flowing around Uriel like a living thing. When he judged that his mind and body were as ready as they could be for the coming fight, he stood and allowed the blood to flow around his body at an accelerated rate.

Though he could see nothing around him, Uriel moved through the basic martial exercises of the Adeptus Astartes, working each of the muscle groups to empower them for combat. Uriel stretched and tensed in long, slow moves, gearing his physique for the stresses and demands of killing.

If anything, the darkness enhanced his exercises, forcing him to rely on his other senses as he spun and advanced, his hands and feet, knees and elbows killing weapons. The pain of his hand was forgotten, the rotten stink of the burned meat a distant memory.

His lungs burned and his heart beat a furious tattoo against his ribs as his body changed from its meditative state to that of a deadly fighting machine. With the basic exercises complete, Uriel moved into more exotic manoeuvres, leaping and twisting in the air as he fought imaginary foes from memory.

At last he dropped to one knee, his fist a millimetre from the ground and released a pent up breath. Uriel stood and ran his hands across his skull, the feel of the bristles unfamiliar, but welcome.

'Light,' said a voice in the darkness and Uriel shielded his eyes as blue fire sprang to life around him. His eyes quickly adjusted to the light and he saw that he was surrounded by a host of silver-armoured warriors. Each warrior carried a tall polearm, the blades sheathed in a haze of energies that were the source of the blue fire.

Twenty-five Grey Knights stood to attention in a circle around him, the plates of their gleaming armour flickering with a shimmering blue-steel glow. Leodegarius marched from the circle of warriors. The leader of the Grey Knights had stripped from his armour and wore a loose-fitting chiton of white, a training uniform similar to that worn by the Ultramarines when not in armour.

'You have put your time to good use, Uriel Ventris,' he said.

'Time spent not honing my skills is wasted time,' replied Uriel.

'Just so,' agreed Leodegarius. 'It has been three days. Let me see your hand.'

Uriel had all but forgotten the pain of his wounded hand, but nodded and lifted it towards Leodegarius without breaking eye contact. A chirurgeon followed the Grey Knight, hissing pipes and gurgling tubes looping from beneath his robes. A brass armature emerged from the chirurgeon's sleeve, bearing a clicking device similar to an Apothecary's narthecium. The device extended towards Uriel's hand, bathing it in a golden glow that felt like warm honey was being poured over his skin.

The light vanished and the chirurgeon nodded to Leodegarius before backing away.

Uriel looked down at his hand and was amazed to see that virtually all trace of the horrific wounding was gone. The flesh was pink and new, raw and tender to be sure, but unmistakably whole once more.

Leodegarius reached out and turned over Uriel's hand, carefully inspecting the flesh. Uriel could tell that the Grey Knight was pleased by what he saw.

'The flesh heals well,' said Leodegarius. 'I do not believe I have ever seen anyone recover from the Ordeal of the Oils as quickly as this.'

'Then, we are ready to fight?' asked Uriel, stepping back.

'You sound eager,' said Leodegarius.

'I am,' replied Uriel, 'not to fight you, but to prove myself.'

Leodegarius nodded. 'I understand,' he said, turning away, 'but we will not be fighting here.'

'Where will we be fighting?'

'Where all can see the Emperor's judgement upon you,' said Leodegarius. 'Follow me.'

URIEL SET OFF after Leodegarius as the Grey Knight led him from his place of confinement. An arched tunnel of dressed ashlar led through what Uriel guessed was the bedrock of the palace. Their route twisted through ancient tunnels, cut in ages past, and adapted by the later builders of the palace.

Rough-hewn tunnels became iron-framed corridors before blending into ceramic-walled chambers with high domes and glaring lights. There appeared to be no sense of order to the subterranean architecture, with passages meandering off at odd angles and the same tunnels returning after too short a time to have led to anything useful.

The Grey Knights marched in perfect step, their pace unhurried, but covering the distance with a kilometre-eating stride. A detachment of warriors went before Uriel, nine behind him and the remainder at his sides. Leodegarius led them and a host of censer bearing acolytes created a living fogbank that moved ahead of their procession.

Storerooms, forgotten chambers, armouries and barracks passed and as they entered a low corridor, Uriel heard a number of voices raised in agitation coming from somewhere ahead.

The tunnel opened up into a wide, circular space with a high ceiling and a grey drum tower in the centre of the chamber. The walls were lined with cells that all faced the circular building and Uriel instinctively recognised this place as a kind of prison.

'It is a Panopticon,' said Leodegarius, guessing Uriel's thoughts. 'Guards are positioned in the building at the centre and the prisoners have no way of knowing when they are being watched, because they cannot see inside. They have no way to avoid being seen, so must control their baser impulses lest they suffer punishment.'

'So fear of retribution, not devotion to the Emperor ensures obedience?'

'Just so,' agreed Leodegarius with distaste. 'Something that might very well be said for this entire planet.'

'Why are we here?' asked Uriel.

'To gather your companion.'

'Pasanius?'

'Yes, he has been kept here since he too passed through the ordeals.'

'He's going to fight you too?'

'He will fight alongside you,' nodded Leodegarius, crossing the chamber to stand before a cell where the welcome sight of Pasanius greeted Uriel.

His friend was unbowed and Uriel saw that his remaining hand was as raw and pink as his own, but clearly healed from its immersion in the boiling oils.

'Uriel!' cried Pasanius, his relief obvious. 'Your hand?'

'Almost as good as yours,' said Uriel as the door slid open and Pasanius stepped from the cell. The two warriors embraced, relieved beyond words to find each other alive, and Uriel released his friend from a crushing bear hug.

'Are you ready for this?' asked Uriel.

'You're damn right I'm ready for this,' said Pasanius, angling his head towards Leodegarius. 'No disrespect intended, but these bastards questioned our loyalty. I'm ready for whatever it takes to prove we're not traitors.'

'Your sergeant has been fiercely loyal to you, Captain Ventris,' said Leodegarius, and Uriel couldn't help but notice that his name had now been prefixed by his rank. That had to be a good sign.

'He is my friend,' said Uriel, 'and that is what friends do.'

Leodegarius turned towards the chamber's exit, a tall arch of black stone that led upwards.

'Then let us hope that is enough.'

Flanked by the Grey Knights, Uriel and Pasanius followed them through another series of winding tunnels that eventually opened up to a fortified gateway lined with gunports and which ended at a tall bronze gate.

The gate was open, daylight streaming inside, and Uriel remembered his joy at seeing true light when they had arrived on Salinas. The feeling of being outside again after so long, although it had only been for a few days at most, was sublime and as he marched down a sloping causeway, he was filled with a sense of hope.

That hope was snatched away as soon as he set foot outside and felt the crushing weight of gloom that filled his lungs with each breath. The air was leaden and heavy, the sky pressing down like a monstrous weight upon the day. Threatening clouds scudded above and Uriel was filled with a dreadful sense of melancholy that put him in mind of the ruins of Khaturian.

Once again, he and Pasanius were in the vast flat space where Restoration Day had been declared. The inhospitable parade ground was filled with at least two hundred soldiers and a tight knot of the planet's dignitaries.

A gleaming silver Thunderhawk gunship sat with its assault ramp open behind the dignitaries and Uriel smiled at the sight of such a reassuringly familiar object. Even though the gunship was not in the colours of the Ultramarines, the potent symbol of the power of the Adeptus Astartes lifted Uriel's spirits from the ugly atmosphere saturating the day.

Uriel saw the tower of the Janiceps at the far end of the space and on his right was the decrepit, yet wondrous, Gallery of Antiquities. Craning his neck over his shoulder, he saw the high towers and bleak spires of the Imperial palace.

'Never liked this place,' said Pasanius. 'Now I like it even less.'

'We are to fight here?' Uriel asked Leodegarius. 'What has happened to this place? It feels… dead.'

'The fight will be held before the proper planetary authorities, both secular and holy,' said Leodegarius. 'In order for the *Judicium Imperator* to mean anything, it must be witnessed. As to what has happened since your incarceration… We will speak of it if you survive.'

On that grim pronouncement, they followed Leodegarius into the centre of the parade ground and Uriel saw many familiar faces gathered to witness the fight. Cardinal Togandis sweated beneath his ceremonial robes of office and Daron Nisato was resplendent in his gleaming black enforcer's armour.

Leto Barbaden was seated on a tall podium, looking simultaneously bored and angered by the proceedings, despite the fact that the fate of two of humanity's greatest protectors was to be decided before his very eyes.

Leodegarius halted before the podium and gave a curt nod of acknowledgement to Leto Barbaden before turning to Uriel and Pasanius.

'Governor Barbaden, these two warriors have passed through the trials of purity as determined by my order and I present them before you that you might bear witness to the Emperor's judgement upon them. No higher authority than the Emperor exists and thus He will have the final say in their fate.'

Uriel blinked in surprise at the Grey Knight's choice of words, recognising in them an implicit threat that Uriel's fate was not Barbaden's to decide. Had the governor demanded their execution in the last few days? Given their previous dealings, it was not beyond the realms of possibility, but Leodegarius's words suggested that such a decision was not Barbaden's to make, not when the Grey Knights were involved.

The Adeptus Astartes stood apart from the rigid hierarchy of the Imperium in a way that some found distasteful, but the Grey Knights were an authority beyond even the autonomy of most Chapters. Their authority was absolute and no one who valued their life would dare to go against their dictates.

It seemed that Leto Barbaden was no exception to this, and Uriel could see that it sat ill with the governor to have to bow before the authority of what he no doubt saw as interlopers.

Barbaden nodded and said, 'These two have brought nothing but trouble to my world, but if your order decrees this combat to be a just and proper trial then I will bear witness to it.'

Uriel hid his amusement at Barbaden's transparent ill-grace, meeting his hostile gaze and returning it with one of his own. His dislike for the governor of Salinas had intensified the more he learned about him. Barbaden's disregard for human life and his actions during the conquest of Salinas were unconscionable and Uriel knew that his crimes must be addressed in the fullness of time.

Leodegarius turned to him and said, 'Follow me to the place of battle.'

Uriel nodded and both he and Pasanius followed the Grey Knight to the centre of a circle that had been etched in silver, like the protective one carved in the stone chamber where he had undergone the ordeals, albeit this was considerably larger. Grey Knights in power armour took up positions around the circle, the shimmering blades of their tall polearms crackling in the sunlight.

'We fight hand-to-hand, no weapons,' said Leodegarius, 'the two of you against me.'

'That's it?' asked Pasanius.

'What more did you expect?'

'I don't know,' admitted Pasanius. 'I just thought there would be a lot more… ritual.'

'Rituals are for heathen corpse-whisperers and sorcerers,' said Leodegarius, assuming a fighting pose. 'I prefer more direct action.'

Uriel let his mind and body slip into the rhythm of combat, allowing his metabolism to speed up and heighten his senses and reaction times.

'So what are the rules?' he asked.

'You are such an Ultramarine,' grinned Leodegarius, launching a thunderous jab at Uriel's face. The Grey Knight's fist was like a steel piston, bludgeoning Uriel backwards as though struck by a dreadnought.

Blood arced from his split cheek and stars exploded behind his eyes at the force, but Uriel had been hit before and he knew how to ride with the pain of impact. He lowered his shoulder and rolled his neck, twisting his head out of the way of Leodegarius's follow-up hook.

His arm came up of its own accord, blocking a right cross and he launched an uppercut into his attacker's torso. His other fist slammed into the Grey Knight's side and he heard a satisfying whoosh of breath. His burned hand was bathed in fiery heat, the flesh split where it had not fully healed, but Uriel pushed the pain to the back of his mind.

Pasanius swung with his left, but Leodegarius easily dodged the off-balance blow. Leodegarius's elbow hammered into Pasanius's side and his fist slammed like a club into his midriff, driving the sergeant to his knees.

Uriel surged forwards, his fist arcing towards Leodegarius's head, but the Grey Knight had been expecting his attack. With a speed that seemed impossible for such a huge warrior, Leodegarius swayed aside and seized Uriel's wrist. He pivoted smoothly and slammed his hip into Uriel, using the momentum of the charge to hurl him from his feet.

The ground came up hard and Uriel slammed into it with pile-driving force. The breath exploded from his lungs and he looked up in time to see a slashing foot descending on him. Uriel rolled aside as the heel smashed down and split the stone. He twisted to his feet as Pasanius took another punishing blow to the head.

Uriel shook his head clear of the ringing impact with the ground and spat a mouthful of blood. He knew he had underestimated his opponent's resolve. Leodegarius might have wanted to show that they were innocent, but he wasn't about to compromise the integrity of the *Judicium Imperator* to get his way.

Leodegarius turned from Pasanius as Uriel circled around to his left and the cheering soldiers looked on. The officials of Salinas watched the fight with studied interest, but the soldiers of the Falcatas were showing no such restraint. Uriel risked a quick glance down at Pasanius, who reeled on the ground, as though still dazed from the blow to the head.

Uriel caught a glimmer of guile from his friend and reversed his circling, bringing Leodegarius back closer to Pasanius. The Grey Knight glanced down, unconcerned, at the groggy, struggling form of Pasanius as Uriel feinted left and punched right.

The blow caught Leodegarius on the shoulder, not hurting him, but putting him off balance for the briefest of seconds. Uriel quickly followed with a series of high jabs, one of which penetrated Leodegarius's defences to open a cut above his right eye.

A slashing riposte thundered into Uriel's jaw, but he had seen it coming. He let his guard drop a fraction and Leodegarius stepped off lightly to deliver a crushing blow.

Before the blow landed, Pasanius pushed himself onto his side and delivered a slashing, scissor kick to Leodegarius's leg, just above the knee. Pasanius's foot was like a steel club, hammering the Grey Knight's peroneal nerve and chopping the leg out from under him.

Leodegarius collapsed and Uriel surged in, pounding his fists against the warrior's face, hating the fact that he was drawing the blood of an Imperial hero, but knowing that he had no choice but to fight with all his strength.

He drew back his fist to strike again, when Leodegarius surged to his feet and slammed the heel of his left hand into Uriel's solar plexus. Almost in the same motion, his right chopped down on Pasanius's neck.

Pasanius gave a strangled cry of pain and his eyes rolled back in their sockets.

Uriel staggered back, struggling for breath as his diaphragm went into spasm and pain from the strike to his solar plexus almost blinded him. He could not draw air into his lungs.

Leodegarius rose to his feet, like a colossus from the depths, and

Uriel was amazed that he had recovered so quickly from Pasanius's strike. A blow of such power would have shattered the leg of a mortal warrior and rendered even a Space Marine immobile for several minutes.

Leodegarius fought as if the blow had never landed and Uriel knew that they were fighting one of the mightiest warriors of the Imperium. Uriel raised his fists, but he was too hurt and too slow to avoid the hammer-blows that rang from his skull as Leodegarius closed on him. He desperately circled in an attempt to put some distance between him and his opponent.

Uriel could not resist the fury of the attack and he saw the blow that would finish him a split second before it landed. The Grey Knight's fist arced around his guard and smashed into his face with the power of a thunderbolt.

Uriel was hurled backwards and landed in a heap next to Pasanius, his face a bloody ruin and his torso a mass of ugly bruises that were already swelling and purpling.

He knew he had to get to his feet, but the strength had been battered from him and he slumped back, unable to rise or fight or do anything other than lie bleeding. His breath came in short, painful gasps and he tasted blood and defeat in his mouth.

Was this how his life was to end? Beaten to a bloody pulp by a warrior he should be fighting shoulder to shoulder with? The indignity and horror of it was unbearable.

Uriel looked up through a mist of blood and swellings to see Leodegarius standing over him. 'Kill us and be done with it,' he snapped, 'but you are only helping the Emperor's enemies by doing so.'

Leodegarius shook his head and offered Uriel his hand. 'No,' he said, 'I am not going to kill you. The *Judicium Imperator* is over and you have proved to me that you are loyal servants of the Imperium.'

Uriel took the proffered hand and drew himself unsteadily to his feet. 'But we lost.'

'The *Judicium Imperator* is not about winning or losing,' said Leodegarius, 'it is about the struggle. I am a warrior of the Grey Knights and I carry the Emperor's fire into the dark corners of the galaxy. Only a servant of the Ruinous Powers can defeat me. Had you bested me, it would have shown that you were an enemy of the

Emperor and my warriors would have gunned you down.'

'Then we were meant to lose?' asked Uriel, horrified at the implication.

'Meant to?' shrugged Leodegarius. 'No, but the Emperor was with me and I was confident I could defeat the pair of you, thus proving that you were not servants of evil.'

Pasanius pushed himself up onto his elbow. 'What happened?' he asked groggily. 'Did we win?'

'I think we did,' said Uriel.

'Good,' said Pasanius, sliding back down into unconsciousness. 'I knew we could take him.'

THE FEEL OF the fresh bodyglove against his skin was sublime and the sense of anticipation was almost unbearable. Uriel felt his heartbeat quicken as the Grey Knights' artificers lifted the blue breastplate of the power armour from the battle flag and manoeuvred it towards his chest.

The movement was accompanied with solemn chants from the hooded acolytes, who, since Uriel and Pasanius's vindication, had taken on an altogether less threatening aspect.

Uriel and Pasanius stood on a raised dais before the assembled warriors of the Grey Knights and Curator Lukas Urbican in one of the grand halls of the Gallery of Antiquities. The Grey Knights were clad in their battle gear, each plate and vambrace garlanded with purity seals.

With Uriel and Pasanius's loyalty to the Golden Throne established by the *Judicium Imperator*, the Grey Knights had borne them into the Thunderhawk, where chirurgeons and Apothecaries had treated their wounds. No words were spoken and Leodegarius refused to answer any questions until they were fit to stand before him as fellow Astartes.

The already healing burns on their hands were cleaned with sterile jellies and repaired with synth-skin bandages, the swelling bruises and lumps earned in the *Judicium Imperator* with ice and pain medication.

Where Uriel had been branded on the shoulder, the clicking mechanisms of a reconstruction servitor implanted in the wall of the Thunderhawk's medicae bay rapidly removed the burn scars and rebuilt the underlying tissue and epidermis.

Within the space of an hour, both Uriel and Pasanius were declared fit for service and had been issued with fresh under-suits for power armour. Leodegarius had marched them from the Thunderhawk and, together with an escort of Grey Knights, crossed the empty parade ground towards the Gallery of Antiquities.

Curator Urbican had been waiting for them, a broad smile plastered across his open features as he welcomed them back into the gallery. Once again they made their way through the shadowed halls until they found themselves before the suits of power armour belonging to the Sons of Guilliman.

Eighteen of the suits were arranged in battle formation behind a dais. The nineteenth, the armour Uriel had chosen, or which had chosen him, was broken down into its component parts and arranged on one of the great battle flags of Salinas taken down from the walls. The armour was exactly as Uriel remembered it, freshly painted in the colours of the Ultramarines, with only the helmet remaining in the blue and white of the Sons of Guilliman.

Arranged beside this suit of armour was another, this one in the familiar livery and iconography of the Ultramarines. Uriel had seen Pasanius's pride at the restoration of their Chapter symbols earlier, but his joy at seeing them again was no less dimmed.

'Prepare to receive your armour, warriors of the Emperor,' said Leodegarius.

Uriel and Pasanius had mounted the dais, and the artificers lifted the first plates of the armour towards their bodies with great reverence. First came the greaves, cuisse and knee guards, followed by the power coils of the midsection.

Piece by piece, the armour was layered upon them and as each segment was fastened into place, Uriel felt as though his soul was being rebuilt. Segments of his armour were fixed in place over his upper arms and then came the vambrace and gauntlets.

The damaged section of Pasanius's armour had been repaired with an end cap to seal his armour at the elbow. His friend had declined the Grey Knight's offer of a temporary augmetic, sheepishly saying that he would rather have one fitted by the Techmarines of Macragge.

Adjustments were made, pieces added and each facet of the armour polished and anointed with sacred oils and unguents until all that remained was the final piece. The artificers slotted the breastplate into position and Uriel felt the familiar hiss and whir of the armour coming to life around him.

Fur-lined cloaks of purest white were fastened around their shoulders and secured with golden eagle clips to their breastplates as the gorget clamped around his neck, tight, but not restricting. As the pressure seals engaged, Uriel could feel the internal workings of the armour revitalise his physique, thrumming with incredible potential energy.

Questing bio-implants unwound from inside the armour and connected with the sockets in his body, meshing his organic structure with that of the ceramite plates and indescribably complex workings of Space Marine armour.

Uriel felt the power of wearing such a magnificent suit of armour, his strength boosted, his endurance enhanced and his ability to smite the enemies of the Imperium increased exponentially.

With Uriel and Pasanius's armour in place, Leodegarius stepped forward and handed them gleaming bolters. The flat plates of the weapons were etched in gold and their length was worked with incredibly detailed lettering. The weapons were freshly oiled, each with a magazine of bolter shells fitted snugly into the space before the trigger.

Uriel nodded as he hefted the bolter, the weapon feeling as though it weighed nothing at all. Strength coursed through the armour and he could feel the channels of energy running through it as surely as though it was a second skin.

A Space Marine was more than any one thing, however, more than his armour, his weapons or his training and dedication. Each of these things combined to create something greater than the sum of its parts.

A warrior without a weapon or armour could be killed by his enemies and a warrior without faith and training would fall to petty vices that led to gross treachery.

Uriel had seen, first hand, what a warrior who was not fully equipped, physically and spiritually, could become, and he had walked perilously close to the precipice that others had fallen from. Images of the Warsmith Honsou and Ardaric Vaanes drifted across his mind, but they were fleeting, ghost images, reminders of a dark time that was now passed.

Uriel turned his head to look at the armour, seeing a thick wad of crimson wax attached to the edge of his shoulder guard. A fluttering length of parchment hung from the wax seal, and written upon it in a fine, cursive script was a line from a sermon familiar to Uriel:

He must put a white cloak upon his soul, that he might climb down into the filth, yet may he die a saint.

Leodegarius stepped back and bowed to them both.

'Welcome back, warriors of Ultramar,' he said.

EIGHTEEN

Fury blazed in Leto Barbaden's eyes as Uriel and Pasanius marched into his private library alongside Leodegarius and a robed acolyte bearing a scented rosewood box. The Grey Knight was clad in a pale cream tunic, over which he wore a shirt of silver mail trimmed in ermine, yet he was no less impressive for lack of his armour.

At the heels of the Space Marines came four others, hastily assembled by the orders of Leodegarius. Cardinal Shavo Togandis came first, sweating beneath his robes of office, which hung loosely on him where they had been fastened incorrectly in his haste to obey the immediate summons to the palace.

Serj Casuaban walked alongside the cardinal, his expression betraying a mix of irritation and curiosity at having been dragged from his works at the House of Providence. The medicae wore a long, dark coat over his functional clothes and his grey hair was combed neatly for perhaps the first time in years.

Daron Nisato and Pascal Blaise walked behind Casuaban, the latter looking deeply uncomfortable in a set of iron restraint cuffs and the former uncomfortable at the idea of them being there, while knowing that they had to be for now.

The governor of Salinas sat in his chair nursing a large glass of port as this procession invaded his inner sanctum, and Uriel felt a flutter of satisfaction at the man's annoyance. He could see the effort of will it was taking the governor to keep a civil tongue in his head, but not even Leto Barbaden would openly risk the wrath of the Grey Knights by refusing an audience.

There was no denying the sense of renewed purpose that filled Uriel. Now that he was once again armoured as a Space Marine, he was ready to stand alongside such heroic warriors as Leodegarius and Pasanius in defence of the Imperium. Though he had no idea what Leodegarius was to say to the assembly, Uriel could feel the tension in the air and the unbearable sense of expectation.

In the wake of the Unfleshed's rampage through Barbadus, the citizens had taken to the streets to variously demand action, recompense or retaliation. Quite who any such action was to be taken against wasn't clear, but the need for something to be done was reaching critical mass. Several buildings had been burned to the ground and widespread looting had gripped the entire north-east quarter of the city.

Daron Nisato's enforcers had taken to the streets in whatever armoured vehicles remained to them, supported by the few soldiers who were willing to patrol the streets after the massacre at the Screaming Eagle's barracks.

The mood on the streets of the city was ugly and all it would take to ignite a city-wide epidemic of bloodshed was a single spark.

Events of great import were in motion and Uriel knew that many of the players in this drama would not live to see its end were they to misstep but a little. The acolyte with the box placed it on the table in the centre of the room and Barbaden spared it the briefest glance before saying, 'Brother Leodegarius, are you sure that this gathering is absolutely necessary? There is chaos on the streets of my city!'

'You are more right than you know, governor,' said Leodegarius darkly, 'and yes, I am sure that this is necessary. Believe me, things are likely to get worse before they get better.'

'Very well,' muttered Barbaden, taking a sip of his port and sending a poisonous glance towards Pascal Blaise. 'Since this… motley band has assembled, might I enquire why you required the presence of a known terrorist, Brother Leodegarius?'

'I'm no terrorist!' snapped Pascal Blaise. 'You're the terrorist, Barbaden.'

'Whatever,' said Barbaden. 'I'll have you executed before the day is out.'

'No, you won't,' said Daron Nisato, resting his hand on the butt of his pistol. 'If we are ever to have peace on Salinas, we will need this man alive.'

Barbaden ignored Nisato, as though he were not even worth bothering with, although Uriel saw his face darken at the unaccustomed sight of a weapon in his presence.

'I will get to that in good time, Governor Barbaden,' answered Leodegarius, looking into the face of every man present, and Uriel had the distinct impression that the Grey Knight was seeing beyond their physical appearance to some hidden quality that only he could discern.

'This motley band, as you call it, is a very singular body, and you are all here because I have seen that you all have a part to play in this planet's future, or rather, whether it has one at all.'

'That sounds like a threat,' observed Barbaden.

'Perhaps it is, governor,' admitted Leodegarius, lifting the rosewood box from the table. 'I am well aware of the unrest in your city, but it can wait, for a potentially far greater threat to your world builds unseen in the darkness.'

'What threat?' demanded Barbaden.

'In time,' said Leodegarius, and Uriel heard the unmistakable tone of one who is growing weary of answering questions. Barbaden heard it too and wisely kept his mouth shut as the Grey Knight opened the box and removed what looked like a pack of cards.

'The art of cartomancy is ancient,' began Leodegarius. 'It predates the Imperium and has been used as a tool of divination by the earliest tribes to crawl across the surface of Old Earth.'

'Are we to receive a history lesson while my city burns?' sneered Barbaden and Uriel was again struck by the man's bravery or stupidity in the face of so mighty a warrior as Leodegarius.

Leodegarius displayed no irritation at the interruption and said, 'Everything comes back to history, governor. What is happening now is a direct result of mistakes made in the past. Only by studying the past can we learn from it.'

Barbaden appeared far from convinced, but nodded as Leodegarius continued. 'I have gathered this group together because you are all intimately linked with what is happening on Salinas. I know this because the cards tell me it is so. Gather round.'

Uriel and Pasanius stood at either shoulder of the Grey Knight as the others approached the table. Predictably, Barbaden was last to arrive, casting a hostile stare at Uriel as he did so.

'Observe,' said Leodegarius, selecting cards at random from the deck and setting it before Daron Nisato. The card was that of a robed man sitting upon a throne. In one hand he carried a sword and in the other a set of golden scales. On the base of the card was written, 'Justice'.

'This is you, Enforcer Nisato,' said Leodegarius. 'Whatever your past has been, the time has come to reflect on the choices you have made along the way. There are wrongs you plan to make amends for and there are people who have brought you distress, but you are wise enough to deal with them in an intelligent way. Your only thought is of making things better and this card shows that those wrongs will be put right.'

'You can get all that from a card?' asked Daron Nisato.

'From the card and from you,' answered Leodegarius, drawing another card and laying it before the man standing next to Nisato. This card depicted a man hung by his ankles from a gibbet attached to an Imperial temple.

'That doesn't look very encouraging,' said Pascal Blaise. 'Is this going to be some kind of justification for executing me?'

'We need no justification for that,' hissed Barbaden. 'The lives you took in your pointless, silly resistance are all the justification I need.'

Leodegarius spoke again before Blaise could reply. 'Things have not reached fruition in your life and you must be patient. Keep your own counsel, let go of your hate, and trust your instincts in the days ahead. They will serve you well.'

Another card was turned up: a robed man sitting between two pillars with a pair of keys lying crossed at his feet.

'Cardinal Togandis, this is you, the Hierophant,' said Leodegarius. 'He symbolises the ruling power of religion and faith, the teachings that are palatable to the masses. This represents your love of ritual and ceremony, but also your need for approval from others. The Hierophant indicates the importance of conformity.'

The sweating cardinal did not answer, and Leodegarius went on.

The next card showed an old, grey-haired man on the edge of a snow-capped cliff, looking out upon the world. In one hand he carried a lantern and in the other, a winged, snake-wrapped staff.

'The Hermit,' said Leodegarius, looking at Serj Casuaban. 'On the long dark nights of the soul, the Hermit is there to guide us towards wisdom and knowledge. From the Hermit we can receive wisdom from the Emperor. The Hermit can guide us in our upcoming endeavours. He reminds us that our goals can be attained, but that the journey will not be smooth or easy.'

'I suppose I have a card?' asked Barbaden, affecting an air of studied boredom, but Uriel could see that he was intrigued to see which card would represent him.

'Indeed you do, governor,' said Leodegarius, slapping another card on the table.

The man on the card wore a long robe and stood before a table, upon which lay a cup, a wand, a sword and a pentacle. Flowers surrounded him, and above his head was a symbol that Uriel recognised as that representing Infinity.

'The Sorcerer,' said Leodegarius.

'A sorcerer?' snorted Barbaden, although there was a hint of unease in his tone. 'I may be many things, Brother Leodegarius, but I am no sorcerer. I can assure you of that.'

Leodegarius shook his head. 'You misread the card, Governor Barbaden. The Sorcerer is not literally a wielder of magic. He represents a man always in control of the choices that surround him. He holds his wand up to the heavens, and yet the opposite hand points to the earth. The Sorcerer is a warning of opportunity and, reversed like this, it indicates a person who is a perfectionist, a man who handles every situation calmly and coolly, but who uses power for destructive and negative purposes.'

'That is absurd,' said Barbaden, although from the look of those around him it was clear that they agreed with the Grey Knight's reading of the card.

'There is one final card to be dealt,' said Leodegarius, 'and that it yours, Captain Ventris.'

Uriel nodded. He had expected this, but he didn't know whether to anticipate or dread the card that Leodegarius would draw.

The card placed before Uriel displayed a tower standing high on a mountain, its structure blown apart by a lightning bolt from the heavens. A pair of figures fell from the tower.

'What does it mean?' asked Uriel.

'The fall of the tower reminds us that if we use our knowledge and strength for evil purposes, then destruction will be wrought upon us,' explained Leodegarius. 'When the Tower appears, it indicates changes, conflict and catastrophe. Not only that, but there will be an overthrow of existing ways of life.'

'Sounds just like you,' observed Pasanius dryly.

Uriel scowled as Leodegarius continued his reading. 'However, with destruction comes enlightenment. The Tower shows us that selfish ambition and greed will ultimately bring us nothing of value.'

Uriel released the breath he was holding and looked at the faces around the table. He knew them all, with the exception of Serj Casuaban, and he could see that the cartomancy had unsettled them all, even Governor Barbaden.

'So you see that you are all necessary to the coming conflict,' said Leodegarius. 'How, I do not yet know, but your destinies are linked to the fate of this world.'

'What did you mean that there was a greater threat to Salinas?' asked Uriel. 'It sounds like you are saying that what's happening now is a symptom of something more serious.'

'It is indeed, Captain Ventris, but to answer that I will need to instruct you in the history of Salinas.'

'We already know the history of Salinas,' said Leto Barbaden. 'We have a Gallery of Antiquities devoted to it should anyone feel the need to be bored rigid.'

'I meant the history of Salinas as it is known by *my* order,' said Leodegarius.

BEFORE LEODEGARIUS BEGAN his tale, he spoke into a wrist-mounted vox-unit and would say nothing until the seven Null-Servitors entered and took up positions around the edges of the room. They began their droning chant and Uriel saw that their dreadful appearance was a shock to everyone in the room. Even Barbaden recoiled in loathing at the sight of them.

'There are truths that must be spoken here,' said Leodegarius. 'And truth is powerful, it can reach beyond the realms of Men. I must speak words that should not escape into the world beyond this chamber.'

Uriel felt his skin crawl at the sight of the blank, empty-faced servitors, feeling the familiar dullness blunt his senses as their chant continued and Leodegarius began to speak.

'To understand what is happening on Salinas, you must understand a measure of the foe ranged against us. In this region of space, the walls between the material realm and the heaving madness of the Warp are thin. The currents within the Sea of Souls are felt in this world and stir the dreams and nightmares of mortals, goading their fractious hearts to discord. Voracious predator creatures lurk in the depths of the warp, and in most places, such creatures cannot force themselves from their abode of the damned to our world without willing conduits or debased followers to ease their passage. But here... here daemonic beings of great power can force themselves through on their own.'

Leodegarius paused and Uriel felt the skin beneath his armour crawl at the thought of the denizens of the warp. He had faced such creatures and knew well the havoc they could wreak.

'One such being was able to manifest on Salinas just over four thousand years ago, a fell Daemon Prince of Chaos named Ustaroth; a thousand curses upon its damned name. This prince of mayhem was a creature of almost limitless power and incalculable malice, and the stress of its passage from the warp allowed others of its kind to follow in the froth of its immaterial wake. Great was the slaughter unleashed, and hundreds died in the first hours of their arrival, thousands in the days following. In desperation, the Imperial Commander called for aid and a detachment of warriors from the Sons of Guilliman heard his plea. Though they knew there was little hope of victory, they diverted to provide what aid they could, for what warrior of honour could stand idly by while the forces of the Archenemy made sport with loyal servants of the Emperor?'

Uriel's heart filled with pride at the heroism of his brothers of the blood and he made a solemn vow that he would do honour to this armour, which had belonged to one of those heroes of long ago.

'The Sons of Guilliman fought alongside the planetary armies, but they were no match for the host of the Daemon Prince, who swept them aside and slew them in a great battle fought within a city in the shadow of the mountains.'

Uriel and Pasanius shared a glance with one another, and they could see that everyone in the room knew, without knowing how they knew, that the Sons of Guilliman had died in Khaturian.

The Killing Ground was, it seemed, a magnet for death.

'Death, unimaginable bloodshed and slavery followed for a decade before warriors from the Grey Knights arrived at the head of a crusade force. My order met the Prince of Chaos in battle and the great Ignatius defeated it, hurling its unclean flesh back to the hell from whence it had come. Salinas was cleansed of taint and displaced peoples from across the sector were brought in to repopulate the planet. Within three generations, what little evidence remained of the invasion had been eradicated and the planet was on its way to becoming a world of the Emperor once more.'

Leodegarius paused, his eyes closed as though remembering and doing honour to the brave hero who had defeated the mighty daemon prince. The Grey Knight opened his eyes and took up the tale once more.

'Salinas was freed from the grip of the daemonic, but great was the damage done beyond the merely physical. Though no trace of the warp remained, the very presence of so powerful a creature is anathema to the fabric of reality, and the invisible walls that separate our realm of existence from that of the immaterium were worn dangerously thin. And the daemonic will always seek to return to the places they once trod.'

'So you've been watching Salinas ever since?' asked Pasanius suddenly. 'That's why you're here now, isn't it?'

'Indeed,' said Leodegarius. 'Since that great victory, we have maintained a secret outpost, hidden from all, that we might stand vigil on Salinas and watch for the return of the daemon prince banished by the great Ignatius.'

'You intercepted our astropathic message,' said Uriel, understanding how the Grey Knights could have known of their whereabouts. 'You heard the call of the Janiceps.'

Leodegarius nodded. 'We did and our warp-seers felt the surge in the warp caused by your arrival. Vast quantities of dangerous energies were released by the machine that brought you here and they have been seized upon by a dark presence lurking on this world.'

'Dark presence?' asked Cardinal Togandis, his voice trembling. 'The daemon prince?'

'Thankfully not,' said Leodegarius, and Togandis visibly sagged against the table, 'but there are powers at work on Salinas that are drawing on that energy and that is further weakening the barriers between us and the warp.'

'What are these powers?' asked Daron Nisato. 'And how do we stop them?'

'We all know what it is,' blurted Togandis, his eyes filling with tears. 'Don't we? Come on, admit it, we've all seen them, haven't we? Daron? Leto? Serj... I know you have!'

'What are you babbling about, Shavo?' snapped Barbaden.

'The dead!' shrieked Togandis. 'The dead of Khaturian! They won't let go of their anger! They want to punish us for what we did... for what we allowed to happen.'

TOGANDIS FELL TO his knees, and Uriel reached out to grab him. The cardinal held onto Uriel's arm for support, fat tears streaming down his glossy cheeks.

'We were there,' whispered the cardinal. 'We were there.'

'Shavo, shut up,' said Barbaden.

Shavo Togandis looked up at the governor, and Uriel was surprised at the steel he saw in the cardinal's eyes. 'No, Leto,' said Togandis, 'not any more. You did it. You doomed us all that day. I must confess. I have to speak!'

Before Togandis could say more, Eversham moved from behind Barbaden with his pistol drawn. Uriel was too far away to react, but there was a flash of silver mail followed by a heavy crunch and Eversham dropped to the floor.

'Emperor's blood!' swore Uriel as he saw Barbaden's equerry lying crumpled on the carpet, blood leaking from the enormous crater that Leodegarius had punched in the side of his head. The man's legs twitched and his eyes fluttered as though he couldn't quite comprehend that he had been killed.

Everyone backed away from the corpse and Leodegarius loomed over Leto Barbaden.

'What has to be said here will be said,' commanded the Grey Knight.

'Of course,' replied Barbaden, looking down at the corpse and for once appearing to be cowed by the warrior.

Leodegarius turned back to the shaking cardinal and took hold of his shoulder, lifting him to his feet as though he weighed no more than a child. He marched the unresisting Togandis towards the room's only chair, and the sweating cardinal gratefully sank into the plush leather.

'Was... Was he going to kill me?' asked Togandis, his gaze switching between the corpse and the warrior who had spilled its blood and brains over the floor.

'He was,' nodded Leodegarius, 'to protect his master.'

All eyes turned on Leto Barbaden and the governor drew himself up to his full height, pulling his coat tightly around him and folding his arms.

'I apologise for nothing,' he stated. 'I did what I had to do. Any commander would have done likewise.'

'No,' said Uriel, rounding on the governor, 'they would not. You murdered the population of Khaturian just because it was the quickest and easier solution. A whole city, tens of thousands dead just to get to one man.'

'Khaturian was a legitimate military target,' said Barbaden.

'Military target?' exclaimed Pascal Blaise, his face purpling with rage and only prevented from launching himself at Barbaden by Daron Nisato's restraining hand. 'There were never any weapons or supplies in Khaturian! We deliberately kept it out of the troubles so there would be somewhere safe for our families to live. You murdered them all!'

'The city was harbouring wanted terrorists and its people shot at my soldiers, so I don't know why you're throwing words like murder around.'

'No!' cried Togandis, rising to his feet. 'You knew, Leto. You knew that many of the Sons of Salinas had families in Khaturian. That was why you picked it. You knew before the first tank rolled that you were going to raze the city to the ground. You sent in Verena Kain and she killed them all. Just to drive Sylvanus Thayer mad with grief and rage and draw him into battle.'

'It worked, didn't it?' snarled Barbaden. 'Why don't any of you see that? We destroyed him and the Sons of Salinas. We brought peace!'

'Brought peace?' laughed Serj Casuaban bitterly. 'You are a fool if you think that, Leto. Spend a day in the House of Providence and you will see what your "peace" has brought to Salinas.'

'So that's it,' laughed Barbaden. 'This is all some grand charade to condemn me, is that it? Gather up all the weaklings who didn't have the spine or will to do what needed to be done and have them all point their grubby little fingers at me?'

Leto Barbaden moved to his drinks cabinet and poured a fresh glass of port. 'We were at war with these people,' he said, carefully enunciating every word, as though speaking to a roomful of simpletons, 'and people die in wars.'

'That's your excuse for mass murder?' asked Uriel.

'Mass murder, military necessity, genocide,' said Barbaden, shrugging, 'it's all the same thing, isn't it? The great Solar Macharius did not shy away from tough decisions that needed to be made, Captain Ventris. He left worlds burning in his wake and entire planets were destroyed in his campaigns, and he is a hero. His name is lauded throughout the Imperium and his generals are revered as saints. Would you have levelled the same accusations at him? Wars are won by the side that is willing to go the furthest, to take the decisions their foes are too squeamish to take. Or have you been so long away from your Chapter that you have forgotten that elementary fact?'

'You are wrong, governor,' said Uriel. 'I have seen my share of death, both honourable and despicable, and yes, I know that war is a brutal, bloody business capable of bringing out the best and worst in men. This is a harsh, dangerous galaxy, with untold terrors lurking in the dark to devour us, but the minute we turn on our own kind and murder them, we might as well take a blade to our throats.'

'I never thought to hear one of the Adeptus Astartes say something so naïve,' spat Barbaden. 'We were at war with an enemy that fought in the shadows with the tactics of terror. How were we to win the war if not by using their own methods against them?'

'You were once a man, Leto, but you are a monster now,' said Shavo Togandis. 'I was once proud to serve you, but what we did that day was wrong, and we have to pay for it.'

'Pay for it?' said Barbaden. 'And who is there to make me?'

'I told you, the dead seek their vengeance.'

Barbaden laughed. 'The dead? Frankly I don't think I need fear them. I think I'm somewhat beyond their jurisdiction.'

'You're wrong,' said Togandis. 'I've seen them. I've felt their cold breath and the touch of their dead hands. They want us all to pay for what we did. Hanno Merbal couldn't take it any more and took his own life right in front of Daron, and I wish I had his courage. For the love of the Emperor, the dead have already killed Mesira and Verena and the Screaming Eagles! And we're next, you, me and Serj. We're all that's left.'

Leodegarius lifted a hand, stopping Barbaden's reply. 'The cardinal is correct, the dead *are* here. I have felt them and one does not need to be a psychic to feel the dread presence of their spirits. This planet is rank with them.'

'How is that possible?' asked Uriel. 'How can the dead remain after they are gone?'

'Each of us has a spark inside us, a spirit or soul, call it what you will, and when we die it is released from our bodies to dissipate into the warp,' said Leodegarius, 'but when so large a number of people die, gripped by such rage and terror as must have been felt by the people of Khaturian, their spirits can remain coherent.'

'What happens to them?' asked Pascal Blaise.

'Normally nothing, for such spirits are as swirling embers in a hurricane, but when there is a focus for them, something to direct their energies, they can influence the realm of the living. Even then, it is usually no more than phantasms and does not last for long, but something or someone is directing the power of these spirits and they are growing stronger with every passing moment.'

'Is that what those monsters were that killed Mesira?' asked Daron Nisato. 'The dead?'

'No, they are creatures of flesh and blood,' said Uriel. 'We encountered them in our travels and were bringing them home. Once they were human children, but they were twisted by the Ruinous Powers into...' Uriel struggled for the right word.

'Into monsters,' said Nisato.

'No, not monsters,' said Uriel. 'They are innocents. The spirits of the dead have taken their bodies for their own. What is happening is not their doing.'

Leto Barbaden laughed. 'So am I to understand that these creatures came to Salinas with you, Captain Ventris? Oh, this is too rich. Then the deaths of the Screaming Eagles, Colonel Kain and Mesira Bardhyl are your fault.'

'No, governor,' said Uriel icily. 'Their deaths are on your head. The Unfleshed could have lived their lives out in peace somewhere safe, if it hadn't been for the horror you unleashed on Khaturian. Now they are pawns in the bloody revenge of your victims.'

'Worse, they may see this world destroyed,' said Leodegarius.

All recriminations stopped.

'Destroyed?' asked Casuaban. 'In the name of all that's holy, why?'

'The stronger the dead become, the more they draw the power of the warp to themselves, further weakening the walls that keep the immaterium from engulfing this world. If we do not stop this soon, the walls will collapse and the entire sector will become a gateway to the realm of Chaos. I will destroy this world before I allow that to happen.'

A heavy silence descended as all gathered suddenly realised the scale of the danger.

'So how do we stop it?' asked Uriel.

'We find what is holding the ghosts here and destroy it,' said Leodegarius.

'What is holding them here?' asked Togandis.

When Leodegarius didn't answer immediately, Barbaden said, 'You don't know, do you?'

'No, I do not, but one of you does.'

'One of us?' asked Uriel. 'Who?'

'Again, I do not know, but the cards have gathered you here for a reason,' said Leodegarius. 'The energy of these spirits must have a focus that binds them here, someone with psychic ability, who is so consumed by rage that he has the power to wield such monstrous energies.'

Again, silence fell, until Pascal Blaise said, 'I know who it is.'

'Who?' demanded Leodegarius. 'Tell us.'

'It's Sylvanus Thayer.'

'Nonsense,' snapped Barbaden. 'That stupid bastard is dead. The Falcatas destroyed him and his traitorous band after Khaturian.'

Serj Casuaban shook his head. 'No, Leto,' he said, 'he's alive. What's left of him is hooked up to machines in the House of Providence, though to call what he has "life" is stretching the term somewhat.'

'You knew Thayer was alive and you kept this from me?' stormed Barbaden.

'I did,' admitted Casuaban. 'It was my penance for what we did. He was one man I would not let die through my cowardice.'

Leodegarius interrupted, turning Serj Casuaban around and saying, 'This Sylvanus Thayer? Tell me of him.'

'What do you want to know?'

'You said, "What's left of him", what did you mean by that?'

'I meant that the Falcatas were thorough; they thought they'd killed him and they very nearly did. When Pascal Blaise brought him to me, I thought he was already dead, but he held on to life and just wouldn't let go of it. He'd sustained burns to almost ninety percent of his body and had lost both his legs and one of his arms. His eyes had burned away and he'd lost the power of speech. I think he can hear, but it's hard to tell. A machine breathes for him and another feeds him, while a third takes away his waste. Like I said, it's not much of a life.'

'Imperator, you'd be better off letting him die!' said Pasanius.

'I know,' said Casuaban, his voice close to breaking, 'but I couldn't. After the Killing Ground Massacre, I stayed sane by telling myself that I hadn't killed anyone, hadn't even fired a shot, but if I killed Sylvanus Thayer or just let him die, I'd be as bad as those who had burned Khaturian.'

'If anyone would have enough rage within him it would be the man whose family was killed in Khaturian,' nodded Leodegarius. 'Being trapped in the flesh of his destroyed body… that could have been the catalyst that allowed latent psychic powers to develop.'

Leodegarius gripped Casuaban's shoulders tightly.

'You say this Sylvanus Thayer is in the House of Providence?'

'Yes,' said Casuaban.

'Take us there,' said Leodegarius, 'before it's too late.'

NINETEEN

THE LAND RAIDER'S engine was loud and the stink of its fuel was an acrid, yet amazingly welcome smell to Uriel. Clad in his borrowed armour and riding to battle in one of the most powerful vehicles in the Space Marine inventory was a tangible sign that their enforced exile was at an end.

Pasanius sat next to him, his attention fixed on a pict-slate displaying a grainy image of the Land Raider's exterior, while five other Grey Knights in burnished silver-steel power armour sat opposite him.

Standing at the frontal assault ramp was Leodegarius, who was once again clad in his colossal Terminator armour. The Grey Knight stood with his long polearm clutched tightly in his enormous fist. In place of his wrist-mounted storm bolter, he bore a weapon that he had informed Uriel was a psycannon. Instead of bolt shells, this weapon fired consecrated bolts of purest silver that were the bane of the daemonic and unnatural.

Uriel held the bolter that Leodegarius had given him tightly, the fine lines and exquisite workmanship far exceeding anything he had ever seen. It was a gift of incalculable worth and Uriel hoped he would prove an honourable bearer of such a fine weapon in the coming fight.

He was under no illusions – Blood would be spilled tonight.

No sooner had Uriel stepped from the palace and into the dusk of evening than he had felt the smothering gloom of the looming threat. The presence of the vengeful dead saturated the air and scraped along the nerves like a discordant vibration.

With no time to waste, Leodegarius had mustered his warriors and, together with Uriel and Pasanius and Serj Casuaban, they had set off through the streets of Barbadus towards the House of Providence. Two Rhinos followed behind the Land Raider and despite the sheer bulk and terror a Land Raider inspired, it was slow going, for the streets of Barbadus were thronged with people: shouting, agitated and scared people.

'It's a mess out there,' said Pasanius, looking at the pict-slate.

'No one knows what's happening, but they know that something is terribly wrong,' said Uriel.

'Aye, you're right, you *don't* need to be psychic to know that,' agreed Pasanius, looking towards Leodegarius's vast bulk. The warrior's blade gleamed red in the light of the troop compartment and Uriel shivered as he felt its potency as a shrill prickling along the length of his spine.

'It is a Nemesis weapon,' said Leodegarius, as if sensing Uriel's scrutiny, 'a blade forged by the finest artificers of Titan and quenched in the blood of a daemon.'

'The Unfleshed?' asked Uriel. 'Will it kill them?'

'It killed two of them in the plaza before the building I pulled you out of.'

'Two,' said Uriel sadly, 'that leaves maybe five or six left.'

'You feel sympathy for them?' asked Leodegarius.

'I do,' agreed Uriel. 'They didn't deserve this.'

'Perhaps not, but few people in this galaxy get what they deserve.'

'He will,' said Pasanius, jerking his thumb at Serj Casuaban, looking wretched and miserable in the far corner of the compartment.

Pasanius turned away from the dejected medicae and addressed Leodegarius. 'I still say we should bomb this place from orbit. You've got a ship up there, haven't you?'

'I have,' said Leodegarius without turning, 'and if we cannot stop Thayer then I will order a lance strike from orbit.'

'No, you can't!' cried Serj Casuaban. 'There are innocents in the House of Providence, not to mention all the people you'd kill and maim in the city with a strike like that! Give that order and you're no better than Barbaden.'

'Or you,' said Pasanius. 'You were at Khaturian as well.'

'I killed no one,' said Casuaban defensively.

'You let Barbaden give the order,' said Pasanius. 'Did you even try to stop him?'

'You don't know him. Once Leto has his mind made up, there's not a thing in the world can make him change it.'

'Fine,' said Pasanius, turning to Uriel, 'then why don't we give these dead folk what they want? Barbaden and Togandis are locked up in the cells and we have this one here, so why not just put a bullet in the backs of their heads? Wouldn't that solve the problem?'

'You'd kill me in cold blood?' demanded Casuaban.

'If it would save the planet, aye,' nodded Pasanius, 'in a heartbeat.'

'Pasanius, enough,' snapped Uriel. 'We're not shooting anyone. This is about justice, not revenge. We stop Sylvanus Thayer and then the three of them will face a court martial for war crimes.'

Uriel paused as a sudden thought came to him and turned to face Leodegarius. 'Is it safe to keep Barbaden and Togandis in the palace cells? Won't the dead be able to get to them there?'

'No, I am maintaining an aegis sanctuary over them,' said Leodegarius. 'No power of the warp will be able to touch them.'

Uriel wanted to ask more, but the Grey Knight held up his hand. 'We are here,' he said.

'How does it look?'

'Bad.'

DESPITE THE FACT that he was languishing in a cell beneath the rock of the Imperial Palace, Shavo Togandis was more at peace than he had been in the last ten years. All the guilt was, if not gone, at least less of a burden now that the truth of the Killing Ground was known.

The air in the circular prison complex was cold, and for the first time in as long as he could remember, Togandis was not sweating. Stripped of his ceremonial robes, he had been permitted to retain the undergarments of his vestments, as none of the prison issue tunics were large enough for him.

He knelt before the bars of his cell, facing the featureless guard building in the centre of the chamber, his hands clasped before him, reciting prayers that rushed to fill the void in his mind that had been left by the fear of discovery.

'You think praying will do any good?' asked Leto Barbaden from the cell next to his.

Togandis finished his prayer and turned his head to face the man who had lived in his nightmares for the past decade. Looking at him now, he wondered what he had found so terrifying. Leto Barbaden might be a monster on the inside, but to look at him he was just an ordinary man. Not too strong and not too clever, just an ordinary man.

Just as he was an ordinary man.

Which only made the scale of their crimes all the more horrifying.

How could anyone believe that such evil could come from such unremarkable specimens?

Surely the slaughter of so many innocent lives could only have been at the behest of some winged, fire-breathing daemon or undertaken by a host of bloodthirsty orks.

No, it had been done by men and women.

They had done it, and the nearness of the punishment was a blessed relief to the former cardinal.

'I think prayer can't hurt, Leto,' he answered. 'We are going to pay for what we did and I need to get right with the Emperor before then.'

'They can cook up a farce of a trial, but I won't apologise. They'll get nothing from me.'

'Even now, with everything in the open, you still don't think we did anything wrong?'

'Of course not,' snapped Barbaden.

'Then you are truly lost, Leto,' said Togandis with a shake of his head. 'I always knew you were a very dangerous man, but I don't think I realised why until now.'

'What are you babbling about?'

'You are the dark heart of man, Leto,' answered Togandis. 'You are the evil that can lurk in any of us, the potential to commit the most heinous acts and do it with a smile on our faces. There is a wall of conscience between acts of good and evil inside most of us, but that's missing in you. I don't know why, but for you there is no concept of evil, just results.'

The words flowed from Togandis and he felt the catharsis of them as he spoke.

He closed his eyes and smiled as he smelled the faint, but distinct aroma of burning flesh.

'They're coming, Leto.'

Togandis turned his head and looked out beyond the bars as he heard shouts and cries of alarm from the other prisoners.

A mist of shimmering light was forming in the chamber, as though some ductwork had split open and was pouring hot steam into the gaol. Togandis knew it was no such thing and smiled as he saw a host of jostling, ghostly forms in the mist.

First to emerge from the acrid smoke was a small girl, her dress blackened and smouldering. Her flesh was burned and hung from her body in melted strips.

Other forms joined the girl: men, women and more children. On they came until it seemed as though the chamber was filled with the dead.

They moved as though blown by a gentle breeze, drawing near to the cells. Togandis welcomed them, knowing that neither he nor Leto Barbaden would ever stand before a court martial.

Togandis looked over at Leto Barbaden and didn't know whether to be impressed or revolted at his lack of emotion. The former governor of Salinas appeared as unmoved by these apparitions of death as he did by everything else in life.

How grey life must be to him, thought Togandis.

The young girl turned her face to Barbaden and said, 'You were there.'

'Damn right I was,' snarled Barbaden. 'I killed you and I am not sorry.'

The girl's face twisted, the flesh of her face rippling with light and undulant motion as she launched herself towards Leto Barbaden.

Searing blue lightning flashed from the bars of the cell and Togandis blinked in surprise as the girl was hurled back. Her substance faded and vanished into the mist as though she had never existed.

Barbaden laughed. 'It seems these phantoms of Thayer's are not so powerful after all.'

'What do you mean?' gasped Togandis, willing the spirits of the dead to come for him and end his miserable existence.

'I think Leodegarius really wants us alive to stand trial.'

Then Togandis understood.

BAD DIDN'T EVEN begin to cover it.

The House of Providence was aflame, streamers of cold fire billowing like blazing shrouds from every opening and around every rivet, as though the interiors of the three mighty vehicles were full to bursting with light.

Howling winds, like the shrieking cries of the damned, swirled around their destination carrying tormented screams of anguish so intense that it seemed impossible that they could be wrung from a human throat. Arcs of pellucid lighting crackled and rippled over the metal surfaces of the colossal war engines and a creeping sickness oozed down the hill.

'Still think we shouldn't bomb this place from orbit?' asked Pasanius.

Serj Casuaban looked at what had become of the House of Providence with sick horror, and Uriel could only begin to imagine what he must be feeling. A place of healing had become a place of death and vengeance, and the physician in him rebelled at such a perversion.

Uriel and Leodegarius led the way uphill on foot, the Land Raider's passage onwards blocked by a multitude of burnt out tank chassis dragged onto the road. The Grey Knights followed in five-man combat teams, and Pasanius helped Serj Casuaban to keep up.

'How did these tanks get here?' asked Casuaban. 'They weren't here before.'

'The Unfleshed,' said Uriel, pointing upwards to where five hulking shapes were silhouetted at the ridge of the plateau. No more than midnight-black outlines, their veins ran with light and Uriel saw that the Lord of the Unfleshed had grown more powerful since their last encounter, his flesh monstrously swollen and seething with angry souls.

The creatures vanished from sight behind the ridge and a wave of black despair engulfed Uriel as he knew he would have no choice but to aid the Grey Knights in their destruction. Whatever he had hoped for the Unfleshed was lost. The brutal reality of the galaxy was that there was no place for them, no happy ending, only death.

The winds howling around the House of Providence were getting stronger and the screaming was growing louder. Lightning arced from the middle Capitol Imperialis with a deafening thunderclap, exploding against the hull of a hollowed out Chimera.

'Something's definitely trying to keep us out!' shouted Uriel.

Serj Casuaban clamped his hands over his ears and a hard rain pounded the ground.

Their path wound up the hill, the pace slowed by the need to thread through the maze of burnt and abandoned tanks. Leodegarius hauled those that couldn't be got round out of the way, the incredible power of his Terminator armour able to push tanks from their path as though they weighed nothing at all.

The ridge was approaching and Uriel racked the slide on his bolter, the very notion of going into battle as a Space Marine of the Emperor once more filling him with pride. The Grey Knights spread out, their halberds thrust forward into the storm of light and rain.

Uriel's bolter snapped left and right as he caught fleeting glimpses of darting, ghostly figures at the edge of his vision. A thousand whispering voices rustled like a forest of fallen leaves, the words unintelligible, but all filled with anger.

'You hear them?' asked Leodegarius over the vox.

'I do,' said Uriel, 'but I'm more worried about the Unfleshed.'

'They will be inside,' said Leodegarius, 'waiting for us.'

With that thought uppermost in his mind, Uriel jogged over the ridge, his neck craning upwards as he stood in the enormous shadow of the House of Providence.

Seen from a distance, the three Capitol Imperialis had been hugely impressive symbols of the Imperium, but up close, they were incredible, towering visions of the power to destroy. Their rusted metal flanks soared into the battered sky, the lightning that surrounded them flaring into the heavens as though it was a reactor on the verge of meltdown.

The image was not a comforting one.

As they approached the House of Providence, Uriel's every instinct told him that he was surrounded by foes, yet he could see nothing, nothing solid anyway, for the shrieking winds carried hints of floating phantoms, wisps of bodies as insubstantial as smoke, yet with the presence of a living, breathing being.

Moving towards the House of Providence was proving difficult, as though every step was taken through sucking mud. Even Leodegarius's pace was slowed and Uriel did not want to think of the power that could slow a Terminator.

'How do we get in?' shouted Uriel, looking along the length of the structure for an opening.

'Over there,' said Leodegarius, pointing towards the shadowed form of an arched entrance, partially hidden by mists and unnatural blackness. Uriel peered into the gloom, barely able to discern its outline.

Leodegarius turned to face Serj Casuaban. 'You will lead us to Sylvanus Thayer, medicae. Identify him and then keep out of our way, understand?' he said, his voice easily cutting through the howling gale of the psychic storm.

Casuaban nodded,

Uriel gripped his bolter tightly as Leodegarius said, 'Let's get inside.'

Outside the House of Providence, all was storm-tossed madness, while inside was frozen stillness. No sooner had Uriel entered the towering structure than the noise and light vanished.

Sputtering glow-globes strung from the iron mesh of the ceiling bobbed overhead and steam vented from the backpacks of their armour like breath. The walls were cold iron, streaked with lines of frost, and pools of ice cracked underfoot. Uriel and Pasanius made their way along the narrow entrance corridor, the shoulders of Leodegarius's armour brushing the walls with his every step.

Shadows grew and receded on the glistening walls and Uriel could hear a maddening buzz just below the threshold of hearing. The Grey Knights spread throughout the structures, moving off in teams of five, securing as tight a perimeter as they could around their leaders.

As well as four Grey Knights in power armour, Uriel's group was made up of Leodegarius, Pasanius and Serj Casuaban. The man was shivering, his face pale and his eyes wide. He scratched at the side of his face, shaking his head as though seeking to dislodge something in his ear.

'So many voices,' he whispered, the sound echoing in the cold corridor.

'You can hear them?' asked Uriel.

Casuaban nodded, tears glistening on his cheeks. 'All of them. They're frightened of him. The Mourner, that's what they used to call him.'

'Who?'

'Sylvanus Thayer,' said Casuaban, 'after the massacre.'

'They're frightened of him?'

'Yes... They want to leave, to go to their rest, but he won't let them, not until he's had his vengeance.'

Uriel filed that fact away and set off after Leodegarius.

Their path took them along corridors, through wards filled with terrified people and along open hallways. Wisps of light gathered in the ceiling spaces and the howls of the wounded echoed strangely in the confusing internal architecture of the place.

Desperately injured men, women and children stared at them, some with terror, some with hope, but the Space Marines could not stop to help them. This was a truly wretched place, Uriel thought, the wounded of the decades old conflict left to rot with only the skill and dedication of one man to help them rebuild their lives.

No matter what happened, Uriel vowed that he would do what he could for Serj Casuaban. The man might be guilty, but it was clear that he at least felt some remorse for what he had allowed to happen.

At each junction of corridors, the medicae would point and then set off once more, alert for any sign of the Unfleshed or any other enemy.

Though he saw no threats, Uriel could sense a fearsome potential building, as though a great power was even now gathering its strength. He cursed his vivid imagination and shook off such morbid thoughts as Leodegarius halted.

They had come to a junction with two passages stretching off into the darkness, left and right, while a wide set of iron stairs led up into sputtering, fitful light. Frozen stalactites of ice hung from the brass balustrade.

'Which way, medicae?' demanded Leodegarius.

'Up, we need to go up.'

WHEN THE ATTACK came, it was with a precision that caught everyone by surprise.

The warriors on the right flank came under attack first; a beast with a hunched spine and long arms wrapped in muscles like steel hawsers tore the head from the warrior on point and hurled it back at his comrades.

A creature with a fused exoskeleton like armour barrelled into the warriors on the left, scattering them and crushing two warriors to death with the sheer force and mass of its charge.

As they reached a ramp that led further upwards, Uriel saw a great shadow detach itself from an alcove in the wall ahead, its body pulsing with light as it came at them. This creature was a hybrid of two forms fused into one, a union of flesh that could not possibly be alive, yet had somehow found a way to exist.

Uriel saw the creature's internal twin oozing beneath its newly formed skin, a howling face pressed against its pallid sheath of flesh. Its muscles seethed with light and its fist caved in the helmet of the Grey Knight nearest Uriel in one quick motion.

Blood squirted from the headless corpse and the silence of the House of Providence was brutally ended.

The Grey Knights reacted with all the speed and ferocity that Uriel expected. No sooner had the beast appeared in their midst than every halberd was swinging for it. Storm bolters opened up in a co-ordinated volley of fire. Blazing light and deafening noise filled the space and sprays of light and flesh flew from the Unfleshed as it shuddered under the impacts.

A fist with the mass and force of a lump hammer swung out and smashed the breastplate of a Grey Knight, exiting from the warrior's back in an explosion of blood and ceramite. Uriel ducked the return stroke and opened fire, the bark of his weapon adding to the din.

Serj Casuaban dropped to his knees, his arms pulled in tight as Pasanius stood over him.

Too close to use his psycannon, Leodegarius thrust with his polearm, the glowing blade hammering into the back of the creature. It roared in pain, the shimmering, fiery tip of the blade erupting from its swollen chest. The creature tried to spin around to face its attacker, but Leodegarius's strength and mass was too great and he held it fast.

'Hurry!' shouted Leodegarius. 'Kill it!'

The two surviving Grey Knights moved in, firing as they went, and Uriel was struck by their utter fearlessness in facing this terrifying creature. More bloody craters were gouged in its flesh by a host of mass-reactive shells, yet it appeared not to feel them.

Leodegarius dragged the beast to its knees with a heaving twist of his polearm and Uriel ran to join the Grey Knights, his sword leaping to his hand. Their blades stabbed the creature and its roars of pain echoed from the walls, shaking icicles from the ceiling.

The creature's oozing twin erupted from the Unfleshed's chest in a monstrous parody of birth, its vile, putrescent form slathered in blood and its grasping claws reaching for the nearest warrior. Its claws were sheathed in light and they parted the Grey Knight's armour and flesh as if they were wet paper. The parasitic twin tore through the muscle and bone of the warrior's chest, sundering his heart and ripping the mass of his internal organs to bloody ruin.

The Grey Knight dropped to the ground, breaking the neck of his killer as he fell.

The Unfleshed was weakening and Leodegarius was finally able to bring his psycannon to bear, unleashing a hail of psychically impregnated bolts into the beast.

The effect was instantaneous, and the creature toppled over, a ruined mass of shredded flesh that could not have endured such horrible damage without the power of the dead to sustain it.

Uriel felt no glory at the kill, only regret, but he did not have time to wallow in it.

Fresh foes were upon them.

They came in scads of light from the wards all around them, their shrieking howls of pain screeching along Uriel's nerves. Looking deeper into the light, he saw a host of horrific figures sweeping towards them as though driven by some powerful wind.

They were diseased figures, crippled figures, gaunt, emaciated and burnt forms in billowing surgical gowns: amputees, men with no eyes and women with hideous scars all over their bodies. Every hand was extended as though pleading for alms, and those with eyes were haunted with the angry memory of pain and suffering. A bow wave of frost cracked the walls before them, crazed patterns spreading in waves of white.

'What in the name of the Emperor are they?' screamed Casuaban when he looked up.

'Phantoms,' said Leodegarius, 'the tormented nightmares of the wounded you care for. The power of the warp is getting stronger and they are becoming real.'

'I take it they are dangerous?' said Uriel, raising his sword.

'Lethal,' said Leodegarius. 'Do not let them touch you. They will feed on your life to ease their suffering. Medicae! Which way?'

Casuaban looked around, as though his surroundings were suddenly unfamiliar to him.

'Quickly, man!' shouted Leodegarius.

'Up! Up another level!'

Leodegarius turned away from them and stood in the centre of the corridor directly in the path of the seething horde of nightmares. 'Cheiron, with me! Uriel, get behind us!' he cried. 'Onto the ramp!'

'What are you going to do?' cried Uriel.

'We're going to stop them,' said Leodegarius.

Uriel backed away from the Grey Knights as he tasted the actinic tang of psychic energy and his sword sparked and fizzed in the presence of such power. Hurriedly, he gathered Pasanius and Casuaban and backed onto the ramp that led up to who knew what.

Gunfire roared from the Grey Knights' weapons, Cheiron's bolts appearing to have little effect, but those of Leodegarius tearing through the figures like fire through cloth. As the ghostly nightmares drew ever closer, however, Uriel saw it wouldn't be enough.

'I have to help them!' cried Uriel.

'Wait!' shouted Pasanius, pointing towards the two Grey Knights.

Uriel looked over his shoulder and watched the silver-armoured warriors seem to swell as crackling arcs of lightning flared from the leading edges of their armour.

Both warriors held their polearms upright and their free hands were extended as they chanted the same mantra. 'Foul conjurations of the warp, we know thee. Unclean power from beyond the veil we abhor thee. Fell daemons of the Empyrean we defy thee.'

Leodegarius slammed his polearm onto the metal deck. 'Thrice cursed you are and thrice damned be thee.'

Serj Casuaban cried out and Uriel felt the rush of power as an enormous white fireball exploded into life around the Grey Knights. Wreathed in the flames, Leodegarius and Cheiron shone like angels of the Emperor, the roaring power contained around them by sheer force of will.

'Spawn of evil I cast you from this place!' cried Leodegarius and the blazing white fireball filled the corridor. Billowing flames exploded outwards from the Grey Knights, and the screams of the ghostly figures were swallowed in the seething roar of the fire.

Uriel shielded Serj Casuaban from the flames as their power swirled around them. Metal groaned and hissed under the assault of Leodegarius's purity, the very essence of his soul poured out in the cleansing fire of the Emperor.

In little over a few seconds it was ended, the nightmare howls silenced, and the terrifying roar of the fiery holocaust the two Grey Knights had unleashed at an end.

Uriel looked up to see Leodegarius and Cheiron still standing in the middle of the corridor, their silver armour streaming with scraps of light that faded even as he watched. Leodegarius turned to face him and even though he was clad head to foot in Terminator armour, Uriel could see that he was exhausted.

'Come,' he hissed. 'They will be back. We must move on.'

Uriel nodded as Pasanius dragged Serj Casuaban to his feet.

'Up you said?'

'Yes, Emperor protect me,' said Casuaban, making the sign of the aquila.

Uriel led the way up the ramp, with Pasanius dragging the reluctant medicae behind him. Leodegarius and Cheiron brought up the rear and Uriel could already hear the building screams and howls of more enemies closing on them.

He switched to an internal vox channel within his helmet, hearing shouted commands and the bark of gunfire. Shots sounded in his helmet, throughout the House of Providence, their source impossible to pinpoint as they echoed from the maze-like corridors.

How the other Grey Knights fared, Uriel could not tell, for their commands were spoken in a battle cant unknown to him, but every order was delivered clearly and calmly. To hear warriors in battle communicating with such cool determination under fire was inspiring and Uriel felt a renewed sense of honour to be fighting alongside them.

'This way,' said Serj Casuaban, leading them through a series of low doors that led deeper into the heart of the House of Providence. Some of the doorways proved too small for Leodegarius, but quick, efficient strokes of his Nemesis weapon soon opened a hole large enough for him to squeeze his enormous, armoured bulk through.

At last their route took them into the highest ward in the converted Capitol Imperialis, a long, metal-walled chamber crammed with iron beds arranged along the walls and a wide central nave. Each of the beds was home to a writhing figure, their mouths twisted in rictus grins of pain.

The air was filled with screams and scraps of light, ghostly forms of howling figures that orbited a bed near the centre of the right-hand wall.

There could be no doubt that this was Sylvanus Thayer.

The Lord of the Unfleshed towered over his bed, his mighty form awesome and unbearable to look upon.

♈ TWENTY

Uriel, Leodegarius and Cheiron slowly made their way down through the ward between the rows of beds. Pasanius left Serj Casuaban beside a medical station by the door and followed them. The Lord of the Unfleshed watched them approach, his eyes glowing with fiery light that burned like dead stars.

'So what are we going to do?' asked Uriel over the vox.

'First we fight the beast,' said Leodegarius, 'and then we get to Thayer.'

'Then what?'

'We kill him.'

Uriel nodded. He didn't like the idea of killing a man lying on his deathbed, but Sylvanus Thayer was no innocent, and his unchecked power would kill millions more if they did not stop him. He had kept the dead from their rest and bound them to his hatred, and that was unforgivable.

The Lord of the Unfleshed lowered his head, the jaw working in unfamiliar ways, strings of bloody drool leaking from the corners of his mouth.

'You come here to stop me?' said the Lord of the Unfleshed, in a voice not his own.

'Do I speak with Sylvanus Thayer?' demanded Leodegarius.

'Aye, warrior, you do.'

'Then yes, we come to stop you,' said Leodegarius, taking another step towards the Lord of the Unfleshed. 'Your hatred will doom this world if we do not.'

The creature laughed, the sound barren and repulsive. 'Why would that be a bad thing? Salinas has nothing good left. Barbaden and the Falcatas saw to that.'

'Barbaden is under arrest,' said Uriel at Leodegarius's side. 'Those you haven't already killed will pay for their crimes, I promise you.'

'Pay?' sneered Sylvanus Thayer with the Lord of the Unfleshed's body. 'To languish in a jail cell and live out their lives? That is not nearly enough pain for what they did.'

'Maybe not,' agreed Uriel, 'but it is justice.'

'Justice!' roared Thayer. 'Where was justice when Barbaden's tanks burned my family to death? Where was justice when his soldiers shot fleeing women and children? Where was the justice when he shelled my men to oblivion when we fought to avenge their deaths? Answer me that, warrior!'

'I have no answer to give you,' said Uriel. 'What happened to you and this planet was wrong, but more death is not the answer. Hatred breeds hatred and your actions have only made things worse.'

Serj Casuaban spoke up from behind them, and Uriel turned at the sound of his voice.

'He's right, Captain Ventris, that's not justice,' said the medicae. 'Only our blood will be payment enough. We all know that.'

'Be silent,' ordered Leodegarius. 'I told you to stay out of the way.'

Serj Casuaban lifted his hand and Uriel saw something shining there.

'I did that once before and look where it got me,' said Casuaban, placing a long-bladed scalpel at his throat. 'It's time to pay for what we did, and for what it's worth, I'm sorry.'

'No!' cried Uriel, but it was too late.

Casuaban slashed the blade across his throat, digging deep to sever the jugular. Blood spurted in a crimson fountain and Serj Casuaban dropped to the decking.

Uriel ran over to where he lay, but the medicae had been precise in his cutting and a vast pool of blood already gathered around him. Uriel placed his hands on the wound, but it had been cut too wide and thoroughly to staunch. Blood squirted from between Uriel's fingers and spattered his armour.

Casuaban's eyes were glassy with death and Uriel knew that the man's life was gone. There was no saving him now.

Uriel stood and saw that Leodegarius was within five metres of the enormous form of the Lord of the Unfleshed. The creature stood tall and Uriel was amazed at how powerful his physique had become. The Lord of the Unfleshed had suffered terribly in the fighting of the last few days, but there could be no underestimating the power that still resided in his frame.

Searing lines of light rippled beneath his ashen skin and his mutated flesh was redolent with warp-born power. The Lord of the Unfleshed roared and the ward echoed to the sound of his pain and Thayer's anger.

'Enough blood has been shed,' said Leodegarius, raising his psycannon. 'This ends now.'

'Aye!' bellowed the Lord of the Unfleshed. 'One way or another.'

Before Leodegarius could fire, the Lord of the Unfleshed reached down and heaved, hurling a pair of heavy, iron beds towards them. Consecrated bolts blasted the beds apart and tore their unfortunate occupants to shreds, but were deflected away from their intended target.

The beds crashed down in a heap of twisted iron. A mist of bloodied feathers from the ruptured mattresses filled the air. Uriel ran forward as the Lord of the Unfleshed leapt, his enormous fist smashing into the ward's floor and buckling the metal plates.

Leodegarius took aim once more, but the Lord of the Unfleshed was upon him, towering over the Grey Knight and bathing him in the light that shone beneath his flesh. A backhand blow sent Leodegarius spinning and a hail of bolts from Cheiron's weapon stitched their way up the Lord of the Unfleshed's back.

Pasanius and Cheiron circled behind the towering monster, which battered clubbing fists against the plates of Leodegarius's armour.

Leodegarius fought to keep his attacker at bay, but Terminator armour was designed for protection, not speed, and he could not avoid the Lord of the Unfleshed's savage blows. One shoulder guard was already hanging from sparking cables and torn fibre-bundle muscles, and his breastplate was cracked and leaking fluid.

Uriel vaulted the remains of the shredded beds, offering a silent prayer for the souls who had died upon them. His sword shimmered in the swirling light of the ward and he gripped it two-handed as he joined the fight.

Pasanius fired and Uriel swung his weapon at the Lord of the Unfleshed, the sword a shimmering arc of silver as it struck. The blade scored across the creature's hard body, but no sooner had the blade parted its flesh than the light raced to mend it.

The Lord of the Unfleshed spun and swung his fist at Uriel.

He ducked and rolled beneath the great beast, stabbing his sword up into its groin. The fiery blade bit into the Lord of the Unfleshed's body, and a strike that should have cut the leg from any normal opponent slid clear.

Pasanius and Cheiron kept up a steady barrage, but their weapons were having little effect. The roar of the bolters mingled with the howls of the ghosts and the bellowing of the Lord of the Unfleshed to form one, savage cacophony of battle.

It seemed inconceivable that one opponent could stand before four Space Marines and live, but the Lord of the Unfleshed was not just surviving, he was winning.

Leodegarius fell beneath a crushing blow that tore the Nemesis weapon from his hands. The Grey Knight lifted his other arm, but the Lord of the Unfleshed took hold of it and ripped it from his body with a ghastly tearing sound. Blood jetted from the wound and Uriel heard Leodegarius's bellow of pain over his armour's vox.

Uriel was amazed to see Terminator armour ruptured with such apparent ease, for such revered protection was said to be virtually indestructible. Leodegarius fell back, the pain of his wounding and the exhaustion of his psychic assault below draining him of almost the last of his strength.

Cheiron leapt in, ramming his Nemesis weapon into the Lord of the Unfleshed's back. The creature spun quickly, wrenching the weapon from Cheiron's hands, and smashed the warrior from his feet. The Grey Knight flew across the ward and slammed into the steel wall, falling in an ungainly heap and leaving a huge dent in the metalwork.

Pasanius swept up Leodegarius's fallen Nemesis weapon. Together, he and Uriel circled in opposite directions around the Lord of the

Unfleshed. The creature's body was a mass of cuts and bolt impacts, its back horrifically cratered and running with blood and light.

Uriel could only imagine the pain the Lord of the Unfleshed was feeling, but he knew that he had to suppress any notions of humanity in his opponent.

Pasanius feinted with his polearm, but using such a long, heavy weapon with only one arm was difficult and the Lord of the Unfleshed batted the blade aside. Uriel darted in and hacked his blade down at the Lord of the Unfleshed's knee, hoping to at least slow him down.

Before the blade connected, the Lord of the Unfleshed twisted and clubbed Uriel savagely with an arm like a tree trunk. He flew though the air to land beside the twisted bed frames, the plates of his armour buckled, but unbroken.

He rolled to his feet in time to see Pasanius smashed from his feet. His friend crashed down beside Serj Casuaban's corpse as Leodegarius struggled to pull himself to his feet and Cheiron began to rouse himself from where the Lord of the Unfleshed had hurled him.

URIEL LOOKED OVER at Sylvanus Thayer. The swirling ghosts howled around the man's bed and Uriel could hear the indescribable pain in their agonised utterances. A core of light, white, yet without any purity, was building around his bed. Screams and monstrous shrieks issued from the light and Uriel knew that he was looking at a tear in the very meat of reality, a wound through which all manner of horrors might pour.

He tore his gaze from the burning light, as the Lord of the Unfleshed's roars echoed from the walls, the sound a heartbreaking mix of agony, triumph and regret.

Uriel leapt torn and scattered beds. It went against his every instinct to leave his comrades in battle, but he knew that this fight could not be won through strength of arms as he scrambled over the debris of the chamber towards the bed where Sylvanus Thayer lay.

'I'm with you!' shouted Pasanius, rushing over to join him.

Uriel heard the roar of the Lord of the Unfleshed as Thayer felt his approach, and the howling of the ghosts grew ever louder. A din of battle sounded behind him and Uriel heard the unmistakable sound of something huge coming towards him.

Thayer's bed was just in front of him and Uriel saw the man's body beneath the filmy surgical gauze was as wrecked as Serj Casuaban had said.

His skin was raw and red, wet and horrific. Both legs ended in cauterised stumps in mid-thigh and one arm was missing from the shoulder down. What was left of Thayer's face was a molten ruin of dead flesh. Both eyes were unseeing and useless, artificial lids sutured over the sockets to keep them closed.

Uriel lifted his sword, the blade poised to split Thayer's skull open and end this horror.

There was no glory in this killing, no honour and no reward, only duty.

'Do it!' shouted Pasanius. 'Kill him!'

Then Sylvanus Thayer's eyelids flew open, a fierce light burning within the ravaged sockets, as though every ounce of his hatred of the living had ignited within them.

'Know what I know,' hissed the voice of Sylvanus Thayer in his skull, 'and then judge me.'

Then the world vanished in a searing wall of flames.

URIEL THREW UP his hand as the flames roared over him, expecting his armour's cooling systems to activate in response to the attack, but as he lowered his arms he was amazed to see that he was no longer within the House of Providence. The ruined ward had vanished.

Instead of the grey, metal walls, he and Pasanius stood in a busy city street beneath a warm, spring sun. Hundreds of people thronged the streets, their eyes worried and their movements agitated.

Fear was on the move and the people moved in time with its dance.

Pasanius turned with his borrowed Nemesis weapon at the ready.

'What in the name of the Emperor?' he hissed. 'What just happened? Where are we?'

Uriel had been wondering the same thing, but as his gaze alighted upon a familiar temple with a bronze eagle hanging above the arched entrance, and he suddenly knew.

'Khaturian,' whispered Uriel.

'The Killing Ground,' said Pasanius. 'How is that possible?'

No one appeared to notice them and Uriel said, 'This is not real. It's a memory.'

'A memory? But Thayer wasn't at Khaturian when it was destroyed,' said Pasanius.

'No,' agreed Uriel, indicating the fearful people that filled the streets, 'but they all were.'

A panicked cry went up from somewhere nearby and Uriel looked to the sky as he heard a droning rumble from the direction of the mountains. A trio of cruciform shapes emerged from the clouds, flying low and slowly towards the city.

Uriel's enhanced sight quickly resolved the shapes into flights of Marauder bombers, each cruciform shape comprising of six aircraft.

The people of Khaturian began screaming, even before the first bombs were dropped and Uriel could feel their terror at the sight of the aircraft. Here in the mountains, they had thought themselves safe from the fighting and death that was engulfing the rest of their world.

This day would show them how naïve that belief had been.

'Should we be worried?' asked Pasanius, looking up at the approaching bombers.

Uriel shook his head. 'I do not think so, my friend. Thayer wants us to see what happened here.'

Pasanius looked doubtful, but shrugged. 'Fine. Not a lot we can do anyway.'

Although Uriel knew that what he was seeing was not real and had already happened, the emotions filling the air, panic, terror, disbelief and anger were very real indeed. People ran screaming to their homes, gathering up children and loved ones as they took shelter.

Uriel knew that it would do them no good, as he watched the first clusters of bombs detach from the bellies of the Marauders. Tiny black dots, it seemed inconceivable that they could be the cause of so much misery and death, but as they grew larger their warlike shape became apparent, the snub-nosed warhead and guidance fins spinning them to deliver their payload with greater accuracy.

The first bombs hit in the north of the city, and the ground trembled at the impact. Whooshing shoots of fire erupted skyward and a dark-edged mushroom cloud of smoke billowed upwards. More bombs hit within seconds of the first and a rolling thunderstorm of detonations marched through Khaturian.

Flames and hurricane winds swept over the city, the sound of the explosions merging into one enormous roar of destruction. Buildings collapsed and searing walls of flame roared along the streets. Burning tornadoes seethed like angry elementals, the power of the winds sweeping up those who had not yet found shelter and sucking them back into the burning buildings.

The bombs continued to fall, the destruction wrought around Uriel and Pasanius leaving them untouched. The ground heaved and bucked like a living thing, the pounding of the earth seeming to go on forever as the bombs continued to fall.

The entire city was an inferno, ablaze from its centre to its outskirts. Howling winds carried the flames in every direction, the destruction total and unforgiving. Uriel felt somehow dirty to be immersed in this carnage while immune to it.

For thirty minutes the bombs continued to fall and the city's death scream of collapsing buildings and burning humans seemed never-ending. Uriel felt utterly drained and wished this vision of the apocalypse would end.

'I've seen enough, Thayer!' Uriel shouted into the burning skies.

Everywhere was flames. The sky was ablaze and everything flammable in Khaturian was on fire. Nothing could live in the inferno.

'Emperor's blood,' whispered Pasanius, watching people on fire run screaming from their devastated homes. Burning bodies filled every street and the shriek of the firestorm began to fade as the bombardment finally ended.

'Madness,' hissed Uriel. 'All this for one man.'

Pasanius said nothing, too choked with emotion to speak. Mutilated bodies lay in the wreckage: entire families twisted into grotesque shapes by the heat of the fires.

Though it was surely impossible that people could have lived through such a raging hellstorm, there were, it seemed, survivors. From basements and shelters beneath the city, shell-shocked groups emerged, weeping, into what was left of their city.

Uriel saw that they were bloodied and battered, the skin raw and heat-burned. None had escaped injury and with the noise of the bombardment over, the screams of the citizens of Khaturian began.

'There must be something we can do for them,' said Pasanius, as a man with his arm missing wandered past them in a daze.

'No,' said Uriel. 'They are long dead. The only thing we can do is remember them.'

'I won't forget this,' swore Pasanius.

'Nor I,' agreed Uriel.

'They're getting off easy,' said Pasanius, 'Barbaden and Togandis. You don't have a part in slaughter like this and get to live.'

'They won't,' promised Uriel, his heart hardening to the fate of those who had seen this murder enacted and had either done nothing to stop it or had done nothing to make amends for it.

As they made their way through the devastation, Uriel looked along a rubble-strewn street as he heard the sound of iron treads crushing stone to powder. A dull grey tank in the livery of the Achaman Falcatas rounded the corner. From the burning nozzle protruding from the turret, Uriel recognised it as a Hellhound.

Sheets of flame spouted from the tank, setting ablaze those few parts of the city that had somehow escaped the incendiary bombs dropped by the Marauders. Battle tanks followed in the wake of the Hellhound, spraying bullets indiscriminately along both sides of the street.

Soldiers followed the battle tanks, warriors in red plate armour, who marched beneath a bright banner depicting a screaming, golden eagle against a crimson field. Their guns barked and spat, driving the few survivors into the flames or against the walls where they were executed without mercy.

Uriel could see Leto Barbaden atop the first Leman Russ, his helmet's visor pulled up as he shouted orders to his soldiers. Uriel could see the relish in Barbaden's face, the righteous notion that he was doing the Emperor's work butchering these people. Verena Kain and Sergeant Tremain marched before Barbaden's tank, and Uriel saw the same zealous gleam in their eyes. Uriel wished that Kain's death had been more painful.

He hated himself for such a visceral reaction, but the emotions stirred within him by the knowledge that Barbaden had not only ordered the killings, but had taken such pleasure from them was too powerful to be ignored.

'How do we end this?' asked Pasanius.

'I don't know,' replied Uriel, 'when Thayer thinks we've seen enough.'

'Then I've seen enough,' said Pasanius, 'enough to know that a bullet in the head's too quick a death for Barbaden.'

'Agreed,' said Uriel, 'and I know how this has to end now.'

With those words, the sight before them blurred and shifted, transforming from the burning heart of Khaturian to the devastated House of Providence.

Uriel blinked as his eyes adjusted to the gloom, and he saw the Lord of the Unfleshed towering over him. The killing light in his eyes was undimmed, yet there was no hatred in them, only a sense of profound sadness. Behind the mighty creature, Uriel saw Leodegarius climb to his feet, the entire right-hand side of his armour drenched in blood.

'You know how this has to end?' asked the Lord of the Unfleshed.

Uriel looked down at the ruined, mutilated body of Sylvanus Thayer and nodded.

'I do.'

'How?'

Uriel looked past the mighty creature towards Leodegarius.

'Brother Leodegarius, are you still maintaining your aegis sanctuary over Barbaden and Togandis?'

'I am,' said Leodegarius, and Uriel could hear the exhaustion in the warrior's voice. This hero of the Imperium was wounded nigh unto death and yet still he stood tall. 'What of it?'

'End it,' said Uriel.

THE PRISON WAS in uproar.

Prisoners screamed and shouted for guards, but if any heard their pleas, none dared show their faces in the prison complex. For now, the spirits of the dead ruled the Panopticon.

Shavo Togandis stood before the bars of his cell, mouthing prayers and confessing every base, petty thing he had done in his life. He spoke in words barely above a whisper, knowing that the Emperor would hear them, but unwilling to share them with Leto Barbaden.

The ghostly figures heard his confession in silence and he hoped they understood his regret and pain. They had made no attempt to come closer since the spirit of the young girl had been hurled back by the psychic barrier erected by Leodegarius, but had simply watched, and waited.

His confession done, he said, 'I tread the path of righteousness. Though it be paved with broken glass, I will walk it barefoot. Though it crosses rivers of fire, I will pass over them. Though it wanders wide, the light of the Emperor guides my step.'

'Can't think of words of your own, Shavo?' sneered Barbaden. 'Whose are those? And don't try to tell me they're yours, I know you better than that.'

'They were said by Dolan of Chiros, the man who helped bring down Cardinal Bucharis.'

'Ah, the confessor who stood before the tyrant during the Plague of Unbelief. Is that it? Do you think men will remember you in the same breath as Dolan? You may have been a confessor, Shavo, but you're not a tenth of the man Dolan was,' said Barbaden, lounging unconcerned on his bunk. 'You were always too much of a worm to be granted a place at the Emperor's side.'

'And you think there's a place for you? A murderer?'

Barbaden laughed. 'I'm no murderer, and as soon as this farce of an incarceration is over, I'll be back in the palace. I have the right of appeal to the Sector Governor, and do you think he's going to let me swing for killing a few terrorists?'

'If there is an iota of justice in this galaxy, then yes,' said Togandis, closing his eyes and wishing Leto Barbaden would shut up.

'There is no justice, Shavo. Don't be so foolish. There's no room for justice in this galaxy,' said Barbaden, 'and if you'll permit me to quote back to you, I think you'll find this one illuminating: "When the people forget their duty they are no longer human and become something less than beasts. They have no place in the bosom of humanity nor in the heart of the Emperor. Let them die and be forgotten".'

Then it shall be so.

The voice had sounded right in his ear.

Togandis opened his eyes and he cried out as he saw that their cells were filled with the ghostly figures who had stood, silent and unmoving, beyond the bars, waiting.

Fear clutched at his heart, but it was instantly replaced by a wash of relief. It was over, the waiting, the fear of humiliation and the dread that they would somehow escape retribution.

'Get away from me, damn you!' shouted Barbaden. 'Get away from me, I said!'

Togandis watched as the dead crowded in around the former governor of Salinas, eager to be part of his unmaking. Though they had been called ghosts, they were no phantom apparitions of mist; their nails could tear skin and their teeth could rip flesh from bones.

Barbaden screamed as they plucked at the soft meat of his face, bearing him to the ground and clawing his flesh. His eyes went first, torn from their sockets with a swift jerk of cold, dead hands.

They tore the skin from his face, ripping the muscles from his skull and peeling him back to the frame of bone beneath. His limbs bent and snapped and his screams filled the cells as the dead fought to bloody their hands in his entrails.

Togandis watched in horrified fascination as Leto Barbaden was torn apart before his very eyes, the meat and bone of his existence ripped asunder in a frenzy of vengeance.

In moments it was over and there was nothing left in the cell that even remotely resembled what had once been a human being. All that remained was a jumble of torn offal and a vast lake of blood and snapped bone.

The dead turned their faces to Shavo Togandis.

'Do what must be done,' he said.

The dead came at him and as he felt their hands reach for his eyes, he said, 'I forgive you.'

URIEL KNEW IT was over.

The dead light in the eyes of the Lord of the Unfleshed faded and sudden silence fell upon the House of Providence. The howling of the ghosts ceased and the filmy scraps of light began to fade. Uriel felt a tremendous wave of relief pass through him as the dead began their final journey, their spirits finally allowed to disperse into the warp.

The gloom that had settled upon Salinas was gone in an instant, and Uriel had not fully realised how oppressive it had been until it was removed.

Uriel heard a rasping sigh from the bed next to him and looked down at Sylvanus Thayer as the machine maintaining his life hiked and stuttered. The rhythmic machine noise of his life slowed until it became a single, shrill note that could mean only one thing.

Sylvanus Thayer was dead, and with him the threat to Salinas.

The wound in reality was gone, sealed up without the link between worlds that the former leader of the Sons of Salinas had provided.

Uriel took a deep, cleansing breath, looking around to make sure that he was not imagining things: that it was truly over. Pasanius stood next to him and the injured Leodegarius held himself upright with his one remaining arm.

Cheiron staggered over to his commander and Uriel turned his attention to the Lord of the Unfleshed. The last of the Unfleshed swayed on his feet, unsteady and uncertain, his head turning this way and that as though awakening from a deep slumber.

His eyes, milky and rheumy, focused on Uriel and he dropped to his knees, his massive clawed hands coming up to his face as a heartrending moan of self-loathing issued from deep inside him. Great, wracking sobs burst from the Lord of the Unfleshed's chest and Uriel felt deep sorrow that it had come to this.

Cheiron made his way across the chamber towards the Lord of the Unfleshed with his storm bolter raised, but Uriel shook his head.

'No,' he said, 'you don't need that anymore.'

Cheiron looked down at the hunched, sobbing form of the Lord of the Unfleshed and then back at Uriel. He nodded and returned to Leodegarius.

Uriel knelt beside the Lord of the Unfleshed, whose body had diminished to its former proportions. His flesh was torn with bolter craters and slashes from blades and Uriel was amazed that he was still alive. The creature was still massive, but without the enormous power of the dead, he seemed somehow smaller, more vulnerable, and infinitely sad.

'What do we do now?' asked Pasanius.

Uriel looked up at Pasanius. 'Go with Leodegarius and Cheiron,' he said. 'I have something to do here first.'

'Are you sure?'

Uriel nodded. 'I'm sure, yes.'

Pasanius looked set to argue, but he heard the firmness in Uriel's tone and turned away.

Uriel reached out and placed his hand on the Lord of the Unfleshed's arm. Too late, he remembered that the Unfleshed did not like to be touched, but there was no reaction.

Uriel knelt beside the Lord of the Unfleshed and let him weep.

'Captain Ventris,' said a voice behind him, and he turned to see Leodegarius. The Grey Knight had removed his helmet and his face was pale and wan, drained by the fury of battle and the pain of losing a limb.

Leodegarius said, 'Come to the palace when you are done. Then we shall see about getting you back to Macragge.'

'I will,' promised Uriel.

The Grey Knight held out his hand and Uriel looked down at what he held.

'I think you will be needing this,' said Leodegarius and Uriel nodded.

'Thank you, Brother Leodegarius' said Uriel. 'It was an honour to fight alongside you.'

'No,' said the Grey Knight, 'the honour was mine.'

LEODEGARIUS, PASANIUS AND Cheiron left, leaving Uriel and the Lord of the Unfleshed alone in the ward. The creature he had attempted to rescue from a hideous life of death and misery knelt before the bed of the man who had enslaved him and his tribe and wept.

Uriel could not begin to imagine the horror the memory of what it had been forced to do would be like, and did not intrude on the Lord of the Unfleshed's grief with mere words.

At last, the creature looked up and his gaze fastened on Uriel.

'Unfleshed did very bad things,' he said.

'No,' said Uriel. 'All that hatred and killing, it was not you.'

'Yes, it was. We did it. My hand bloody. Tribe's hands bloody. I saw blood and I tasted blood. Unfleshed bad.'

'No,' repeated Uriel. 'Unfleshed not bad. You were used. It wasn't your fault.'

'Emperor must hate us even more now.'

'He does not hate you,' said Uriel. 'The Emperor loves you. Look.'

Uriel pointed to an aquila fashioned from beaten steel hanging on the wall, the earliest dawn light from a window opposite shining upon it and making it gleam like silver.

The Lord of the Unfleshed looked up at the gleaming eagle, his reflection thrown back at him. As Uriel looked at the distorted image, it appeared to ripple like the surface of a lake, and he found himself looking at the reflection of a handsome young boy, his face alight with youthful mischief.

The Lord of the Unfleshed gave a cry as he too saw the image. 'Emperor loves me!'

Uriel moved to stand behind the Lord of the Unfleshed and raised the psycannon Leodegarius had given him.

'Yes, the Emperor loves you,' said Uriel, and pulled the trigger.

Long is the way, and hard, that out of hell leads up to light.

THE THUNDERHAWK BANKED as it followed the flight-path the ground controllers had indicated. Uriel looked out of the vision port on the side of the roaring gunship, watching as the dazzling white mountains sped by, their soaring, jagged tops wreathed in clouds.

It had been weeks since the battle in the House of Providence and his body and spirit still ached from the time spent on Salinas. Though Uriel's wounds had healed, he could not shake off the melancholy that had settled on him since he had pulled the trigger of the psycannon.

He knew it had been the only option open to him, and if the Lord of the Unfleshed was going to end his days on Salinas, then it was only right that it be at the hands of the man who had led him there.

With the passing of Sylvanus Thayer, the pressure of the dead upon the minds of the living vanished and a strange sense of calm descended upon Barbadus (though *that* name was sure to change). With the announcement of Leto Barbaden's death, that mood of calm had been replaced with one of celebration.

As things turned out, the day after the battle was to be a day of announcements.

Under the supervision of the Grey Knights, an interim governorship was to be formed with Daron Nisato as the new Imperial Commander. While this announcement was greeted with rather less enthusiasm than Leto Barbaden's passing, word that Pascal Blaise supported the former enforcer in his leadership generated a quiet acceptance from the populace.

The days of trouble were far from over for Salinas, but Uriel knew that the planet's course had been turned from disaster, and that its people had a chance to cast off the old hatreds that had almost destroyed them.

It was more than most people got.

Upon the restoration of Imperial control, Leodegarius had walked them to a waiting gunship as it growled on the esplanade before the palace and bid them farewell.

'Remember the Tower,' the Grey Knight said. 'It reminds us that if we use our knowledge and strength for evil purposes, then destruction will be wrought upon us.'

They had said their goodbyes to Lukas Urbican and Daron Nisato and marched aboard the gunship, never to see Salinas again.

Uriel leaned back against the Thunderhawk's fuselage, feeling the power of the engines in the thrumming beat in the metal. He had not dared believe that he would ever make this journey and he kept his eyes shut, as though the reality of it might be snatched away at any moment.

He shared the troop compartment of the gunship with nineteen suits of armour, those belonging to the Sons of Guilliman. Uriel wore a chiton of pale blue and carried his sword across his lap. He had not worn his borrowed armour since the battle in the House of Providence, for he had known that it was not his to wear beyond that immediate need.

Like ghosts, the suits of armour had been strapped into the bench seats in the Thunderhawk as carefully as if they had each contained a living, breathing Space Marine. A message had already been sent to the Sons of Guilliman and the suits of armour would return to their Chapter to protect their battle-brothers once more.

The door to the gun-ship's cockpit opened and Pasanius emerged. Unlike Uriel, Pasanius was fully clad in armour and his face was alight with pleasure.

'You'll want to come up front,' said Pasanius.

Uriel smiled as he rose from his seat and made his way along the troop compartment. He ducked beneath the door to the cockpit, the interior filled with bright sunlight and shadows that moved as the pilots began the gunship's descent into a steep-sided valley of glittering, quartz-rich rocks.

'Look,' said Pasanius, pointing through the armoured glass of the cockpit.

There it was, shimmering atop the mountain like a castle of gold and silver on a cloud.

Uriel found he could barely control his breathing and tears ran unchecked down his face at the sight of the marble towers, mosaic domes and high walls of luminescent stone.

'The Fortress of Hera,' said Pasanius, also in tears.

'Home,' said Uriel.

ABOUT THE AUTHOR

Hailing from Scotland, Graham McNeill worked for over six years as a Games Developer in Games Workshop's Design Studio before taking the plunge to become a full-time writer. In addition to eleven previous novels, Graham's written a host of SF and Fantasy stories and comics, as well as a number of side projects that keep him busy and (mostly) out of trouble. Graham lives and works in Nottingham and you can keep up to date with where he'll be and what he's working on by visiting his website.

Join the ranks of the 4th Company at *www.graham-mcneill.com*

BY GRAHAM McNEILL

WARHAMMER 40,000

THE ULTRAMARINES
OMNIBUS

'Great characters, truck loads of intrigue and an amazing sense of pace.' **Enigma**

GRAHAM McNEILL
NIGHTBRINGER · WARRIORS OF ULTRAMAR · DEAD SKY BLACK SUN

ISBN 978-1-84416-403-5

CHAOS IS UNLEASHED

WARHAMMER
40,000

STORM OF IRON

The must read Chaos novel from Ultramarines author:

GRAHAM McNEILL

ISBN 978-1-84416-571-1

FOR THE EMPEROR

WARHAMMER
40,000

DAN ABNETT

BROTHERS OF THE SNAKE

'He makes war so real that you want to duck!' – SciFi.com

ISBN 978-1-84416-547-6

BY THE BLOOD OF SANGUINIUS!

WARHAMMER
40,000

THE BLOOD ANGELS
OMNIBUS

buy this
omnibus or read
a free extract at
www.blacklibrary.com

'War-torn tales of loyalty and honour.' – SFX

JAMES SWALLOW

ISBN 978-1-84416-559-9

MORE SPACE MARINES

WARHAMMER 40,000

THE SPACE WOLF
OMNIBUS

WILLIAM KING

SPACE WOLF • RAGNAR'S CLAW • GREY HUNTER

'Savage action and adventure with the Space Wolves'. – Enigma

ISBN 978-1-84416-457-8